CASE CLOSED

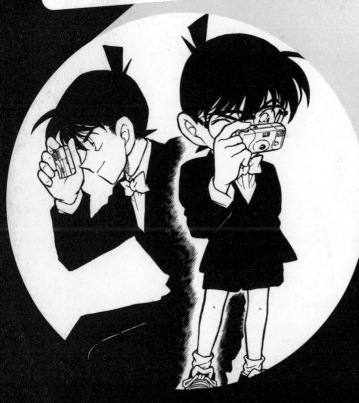

Gosho Aoyama

Case Briefing:

Subject:
Occupation:
Special Skills:
Equipment:

Jimmy Kudo, a.k.a. Conan Edogawa
High School Student/Detective
Analytical thinking and deductive reasoning, Soccer
Bow Tie Voice Transmitter, Super Sneakers,
Homing Glasses, Stretchy Suspenders

The subject is hot on the trail of a pair of suspicious men in black when he is attacked from behind and administered a strange substance which physically transforms him into a first grader. When the subject confides in the eccentric inventor Dr. Agasa, they decide to keep the subject's true identity a secret for the safety of everyone around him. Assuming the new identity of first-grader Conan Edogawa, the subject continues to assist the police force on their most baffling cases. The only problem is that most crime-solving professionals won't take a little kid's advice!

Table of Contents

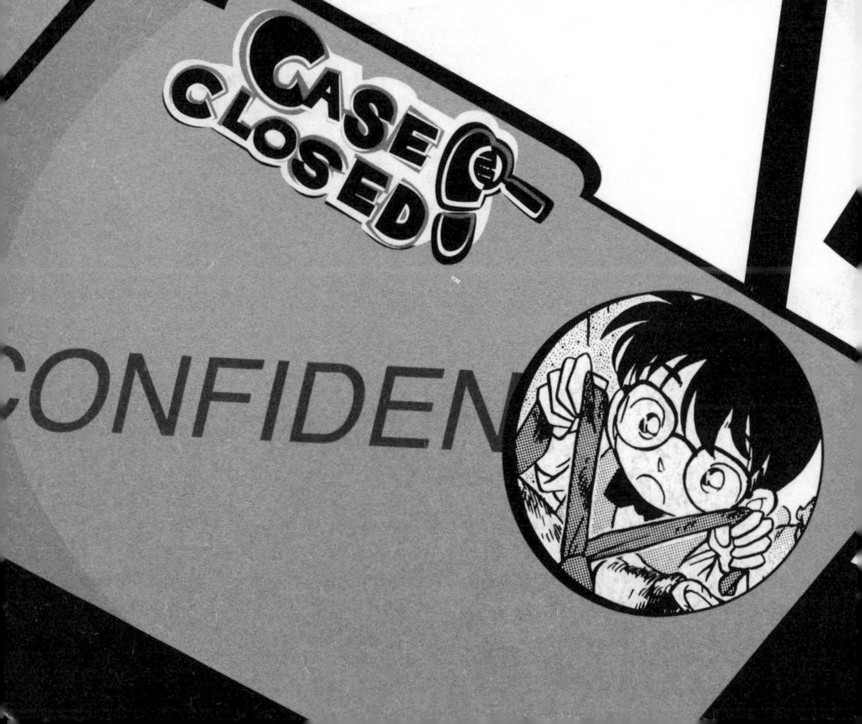

CASE CLOSED
CONFIDEN

CASE CLOSED

Volume 30 • VIZ Media Edition

GOSHO AOYAMA

Translation
Tetsuichiro Miyaki

Touch-up & Lettering
Freeman Wong

Cover & Graphic Design
Andrea Rice

Editor
Shaenon K. Garrity

Editor in Chief, Books **Alvin Lu**
Editor in Chief, Magazines **Marc Weidenbaum**
VP, Publishing Licensing **Rika Inouye**
VP, Sales & Product Marketing **Gonzalo Ferreyra**
VP, Creative **Linda Espinosa**
Publisher **Hyoe Narita**

MEITANTEI CONAN 30 by Gosho AOYAMA © 2001 Gosho AOYAMA
All rights reserved.
Original Japanese edition published in 2001 by Shogakukan Inc., Tokyo.
The stories, characters and incidents mentioned in this publication are entirely fictional.

www.viz.com

Printed in the U.S.A.
Published by VIZ Media, LLC
P.O. Box 77010
San Francisco, CA 94107

10 9 8 7 6 5 4 3 2 1
First printing, July 2009

FILE 1: THE DIRECT APPROACH

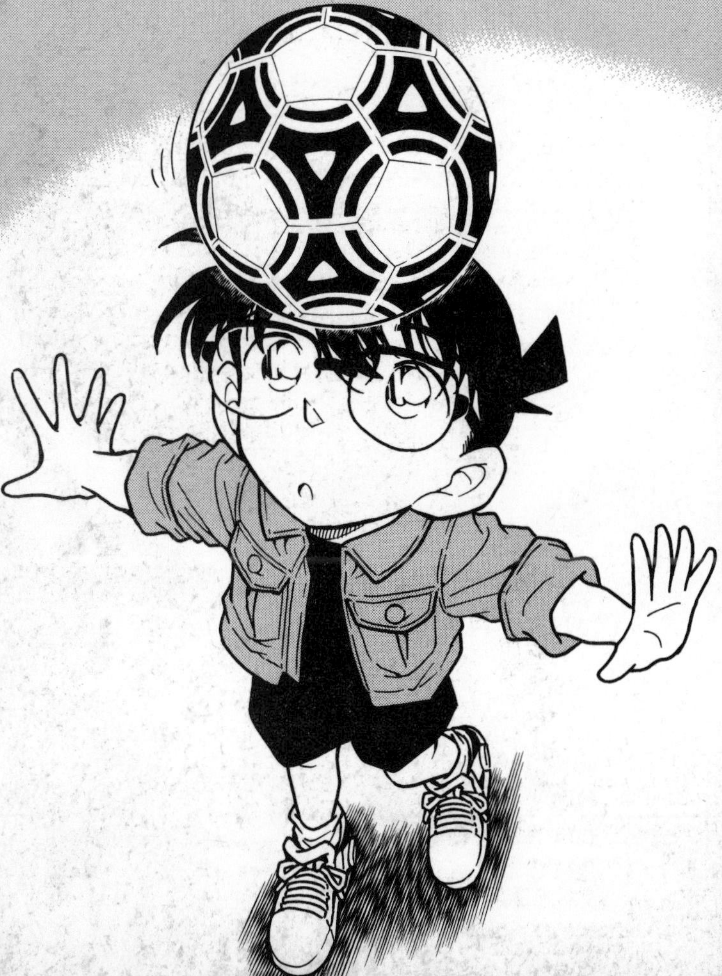

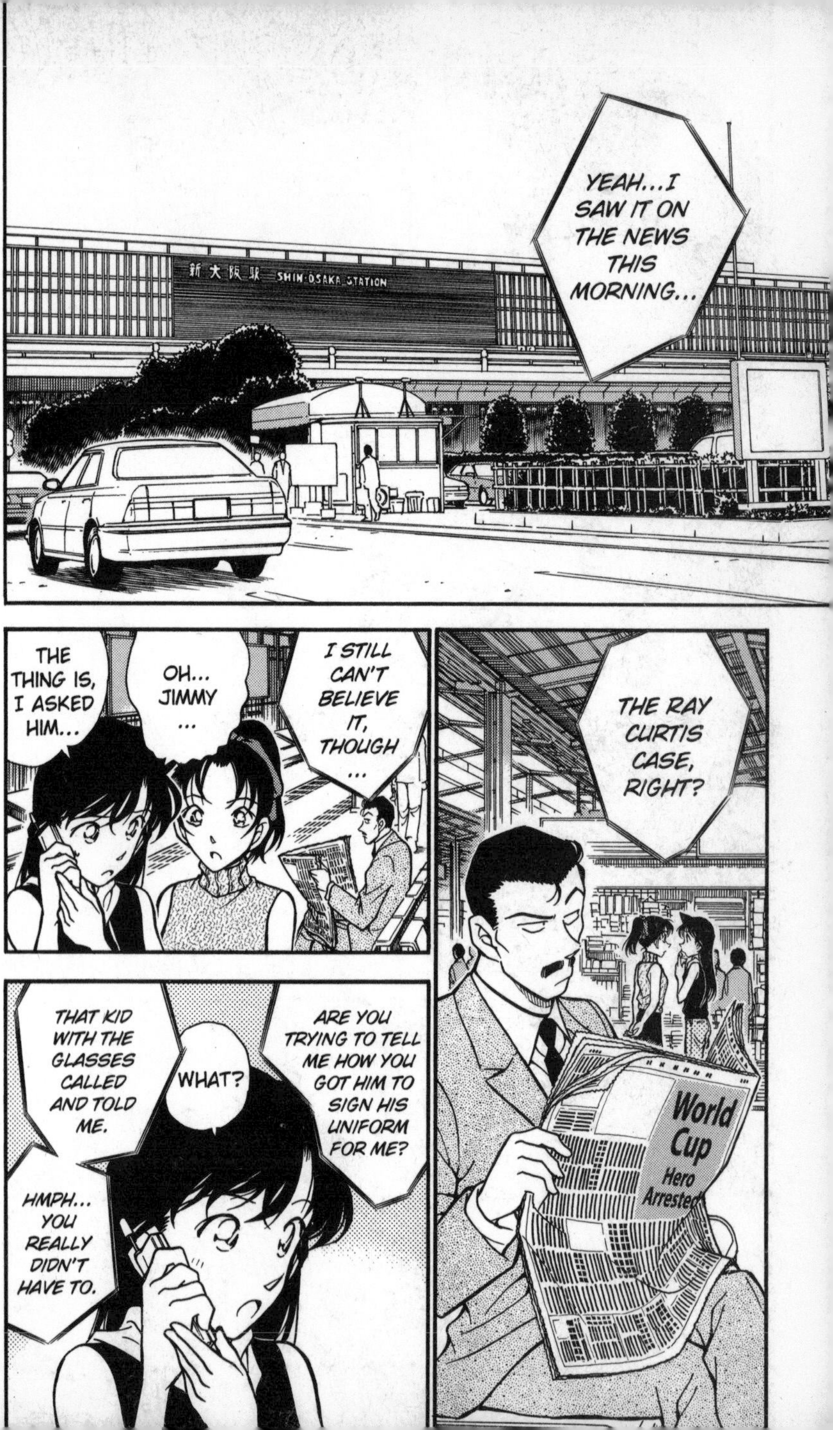
新大阪駅 SHIN-OSAKA STATION
YEAH...I SAW IT ON THE NEWS THIS MORNING...
THE RAY CURTIS CASE, RIGHT?
World Cup Hero Arrested
I STILL CAN'T BELIEVE IT, THOUGH...
OH... JIMMY...
THE THING IS, I ASKED HIM...
ARE YOU TRYING TO TELL ME HOW YOU GOT HIM TO SIGN HIS UNIFORM FOR ME?
WHAT?
THAT KID WITH THE GLASSES CALLED AND TOLD ME.
HMPH... YOU REALLY DIDN'T HAVE TO.

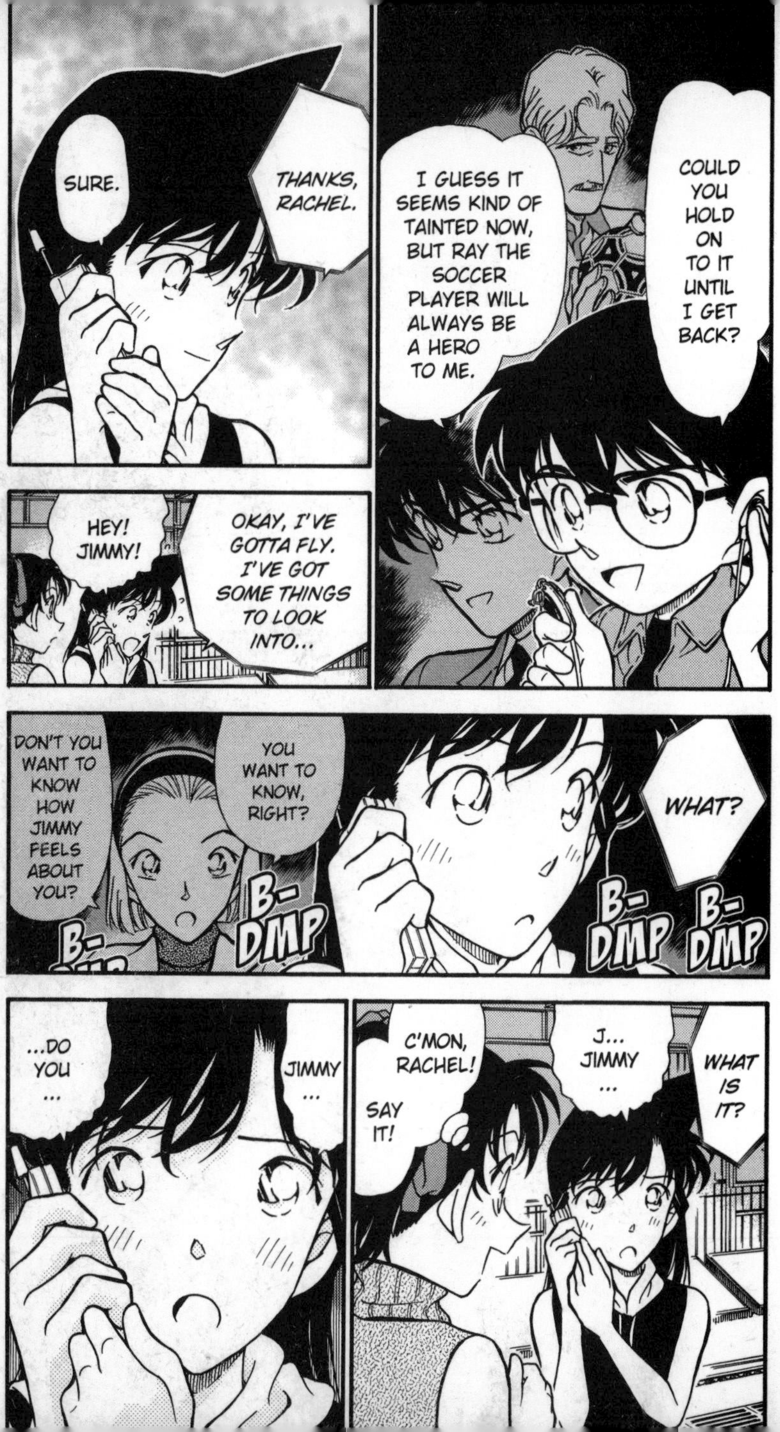
COULD YOU HOLD ON TO IT UNTIL I GET BACK?
I GUESS IT SEEMS KIND OF TAINTED NOW, BUT RAY THE SOCCER PLAYER WILL ALWAYS BE A HERO TO ME.
THANKS, RACHEL.
SURE.
OKAY, I'VE GOTTA FLY. I'VE GOT SOME THINGS TO LOOK INTO...
HEY! JIMMY!
WHAT?
B-DMP
B-DMP
YOU WANT TO KNOW, RIGHT?
DON'T YOU WANT TO KNOW HOW JIMMY FEELS ABOUT YOU?
WHAT IS IT?
J... JIMMY...
C'MON, RACHEL!
SAY IT!
JIMMY...
...DO YOU...

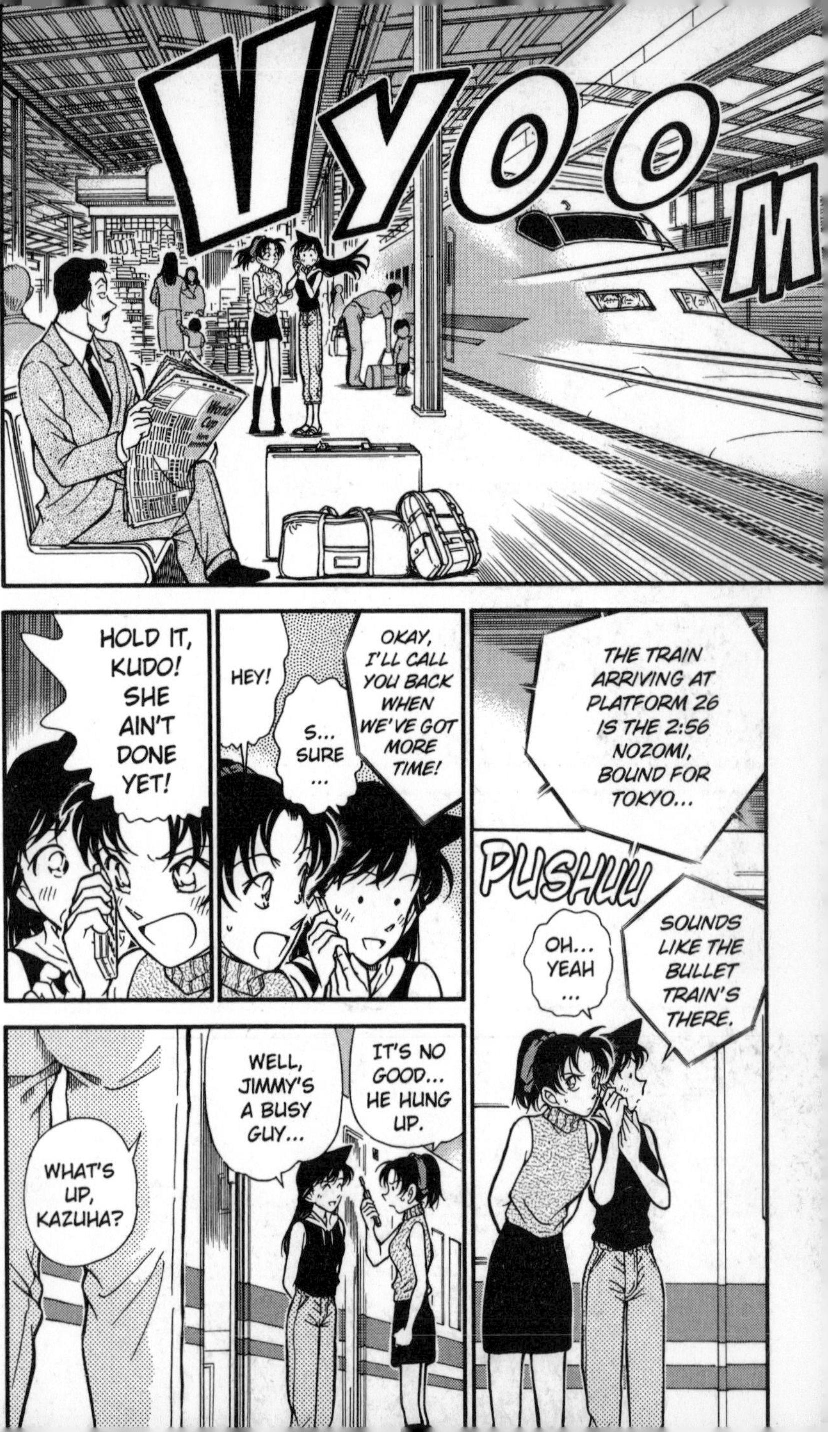
VYOOOM
World Cup
THE TRAIN ARRIVING AT PLATFORM 26 IS THE 2:56 NOZOMI, BOUND FOR TOKYO...
PUSHUU
SOUNDS LIKE THE BULLET TRAIN'S THERE.
OH... YEAH ...
OKAY, I'LL CALL YOU BACK WHEN WE'VE GOT MORE TIME!
HEY!
S... SURE ...
HOLD IT, KUDO! SHE AIN'T DONE YET!
IT'S NO GOOD... HE HUNG UP.
WELL, JIMMY'S A BUSY GUY...
WHAT'S UP, KAZUHA?

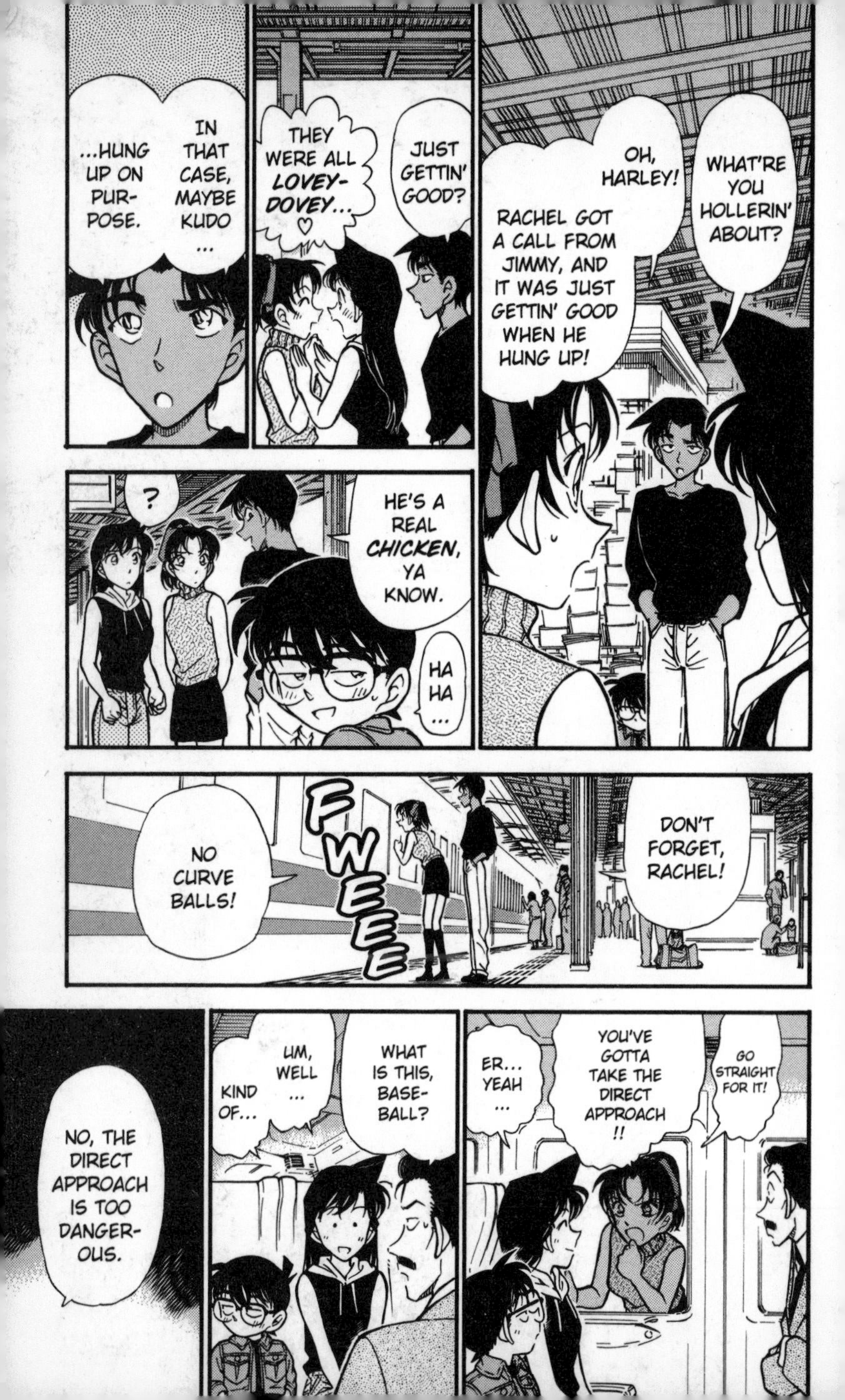
WHAT'RE YOU HOLLERIN' ABOUT?
OH, HARLEY!
RACHEL GOT A CALL FROM JIMMY, AND IT WAS JUST GETTIN' GOOD WHEN HE HUNG UP!
JUST GETTIN' GOOD?
THEY WERE ALL LOVEY-DOVEY... ♡
IN THAT CASE, MAYBE KUDO ...
...HUNG UP ON PURPOSE.
HE'S A REAL CHICKEN, YA KNOW.
HA HA ...
?
DON'T FORGET, RACHEL!
FWEEEE
NO CURVE BALLS!
GO STRAIGHT FOR IT!
YOU'VE GOTTA TAKE THE DIRECT APPROACH !!
ER... YEAH ...
WHAT IS THIS, BASEBALL?
UM, WELL ...
KIND OF...
NO, THE DIRECT APPROACH IS TOO DANGEROUS.

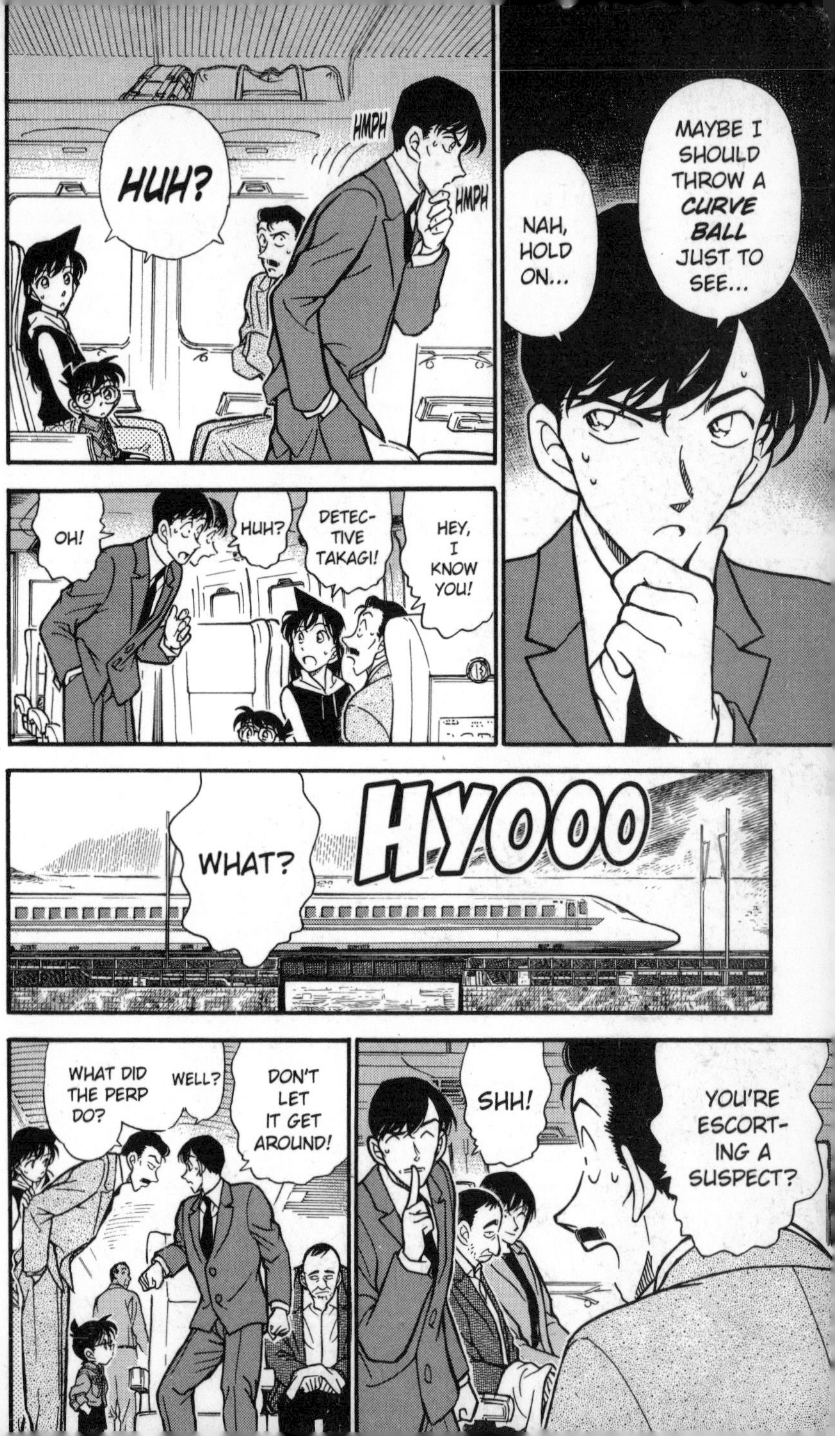
MAYBE I SHOULD THROW A CURVE BALL JUST TO SEE...
NAH, HOLD ON...
HMPH
HMPH
HUH?
HEY, I KNOW YOU!
DETECTIVE TAKAGI!
HUH?
OH!
HYOOO
WHAT?
YOU'RE ESCORTING A SUSPECT?
SHH!
DON'T LET IT GET AROUND!
WELL?
WHAT DID THE PERP DO?

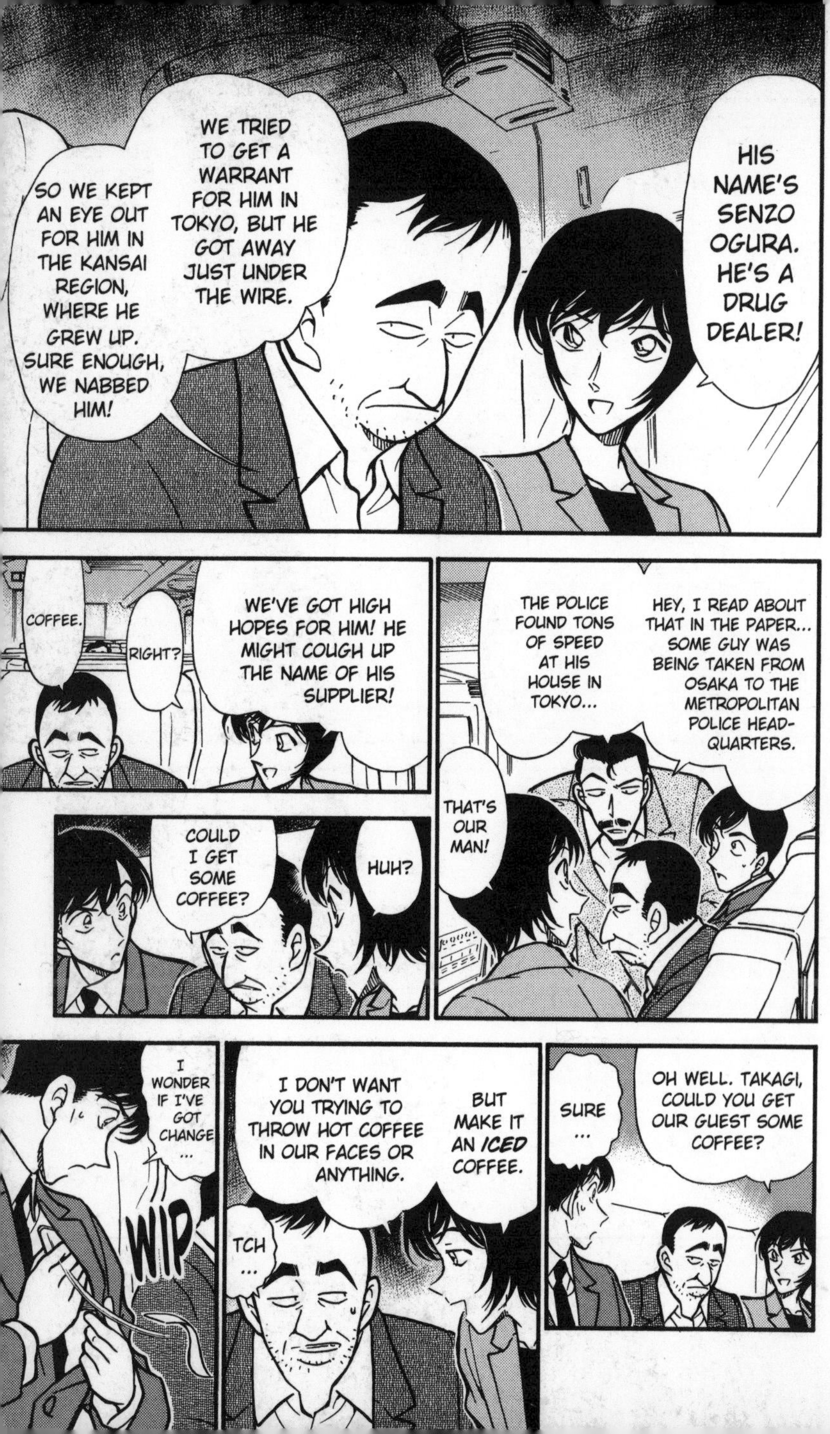
HIS NAME'S SENZO OGURA. HE'S A DRUG DEALER!
WE TRIED TO GET A WARRANT FOR HIM IN TOKYO, BUT HE GOT AWAY JUST UNDER THE WIRE.
SO WE KEPT AN EYE OUT FOR HIM IN THE KANSAI REGION, WHERE HE GREW UP. SURE ENOUGH, WE NABBED HIM!
HEY, I READ ABOUT THAT IN THE PAPER... SOME GUY WAS BEING TAKEN FROM OSAKA TO THE METROPOLITAN POLICE HEAD-QUARTERS.
THE POLICE FOUND TONS OF SPEED AT HIS HOUSE IN TOKYO...
THAT'S OUR MAN!
WE'VE GOT HIGH HOPES FOR HIM! HE MIGHT COUGH UP THE NAME OF HIS SUPPLIER!
RIGHT?
COFFEE.
HUH?
COULD I GET SOME COFFEE?
OH WELL. TAKAGI, COULD YOU GET OUR GUEST SOME COFFEE?
SURE ...
BUT MAKE IT AN ICED COFFEE.
I DON'T WANT YOU TRYING TO THROW HOT COFFEE IN OUR FACES OR ANYTHING.
TCH ...
I WONDER IF I'VE GOT CHANGE ...
WIP

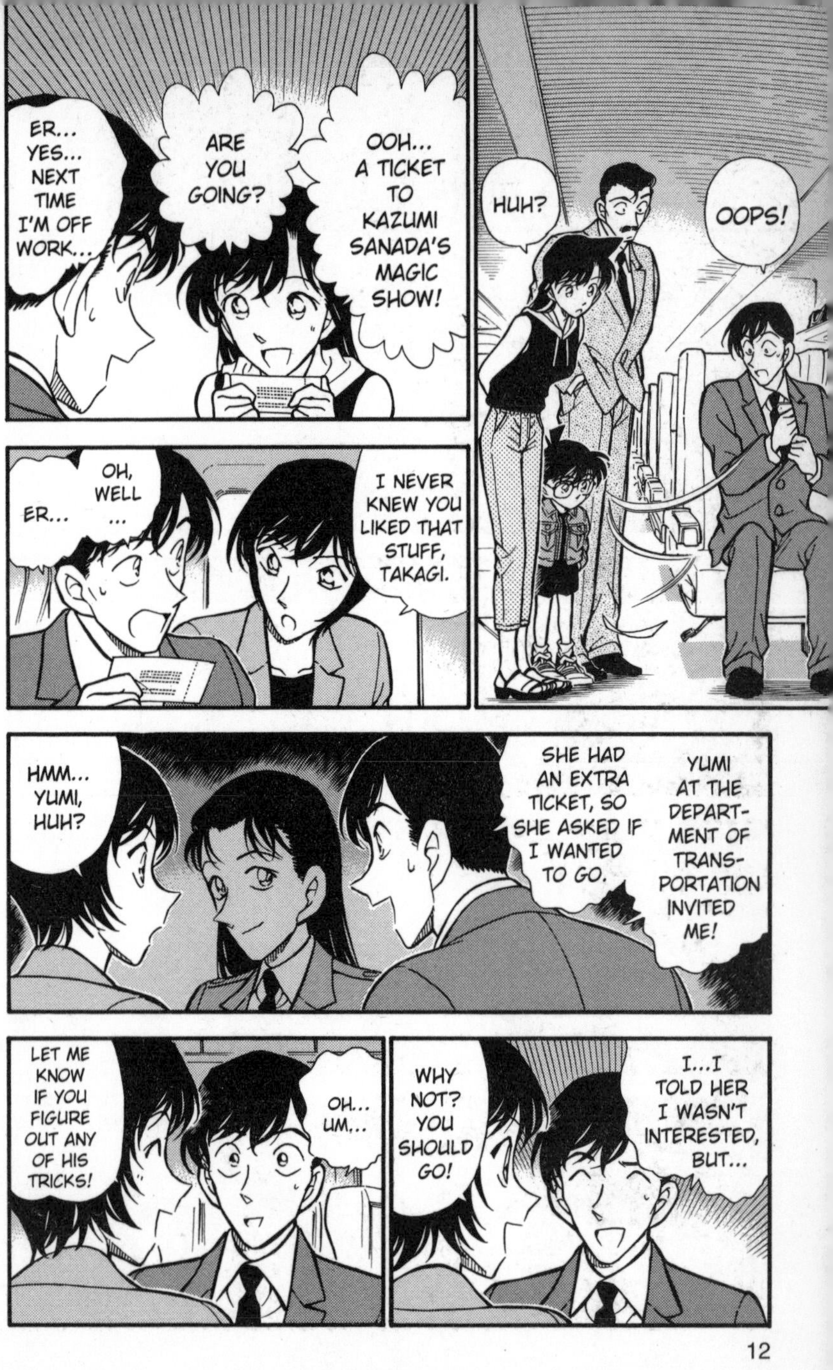
OOPS!
HUH?
OOH... A TICKET TO KAZUMI SANADA'S MAGIC SHOW!
ARE YOU GOING?
ER... YES... NEXT TIME I'M OFF WORK...
I NEVER KNEW YOU LIKED THAT STUFF, TAKAGI.
OH, WELL ...
ER...
YUMI AT THE DEPARTMENT OF TRANSPORTATION INVITED ME!
SHE HAD AN EXTRA TICKET, SO SHE ASKED IF I WANTED TO GO.
HMM... YUMI, HUH?
I...I TOLD HER I WASN'T INTERESTED, BUT...
WHY NOT? YOU SHOULD GO!
OH... UM...
LET ME KNOW IF YOU FIGURE OUT ANY OF HIS TRICKS!

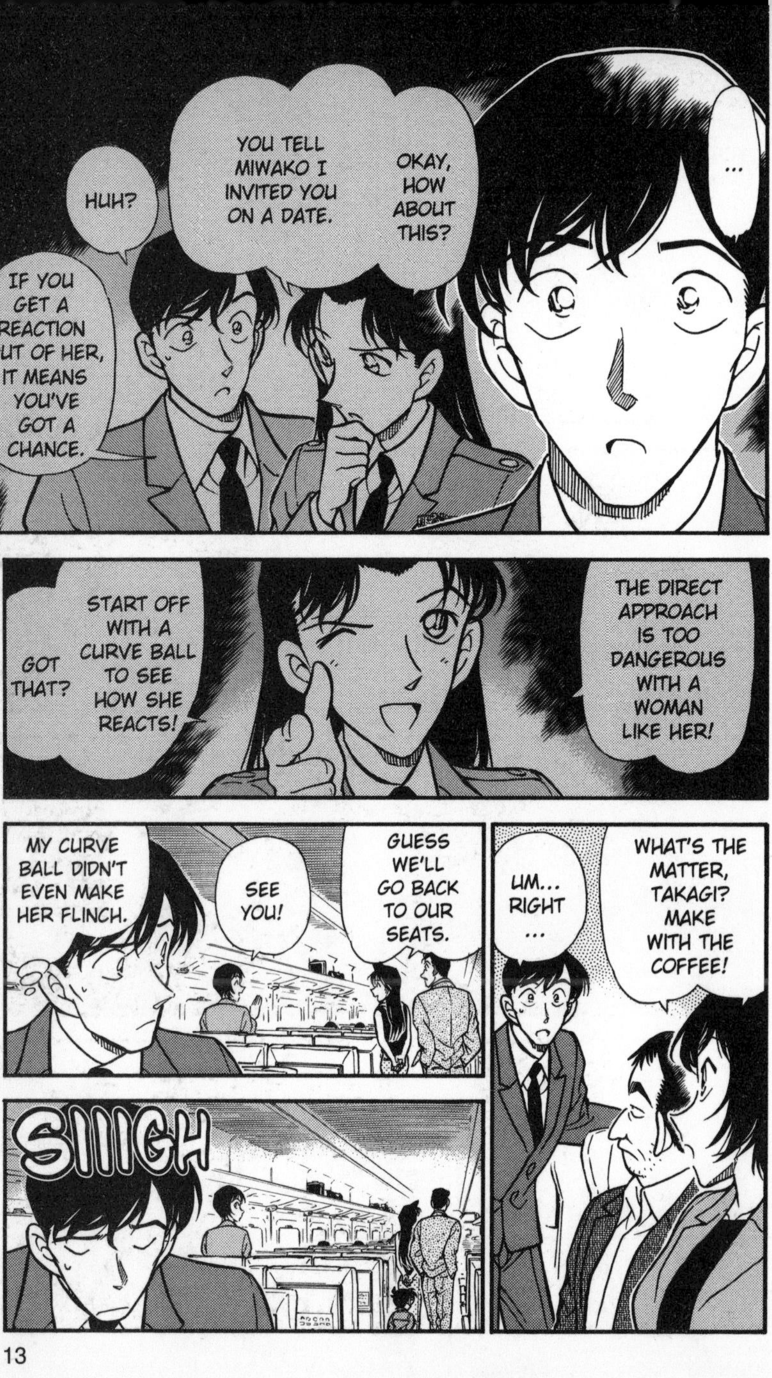
...
OKAY, HOW ABOUT THIS?
YOU TELL MIWAKO I INVITED YOU ON A DATE.
HUH?
IF YOU GET A REACTION OUT OF HER, IT MEANS YOU'VE GOT A CHANCE.
THE DIRECT APPROACH IS TOO DANGEROUS WITH A WOMAN LIKE HER!
START OFF WITH A CURVE BALL TO SEE HOW SHE REACTS!
GOT THAT?
WHAT'S THE MATTER, TAKAGI? MAKE WITH THE COFFEE!
UM... RIGHT ...
GUESS WE'LL GO BACK TO OUR SEATS.
SEE YOU!
MY CURVE BALL DIDN'T EVEN MAKE HER FLINCH.
SIIIGH

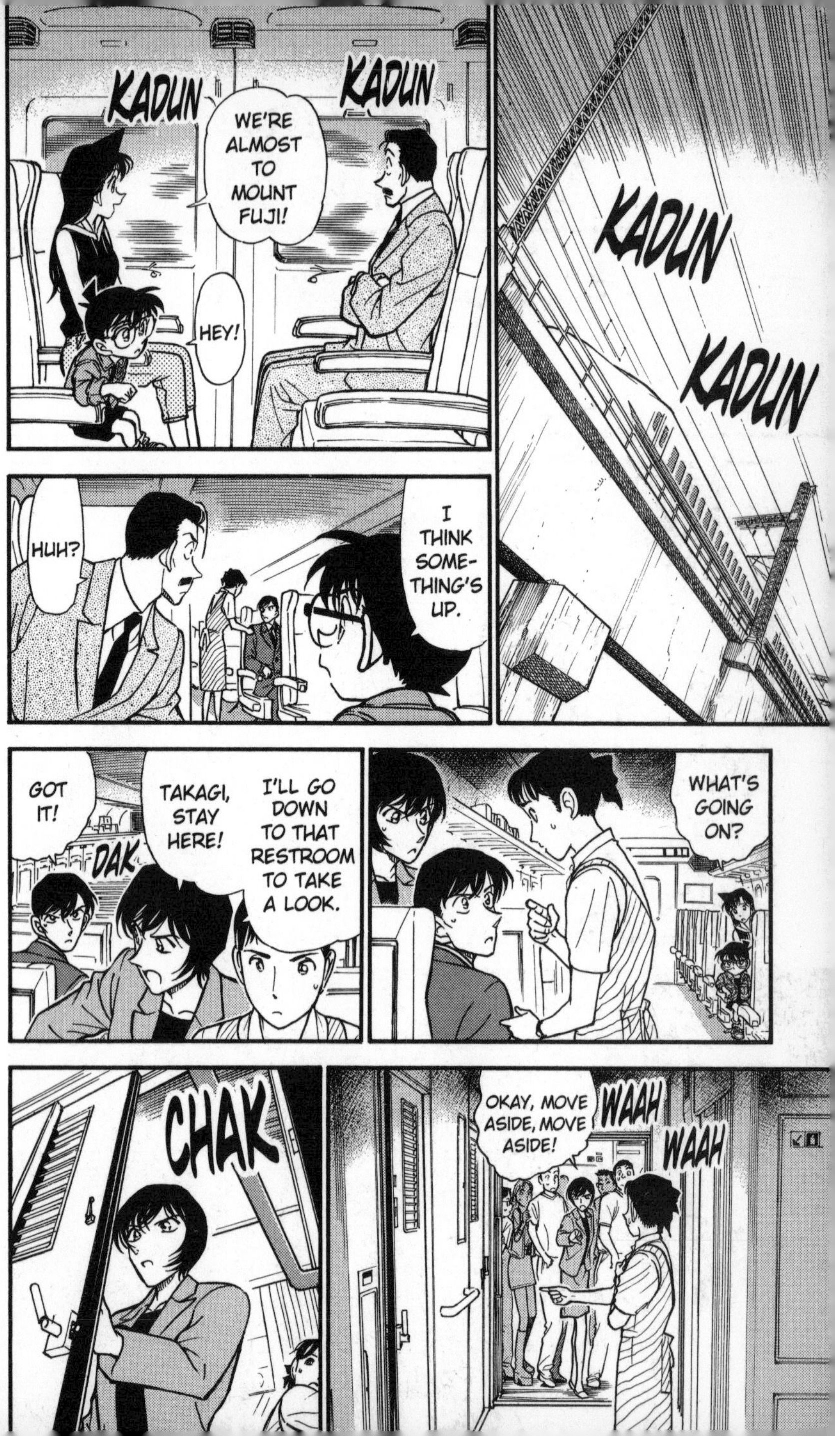
KADUN
KADUN
KADUN
WE'RE ALMOST TO MOUNT FUJI!
KADUN
HEY!
I THINK SOME-THING'S UP.
HUH?
WHAT'S GOING ON?
I'LL GO DOWN TO THAT RESTROOM TO TAKE A LOOK.
TAKAGI, STAY HERE!
GOT IT!
DAK
WAAH
WAAH
OKAY, MOVE ASIDE, MOVE ASIDE!
CHAK

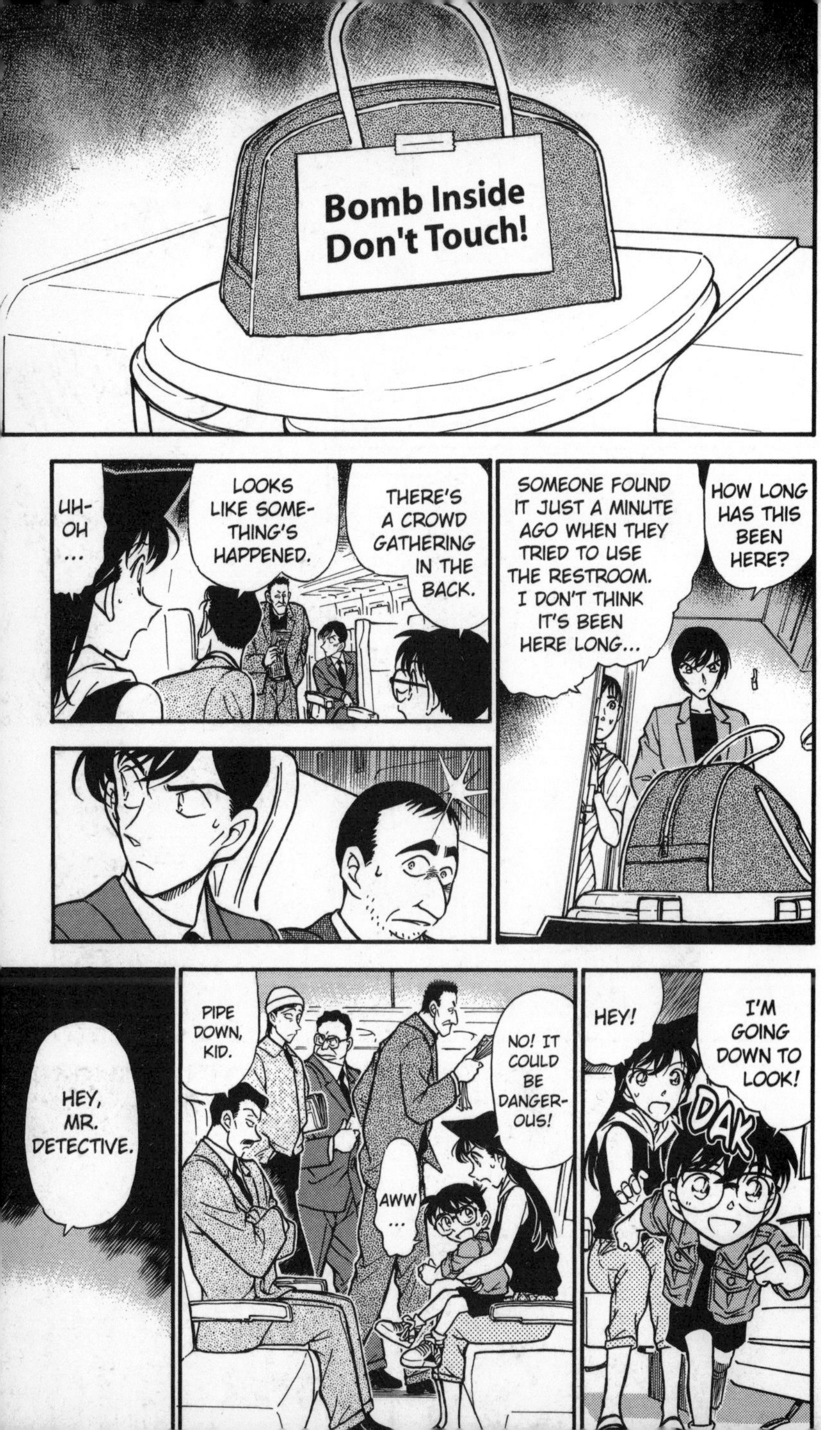
Bomb Inside Don't Touch!
HOW LONG HAS THIS BEEN HERE?
SOMEONE FOUND IT JUST A MINUTE AGO WHEN THEY TRIED TO USE THE RESTROOM. I DON'T THINK IT'S BEEN HERE LONG...
THERE'S A CROWD GATHERING IN THE BACK.
LOOKS LIKE SOME-THING'S HAPPENED.
UH-OH ...
I'M GOING DOWN TO LOOK!
HEY!
DAK
NO! IT COULD BE DANGER-OUS!
PIPE DOWN, KID.
AWW ...
HEY, MR. DETECTIVE.

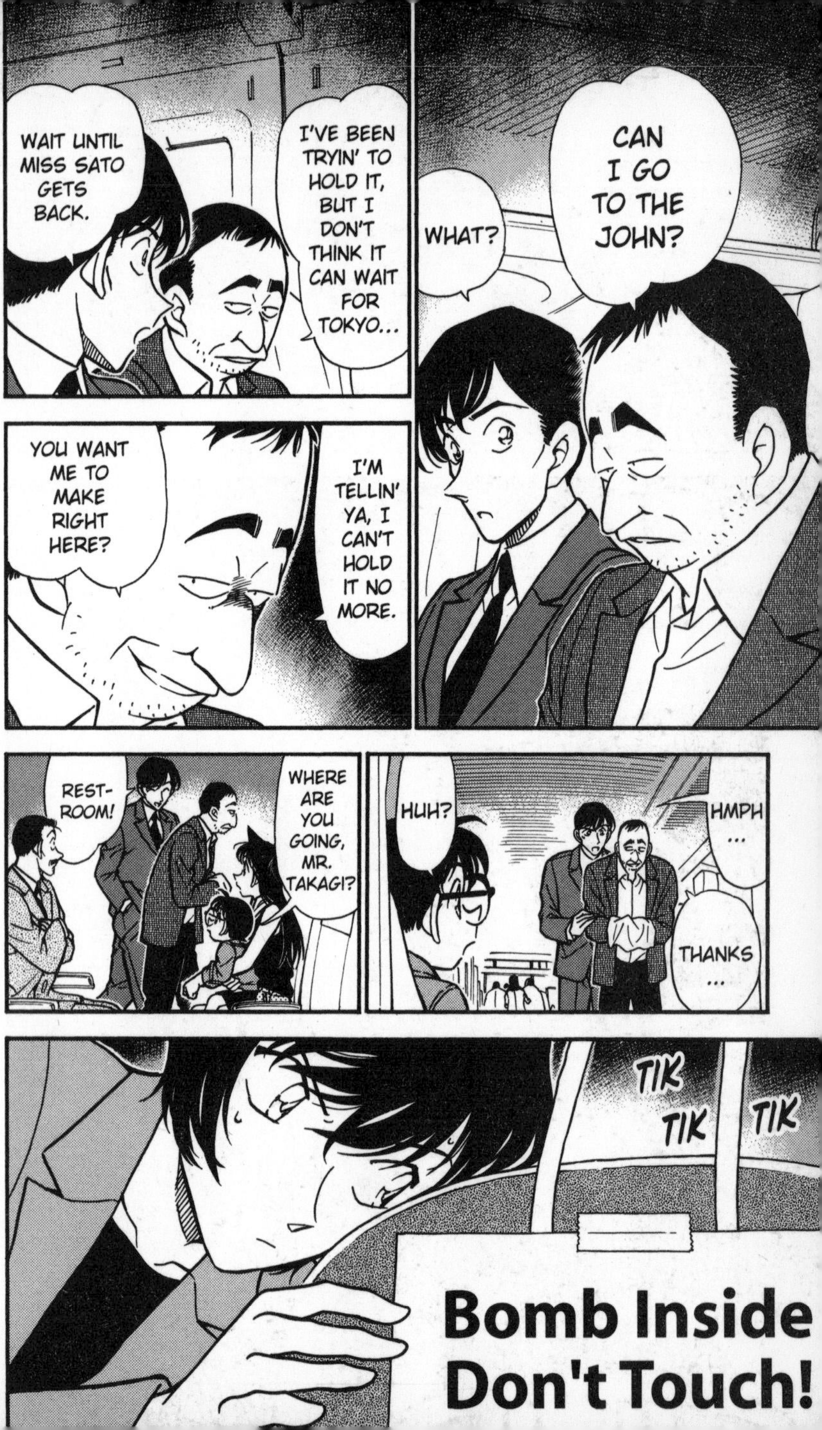

CAN I GO TO THE JOHN?
WHAT?
I'VE BEEN TRYIN' TO HOLD IT, BUT I DON'T THINK IT CAN WAIT FOR TOKYO...
WAIT UNTIL MISS SATO GETS BACK.
I'M TELLIN' YA, I CAN'T HOLD IT NO MORE.
YOU WANT ME TO MAKE RIGHT HERE?
HMPH ...
THANKS ...
HUH?
WHERE ARE YOU GOING, MR. TAKAGI?
REST-ROOM!
TIK
TIK
TIK
Bomb Inside
Don't Touch!

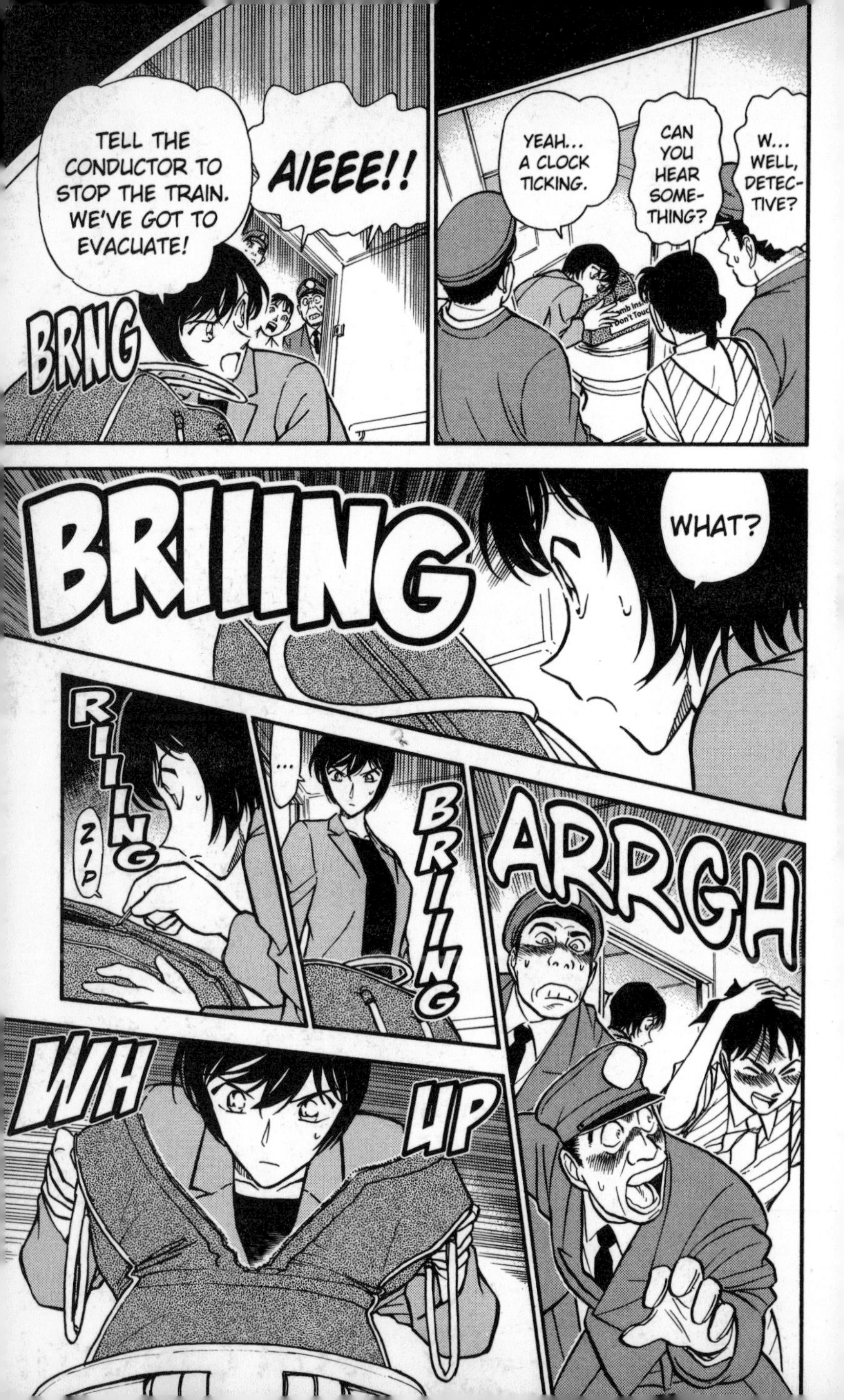

W... WELL, DETECTIVE?
CAN YOU HEAR SOMETHING?
YEAH... A CLOCK TICKING.
AIEEE!!
TELL THE CONDUCTOR TO STOP THE TRAIN. WE'VE GOT TO EVACUATE!
BRNG
WHAT?
BRIIING
ARRGH
...
BRIING
RIIING
ZIP
WHUP

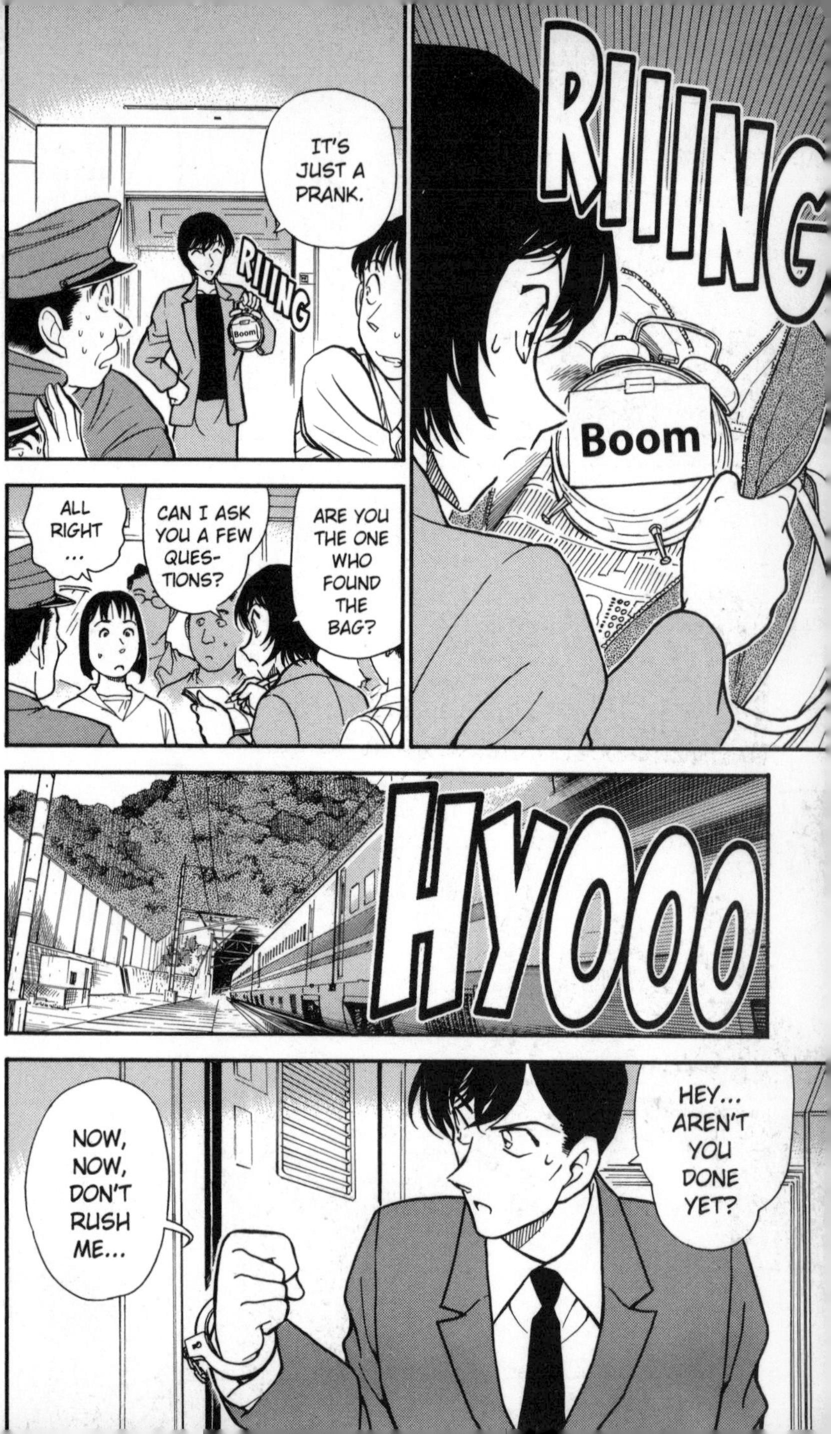
RIIING
Boom
IT'S JUST A PRANK.
RIIING
Boom
ARE YOU THE ONE WHO FOUND THE BAG?
CAN I ASK YOU A FEW QUES-TIONS?
ALL RIGHT ...
HYOOO
HEY... AREN'T YOU DONE YET?
NOW, NOW, DON'T RUSH ME...

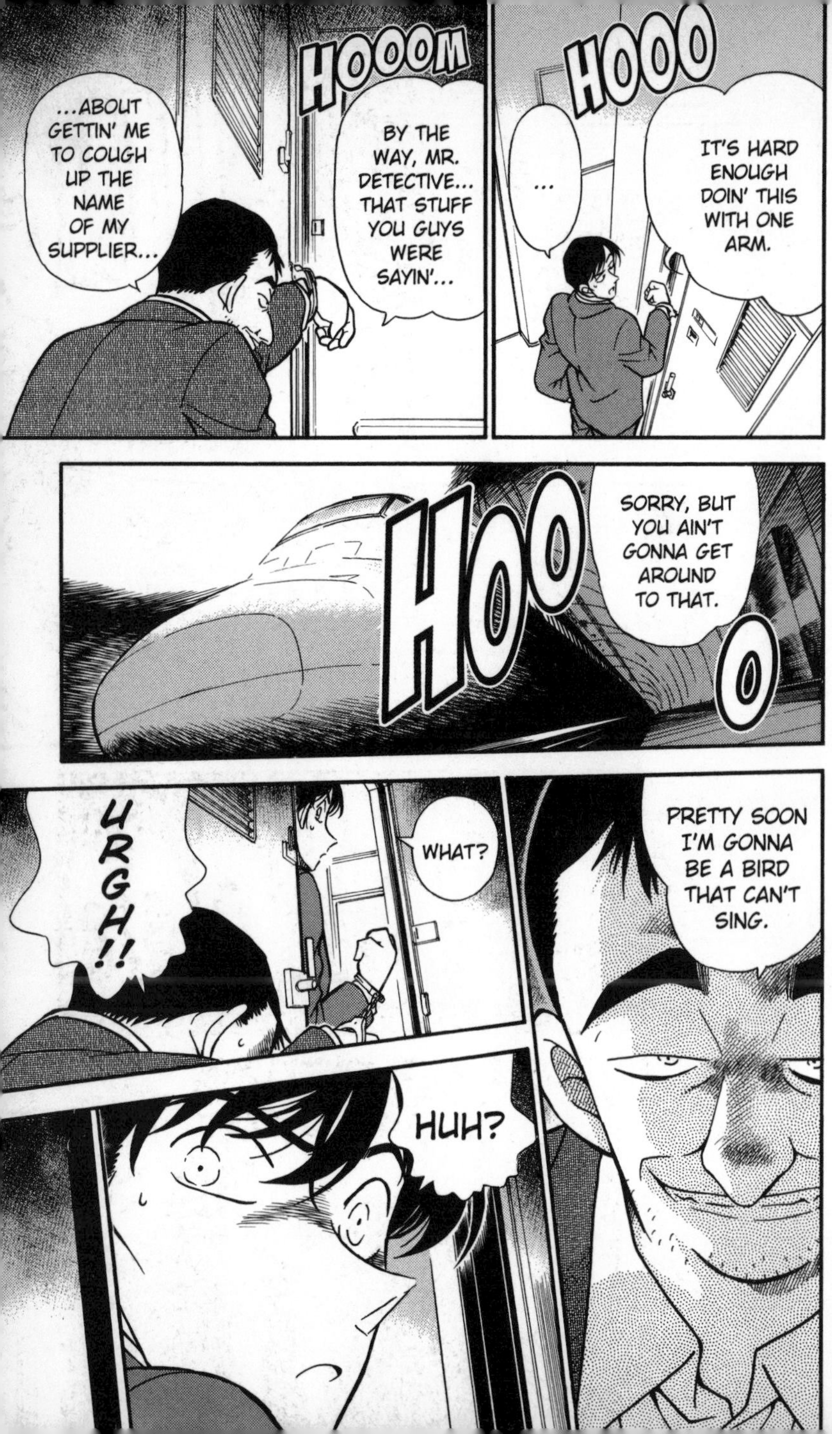
HOOO
IT'S HARD ENOUGH DOIN' THIS WITH ONE ARM.
...
HOOOM
BY THE WAY, MR. DETECTIVE... THAT STUFF YOU GUYS WERE SAYIN'...
...ABOUT GETTIN' ME TO COUGH UP THE NAME OF MY SUPPLIER...
SORRY, BUT YOU AIN'T GONNA GET AROUND TO THAT.
HOOO
PRETTY SOON I'M GONNA BE A BIRD THAT CAN'T SING.
WHAT?
URGH!!
HUH?

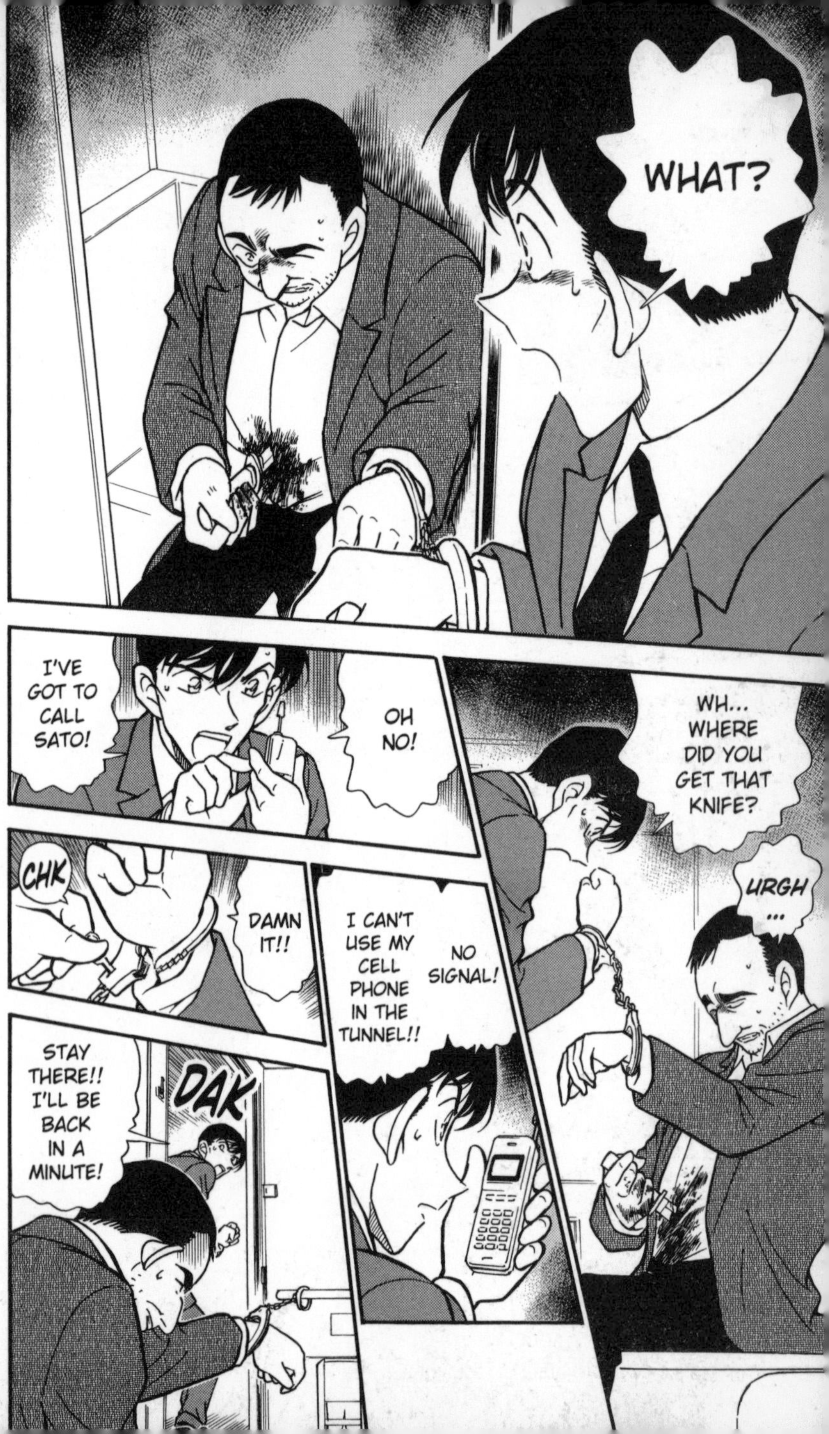
WHAT?
WH... WHERE DID YOU GET THAT KNIFE?
URGH...
OH NO!
I'VE GOT TO CALL SATO!
NO SIGNAL!
I CAN'T USE MY CELL PHONE IN THE TUNNEL!!
DAMN IT!!
CHK
DAK
STAY THERE!! I'LL BE BACK IN A MINUTE!

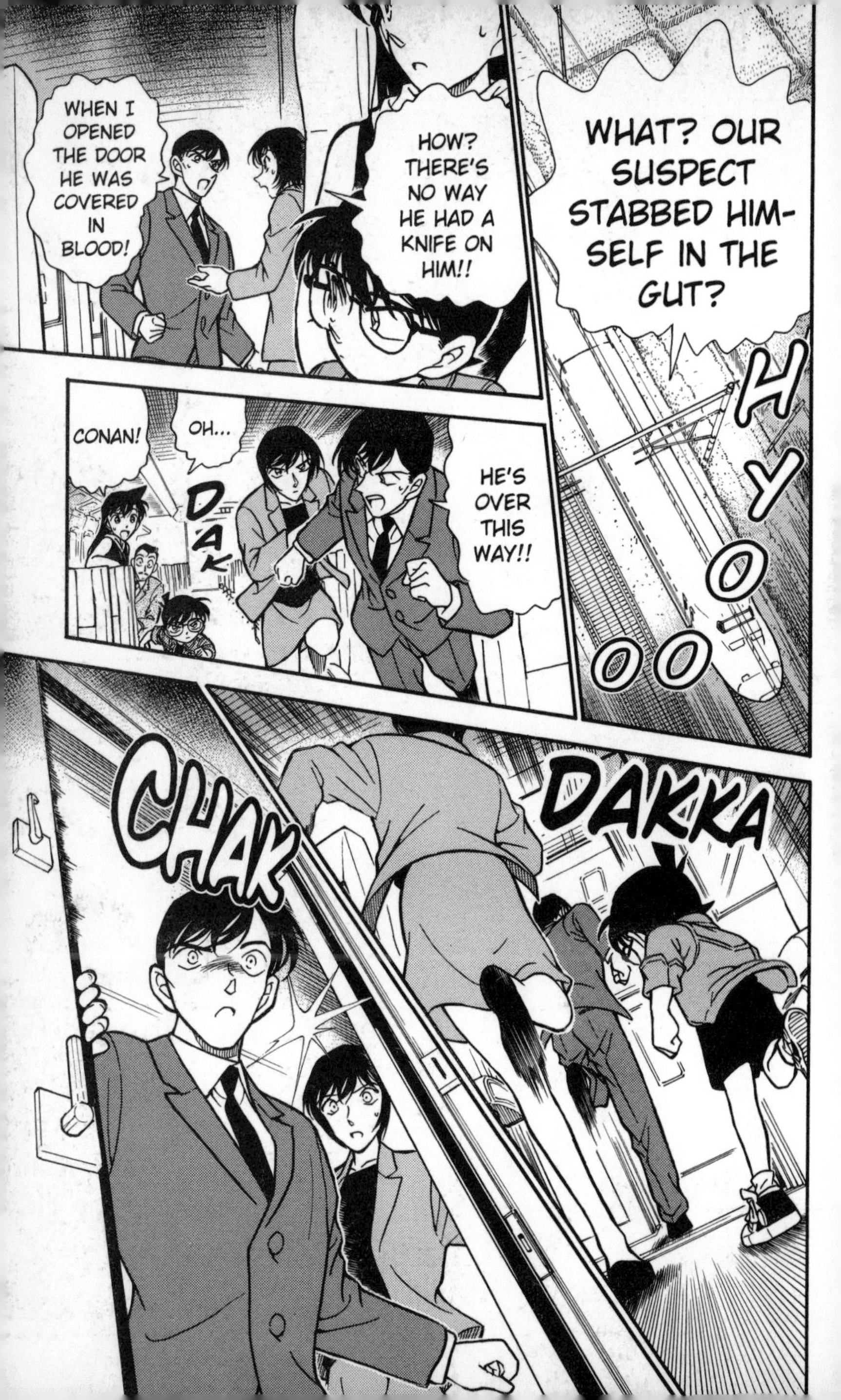
WHAT? OUR SUSPECT STABBED HIM-SELF IN THE GUT?
HYOOOO
HOW? THERE'S NO WAY HE HAD A KNIFE ON HIM!!
WHEN I OPENED THE DOOR HE WAS COVERED IN BLOOD!
HE'S OVER THIS WAY!!
OH...
CONAN!
DAK
DAKKA
CHAK

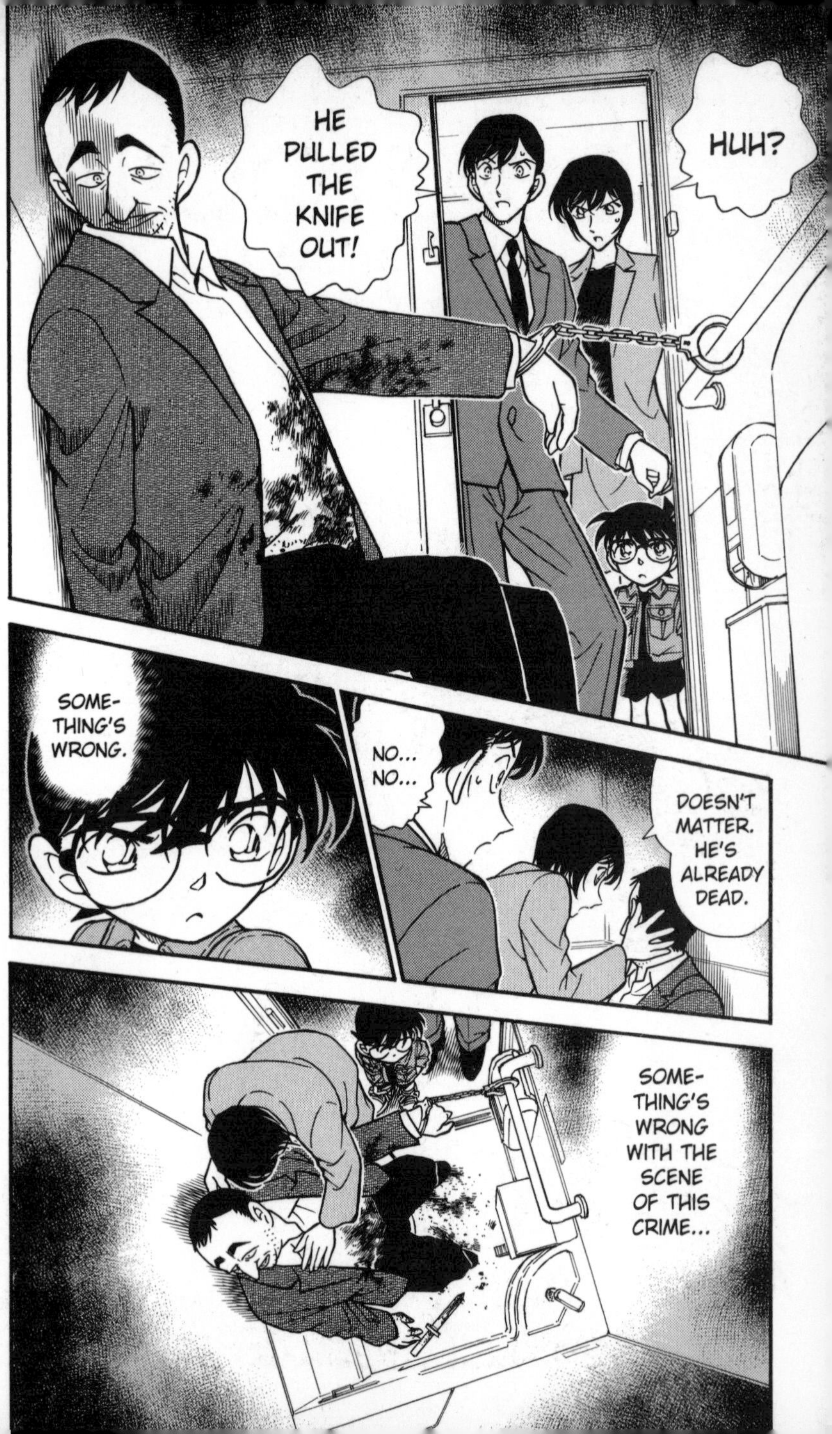
HUH?
HE PULLED THE KNIFE OUT!
DOESN'T MATTER. HE'S ALREADY DEAD.
NO... NO...
SOME-THING'S WRONG.
SOME-THING'S WRONG WITH THE SCENE OF THIS CRIME...

FILE 2: THE OPEN LOCKED ROOM

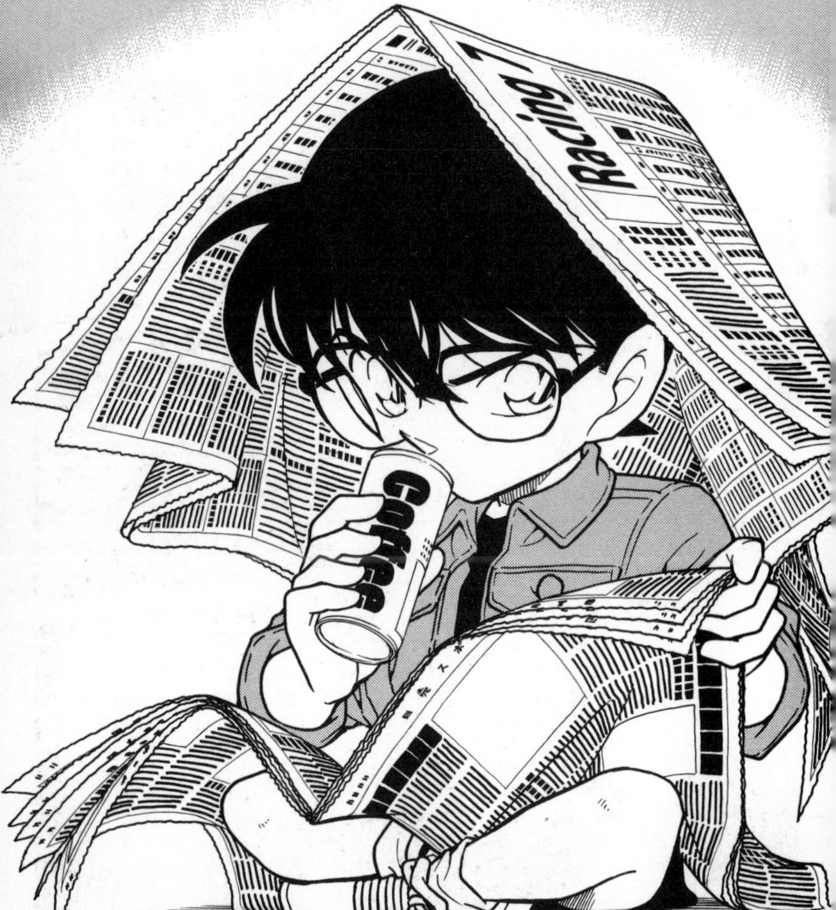
Racing
Coffee

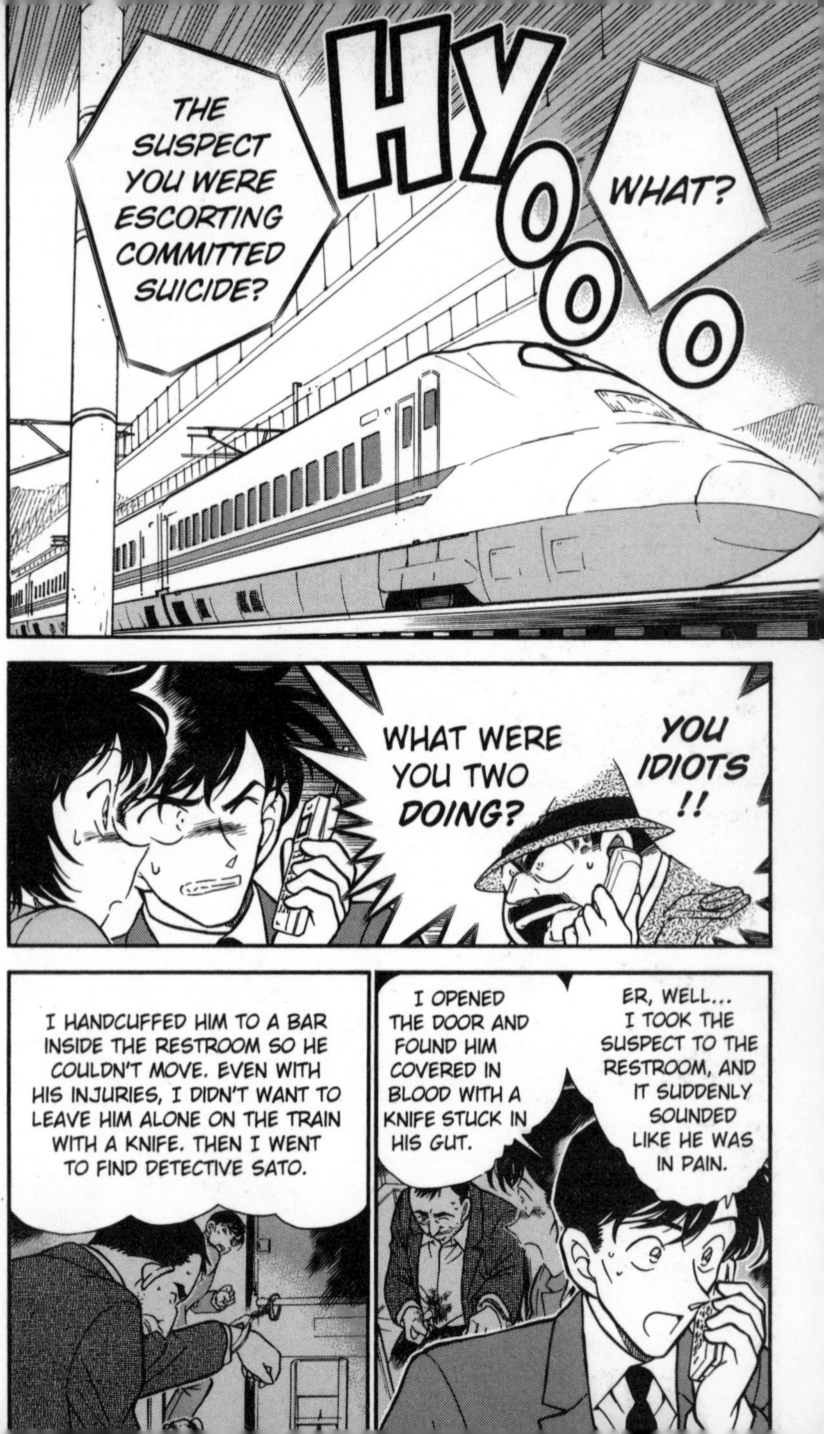
WHAT?
HYOOOO
THE SUSPECT YOU WERE ESCORTING COMMITTED SUICIDE?
YOU IDIOTS !!
WHAT WERE YOU TWO DOING?
ER, WELL... I TOOK THE SUSPECT TO THE RESTROOM, AND IT SUDDENLY SOUNDED LIKE HE WAS IN PAIN.
I OPENED THE DOOR AND FOUND HIM COVERED IN BLOOD WITH A KNIFE STUCK IN HIS GUT.
I HANDCUFFED HIM TO A BAR INSIDE THE RESTROOM SO HE COULDN'T MOVE. EVEN WITH HIS INJURIES, I DIDN'T WANT TO LEAVE HIM ALONE ON THE TRAIN WITH A KNIFE. THEN I WENT TO FIND DETECTIVE SATO.

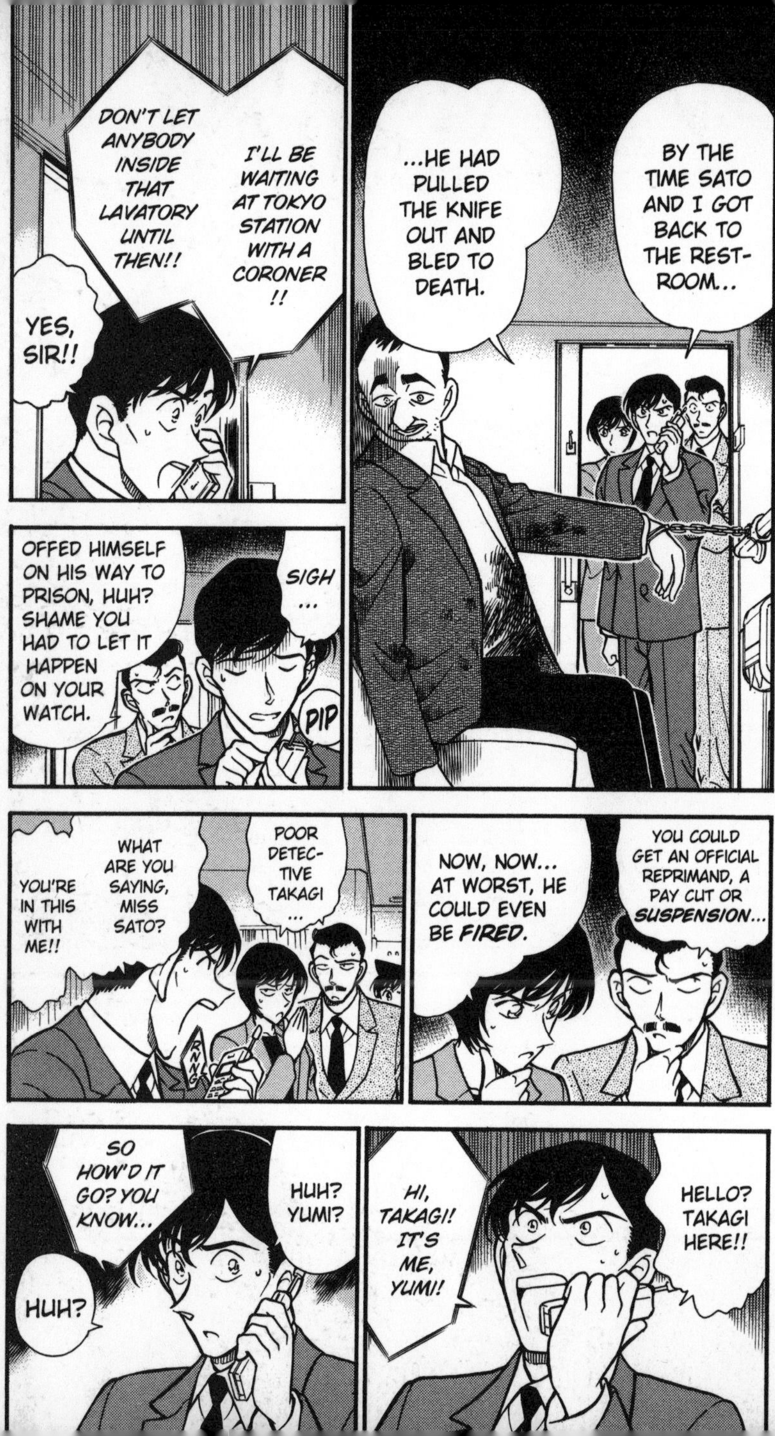
BY THE TIME SATO AND I GOT BACK TO THE REST-ROOM...
...HE HAD PULLED THE KNIFE OUT AND BLED TO DEATH.
I'LL BE WAITING AT TOKYO STATION WITH A CORONER!!
DON'T LET ANYBODY INSIDE THAT LAVATORY UNTIL THEN!!
YES, SIR!!
SIGH...
PIP
OFFED HIMSELF ON HIS WAY TO PRISON, HUH? SHAME YOU HAD TO LET IT HAPPEN ON YOUR WATCH.
YOU COULD GET AN OFFICIAL REPRIMAND, A PAY CUT OR SUSPENSION...
NOW, NOW... AT WORST, HE COULD EVEN BE FIRED.
POOR DETECTIVE TAKAGI...
WHAT ARE YOU SAYING, MISS SATO?
YOU'RE IN THIS WITH ME!!
RNNG
HELLO? TAKAGI HERE!!
HI, TAKAGI!! IT'S ME, YUMI!
HUH? YUMI?
SO HOW'D IT GO? YOU KNOW...
HUH?

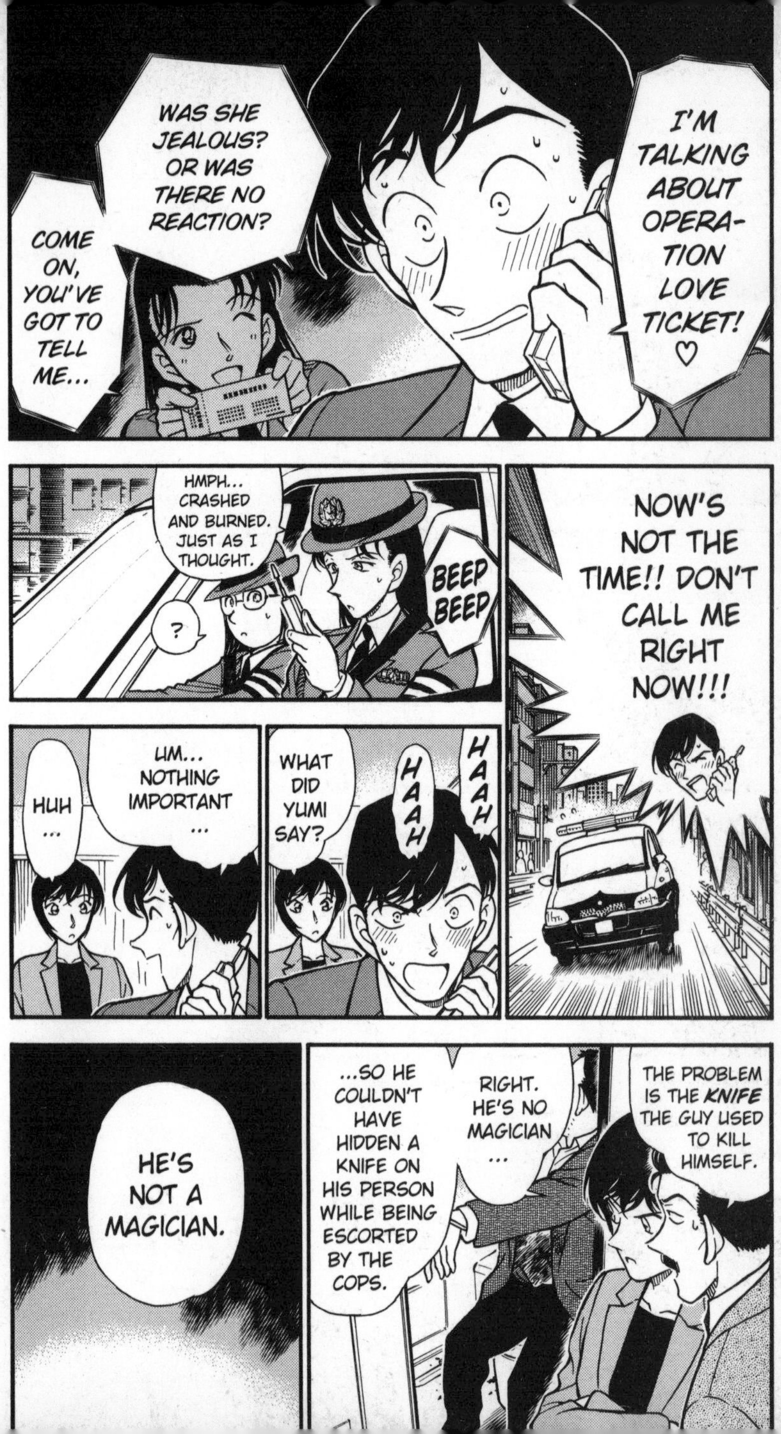
I'M TALKING ABOUT OPERATION LOVE TICKET! ♡
WAS SHE JEALOUS? OR WAS THERE NO REACTION?
COME ON, YOU'VE GOT TO TELL ME...
NOW'S NOT THE TIME!! DON'T CALL ME RIGHT NOW!!!
BEEP BEEP
HMPH... CRASHED AND BURNED. JUST AS I THOUGHT.
?
HAAAH
WHAT DID YUMI SAY?
UM... NOTHING IMPORTANT ...
HUH ...
THE PROBLEM IS THE *KNIFE* THE GUY USED TO KILL HIMSELF.
RIGHT. HE'S NO MAGICIAN ...
...SO HE COULDN'T HAVE HIDDEN A KNIFE ON HIS PERSON WHILE BEING ESCORTED BY THE COPS.
HE'S NOT A MAGICIAN.

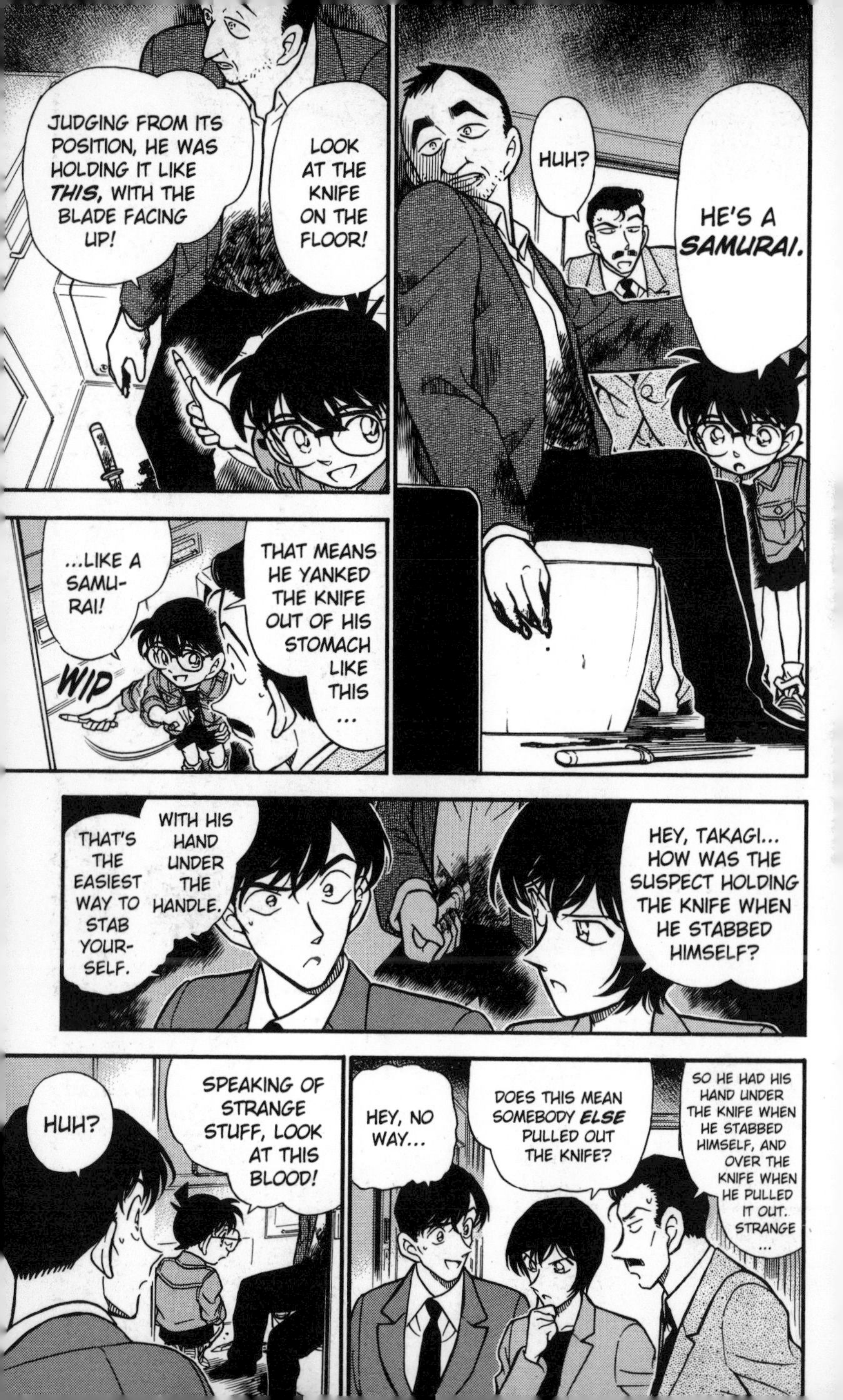
HE'S A SAMURAI.
HUH?
LOOK AT THE KNIFE ON THE FLOOR!
JUDGING FROM ITS POSITION, HE WAS HOLDING IT LIKE THIS, WITH THE BLADE FACING UP!
THAT MEANS HE YANKED THE KNIFE OUT OF HIS STOMACH LIKE THIS...
...LIKE A SAMURAI!
WIP
HEY, TAKAGI... HOW WAS THE SUSPECT HOLDING THE KNIFE WHEN HE STABBED HIMSELF?
WITH HIS HAND UNDER THE HANDLE.
THAT'S THE EASIEST WAY TO STAB YOURSELF.
SO HE HAD HIS HAND UNDER THE KNIFE WHEN HE STABBED HIMSELF, AND OVER THE KNIFE WHEN HE PULLED IT OUT. STRANGE...
DOES THIS MEAN SOMEBODY ELSE PULLED OUT THE KNIFE?
HEY, NO WAY...
SPEAKING OF STRANGE STUFF, LOOK AT THIS BLOOD!
HUH?

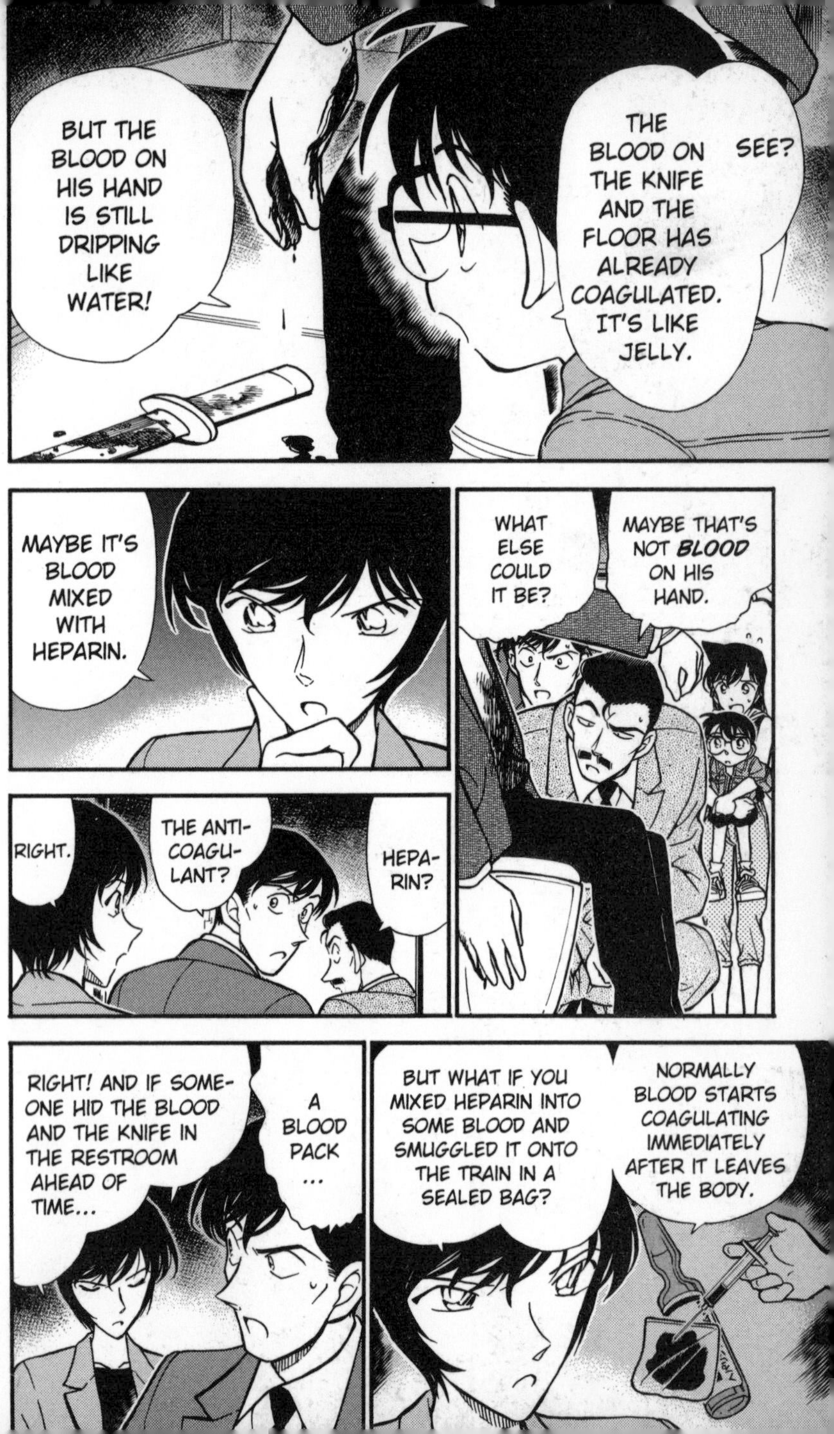
SEE?
THE BLOOD ON THE KNIFE AND THE FLOOR HAS ALREADY COAGULATED. IT'S LIKE JELLY.
BUT THE BLOOD ON HIS HAND IS STILL DRIPPING LIKE WATER!
MAYBE THAT'S NOT **BLOOD** ON HIS HAND.
WHAT ELSE COULD IT BE?
MAYBE IT'S BLOOD MIXED WITH HEPARIN.
HEPA-RIN?
THE ANTI-COAGU-LANT?
RIGHT.
NORMALLY BLOOD STARTS COAGULATING IMMEDIATELY AFTER IT LEAVES THE BODY.
BUT WHAT IF YOU MIXED HEPARIN INTO SOME BLOOD AND SMUGGLED IT ONTO THE TRAIN IN A SEALED BAG?
A BLOOD PACK...
RIGHT! AND IF SOME-ONE HID THE BLOOD AND THE KNIFE IN THE RESTROOM AHEAD OF TIME...

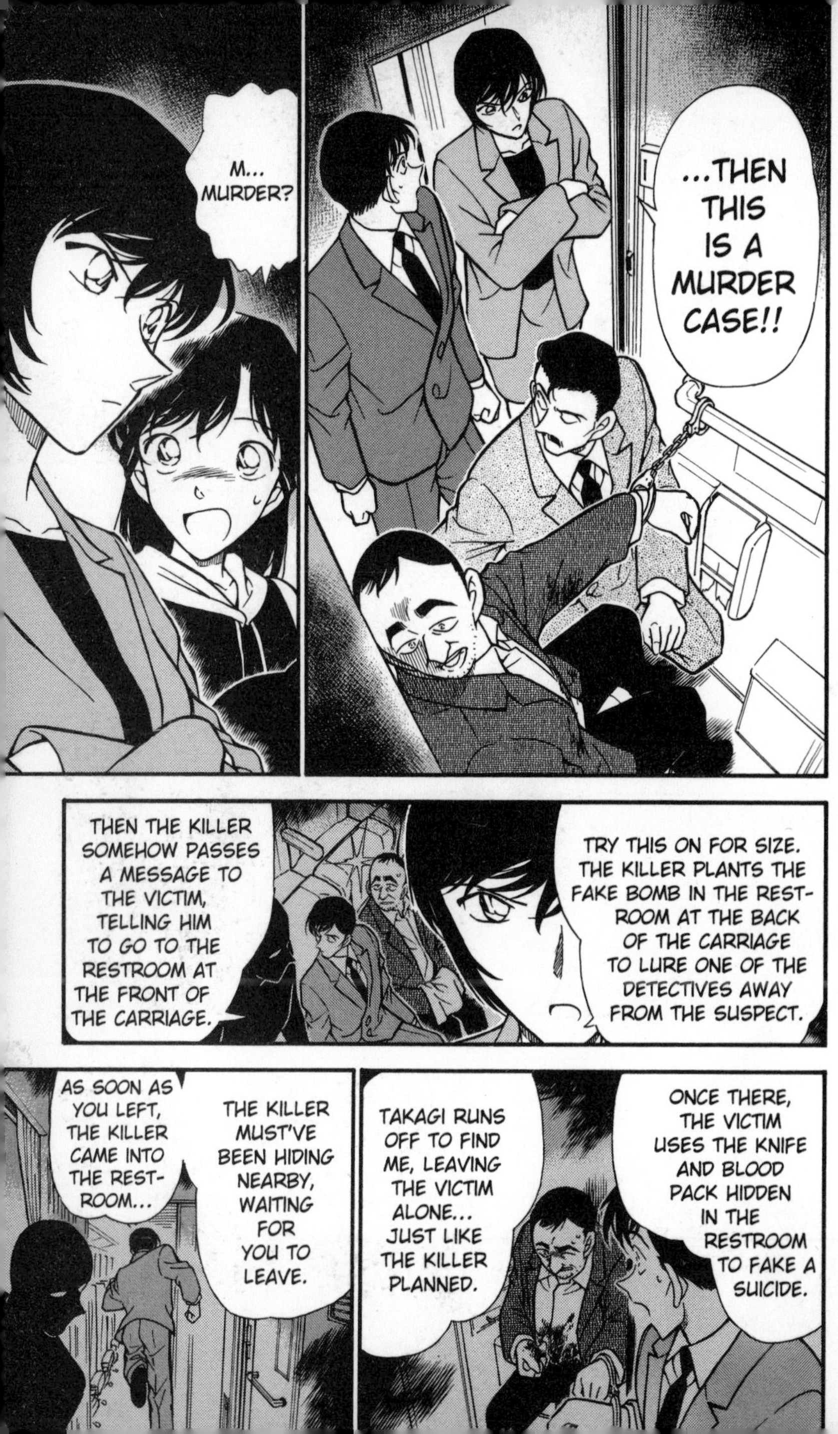
...THEN THIS IS A MURDER CASE!!
M... MURDER?
TRY THIS ON FOR SIZE. THE KILLER PLANTS THE FAKE BOMB IN THE REST-ROOM AT THE BACK OF THE CARRIAGE TO LURE ONE OF THE DETECTIVES AWAY FROM THE SUSPECT.
THEN THE KILLER SOMEHOW PASSES A MESSAGE TO THE VICTIM, TELLING HIM TO GO TO THE RESTROOM AT THE FRONT OF THE CARRIAGE.
ONCE THERE, THE VICTIM USES THE KNIFE AND BLOOD PACK HIDDEN IN THE RESTROOM TO FAKE A SUICIDE.
TAKAGI RUNS OFF TO FIND ME, LEAVING THE VICTIM ALONE... JUST LIKE THE KILLER PLANNED.
THE KILLER MUST'VE BEEN HIDING NEARBY, WAITING FOR YOU TO LEAVE.
AS SOON AS YOU LEFT, THE KILLER CAME INTO THE REST-ROOM...

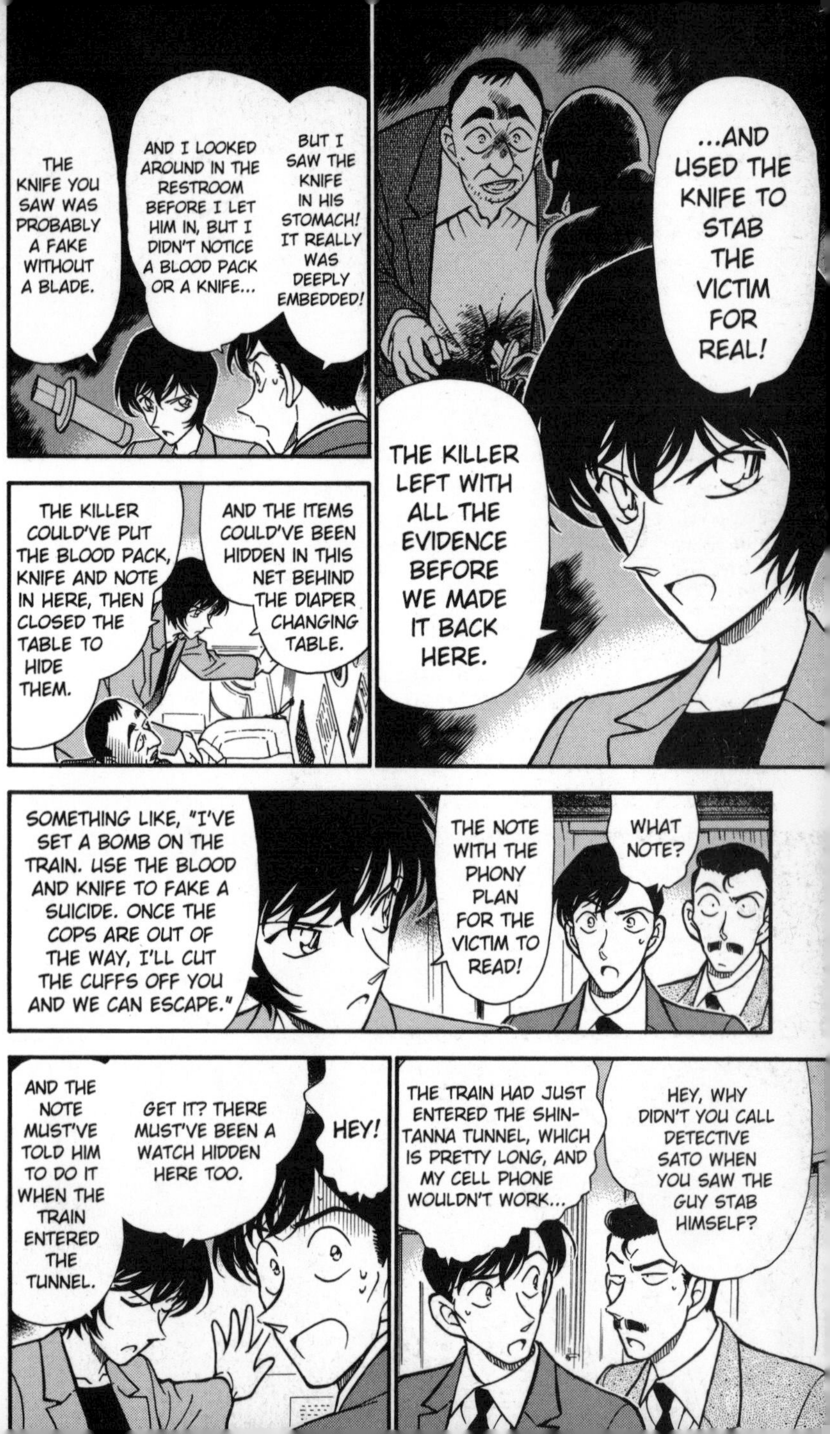
...AND USED THE KNIFE TO STAB THE VICTIM FOR REAL!
THE KILLER LEFT WITH ALL THE EVIDENCE BEFORE WE MADE IT BACK HERE.
BUT I SAW THE KNIFE IN HIS STOMACH! IT REALLY WAS DEEPLY EMBEDDED!
AND I LOOKED AROUND IN THE RESTROOM BEFORE I LET HIM IN, BUT I DIDN'T NOTICE A BLOOD PACK OR A KNIFE...
THE KNIFE YOU SAW WAS PROBABLY A FAKE WITHOUT A BLADE.
AND THE ITEMS COULD'VE BEEN HIDDEN IN THIS NET BEHIND THE DIAPER CHANGING TABLE.
THE KILLER COULD'VE PUT THE BLOOD PACK, KNIFE AND NOTE IN HERE, THEN CLOSED THE TABLE TO HIDE THEM.
WHAT NOTE?
THE NOTE WITH THE PHONY PLAN FOR THE VICTIM TO READ!
SOMETHING LIKE, "I'VE SET A BOMB ON THE TRAIN. USE THE BLOOD AND KNIFE TO FAKE A SUICIDE. ONCE THE COPS ARE OUT OF THE WAY, I'LL CUT THE CUFFS OFF YOU AND WE CAN ESCAPE."
HEY, WHY DIDN'T YOU CALL DETECTIVE SATO WHEN YOU SAW THE GUY STAB HIMSELF?
THE TRAIN HAD JUST ENTERED THE SHIN-TANNA TUNNEL, WHICH IS PRETTY LONG, AND MY CELL PHONE WOULDN'T WORK...
HEY!
GET IT? THERE MUST'VE BEEN A WATCH HIDDEN HERE TOO.
AND THE NOTE MUST'VE TOLD HIM TO DO IT WHEN THE TRAIN ENTERED THE TUNNEL.

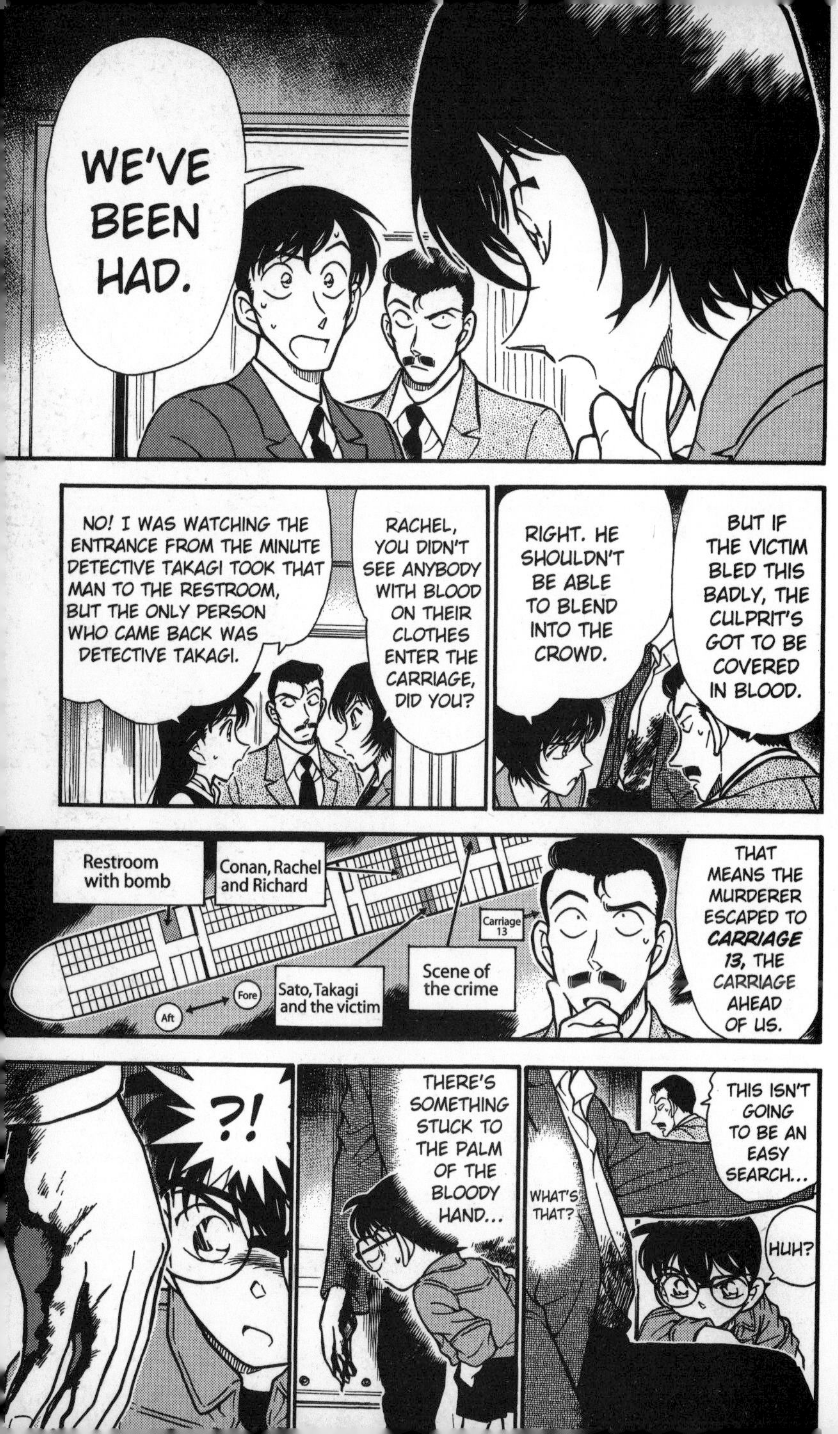
WE'VE BEEN HAD.
BUT IF THE VICTIM BLED THIS BADLY, THE CULPRIT'S GOT TO BE COVERED IN BLOOD.
RIGHT. HE SHOULDN'T BE ABLE TO BLEND INTO THE CROWD.
RACHEL, YOU DIDN'T SEE ANYBODY WITH BLOOD ON THEIR CLOTHES ENTER THE CARRIAGE, DID YOU?
NO! I WAS WATCHING THE ENTRANCE FROM THE MINUTE DETECTIVE TAKAGI TOOK THAT MAN TO THE RESTROOM, BUT THE ONLY PERSON WHO CAME BACK WAS DETECTIVE TAKAGI.
THAT MEANS THE MURDERER ESCAPED TO CARRIAGE 13, THE CARRIAGE AHEAD OF US.
Carriage 13
Conan, Rachel and Richard
Restroom with bomb
Scene of the crime
Sato, Takagi and the victim
Fore
Aft
THIS ISN'T GOING TO BE AN EASY SEARCH...
HUH?
WHAT'S THAT?
THERE'S SOMETHING STUCK TO THE PALM OF THE BLOODY HAND...
?!

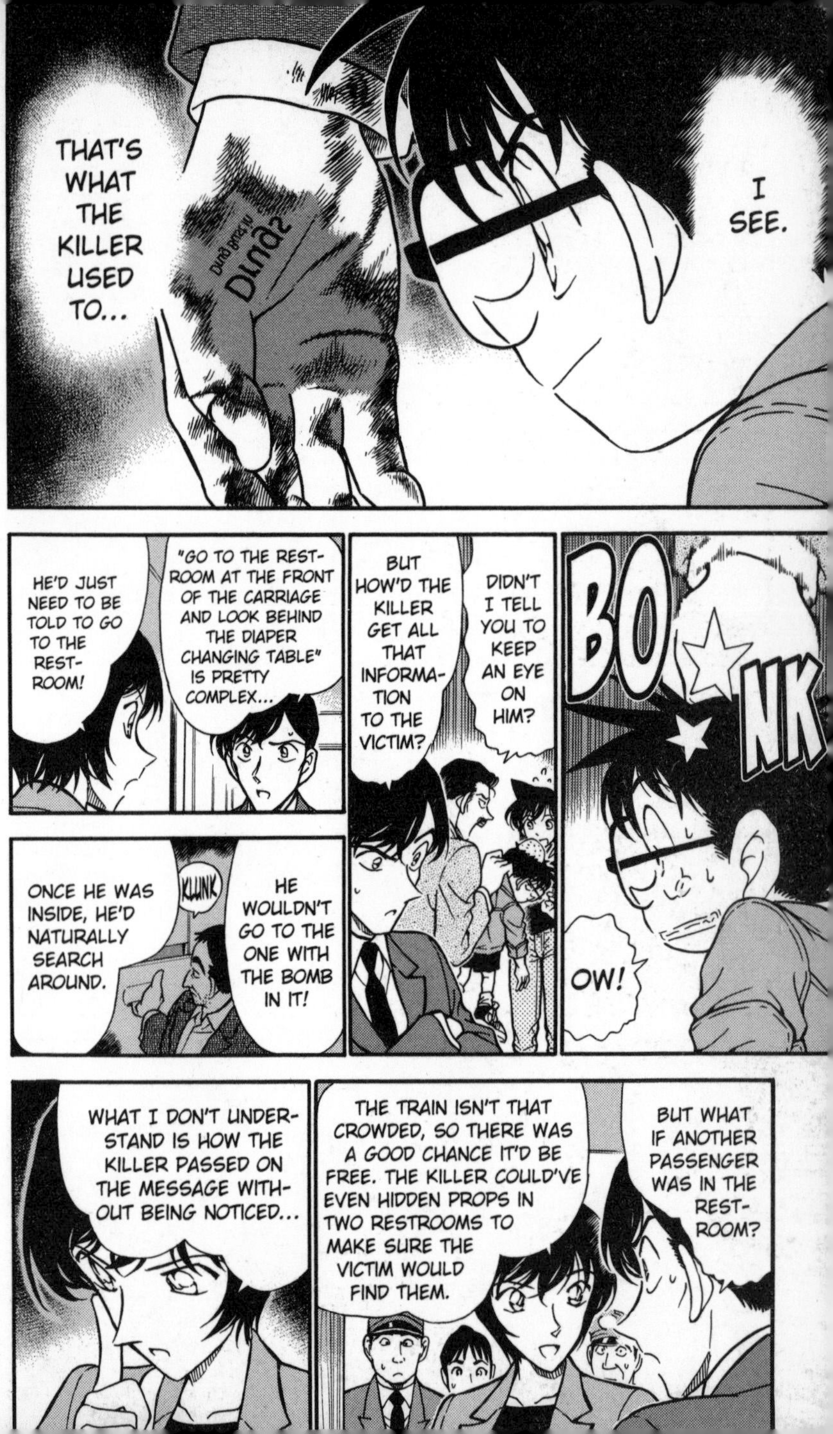
I SEE.
THAT'S WHAT THE KILLER USED TO...
BONK
OW!
DIDN'T I TELL YOU TO KEEP AN EYE ON HIM?
BUT HOW'D THE KILLER GET ALL THAT INFORMATION TO THE VICTIM?
"GO TO THE RESTROOM AT THE FRONT OF THE CARRIAGE AND LOOK BEHIND THE DIAPER CHANGING TABLE" IS PRETTY COMPLEX...
HE'D JUST NEED TO BE TOLD TO GO TO THE RESTROOM!
HE WOULDN'T GO TO THE ONE WITH THE BOMB IN IT!
KLUNK
ONCE HE WAS INSIDE, HE'D NATURALLY SEARCH AROUND.
BUT WHAT IF ANOTHER PASSENGER WAS IN THE RESTROOM?
THE TRAIN ISN'T THAT CROWDED, SO THERE WAS A GOOD CHANCE IT'D BE FREE. THE KILLER COULD'VE EVEN HIDDEN PROPS IN TWO RESTROOMS TO MAKE SURE THE VICTIM WOULD FIND THEM.
WHAT I DON'T UNDERSTAND IS HOW THE KILLER PASSED ON THE MESSAGE WITHOUT BEING NOTICED...

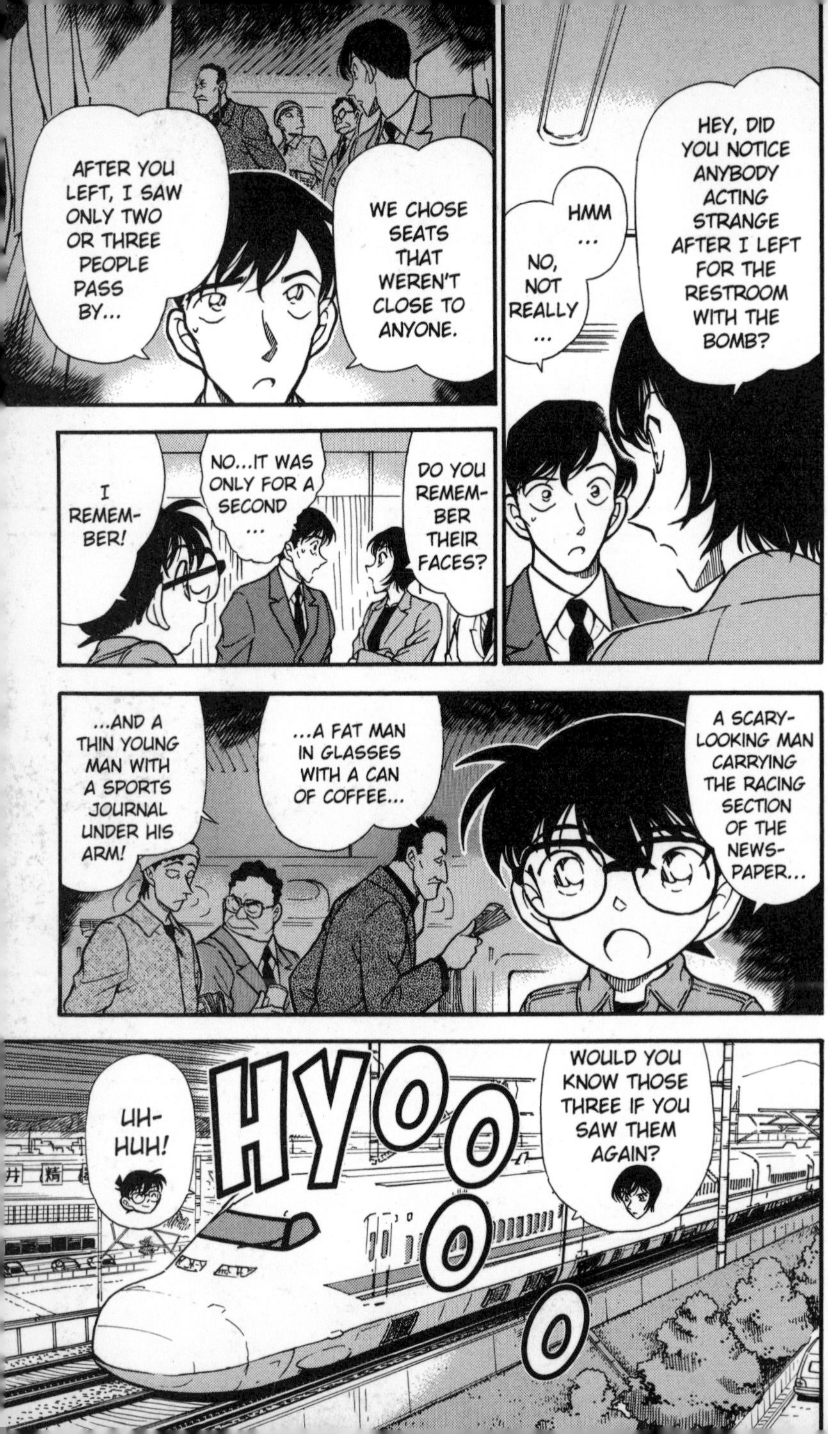
HEY, DID YOU NOTICE ANYBODY ACTING STRANGE AFTER I LEFT FOR THE RESTROOM WITH THE BOMB?
HMM ...
NO, NOT REALLY ...
WE CHOSE SEATS THAT WEREN'T CLOSE TO ANYONE.
AFTER YOU LEFT, I SAW ONLY TWO OR THREE PEOPLE PASS BY...
DO YOU REMEMBER THEIR FACES?
NO...IT WAS ONLY FOR A SECOND ...
I REMEMBER!
A SCARY-LOOKING MAN CARRYING THE RACING SECTION OF THE NEWSPAPER...
...A FAT MAN IN GLASSES WITH A CAN OF COFFEE...
...AND A THIN YOUNG MAN WITH A SPORTS JOURNAL UNDER HIS ARM!
WOULD YOU KNOW THOSE THREE IF YOU SAW THEM AGAIN?
HYOOOOOO
UH-HUH!

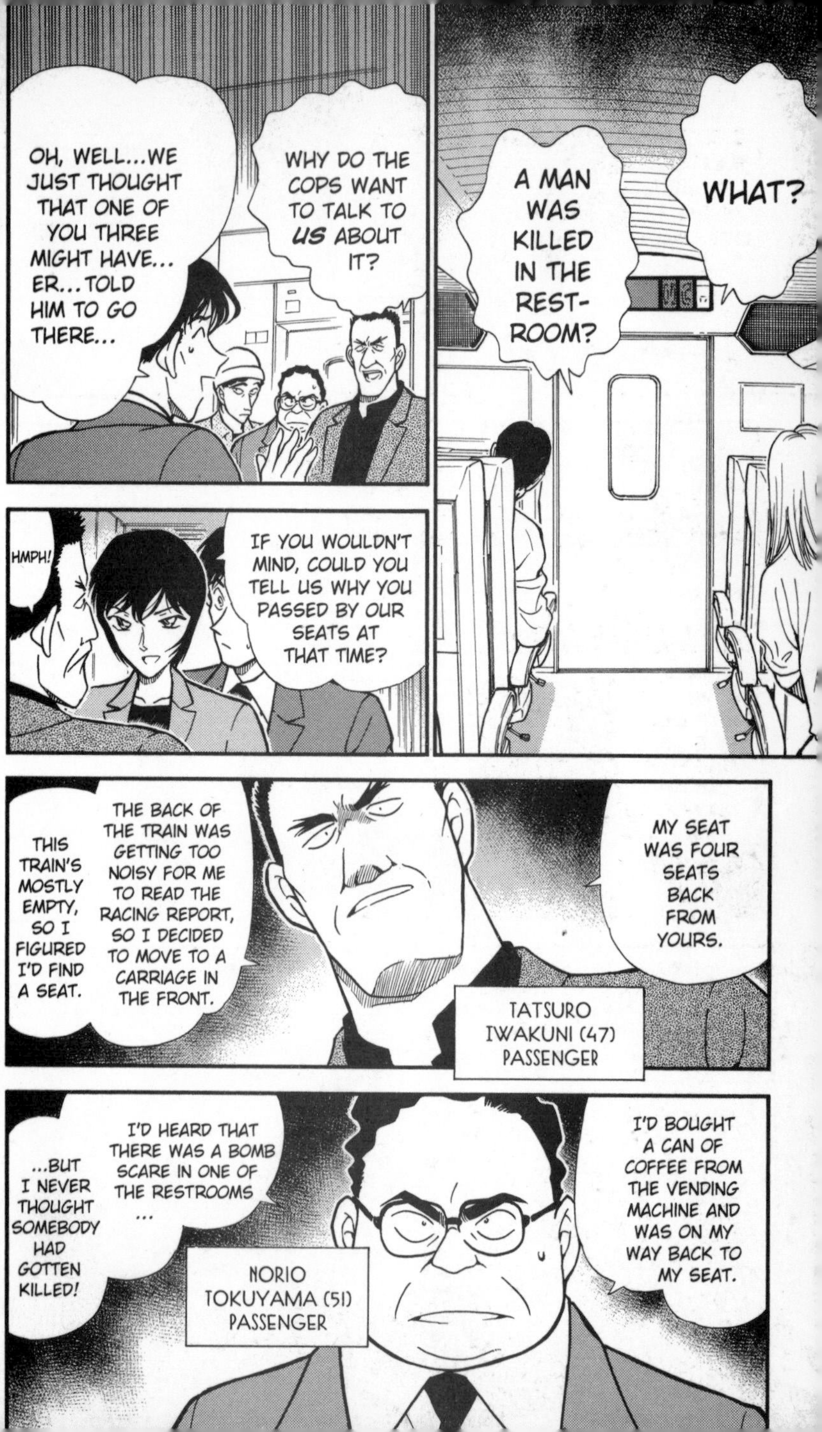
WHAT?
A MAN WAS KILLED IN THE REST-ROOM?
WHY DO THE COPS WANT TO TALK TO US ABOUT IT?
OH, WELL...WE JUST THOUGHT THAT ONE OF YOU THREE MIGHT HAVE... ER...TOLD HIM TO GO THERE...
IF YOU WOULDN'T MIND, COULD YOU TELL US WHY YOU PASSED BY OUR SEATS AT THAT TIME?
HMPH!
MY SEAT WAS FOUR SEATS BACK FROM YOURS.
THE BACK OF THE TRAIN WAS GETTING TOO NOISY FOR ME TO READ THE RACING REPORT, SO I DECIDED TO MOVE TO A CARRIAGE IN THE FRONT.
THIS TRAIN'S MOSTLY EMPTY, SO I FIGURED I'D FIND A SEAT.
TATSURO IWAKUNI (47) PASSENGER
I'D BOUGHT A CAN OF COFFEE FROM THE VENDING MACHINE AND WAS ON MY WAY BACK TO MY SEAT.
I'D HEARD THAT THERE WAS A BOMB SCARE IN ONE OF THE RESTROOMS ...
...BUT I NEVER THOUGHT SOMEBODY HAD GOTTEN KILLED!
NORIO TOKUYAMA (51) PASSENGER

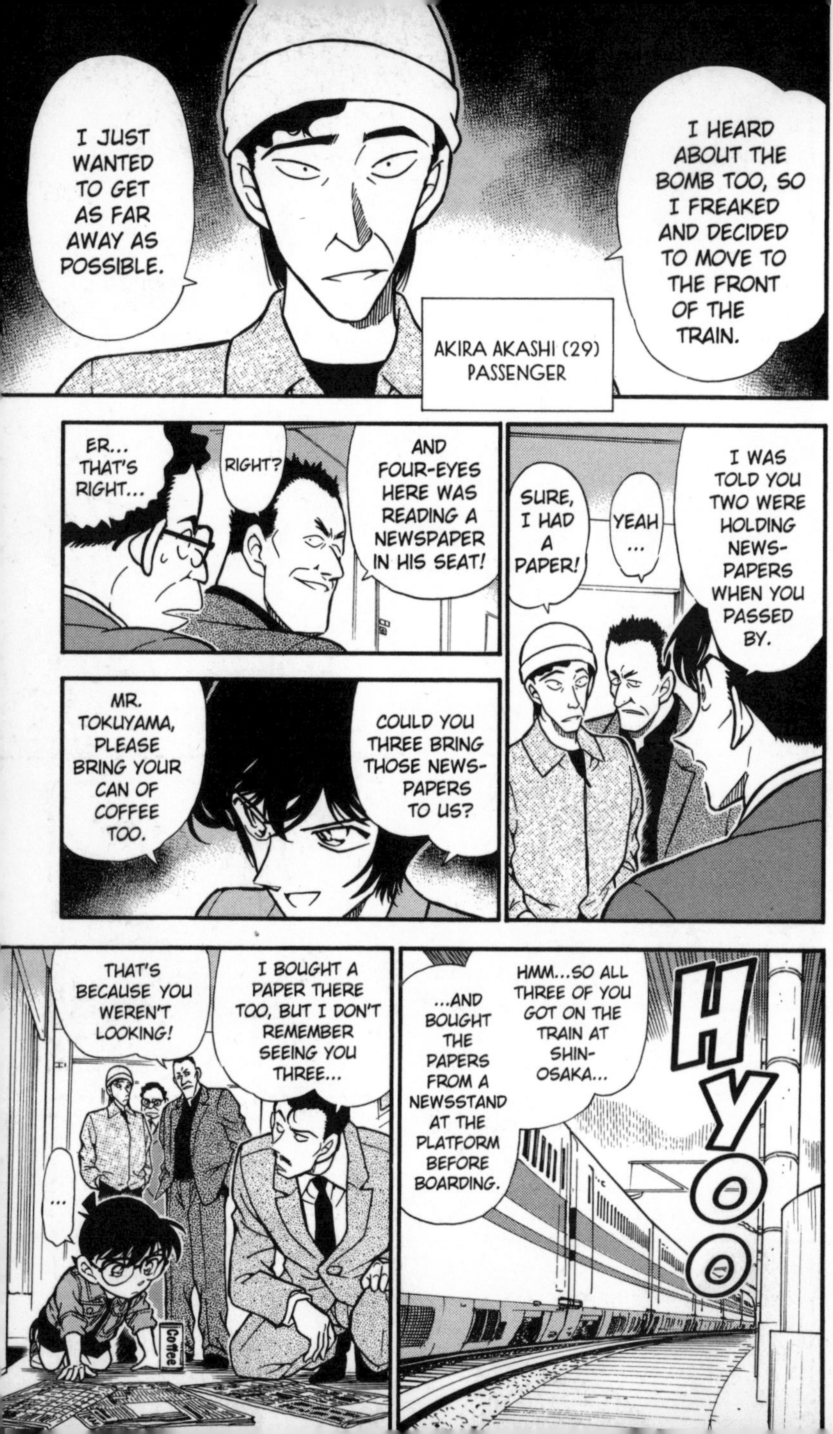
I HEARD ABOUT THE BOMB TOO, SO I FREAKED AND DECIDED TO MOVE TO THE FRONT OF THE TRAIN.
I JUST WANTED TO GET AS FAR AWAY AS POSSIBLE.
AKIRA AKASHI (29) PASSENGER
I WAS TOLD YOU TWO WERE HOLDING NEWS-PAPERS WHEN YOU PASSED BY.
YEAH...
SURE, I HAD A PAPER!
AND FOUR-EYES HERE WAS READING A NEWSPAPER IN HIS SEAT!
RIGHT?
ER... THAT'S RIGHT...
COULD YOU THREE BRING THOSE NEWS-PAPERS TO US?
MR. TOKUYAMA, PLEASE BRING YOUR CAN OF COFFEE TOO.
HYOO
HMM...SO ALL THREE OF YOU GOT ON THE TRAIN AT SHIN-OSAKA...
...AND BOUGHT THE PAPERS FROM A NEWSSTAND AT THE PLATFORM BEFORE BOARDING.
I BOUGHT A PAPER THERE TOO, BUT I DON'T REMEMBER SEEING YOU THREE...
THAT'S BECAUSE YOU WEREN'T LOOKING!
...
Coffee

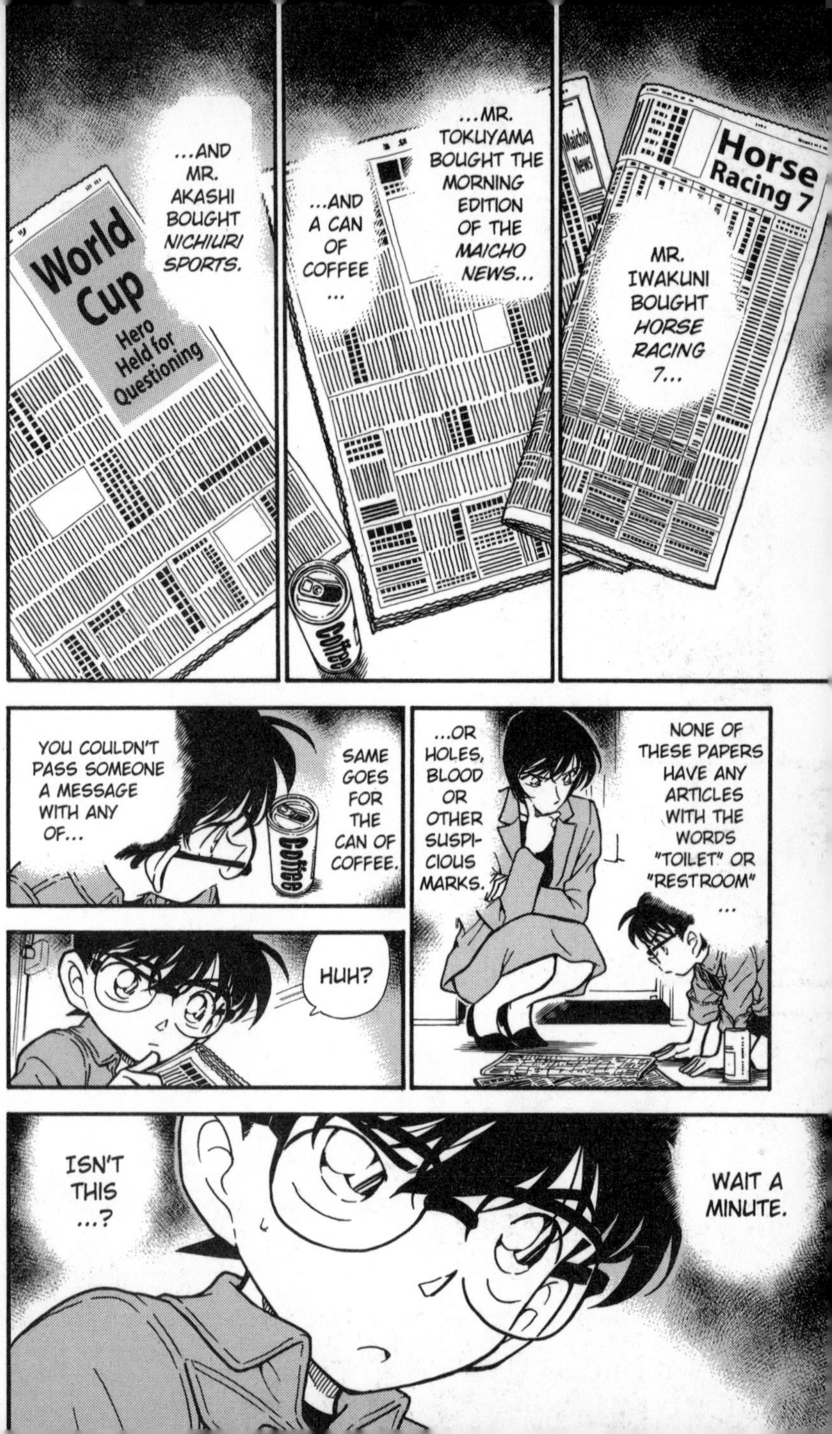
Horse Racing 7
Maicho News
MR. IWAKUNI BOUGHT HORSE RACING 7...
...MR. TOKUYAMA BOUGHT THE MORNING EDITION OF THE MAICHO NEWS...
...AND A CAN OF COFFEE...
Coffee
...AND MR. AKASHI BOUGHT NICHIURI SPORTS.
World Cup
Hero Held for Questioning
NONE OF THESE PAPERS HAVE ANY ARTICLES WITH THE WORDS "TOILET" OR "RESTROOM"...
...OR HOLES, BLOOD OR OTHER SUSPICIOUS MARKS.
SAME GOES FOR THE CAN OF COFFEE.
YOU COULDN'T PASS SOMEONE A MESSAGE WITH ANY OF...
Coffee
HUH?
WAIT A MINUTE.
ISN'T THIS ...?

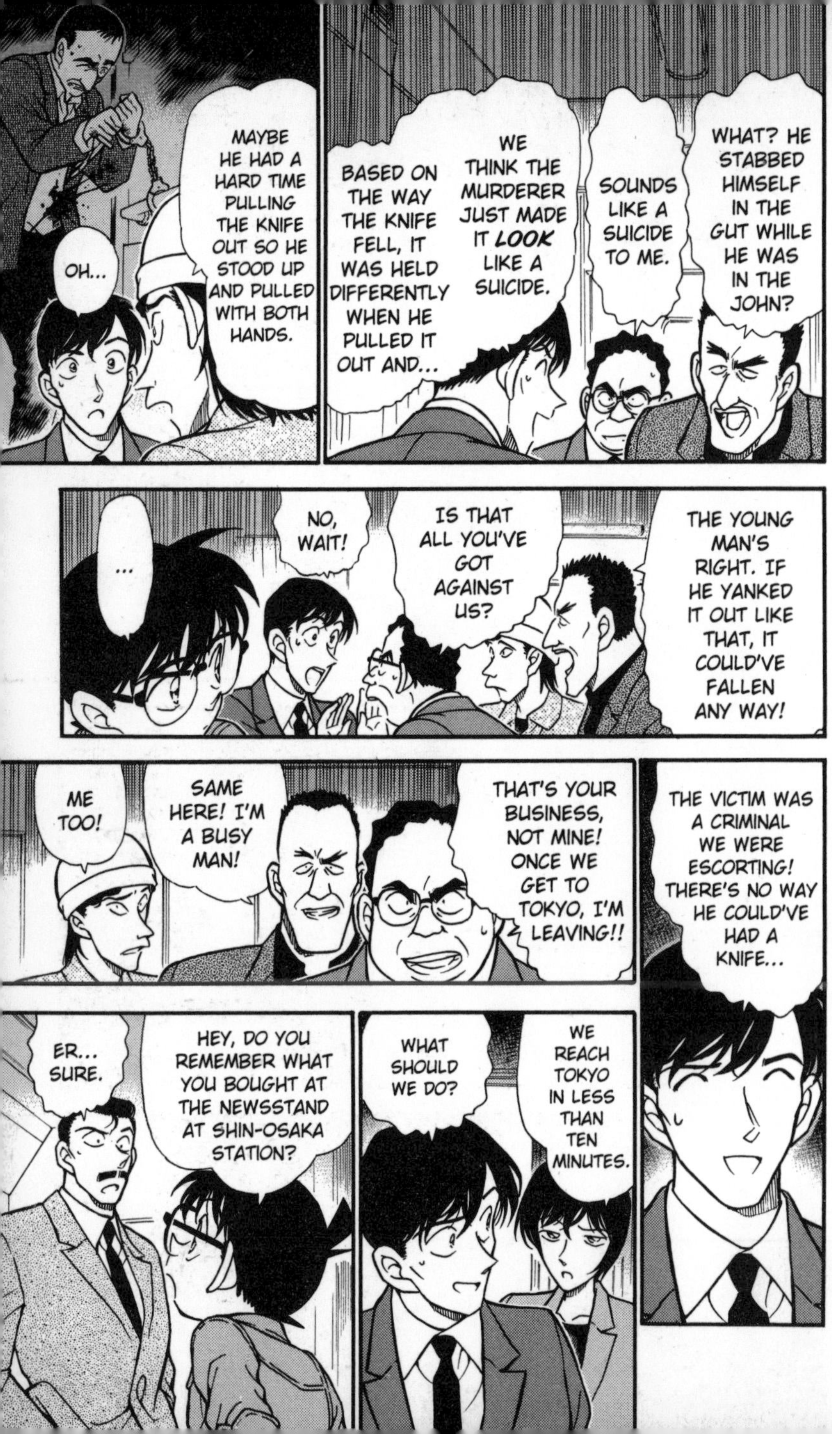
WHAT? HE STABBED HIMSELF IN THE GUT WHILE HE WAS IN THE JOHN?
SOUNDS LIKE A SUICIDE TO ME.
WE THINK THE MURDERER JUST MADE IT *LOOK* LIKE A SUICIDE.
BASED ON THE WAY THE KNIFE FELL, IT WAS HELD DIFFERENTLY WHEN HE PULLED IT OUT AND...
MAYBE HE HAD A HARD TIME PULLING THE KNIFE OUT SO HE STOOD UP AND PULLED WITH BOTH HANDS.
OH...
THE YOUNG MAN'S RIGHT. IF HE YANKED IT OUT LIKE THAT, IT COULD'VE FALLEN ANY WAY!
IS THAT ALL YOU'VE GOT AGAINST US?
NO, WAIT!
...
THE VICTIM WAS A CRIMINAL WE WERE ESCORTING! THERE'S NO WAY HE COULD'VE HAD A KNIFE...
THAT'S YOUR BUSINESS, NOT MINE! ONCE WE GET TO TOKYO, I'M LEAVING!!
SAME HERE! I'M A BUSY MAN!
ME TOO!
WE REACH TOKYO IN LESS THAN TEN MINUTES.
WHAT SHOULD WE DO?
HEY, DO YOU REMEMBER WHAT YOU BOUGHT AT THE NEWSSTAND AT SHIN-OSAKA STATION?
ER... SURE.

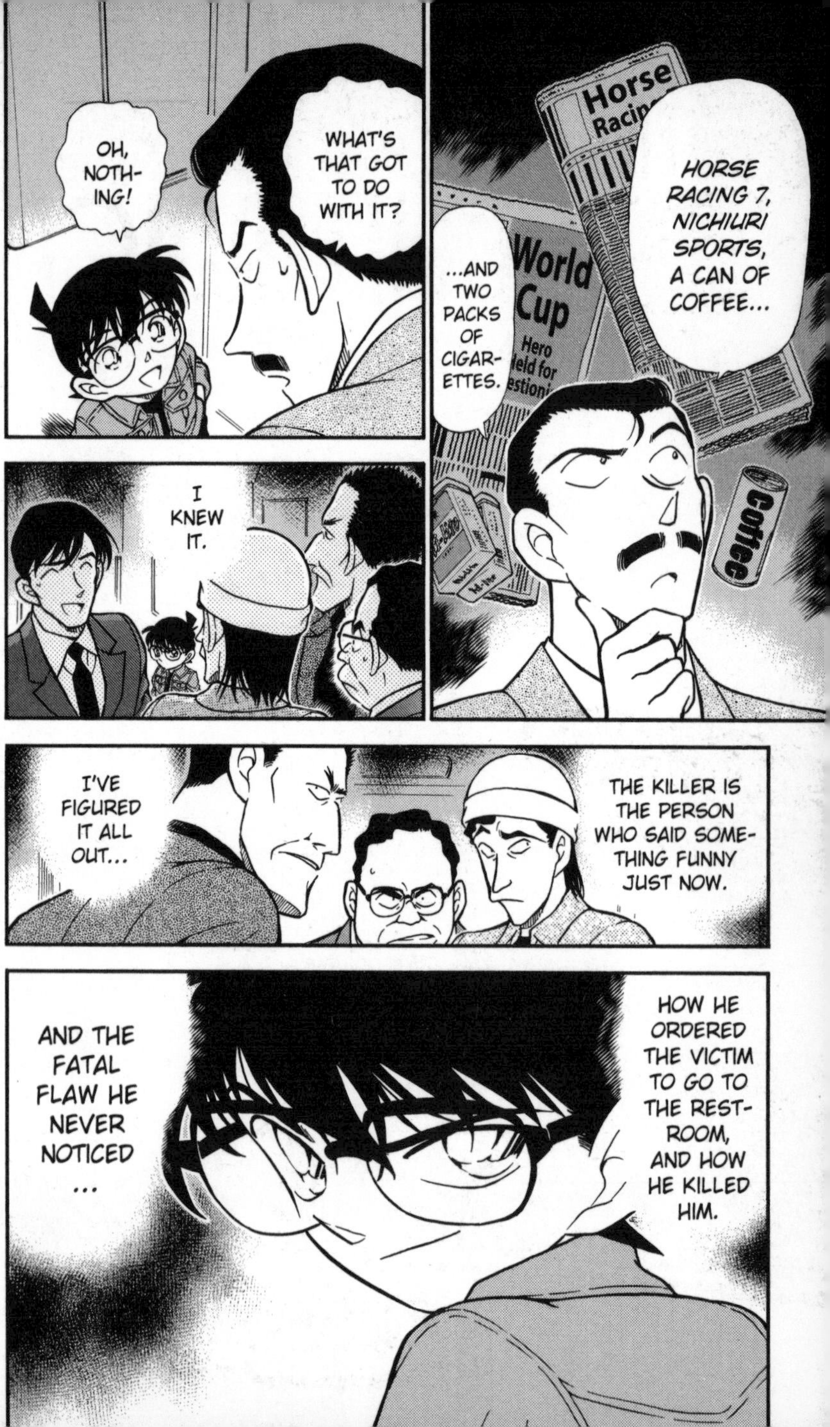
Horse
HORSE RACING 7, NICHIURI SPORTS, A CAN OF COFFEE...
World Cup
Hero
...AND TWO PACKS OF CIGARETTES.
Coffee
WHAT'S THAT GOT TO DO WITH IT?
OH, NOTHING!
I KNEW IT.
THE KILLER IS THE PERSON WHO SAID SOMETHING FUNNY JUST NOW.
I'VE FIGURED IT ALL OUT...
HOW HE ORDERED THE VICTIM TO GO TO THE RESTROOM, AND HOW HE KILLED HIM.
AND THE FATAL FLAW HE NEVER NOTICED...

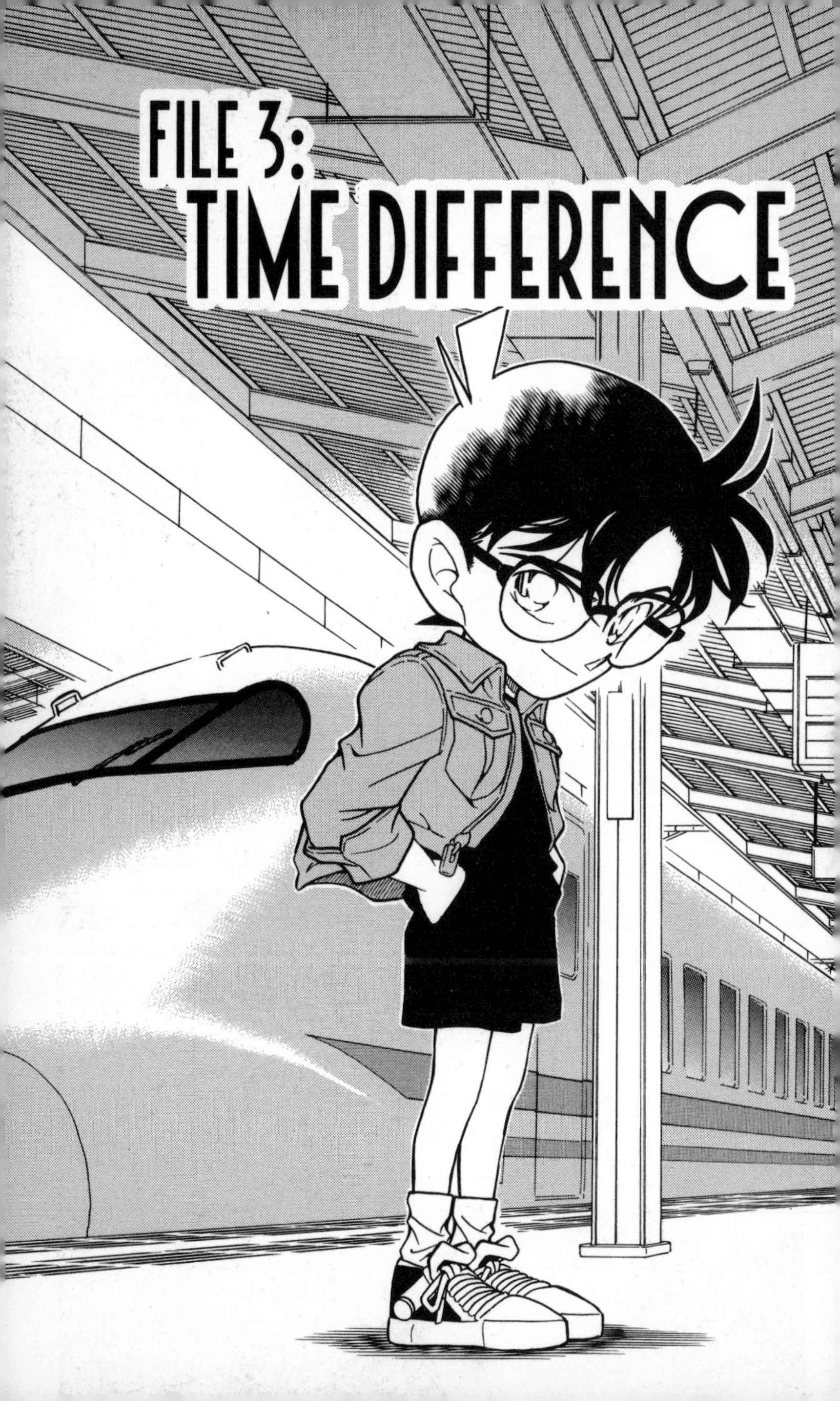
FILE 3:
TIME DIFFERENCE

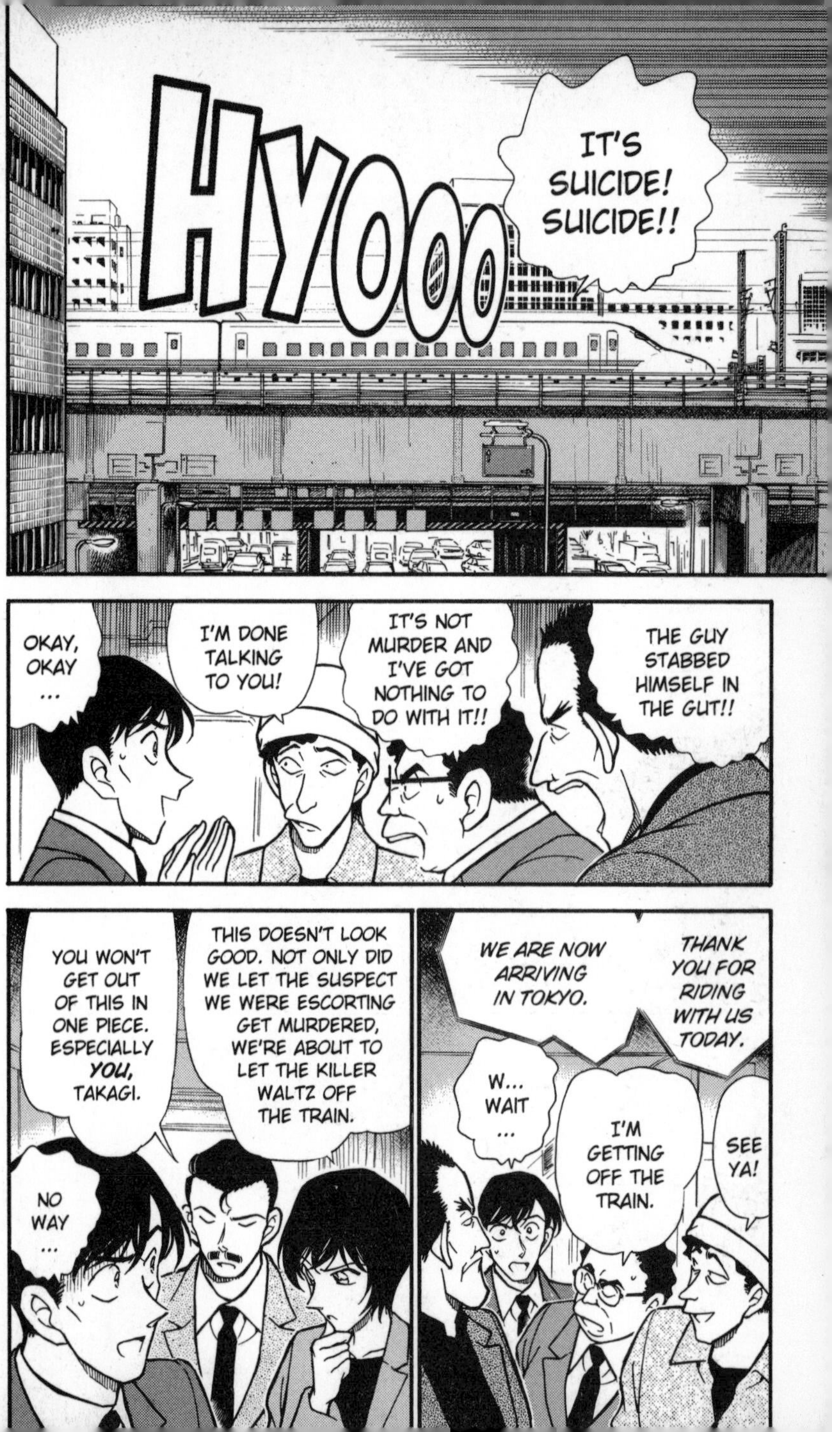
IT'S SUICIDE! SUICIDE!!
HYOOO
THE GUY STABBED HIMSELF IN THE GUT!!
IT'S NOT MURDER AND I'VE GOT NOTHING TO DO WITH IT!!
I'M DONE TALKING TO YOU!
OKAY, OKAY ...
THANK YOU FOR RIDING WITH US TODAY.
WE ARE NOW ARRIVING IN TOKYO.
SEE YA!
I'M GETTING OFF THE TRAIN.
W... WAIT ...
THIS DOESN'T LOOK GOOD. NOT ONLY DID WE LET THE SUSPECT WE WERE ESCORTING GET MURDERED, WE'RE ABOUT TO LET THE KILLER WALTZ OFF THE TRAIN.
YOU WON'T GET OUT OF THIS IN ONE PIECE. ESPECIALLY *YOU,* TAKAGI.
NO WAY ...

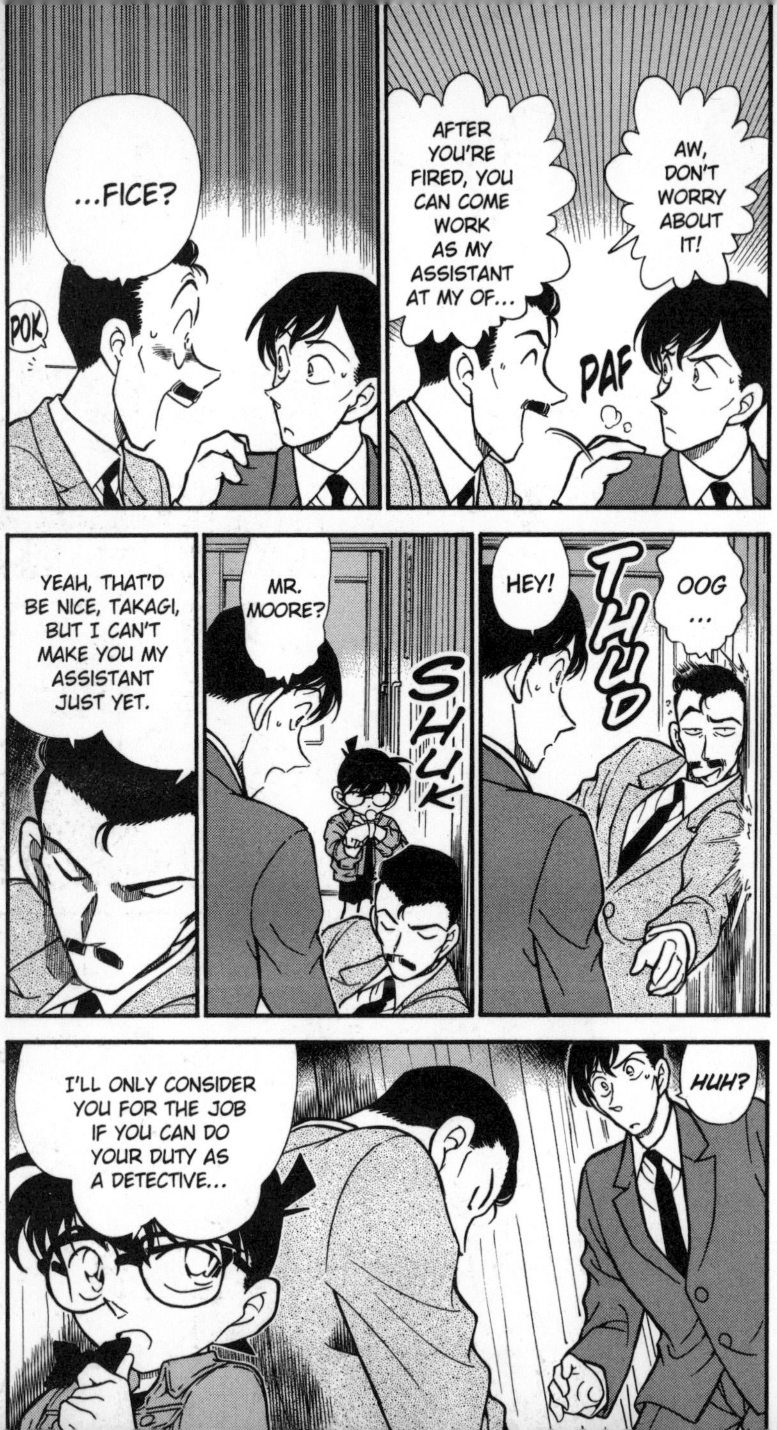
AW, DON'T WORRY ABOUT IT!
AFTER YOU'RE FIRED, YOU CAN COME WORK AS MY ASSISTANT AT MY OF...
PAF
...FICE?
POK
OOG ...
THUD
HEY!
SHUK
MR. MOORE?
YEAH, THAT'D BE NICE, TAKAGI, BUT I CAN'T MAKE YOU MY ASSISTANT JUST YET.
HUH?
I'LL ONLY CONSIDER YOU FOR THE JOB IF YOU CAN DO YOUR DUTY AS A DETECTIVE...

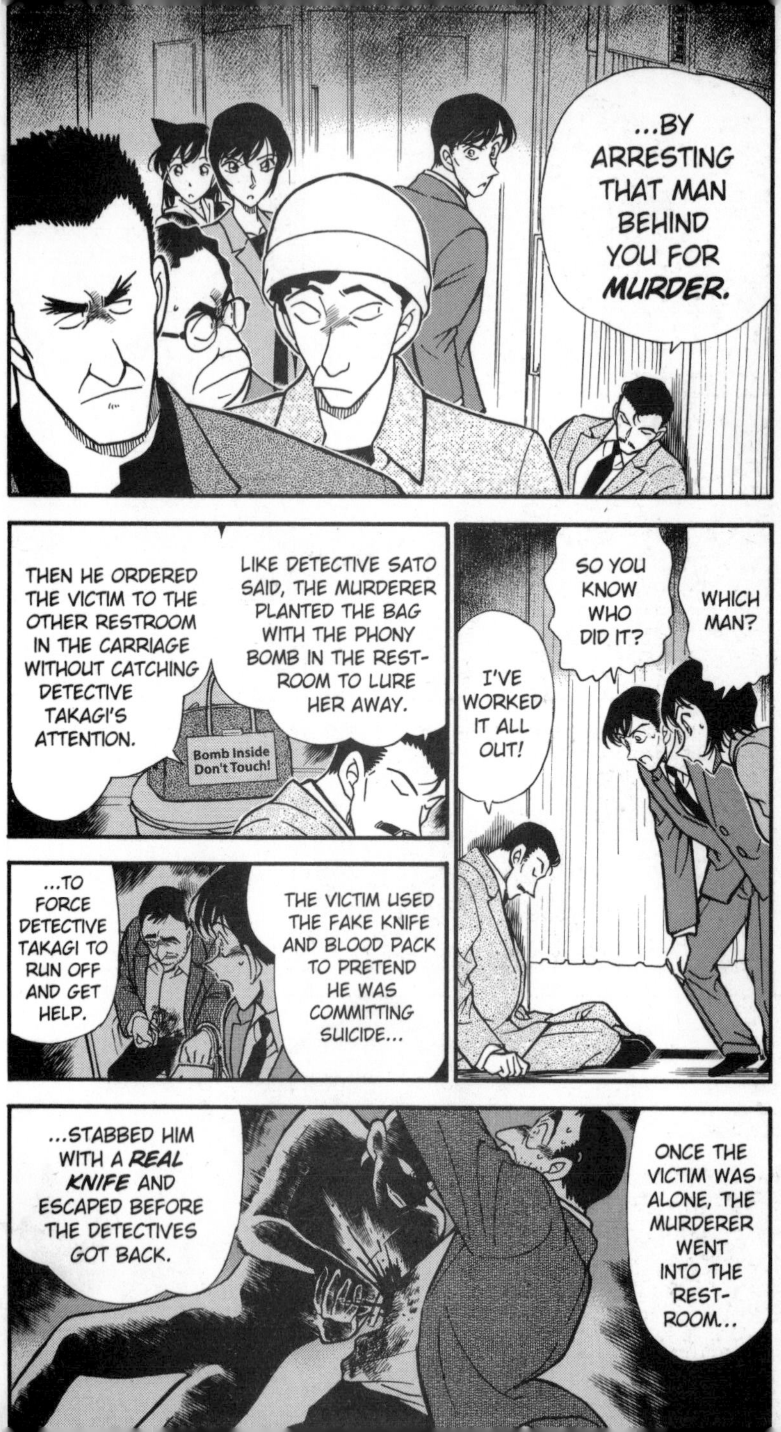
...BY ARRESTING THAT MAN BEHIND YOU FOR *MURDER.*
WHICH MAN?
SO YOU KNOW WHO DID IT?
I'VE WORKED IT ALL OUT!
LIKE DETECTIVE SATO SAID, THE MURDERER PLANTED THE BAG WITH THE PHONY BOMB IN THE REST-ROOM TO LURE HER AWAY.
THEN HE ORDERED THE VICTIM TO THE OTHER RESTROOM IN THE CARRIAGE WITHOUT CATCHING DETECTIVE TAKAGI'S ATTENTION.
Bomb Inside Don't Touch!
THE VICTIM USED THE FAKE KNIFE AND BLOOD PACK TO PRETEND HE WAS COMMITTING SUICIDE...
...TO FORCE DETECTIVE TAKAGI TO RUN OFF AND GET HELP.
ONCE THE VICTIM WAS ALONE, THE MURDERER WENT INTO THE REST-ROOM...
...STABBED HIM WITH A ***REAL KNIFE*** AND ESCAPED BEFORE THE DETECTIVES GOT BACK.

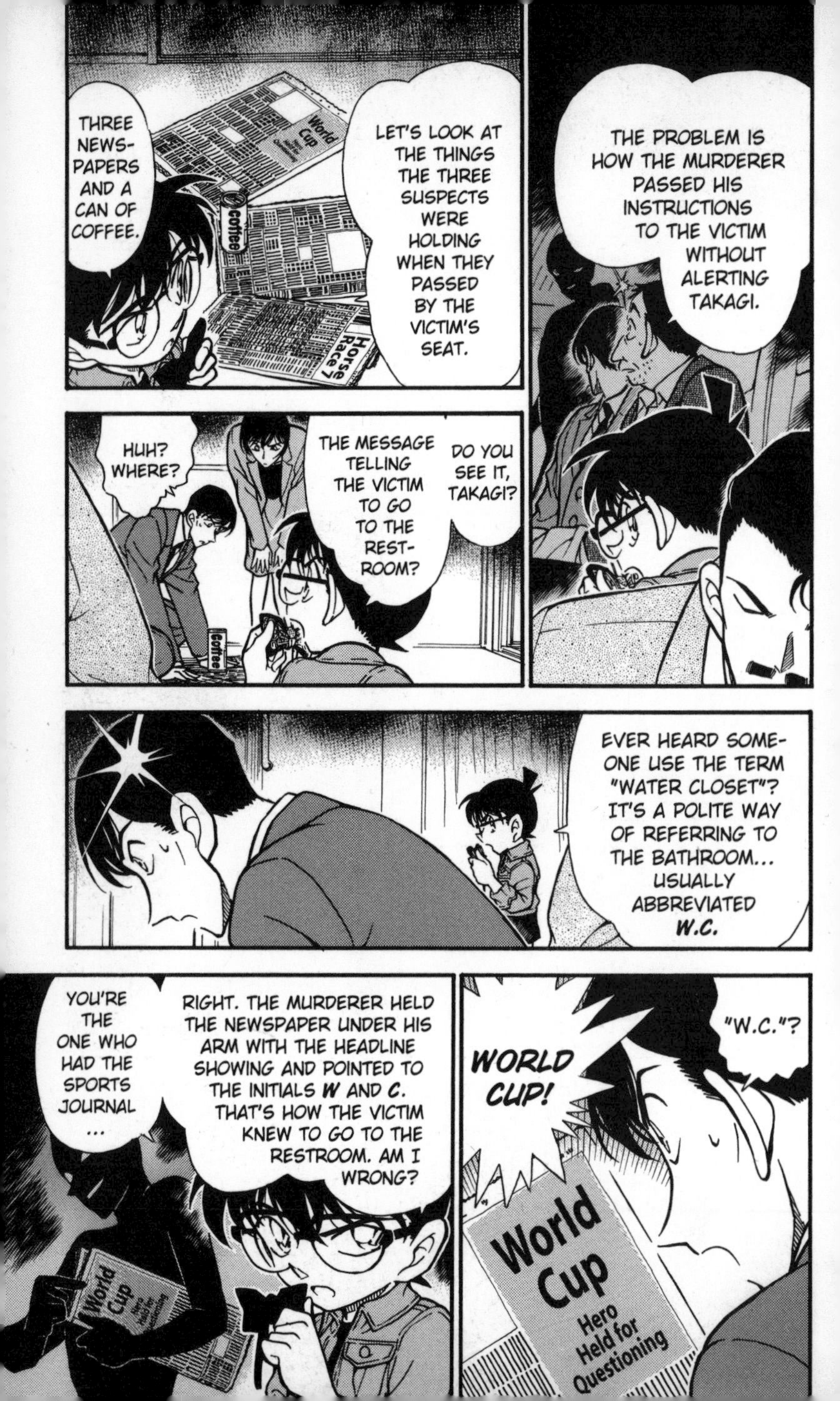
THE PROBLEM IS HOW THE MURDERER PASSED HIS INSTRUCTIONS TO THE VICTIM WITHOUT ALERTING TAKAGI.
LET'S LOOK AT THE THINGS THE THREE SUSPECTS WERE HOLDING WHEN THEY PASSED BY THE VICTIM'S SEAT.
World Cup
coffee
Horse Race 7
THREE NEWS-PAPERS AND A CAN OF COFFEE.
DO YOU SEE IT, TAKAGI?
THE MESSAGE TELLING THE VICTIM TO GO TO THE REST-ROOM?
HUH? WHERE?
coffee
EVER HEARD SOME-ONE USE THE TERM "WATER CLOSET"? IT'S A POLITE WAY OF REFERRING TO THE BATHROOM... USUALLY ABBREVIATED *W.C.*
"W.C."?
WORLD CUP!
World Cup
Hero Held for Questioning
RIGHT. THE MURDERER HELD THE NEWSPAPER UNDER HIS ARM WITH THE HEADLINE SHOWING AND POINTED TO THE INITIALS *W* AND *C*. THAT'S HOW THE VICTIM KNEW TO GO TO THE RESTROOM. AM I WRONG?
YOU'RE THE ONE WHO HAD THE SPORTS JOURNAL ...
World Cup

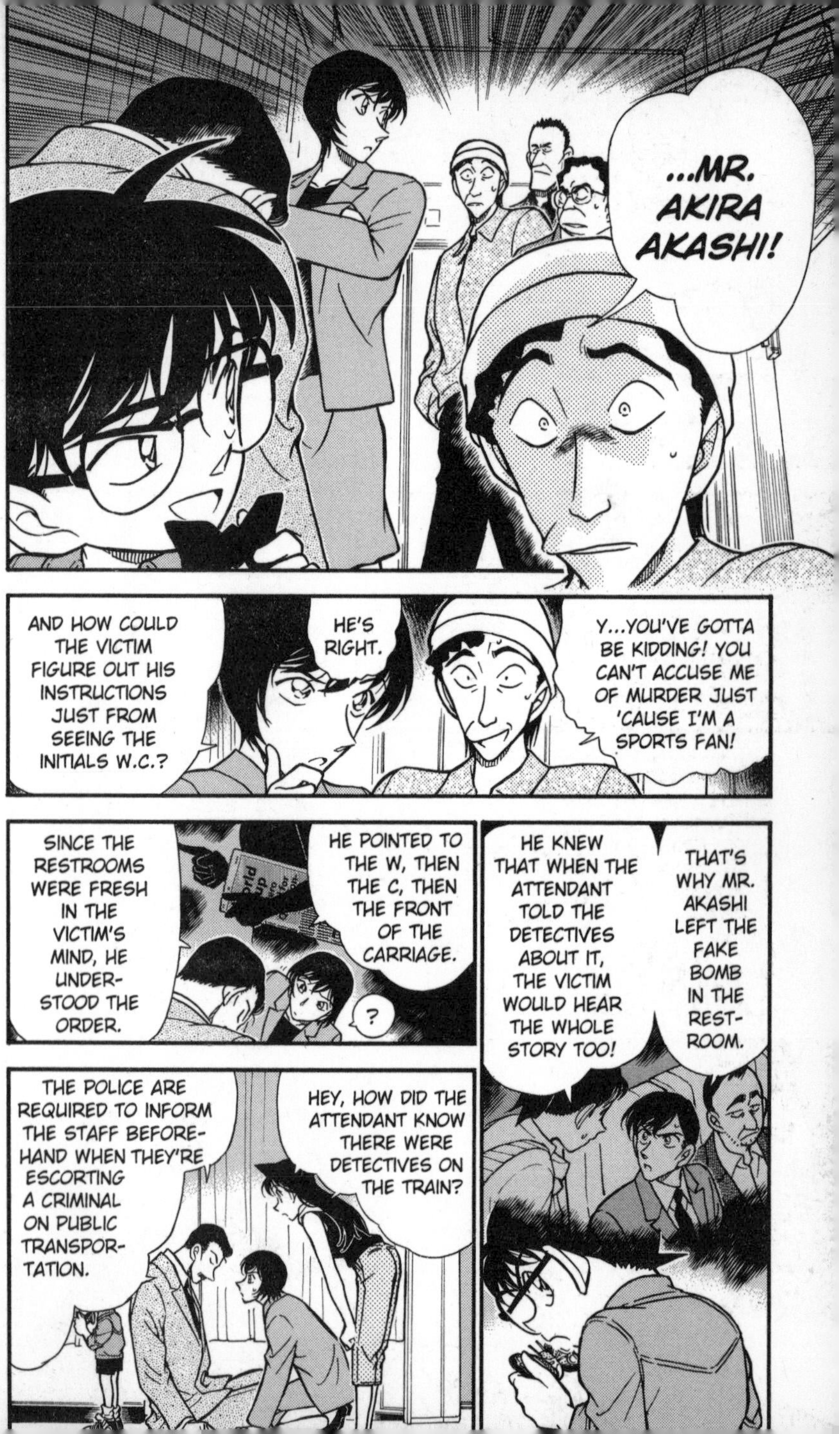
...MR. AKIRA AKASHI!
Y...YOU'VE GOTTA BE KIDDING! YOU CAN'T ACCUSE ME OF MURDER JUST 'CAUSE I'M A SPORTS FAN!
HE'S RIGHT.
AND HOW COULD THE VICTIM FIGURE OUT HIS INSTRUCTIONS JUST FROM SEEING THE INITIALS W.C.?
THAT'S WHY MR. AKASHI LEFT THE FAKE BOMB IN THE REST-ROOM.
HE KNEW THAT WHEN THE ATTENDANT TOLD THE DETECTIVES ABOUT IT, THE VICTIM WOULD HEAR THE WHOLE STORY TOO!
HE POINTED TO THE W, THEN THE C, THEN THE FRONT OF THE CARRIAGE.
SINCE THE RESTROOMS WERE FRESH IN THE VICTIM'S MIND, HE UNDER-STOOD THE ORDER.
?
HEY, HOW DID THE ATTENDANT KNOW THERE WERE DETECTIVES ON THE TRAIN?
THE POLICE ARE REQUIRED TO INFORM THE STAFF BEFORE-HAND WHEN THEY'RE ESCORTING A CRIMINAL ON PUBLIC TRANSPOR-TATION.

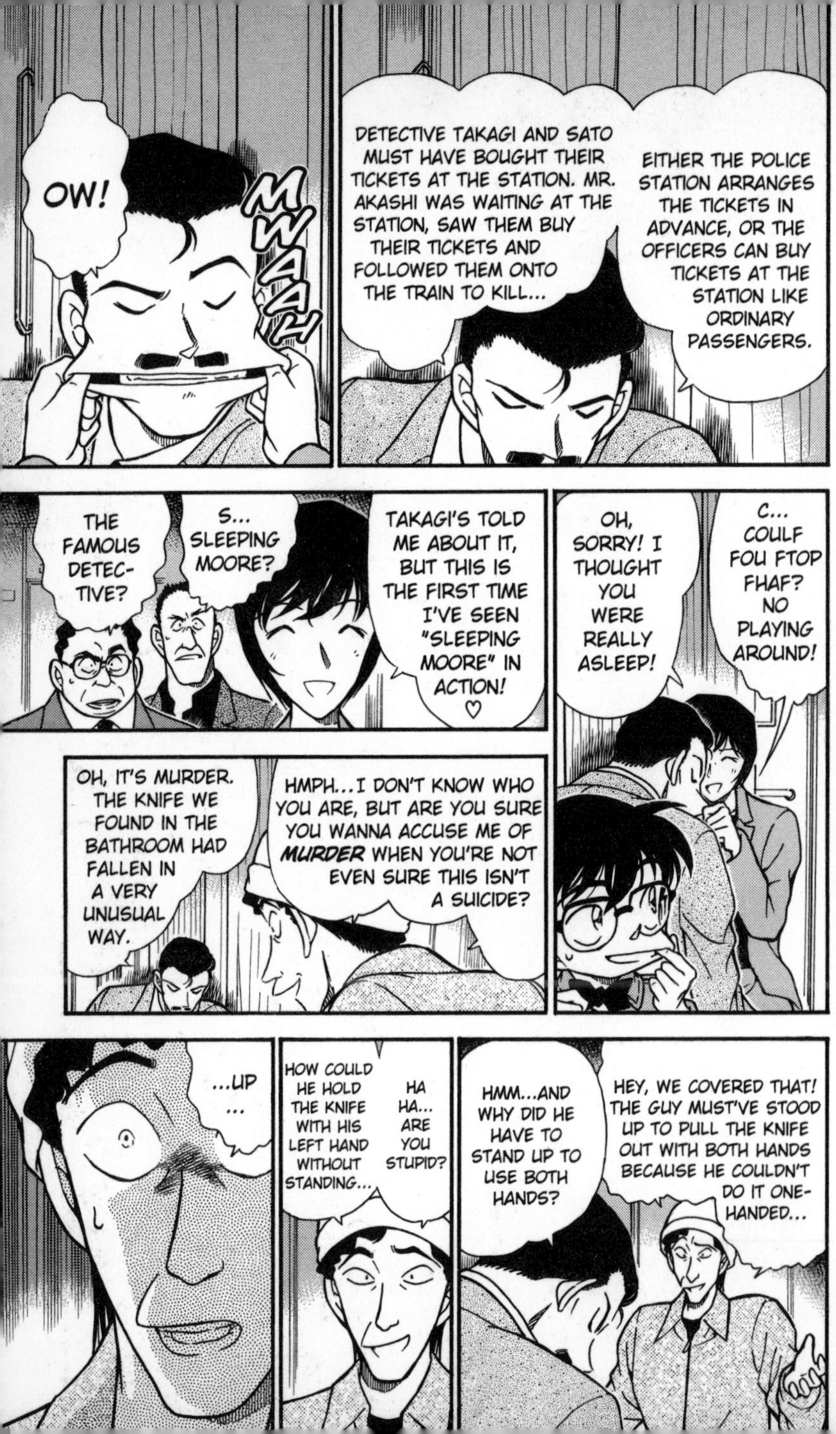
EITHER THE POLICE STATION ARRANGES THE TICKETS IN ADVANCE, OR THE OFFICERS CAN BUY TICKETS AT THE STATION LIKE ORDINARY PASSENGERS.
DETECTIVE TAKAGI AND SATO MUST HAVE BOUGHT THEIR TICKETS AT THE STATION. MR. AKASHI WAS WAITING AT THE STATION, SAW THEM BUY THEIR TICKETS AND FOLLOWED THEM ONTO THE TRAIN TO KILL...
MWAAAH
OW!
C... COULF FOU FTOP FHAF? NO PLAYING AROUND!
OH, SORRY! I THOUGHT YOU WERE REALLY ASLEEP!
TAKAGI'S TOLD ME ABOUT IT, BUT THIS IS THE FIRST TIME I'VE SEEN "SLEEPING MOORE" IN ACTION! ♡
S... SLEEPING MOORE?
THE FAMOUS DETEC-TIVE?
HMPH...I DON'T KNOW WHO YOU ARE, BUT ARE YOU SURE YOU WANNA ACCUSE ME OF MURDER WHEN YOU'RE NOT EVEN SURE THIS ISN'T A SUICIDE?
OH, IT'S MURDER. THE KNIFE WE FOUND IN THE BATHROOM HAD FALLEN IN A VERY UNUSUAL WAY.
HEY, WE COVERED THAT! THE GUY MUST'VE STOOD UP TO PULL THE KNIFE OUT WITH BOTH HANDS BECAUSE HE COULDN'T DO IT ONE-HANDED...
HMM...AND WHY DID HE HAVE TO STAND UP TO USE BOTH HANDS?
HA HA... ARE YOU STUPID?
HOW COULD HE HOLD THE KNIFE WITH HIS LEFT HAND WITHOUT STANDING...
...UP ...

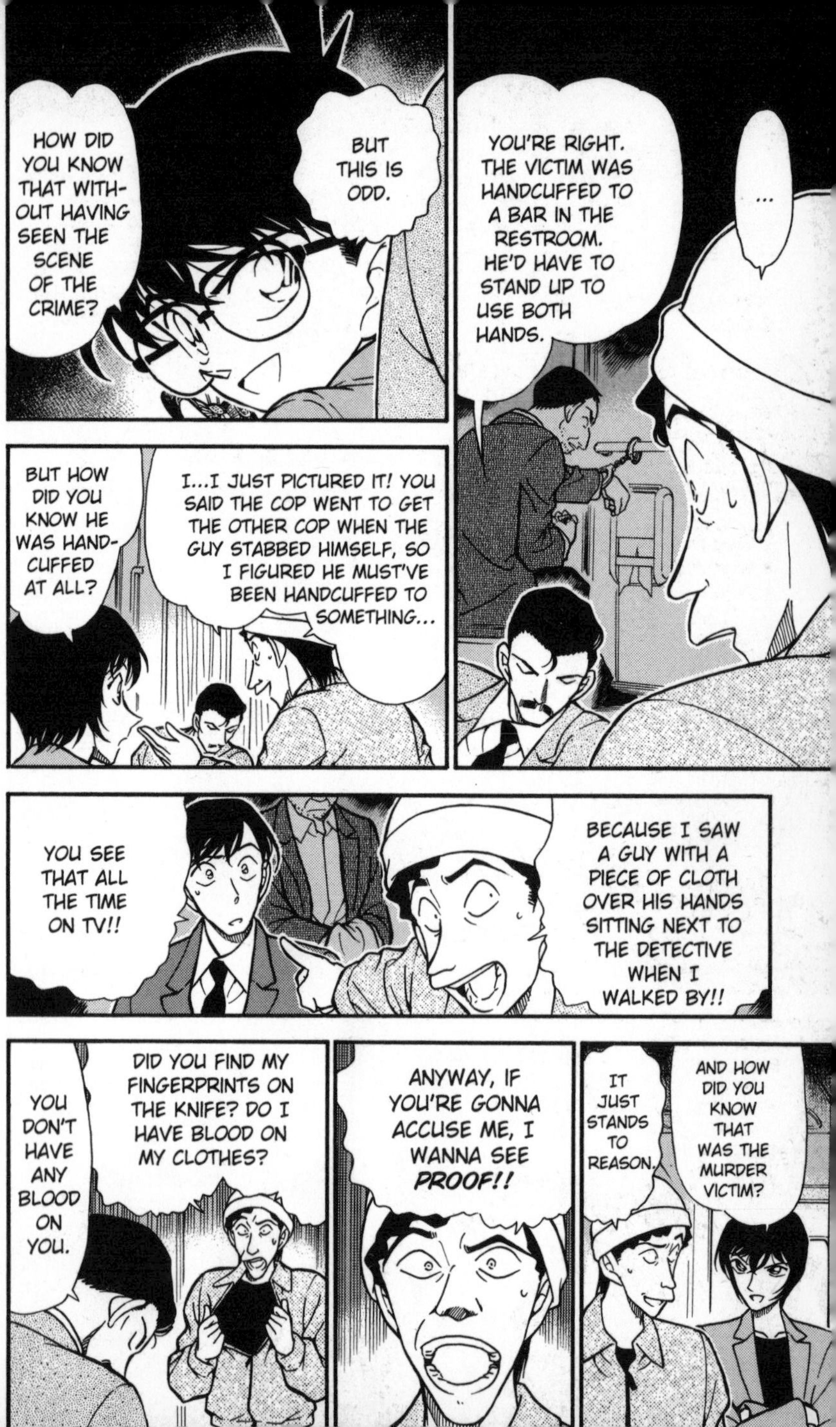
...
YOU'RE RIGHT. THE VICTIM WAS HANDCUFFED TO A BAR IN THE RESTROOM. HE'D HAVE TO STAND UP TO USE BOTH HANDS.
BUT THIS IS ODD.
HOW DID YOU KNOW THAT WITH-OUT HAVING SEEN THE SCENE OF THE CRIME?
I...I JUST PICTURED IT! YOU SAID THE COP WENT TO GET THE OTHER COP WHEN THE GUY STABBED HIMSELF, SO I FIGURED HE MUST'VE BEEN HANDCUFFED TO SOMETHING...
BUT HOW DID YOU KNOW HE WAS HAND-CUFFED AT ALL?
BECAUSE I SAW A GUY WITH A PIECE OF CLOTH OVER HIS HANDS SITTING NEXT TO THE DETECTIVE WHEN I WALKED BY!!
YOU SEE THAT ALL THE TIME ON TV!!
AND HOW DID YOU KNOW THAT WAS THE MURDER VICTIM?
IT JUST STANDS TO REASON.
ANYWAY, IF YOU'RE GONNA ACCUSE ME, I WANNA SEE *PROOF!!*
DID YOU FIND MY FINGERPRINTS ON THE KNIFE? DO I HAVE BLOOD ON MY CLOTHES?
YOU DON'T HAVE ANY BLOOD ON YOU.

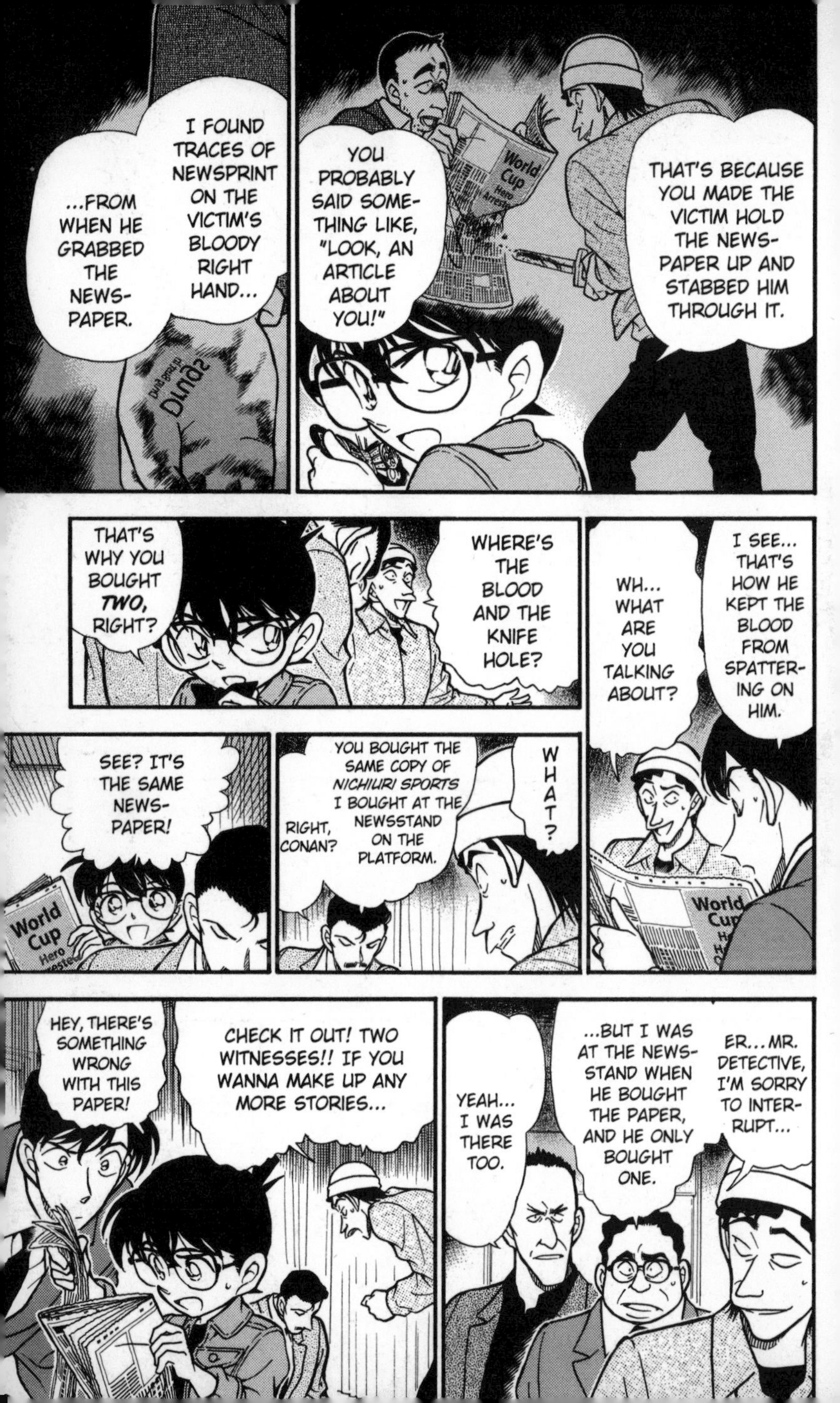
THAT'S BECAUSE YOU MADE THE VICTIM HOLD THE NEWSPAPER UP AND STABBED HIM THROUGH IT.
YOU PROBABLY SAID SOMETHING LIKE, "LOOK, AN ARTICLE ABOUT YOU!"
I FOUND TRACES OF NEWSPRINT ON THE VICTIM'S BLOODY RIGHT HAND...
...FROM WHEN HE GRABBED THE NEWSPAPER.
I SEE... THAT'S HOW HE KEPT THE BLOOD FROM SPATTERING ON HIM.
WH... WHAT ARE YOU TALKING ABOUT?
WHERE'S THE BLOOD AND THE KNIFE HOLE?
THAT'S WHY YOU BOUGHT ***TWO,*** RIGHT?
WHAT?
YOU BOUGHT THE SAME COPY OF *NICHIURI SPORTS* I BOUGHT AT THE NEWSSTAND ON THE PLATFORM.
RIGHT, CONAN?
SEE? IT'S THE SAME NEWSPAPER!
World Cup
ER...MR. DETECTIVE, I'M SORRY TO INTERRUPT...
...BUT I WAS AT THE NEWSSTAND WHEN HE BOUGHT THE PAPER, AND HE ONLY BOUGHT ONE.
YEAH... I WAS THERE TOO.
CHECK IT OUT! TWO WITNESSES!! IF YOU WANNA MAKE UP ANY MORE STORIES...
HEY, THERE'S SOMETHING WRONG WITH THIS PAPER!

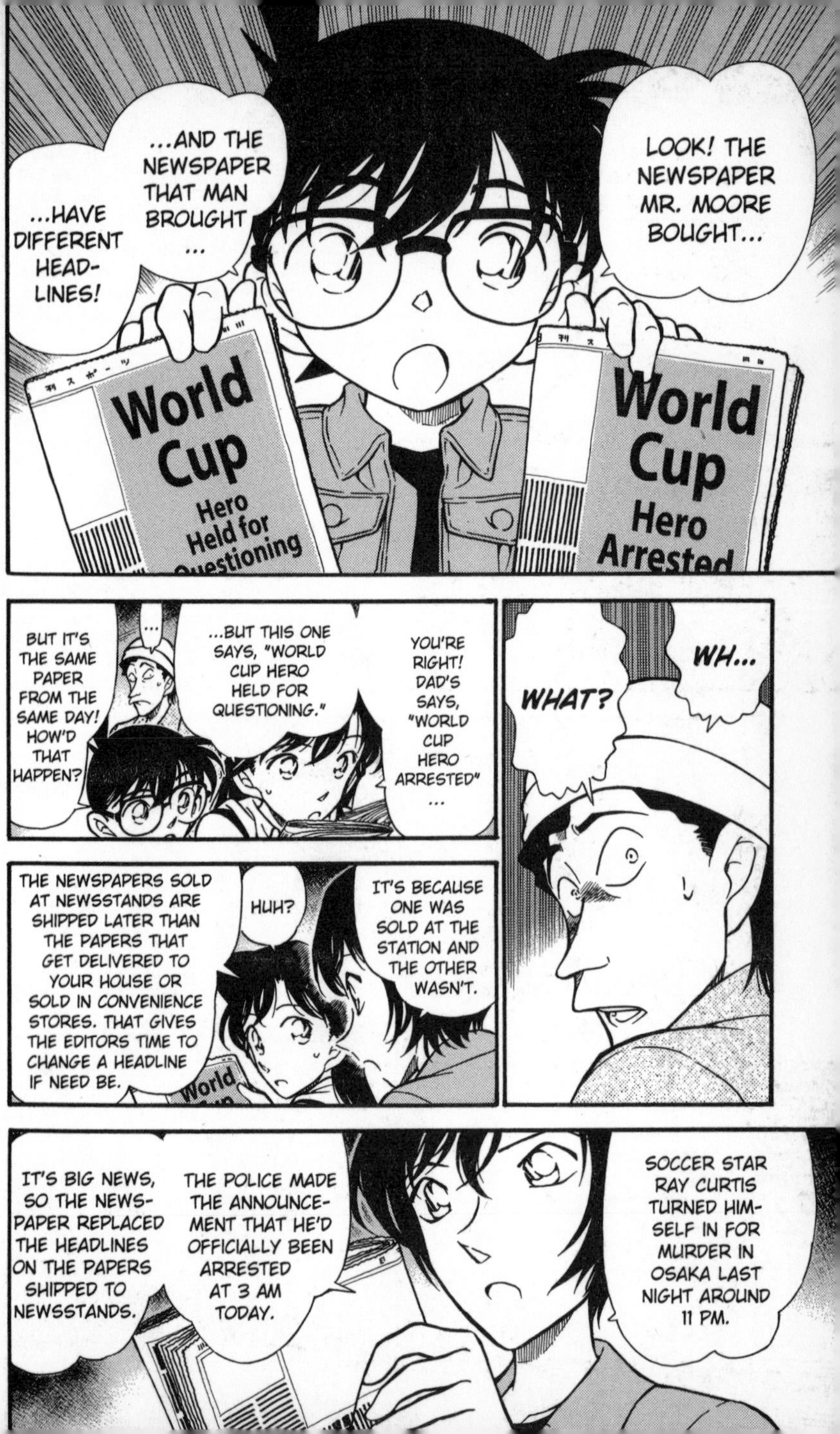
LOOK! THE NEWSPAPER MR. MOORE BOUGHT...
...AND THE NEWSPAPER THAT MAN BROUGHT ...
...HAVE DIFFERENT HEAD-LINES!
World Cup Hero Arrested
World Cup Hero Held for Questioning
WH...
WHAT?
YOU'RE RIGHT! DAD'S SAYS, "WORLD CUP HERO ARRESTED" ...
...BUT THIS ONE SAYS, "WORLD CUP HERO HELD FOR QUESTIONING."
...
BUT IT'S THE SAME PAPER FROM THE SAME DAY! HOW'D THAT HAPPEN?
IT'S BECAUSE ONE WAS SOLD AT THE STATION AND THE OTHER WASN'T.
HUH?
THE NEWSPAPERS SOLD AT NEWSSTANDS ARE SHIPPED LATER THAN THE PAPERS THAT GET DELIVERED TO YOUR HOUSE OR SOLD IN CONVENIENCE STORES. THAT GIVES THE EDITORS TIME TO CHANGE A HEADLINE IF NEED BE.
SOCCER STAR RAY CURTIS TURNED HIM-SELF IN FOR MURDER IN OSAKA LAST NIGHT AROUND 11 PM.
THE POLICE MADE THE ANNOUNCE-MENT THAT HE'D OFFICIALLY BEEN ARRESTED AT 3 AM TODAY.
IT'S BIG NEWS, SO THE NEWS-PAPER REPLACED THE HEADLINES ON THE PAPERS SHIPPED TO NEWSSTANDS.

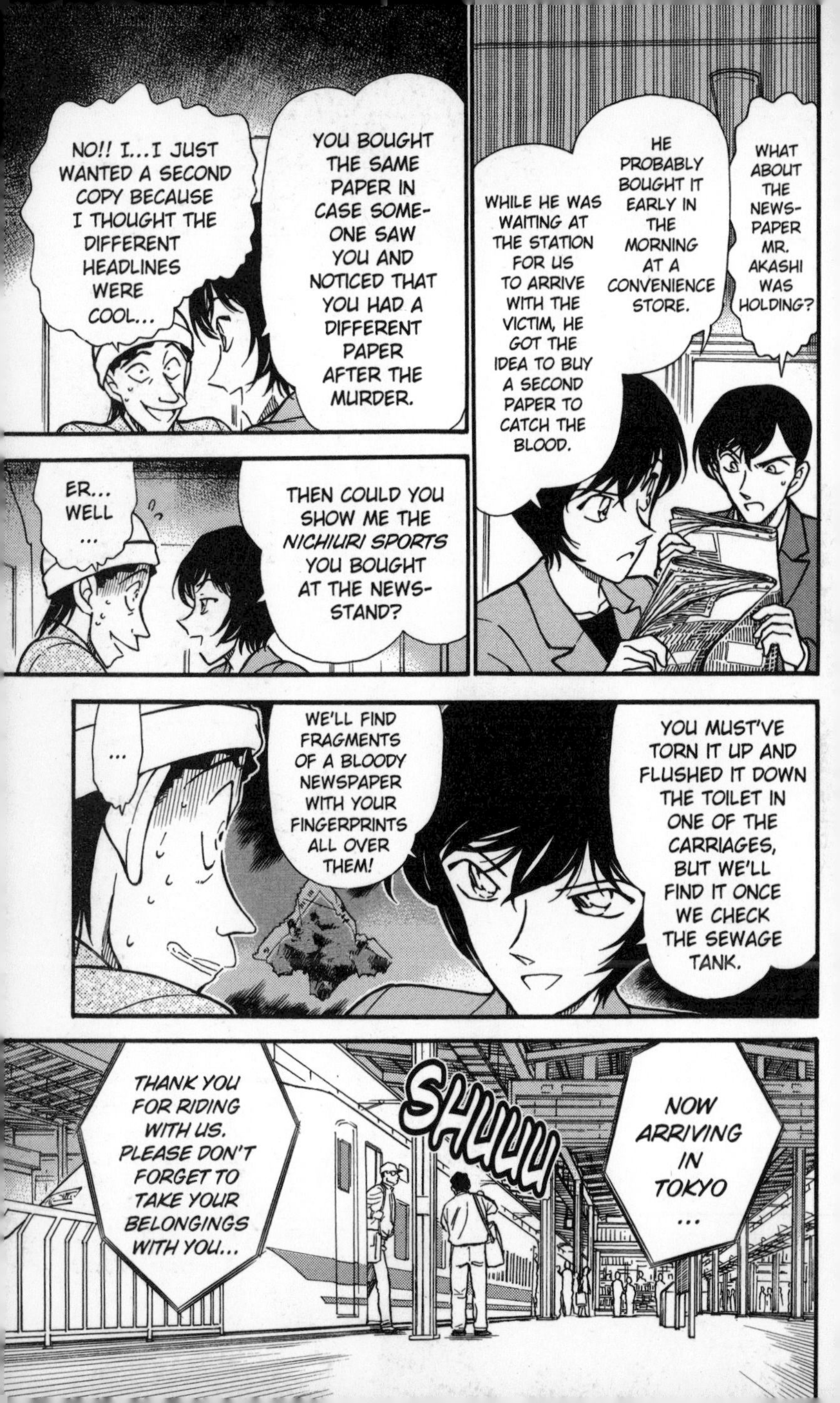
WHAT ABOUT THE NEWSPAPER MR. AKASHI WAS HOLDING?
HE PROBABLY BOUGHT IT EARLY IN THE MORNING AT A CONVENIENCE STORE.
WHILE HE WAS WAITING AT THE STATION FOR US TO ARRIVE WITH THE VICTIM, HE GOT THE IDEA TO BUY A SECOND PAPER TO CATCH THE BLOOD.
YOU BOUGHT THE SAME PAPER IN CASE SOMEONE SAW YOU AND NOTICED THAT YOU HAD A DIFFERENT PAPER AFTER THE MURDER.
NO!! I...I JUST WANTED A SECOND COPY BECAUSE I THOUGHT THE DIFFERENT HEADLINES WERE COOL...
THEN COULD YOU SHOW ME THE *NICHIURI SPORTS* YOU BOUGHT AT THE NEWSSTAND?
ER... WELL...
YOU MUST'VE TORN IT UP AND FLUSHED IT DOWN THE TOILET IN ONE OF THE CARRIAGES, BUT WE'LL FIND IT ONCE WE CHECK THE SEWAGE TANK.
WE'LL FIND FRAGMENTS OF A BLOODY NEWSPAPER WITH YOUR FINGERPRINTS ALL OVER THEM!
...
NOW ARRIVING IN TOKYO...
SHUUU
THANK YOU FOR RIDING WITH US. PLEASE DON'T FORGET TO TAKE YOUR BELONGINGS WITH YOU...

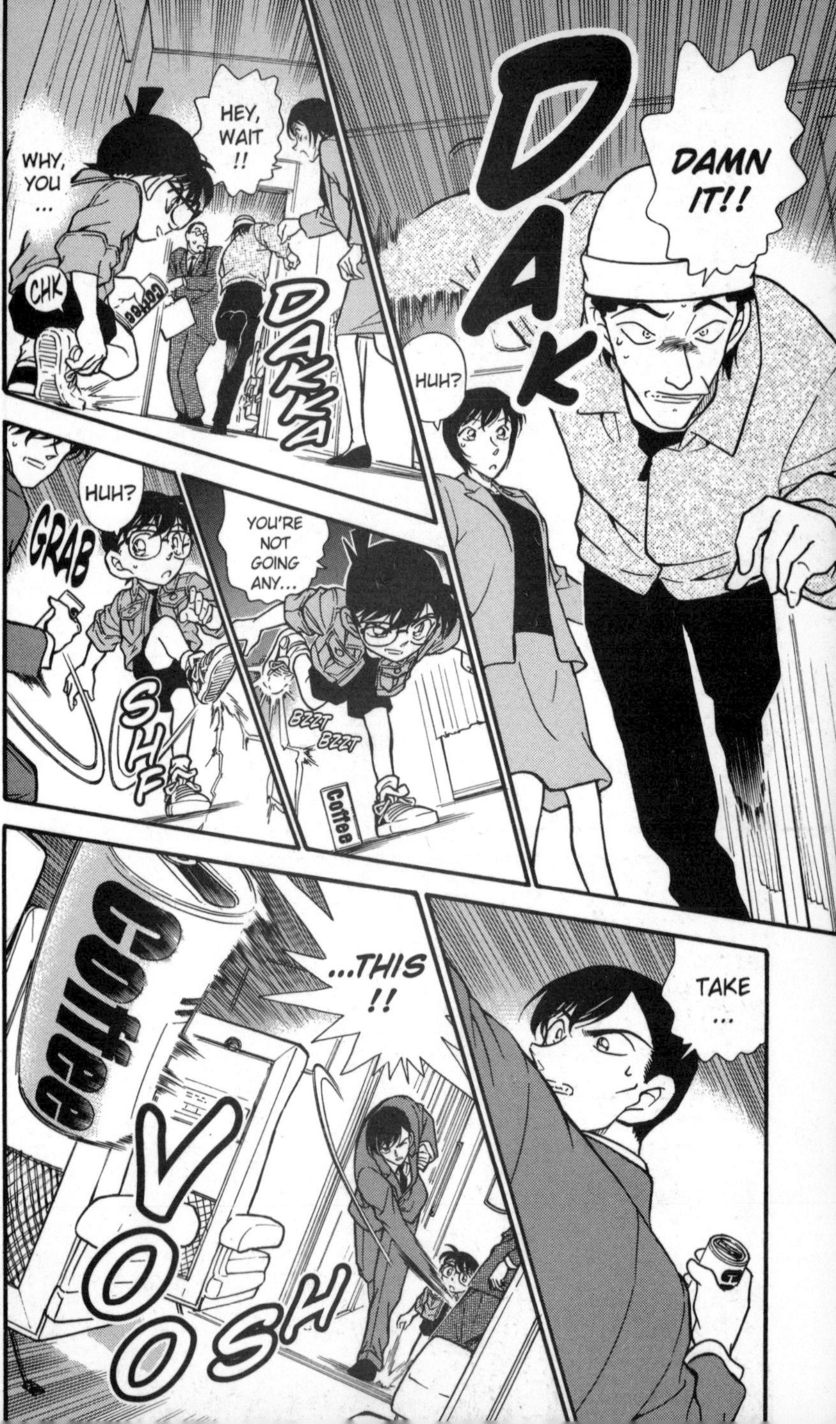
DAMN IT!!
DAK
HUH?
HEY, WAIT!!
WHY, YOU ...
DAKA
CHK
Coffee
YOU'RE NOT GOING ANY...
BZZT BZZT
Coffee
HUH?
GRAB
SHF
TAKE ...
...THIS !!
Coffee
VOOSH

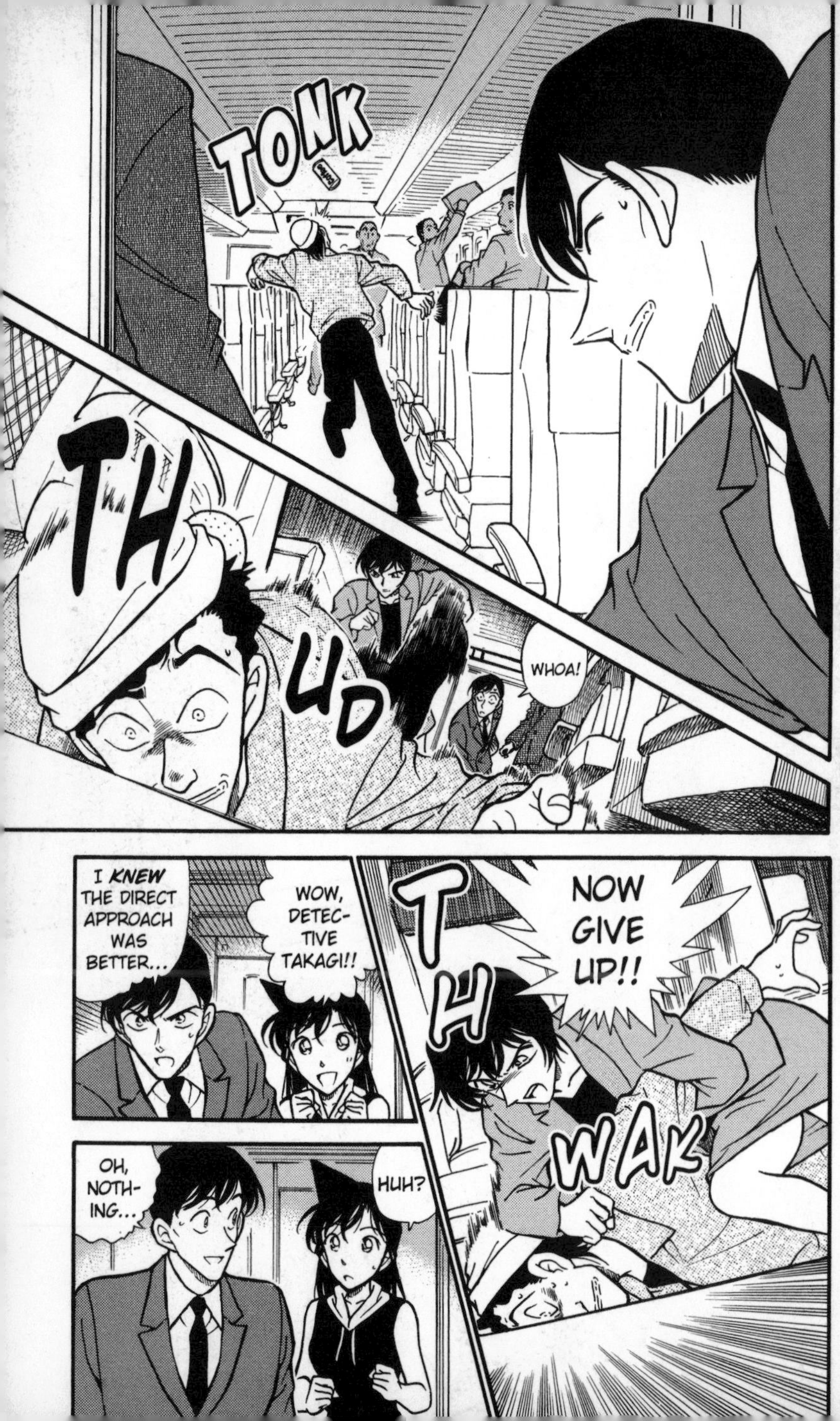
TONK
WHOA!
THUD
NOW GIVE UP!!
THWAK
WOW, DETECTIVE TAKAGI!!
I *KNEW* THE DIRECT APPROACH WAS BETTER...
HUH?
OH, NOTHING...

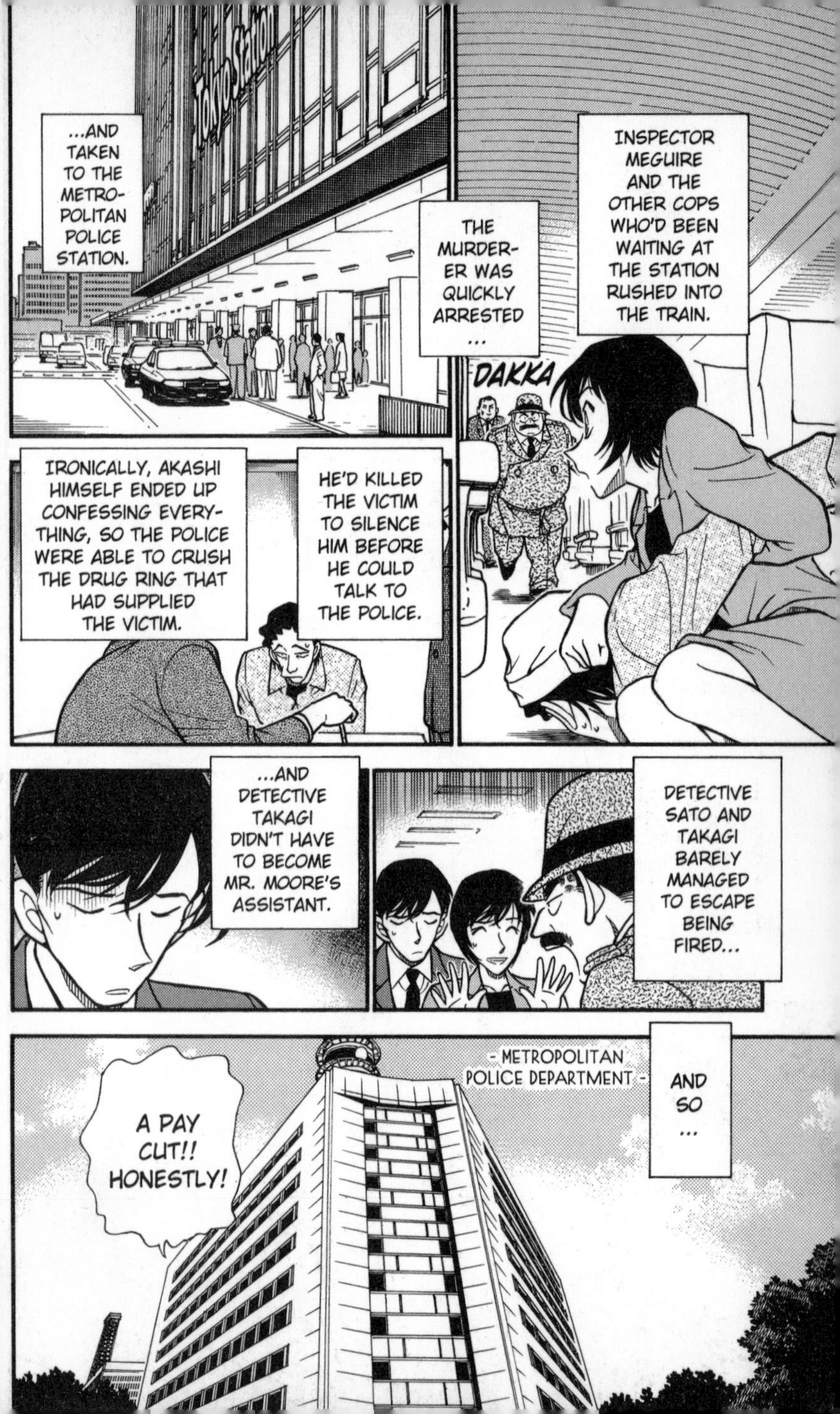
INSPECTOR MEGUIRE AND THE OTHER COPS WHO'D BEEN WAITING AT THE STATION RUSHED INTO THE TRAIN.
THE MURDERER WAS QUICKLY ARRESTED ...
DAKKA
...AND TAKEN TO THE METROPOLITAN POLICE STATION.
HE'D KILLED THE VICTIM TO SILENCE HIM BEFORE HE COULD TALK TO THE POLICE.
IRONICALLY, AKASHI HIMSELF ENDED UP CONFESSING EVERYTHING, SO THE POLICE WERE ABLE TO CRUSH THE DRUG RING THAT HAD SUPPLIED THE VICTIM.
DETECTIVE SATO AND TAKAGI BARELY MANAGED TO ESCAPE BEING FIRED...
...AND DETECTIVE TAKAGI DIDN'T HAVE TO BECOME MR. MOORE'S ASSISTANT.
AND SO ...
- METROPOLITAN POLICE DEPARTMENT -
A PAY CUT!! HONESTLY!

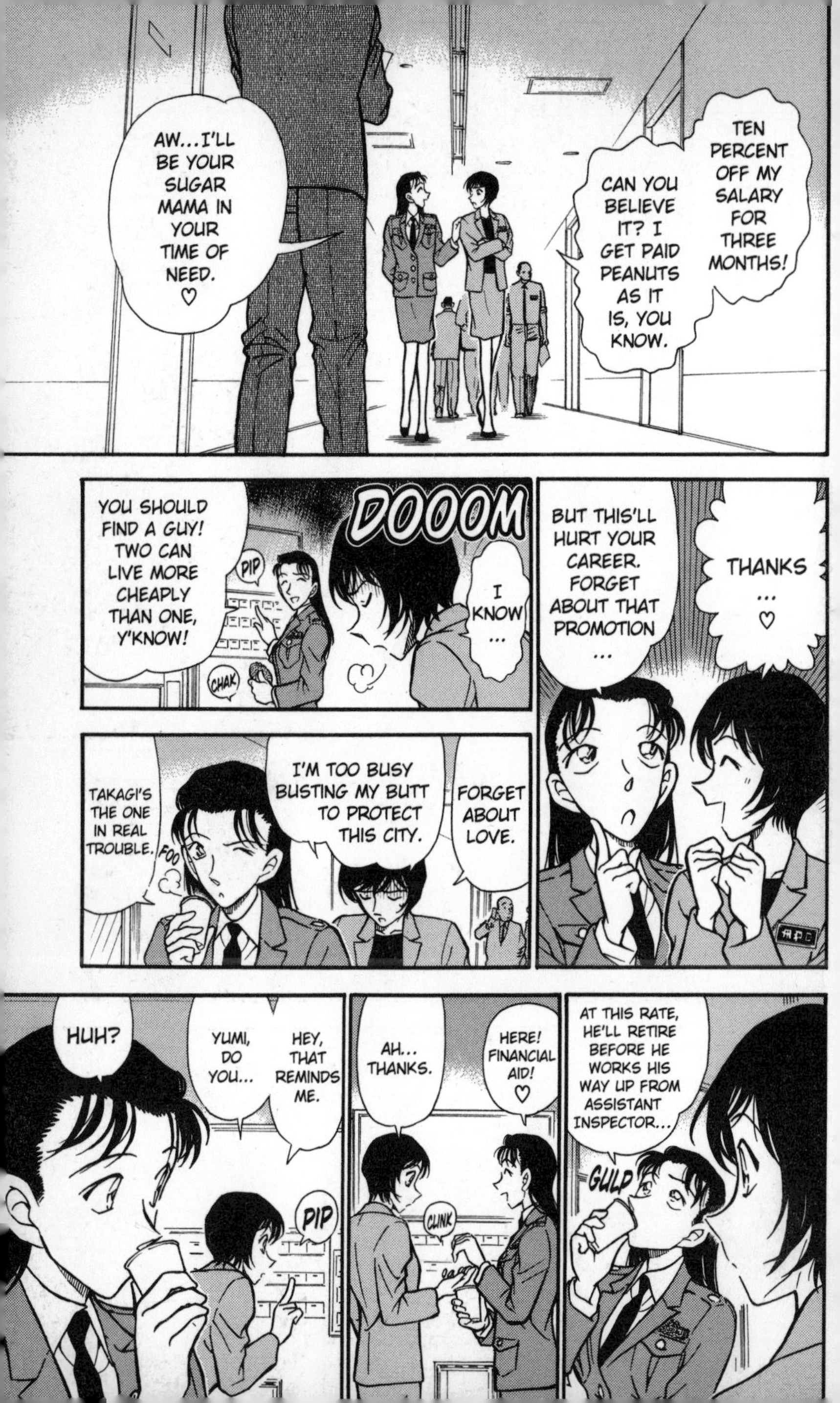
TEN PERCENT OFF MY SALARY FOR THREE MONTHS!
CAN YOU BELIEVE IT? I GET PAID PEANUTS AS IT IS, YOU KNOW.
AW...I'LL BE YOUR SUGAR MAMA IN YOUR TIME OF NEED. ♡
THANKS... ♡
BUT THIS'LL HURT YOUR CAREER. FORGET ABOUT THAT PROMOTION...
DOOOM
I KNOW...
YOU SHOULD FIND A GUY! TWO CAN LIVE MORE CHEAPLY THAN ONE, Y'KNOW!
PIP
CHAK
FORGET ABOUT LOVE.
I'M TOO BUSY BUSTING MY BUTT TO PROTECT THIS CITY.
TAKAGI'S THE ONE IN REAL TROUBLE.
FOO
AT THIS RATE, HE'LL RETIRE BEFORE HE WORKS HIS WAY UP FROM ASSISTANT INSPECTOR...
GULP
HERE! FINANCIAL AID! ♡
AH... THANKS.
CLINK
HEY, THAT REMINDS ME.
YUMI, DO YOU...
HUH?
PIP

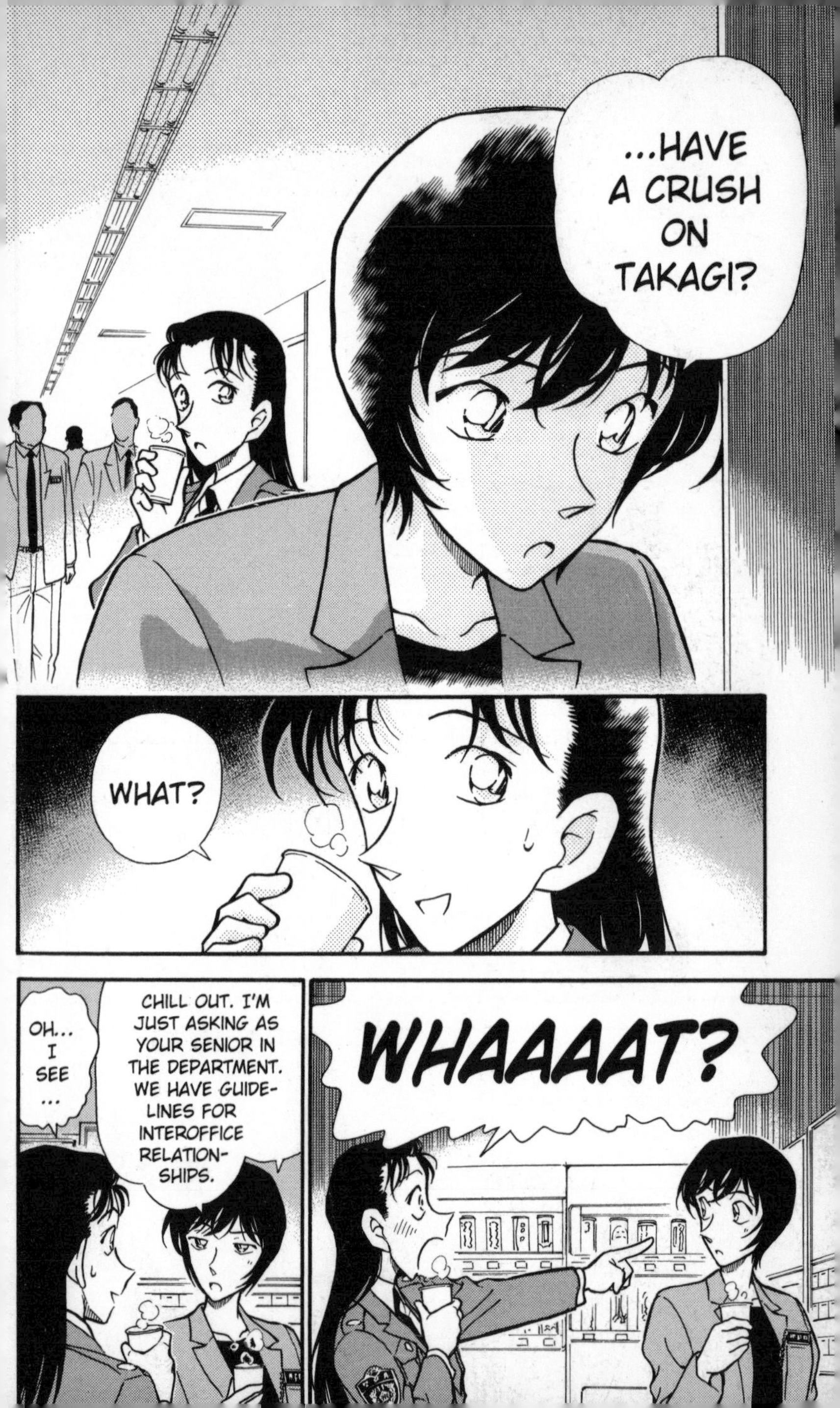
...HAVE A CRUSH ON TAKAGI?
WHAT?
WHAAAAT?
CHILL OUT. I'M JUST ASKING AS YOUR SENIOR IN THE DEPARTMENT. WE HAVE GUIDE-LINES FOR INTEROFFICE RELATION-SHIPS.
OH... I SEE ...

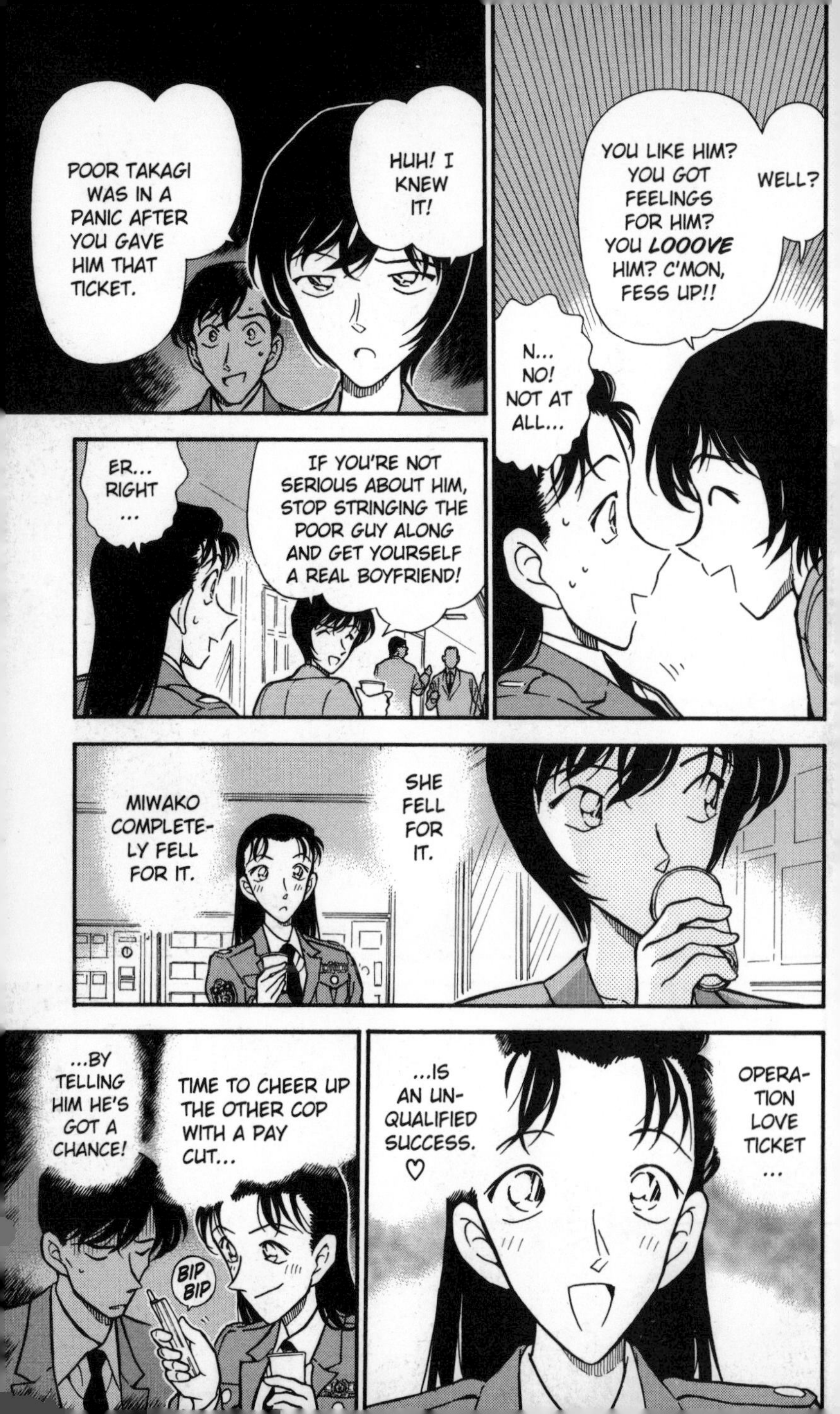
WELL?
YOU LIKE HIM? YOU GOT FEELINGS FOR HIM? YOU ***LOOOVE*** HIM? C'MON, FESS UP!!
N... NO! NOT AT ALL...
HUH! I KNEW IT!
POOR TAKAGI WAS IN A PANIC AFTER YOU GAVE HIM THAT TICKET.
IF YOU'RE NOT SERIOUS ABOUT HIM, STOP STRINGING THE POOR GUY ALONG AND GET YOURSELF A REAL BOYFRIEND!
ER... RIGHT ...
SHE FELL FOR IT.
MIWAKO COMPLETE-LY FELL FOR IT.
OPERA-TION LOVE TICKET ...
...IS AN UN-QUALIFIED SUCCESS. ♡
TIME TO CHEER UP THE OTHER COP WITH A PAY CUT...
...BY TELLING HIM HE'S GOT A CHANCE!
BIP BIP

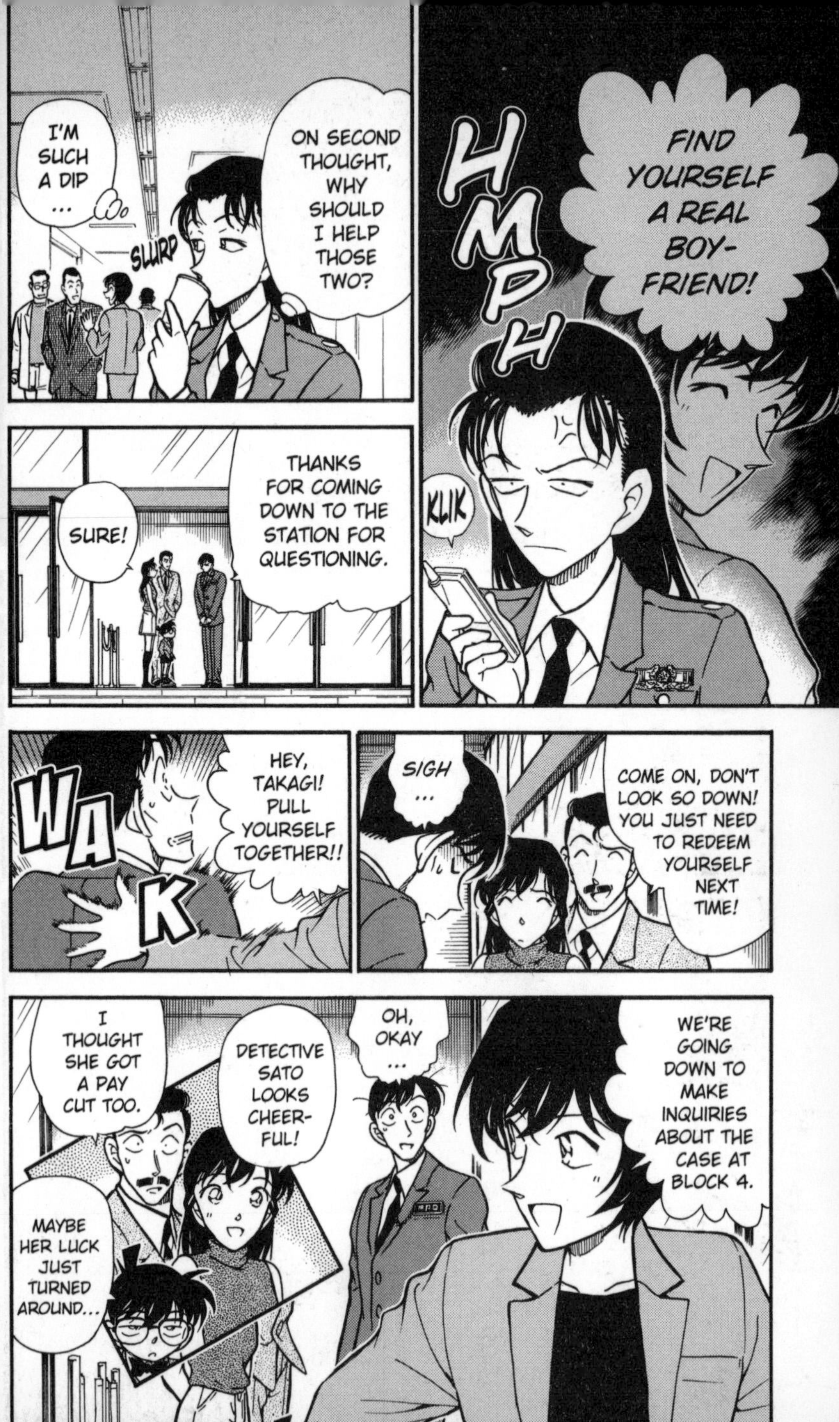
HMPH
FIND YOURSELF A REAL BOY-FRIEND!
KLIK
ON SECOND THOUGHT, WHY SHOULD I HELP THOSE TWO?
I'M SUCH A DIP ...
SLURP
THANKS FOR COMING DOWN TO THE STATION FOR QUESTIONING.
SURE!
COME ON, DON'T LOOK SO DOWN! YOU JUST NEED TO REDEEM YOURSELF NEXT TIME!
SIGH ...
HEY, TAKAGI! PULL YOURSELF TOGETHER!!
WAK
WE'RE GOING DOWN TO MAKE INQUIRIES ABOUT THE CASE AT BLOCK 4.
OH, OKAY ...
DETECTIVE SATO LOOKS CHEER-FUL!
I THOUGHT SHE GOT A PAY CUT TOO.
MAYBE HER LUCK JUST TURNED AROUND...

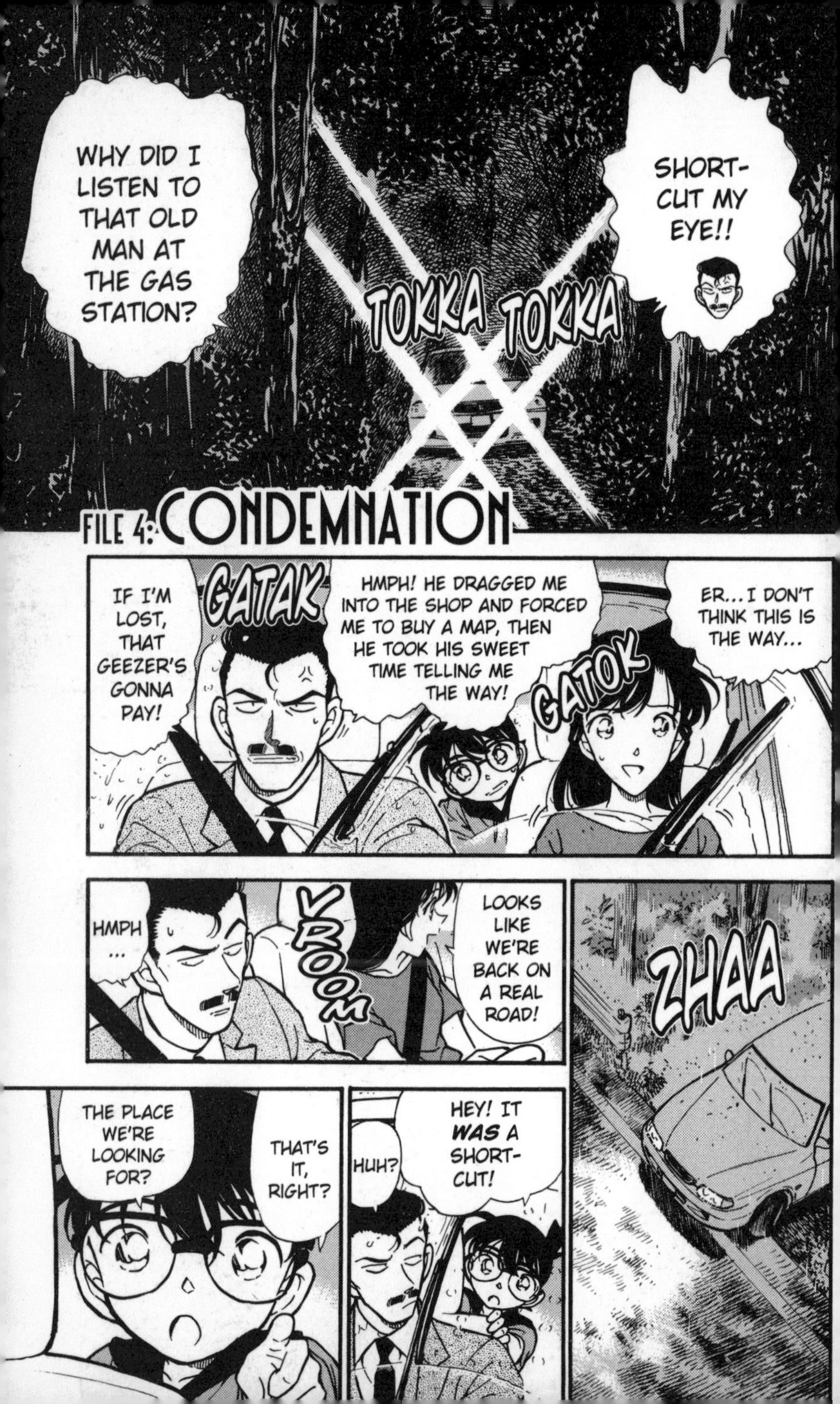
SHORT-CUT MY EYE!!
TOKKA TOKKA
WHY DID I LISTEN TO THAT OLD MAN AT THE GAS STATION?
FILE 4: CONDEMNATION
ER... I DON'T THINK THIS IS THE WAY...
GATOK
HMPH! HE DRAGGED ME INTO THE SHOP AND FORCED ME TO BUY A MAP, THEN HE TOOK HIS SWEET TIME TELLING ME THE WAY!
GATAK
IF I'M LOST, THAT GEEZER'S GONNA PAY!
ZHAA
LOOKS LIKE WE'RE BACK ON A REAL ROAD!
VROOM
HMPH ...
HEY! IT *WAS* A SHORT-CUT!
HUH?
THAT'S IT, RIGHT?
THE PLACE WE'RE LOOKING FOR?

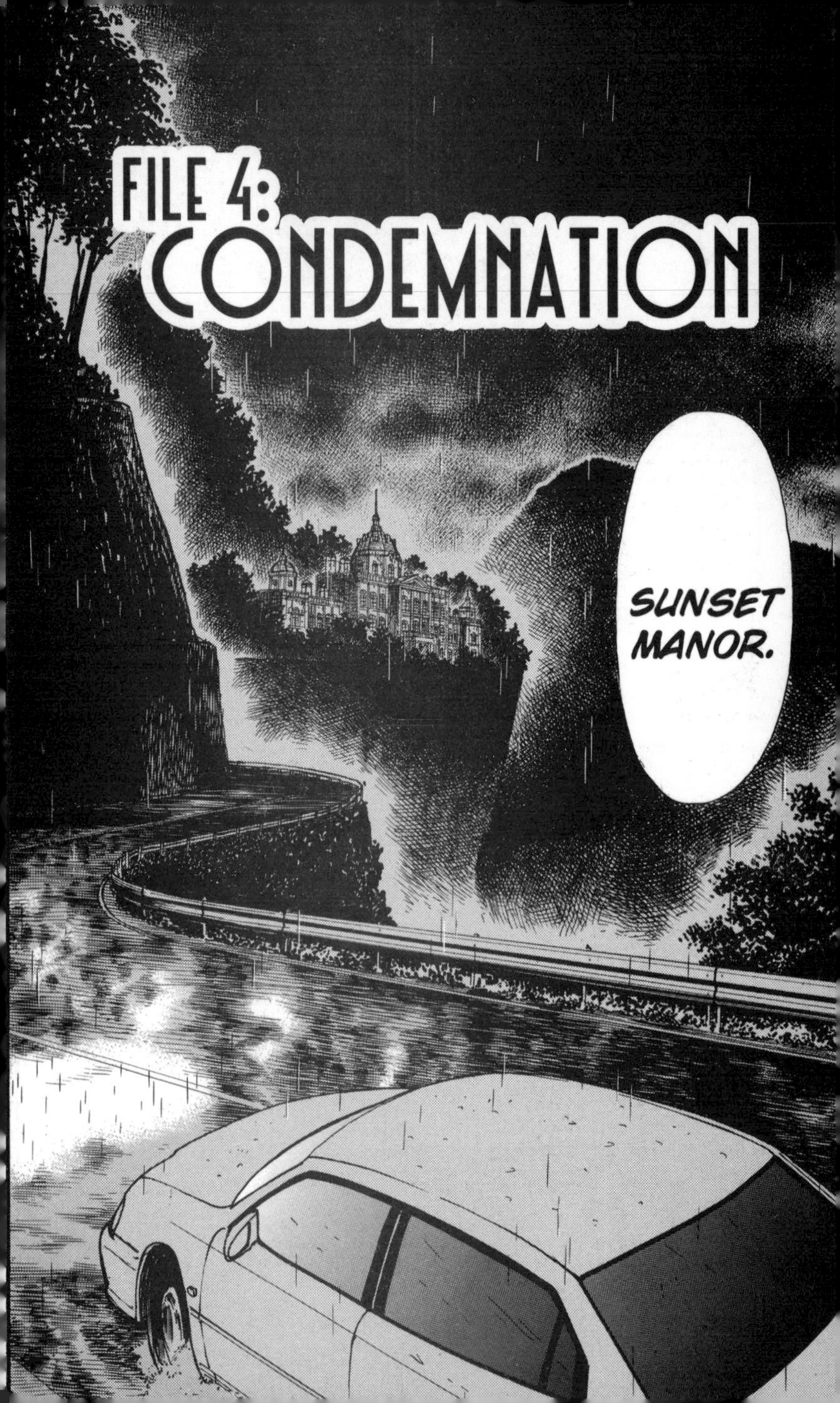
FILE 4: CONDEMNATION
SUNSET MANOR.

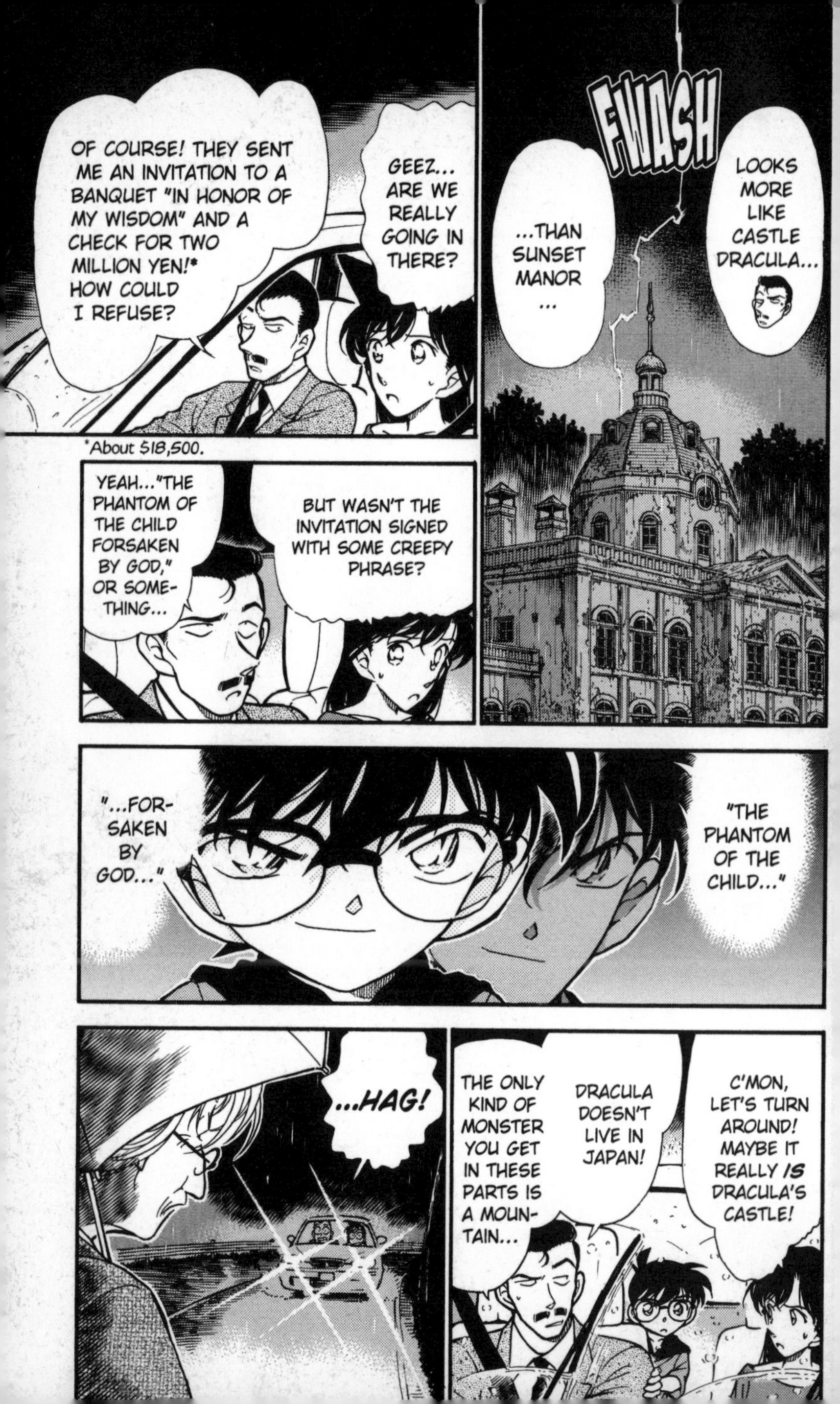
FWASH
LOOKS MORE LIKE CASTLE DRACULA...
...THAN SUNSET MANOR...
GEEZ... ARE WE REALLY GOING IN THERE?
OF COURSE! THEY SENT ME AN INVITATION TO A BANQUET "IN HONOR OF MY WISDOM" AND A CHECK FOR TWO MILLION YEN!* HOW COULD I REFUSE?
*About $18,500.
BUT WASN'T THE INVITATION SIGNED WITH SOME CREEPY PHRASE?
YEAH..."THE PHANTOM OF THE CHILD FORSAKEN BY GOD," OR SOMETHING...
"THE PHANTOM OF THE CHILD..."
"...FORSAKEN BY GOD..."
C'MON, LET'S TURN AROUND! MAYBE IT REALLY *IS* DRACULA'S CASTLE!
DRACULA DOESN'T LIVE IN JAPAN!
THE ONLY KIND OF MONSTER YOU GET IN THESE PARTS IS A MOUNTAIN...
...HAG!

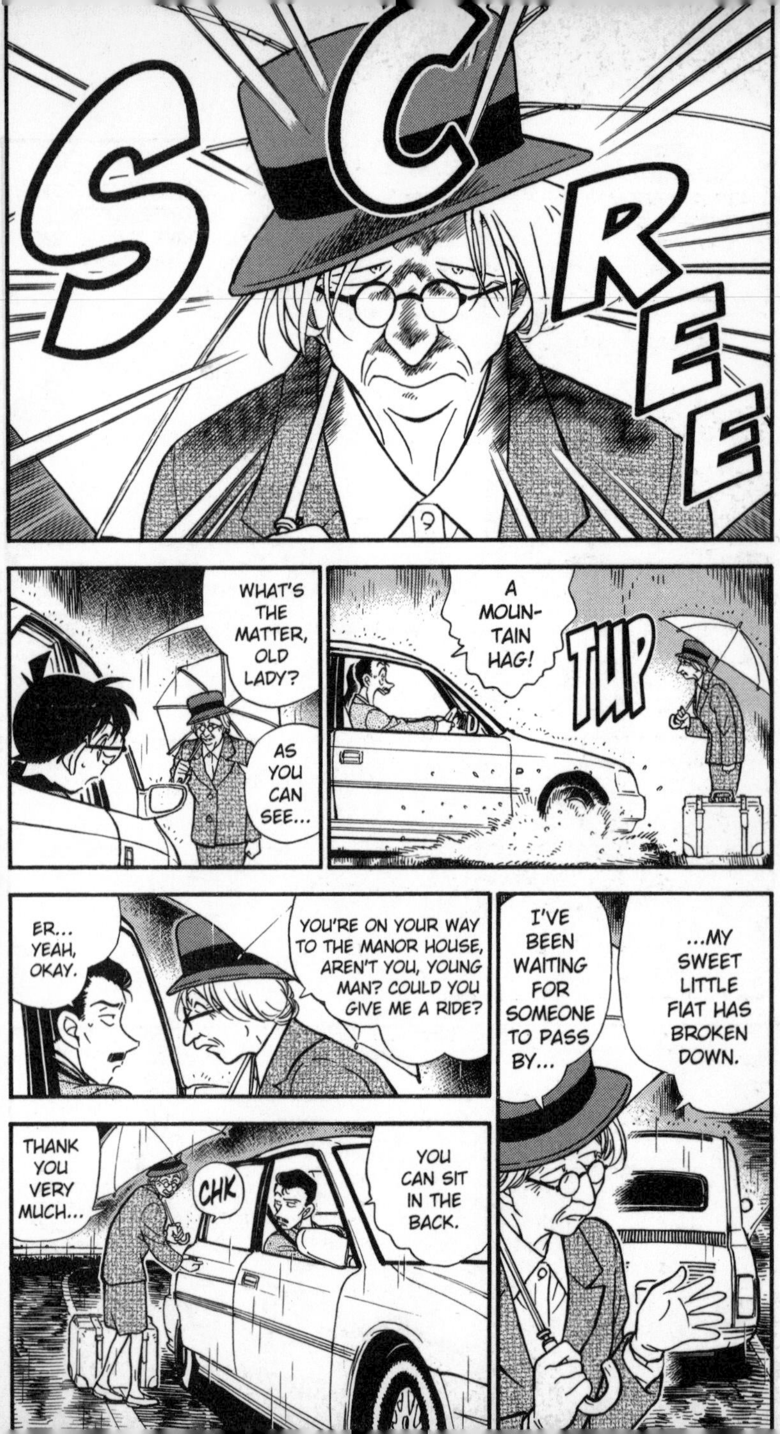
SCREE
A MOUNTAIN HAG!
TUP
WHAT'S THE MATTER, OLD LADY?
AS YOU CAN SEE...
...MY SWEET LITTLE FIAT HAS BROKEN DOWN.
I'VE BEEN WAITING FOR SOMEONE TO PASS BY...
YOU'RE ON YOUR WAY TO THE MANOR HOUSE, AREN'T YOU, YOUNG MAN? COULD YOU GIVE ME A RIDE?
ER... YEAH, OKAY.
YOU CAN SIT IN THE BACK.
CHK
THANK YOU VERY MUCH...

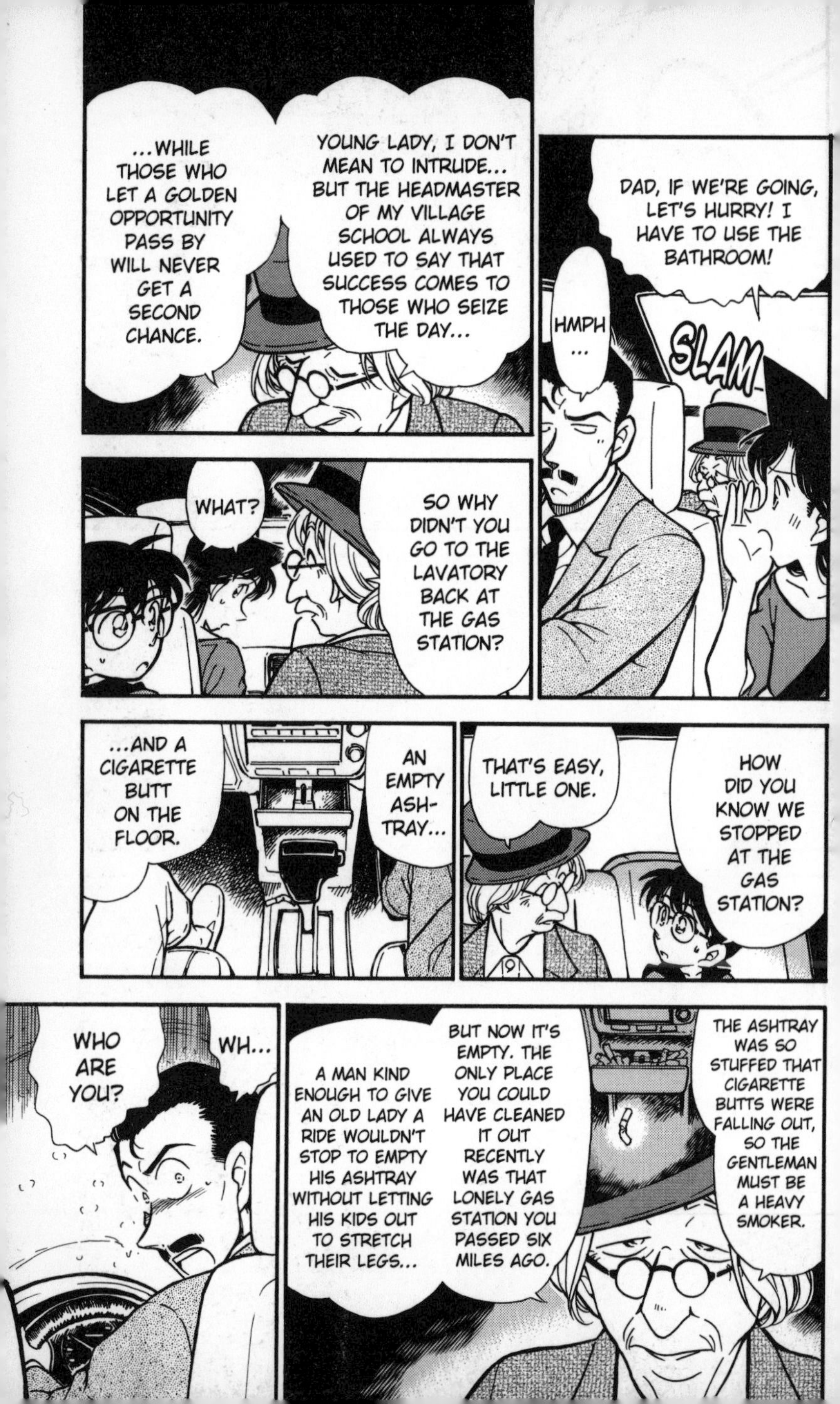
YOUNG LADY, I DON'T MEAN TO INTRUDE... BUT THE HEADMASTER OF MY VILLAGE SCHOOL ALWAYS USED TO SAY THAT SUCCESS COMES TO THOSE WHO SEIZE THE DAY...
...WHILE THOSE WHO LET A GOLDEN OPPORTUNITY PASS BY WILL NEVER GET A SECOND CHANCE.
DAD, IF WE'RE GOING, LET'S HURRY! I HAVE TO USE THE BATHROOM!
SLAM
HMPH...
SO WHY DIDN'T YOU GO TO THE LAVATORY BACK AT THE GAS STATION?
WHAT?
HOW DID YOU KNOW WE STOPPED AT THE GAS STATION?
THAT'S EASY, LITTLE ONE.
AN EMPTY ASH-TRAY...
...AND A CIGARETTE BUTT ON THE FLOOR.
THE ASHTRAY WAS SO STUFFED THAT CIGARETTE BUTTS WERE FALLING OUT, SO THE GENTLEMAN MUST BE A HEAVY SMOKER.
BUT NOW IT'S EMPTY. THE ONLY PLACE YOU COULD HAVE CLEANED IT OUT RECENTLY WAS THAT LONELY GAS STATION YOU PASSED SIX MILES AGO.
A MAN KIND ENOUGH TO GIVE AN OLD LADY A RIDE WOULDN'T STOP TO EMPTY HIS ASHTRAY WITHOUT LETTING HIS KIDS OUT TO STRETCH THEIR LEGS...
WH...
WHO ARE YOU?

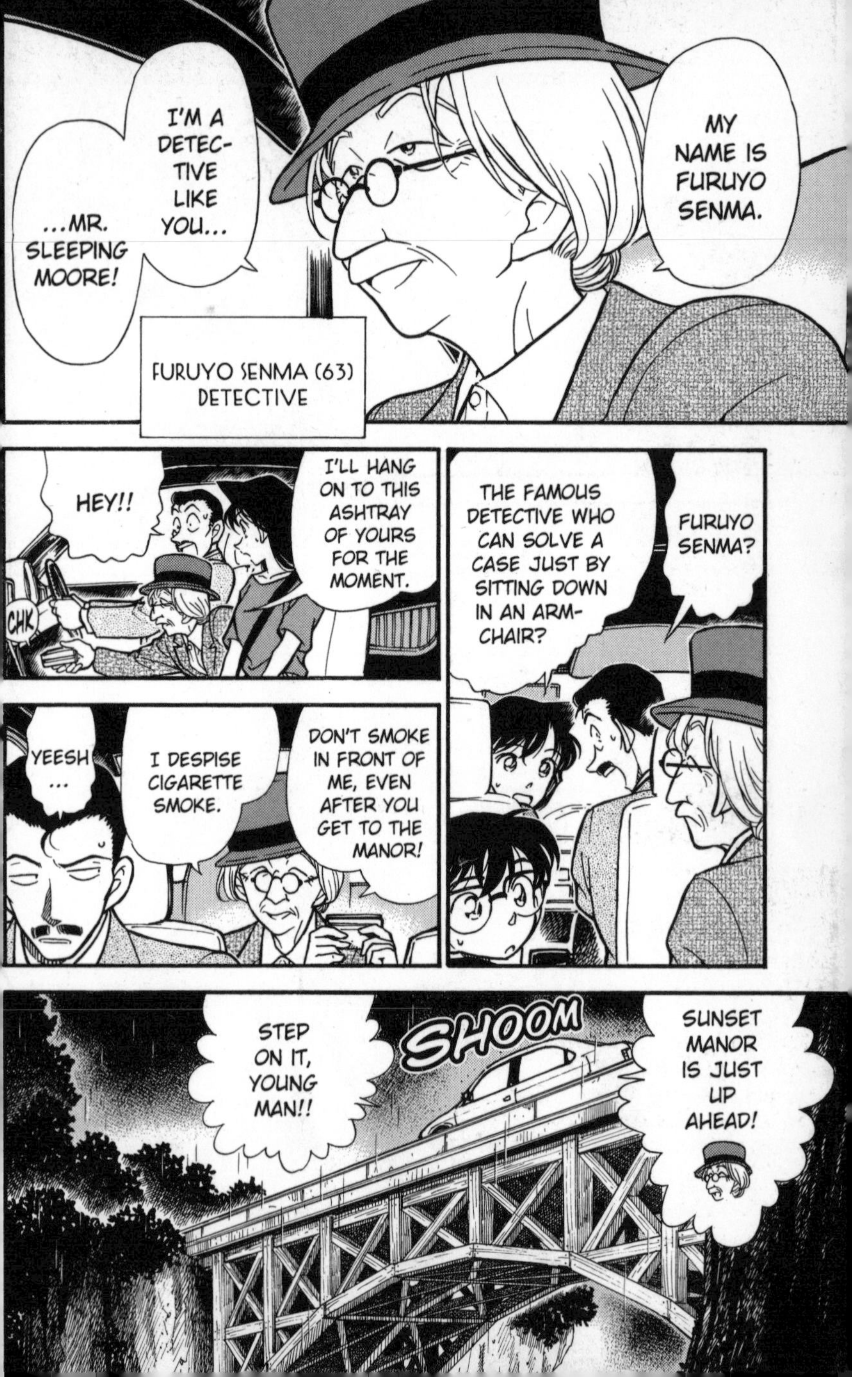
MY NAME IS FURUYO SENMA.
I'M A DETEC-TIVE LIKE YOU...
...MR. SLEEPING MOORE!
FURUYO SENMA (63) DETECTIVE
FURUYO SENMA?
THE FAMOUS DETECTIVE WHO CAN SOLVE A CASE JUST BY SITTING DOWN IN AN ARM-CHAIR?
I'LL HANG ON TO THIS ASHTRAY OF YOURS FOR THE MOMENT.
HEY!!
CHK
DON'T SMOKE IN FRONT OF ME, EVEN AFTER YOU GET TO THE MANOR!
I DESPISE CIGARETTE SMOKE.
YEESH...
SUNSET MANOR IS JUST UP AHEAD!
SHOOM
STEP ON IT, YOUNG MAN!!

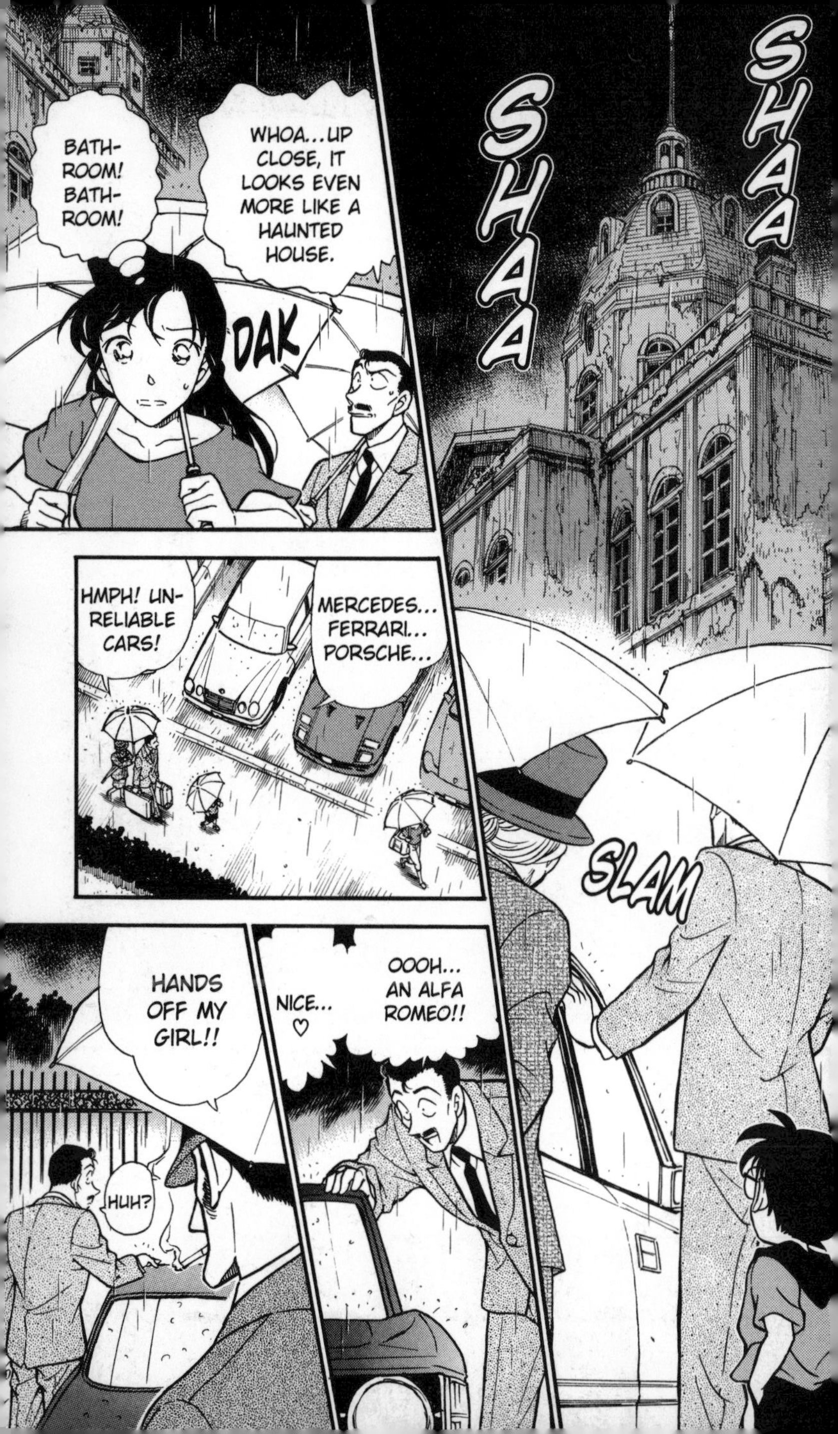
SHAA
SHAA
SLAM
WHOA...UP CLOSE, IT LOOKS EVEN MORE LIKE A HAUNTED HOUSE.
BATH-ROOM! BATH-ROOM!
DAK
MERCEDES... FERRARI... PORSCHE...
HMPH! UN-RELIABLE CARS!
OOOH... AN ALFA ROMEO!!
NICE... ♡
HANDS OFF MY GIRL!!
HUH?

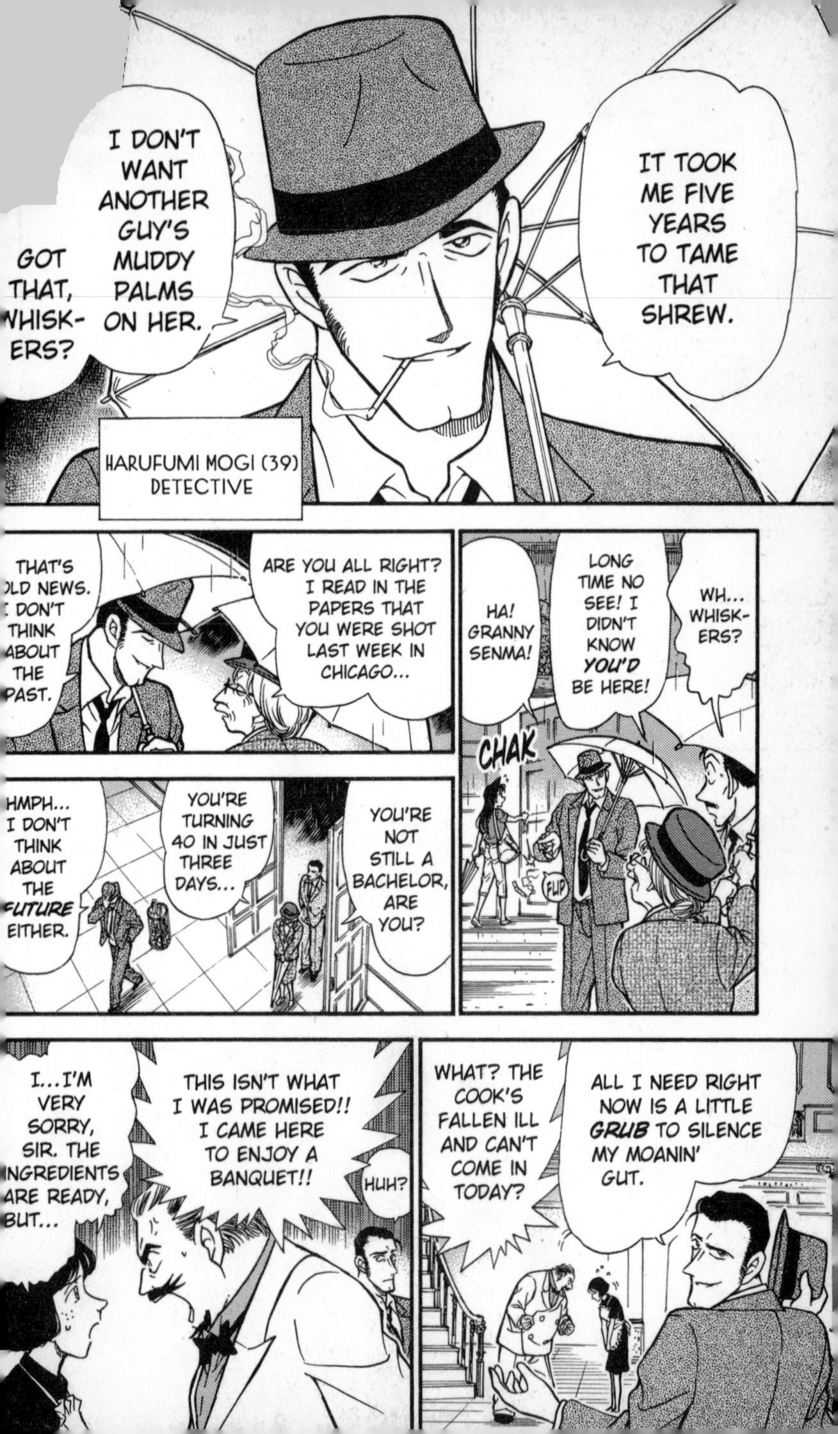

IT TOOK ME FIVE YEARS TO TAME THAT SHREW.
I DON'T WANT ANOTHER GUY'S MUDDY PALMS ON HER.
GOT THAT, WHISKERS?
HARUFUMI MOGI (39) DETECTIVE
WH... WHISKERS?
LONG TIME NO SEE! I DIDN'T KNOW **YOU'D** BE HERE!
HA! GRANNY SENMA!
CHAK
FLIP
ARE YOU ALL RIGHT? I READ IN THE PAPERS THAT YOU WERE SHOT LAST WEEK IN CHICAGO...
THAT'S OLD NEWS. I DON'T THINK ABOUT THE PAST.
YOU'RE NOT STILL A BACHELOR, ARE YOU?
YOU'RE TURNING 40 IN JUST THREE DAYS...
HMPH... I DON'T THINK ABOUT THE **FUTURE** EITHER.
ALL I NEED RIGHT NOW IS A LITTLE **GRUB** TO SILENCE MY MOANIN' GUT.
WHAT? THE COOK'S FALLEN ILL AND CAN'T COME IN TODAY?
THIS ISN'T WHAT I WAS PROMISED!! I CAME HERE TO ENJOY A BANQUET!!
HUH?
I...I'M VERY SORRY, SIR. THE INGREDIENTS ARE READY, BUT...

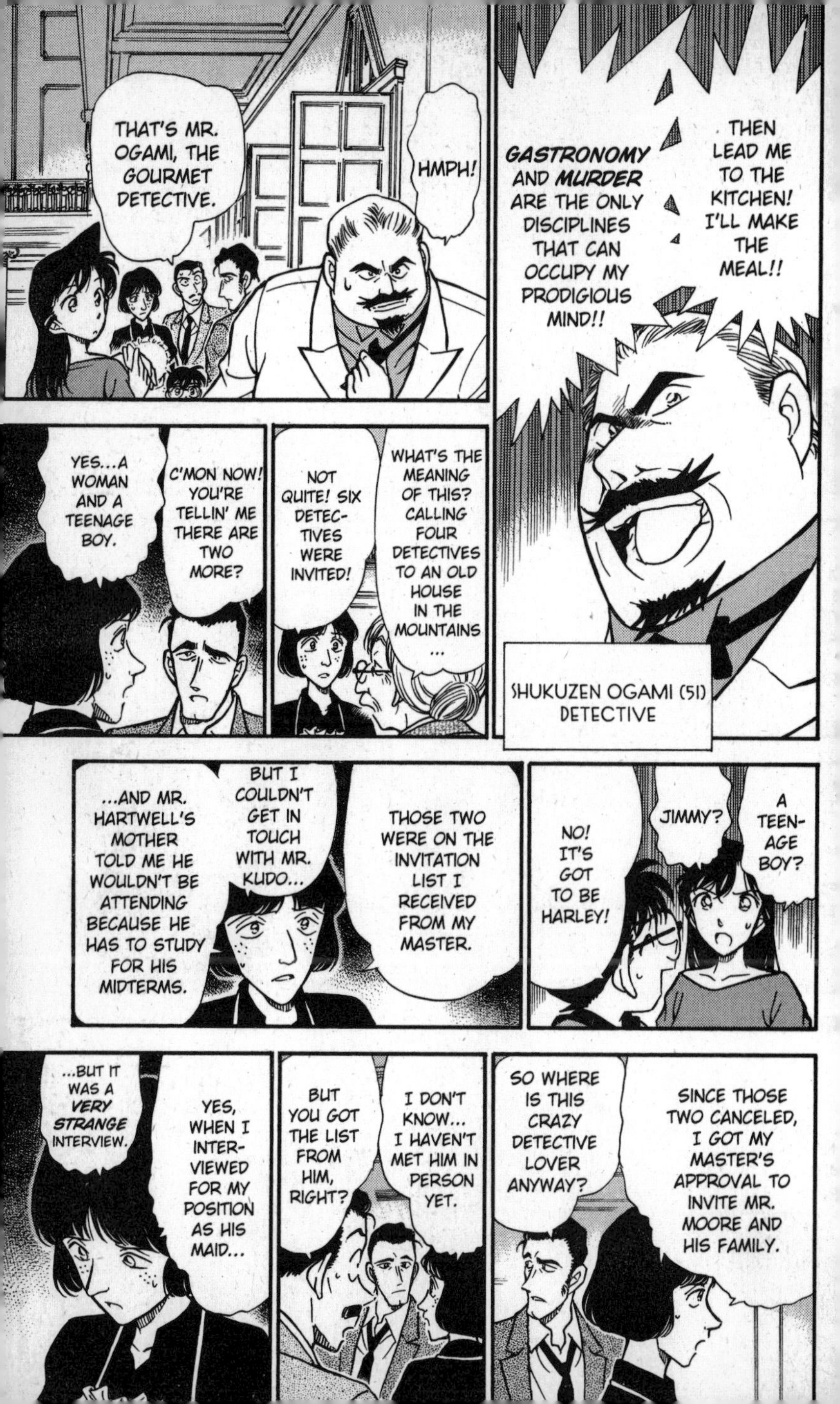
THEN LEAD ME TO THE KITCHEN! I'LL MAKE THE MEAL!!
GASTRONOMY AND MURDER ARE THE ONLY DISCIPLINES THAT CAN OCCUPY MY PRODIGIOUS MIND!!
SHUKUZEN OGAMI (51) DETECTIVE
HMPH!
THAT'S MR. OGAMI, THE GOURMET DETECTIVE.
WHAT'S THE MEANING OF THIS? CALLING FOUR DETECTIVES TO AN OLD HOUSE IN THE MOUNTAINS...
NOT QUITE! SIX DETEC-TIVES WERE INVITED!
C'MON NOW! YOU'RE TELLIN' ME THERE ARE TWO MORE?
YES...A WOMAN AND A TEENAGE BOY.
A TEEN-AGE BOY?
JIMMY?
NO! IT'S GOT TO BE HARLEY!
THOSE TWO WERE ON THE INVITATION LIST I RECEIVED FROM MY MASTER.
BUT I COULDN'T GET IN TOUCH WITH MR. KUDO...
...AND MR. HARTWELL'S MOTHER TOLD ME HE WOULDN'T BE ATTENDING BECAUSE HE HAS TO STUDY FOR HIS MIDTERMS.
SINCE THOSE TWO CANCELED, I GOT MY MASTER'S APPROVAL TO INVITE MR. MOORE AND HIS FAMILY.
SO WHERE IS THIS CRAZY DETECTIVE LOVER ANYWAY?
I DON'T KNOW... I HAVEN'T MET HIM IN PERSON YET.
BUT YOU GOT THE LIST FROM HIM, RIGHT?
YES, WHEN I INTER-VIEWED FOR MY POSITION AS HIS MAID...
...BUT IT WAS A VERY STRANGE INTERVIEW.

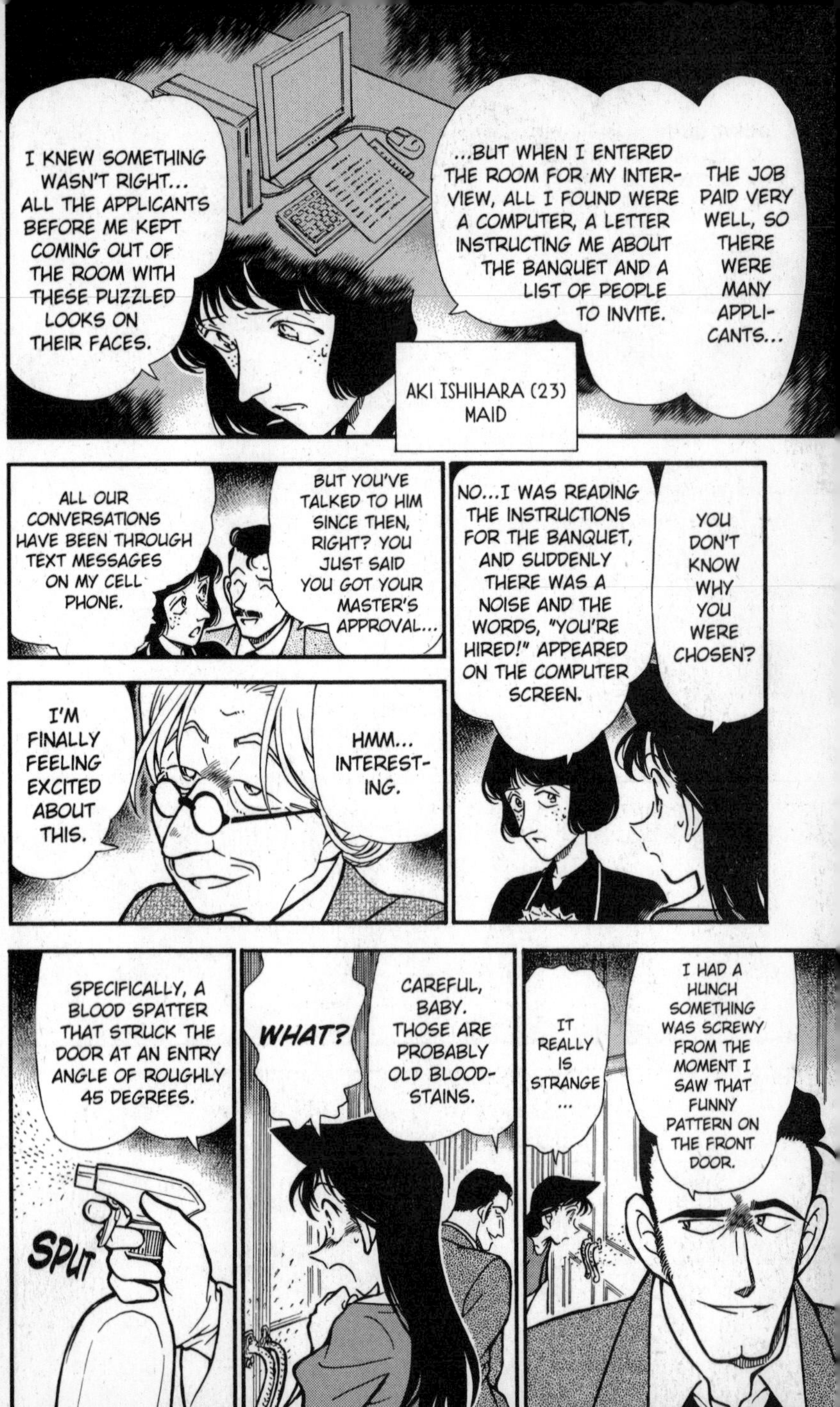
THE JOB PAID VERY WELL, SO THERE WERE MANY APPLICANTS...
...BUT WHEN I ENTERED THE ROOM FOR MY INTERVIEW, ALL I FOUND WERE A COMPUTER, A LETTER INSTRUCTING ME ABOUT THE BANQUET AND A LIST OF PEOPLE TO INVITE.
I KNEW SOMETHING WASN'T RIGHT... ALL THE APPLICANTS BEFORE ME KEPT COMING OUT OF THE ROOM WITH THESE PUZZLED LOOKS ON THEIR FACES.
AKI ISHIHARA (23) MAID
YOU DON'T KNOW WHY YOU WERE CHOSEN?
NO...I WAS READING THE INSTRUCTIONS FOR THE BANQUET, AND SUDDENLY THERE WAS A NOISE AND THE WORDS, "YOU'RE HIRED!" APPEARED ON THE COMPUTER SCREEN.
BUT YOU'VE TALKED TO HIM SINCE THEN, RIGHT? YOU JUST SAID YOU GOT YOUR MASTER'S APPROVAL...
ALL OUR CONVERSATIONS HAVE BEEN THROUGH TEXT MESSAGES ON MY CELL PHONE.
HMM... INTERESTING.
I'M FINALLY FEELING EXCITED ABOUT THIS.
I HAD A HUNCH SOMETHING WAS SCREWY FROM THE MOMENT I SAW THAT FUNNY PATTERN ON THE FRONT DOOR.
IT REALLY IS STRANGE...
CAREFUL, BABY. THOSE ARE PROBABLY OLD BLOODSTAINS.
WHAT?
SPECIFICALLY, A BLOOD SPATTER THAT STRUCK THE DOOR AT AN ENTRY ANGLE OF ROUGHLY 45 DEGREES.
SPUT

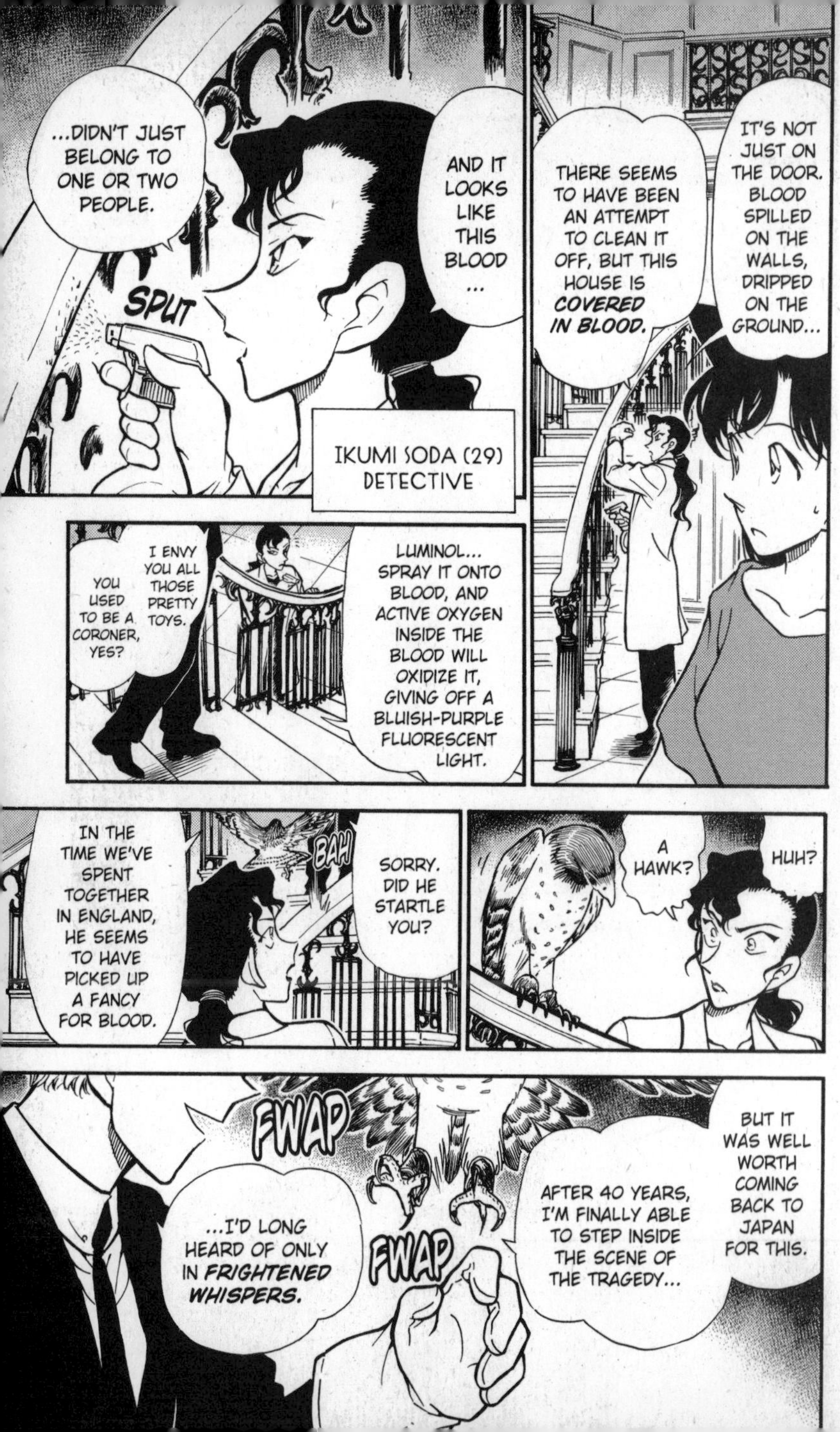
IT'S NOT JUST ON THE DOOR. BLOOD SPILLED ON THE WALLS, DRIPPED ON THE GROUND...
THERE SEEMS TO HAVE BEEN AN ATTEMPT TO CLEAN IT OFF, BUT THIS HOUSE IS ***COVERED IN BLOOD.***
AND IT LOOKS LIKE THIS BLOOD...
...DIDN'T JUST BELONG TO ONE OR TWO PEOPLE.
SPUT
IKUMI SODA (29) DETECTIVE
LUMINOL... SPRAY IT ONTO BLOOD, AND ACTIVE OXYGEN INSIDE THE BLOOD WILL OXIDIZE IT, GIVING OFF A BLUISH-PURPLE FLUORESCENT LIGHT.
I ENVY YOU ALL THOSE PRETTY TOYS.
YOU USED TO BE A CORONER, YES?
HUH?
A HAWK?
SORRY. DID HE STARTLE YOU?
BAH
IN THE TIME WE'VE SPENT TOGETHER IN ENGLAND, HE SEEMS TO HAVE PICKED UP A FANCY FOR BLOOD.
BUT IT WAS WELL WORTH COMING BACK TO JAPAN FOR THIS.
AFTER 40 YEARS, I'M FINALLY ABLE TO STEP INSIDE THE SCENE OF THE TRAGEDY...
FWAP
...I'D LONG HEARD OF ONLY IN ***FRIGHTENED WHISPERS.***
FWAP

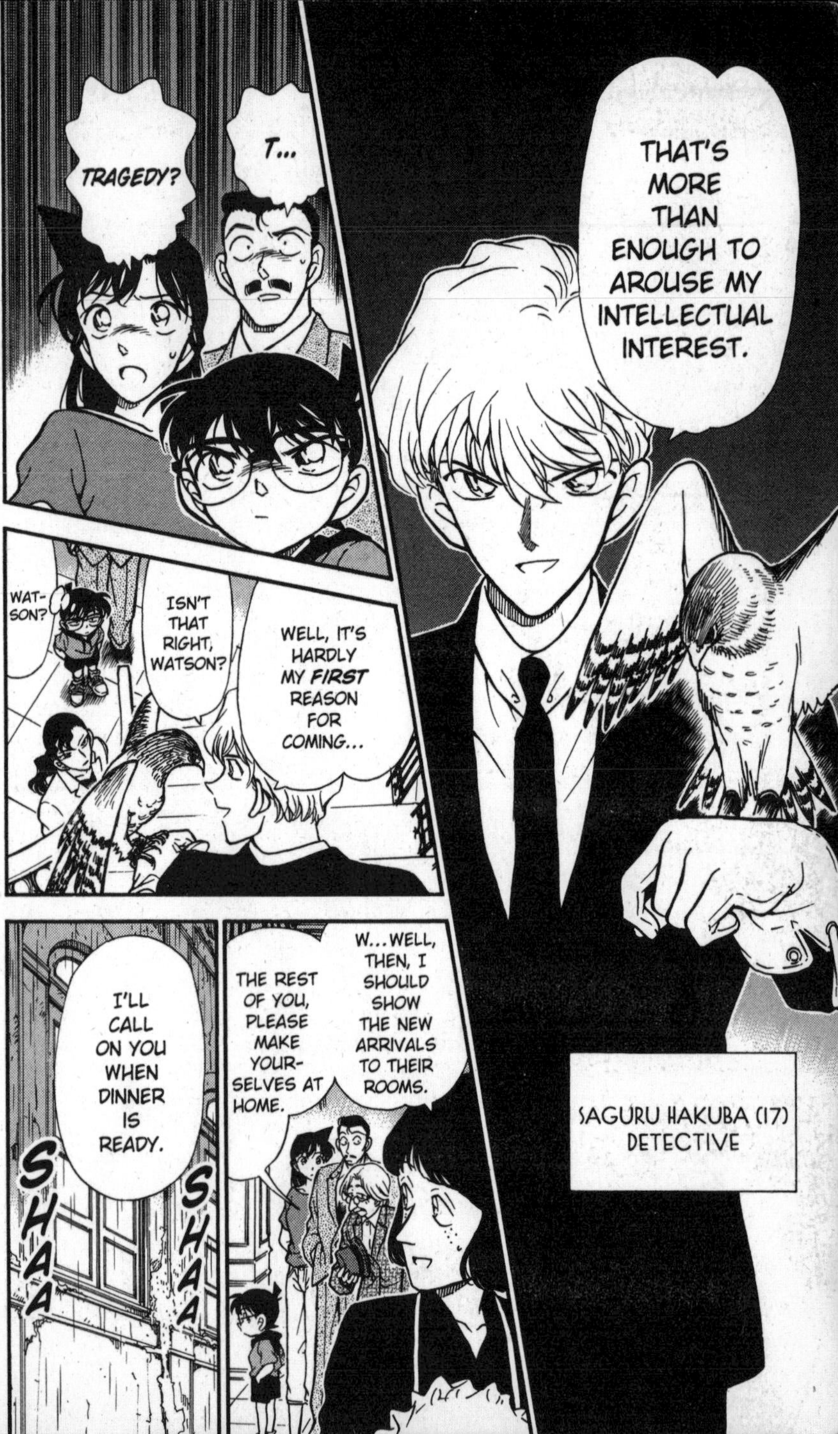
THAT'S MORE THAN ENOUGH TO AROUSE MY INTELLECTUAL INTEREST.
SAGURU HAKUBA (17) DETECTIVE
T...
TRAGEDY?
WELL, IT'S HARDLY MY FIRST REASON FOR COMING...
ISN'T THAT RIGHT, WATSON?
WATSON?
W...WELL, THEN, I SHOULD SHOW THE NEW ARRIVALS TO THEIR ROOMS.
THE REST OF YOU, PLEASE MAKE YOURSELVES AT HOME.
SHAA
I'LL CALL ON YOU WHEN DINNER IS READY.
SHAA

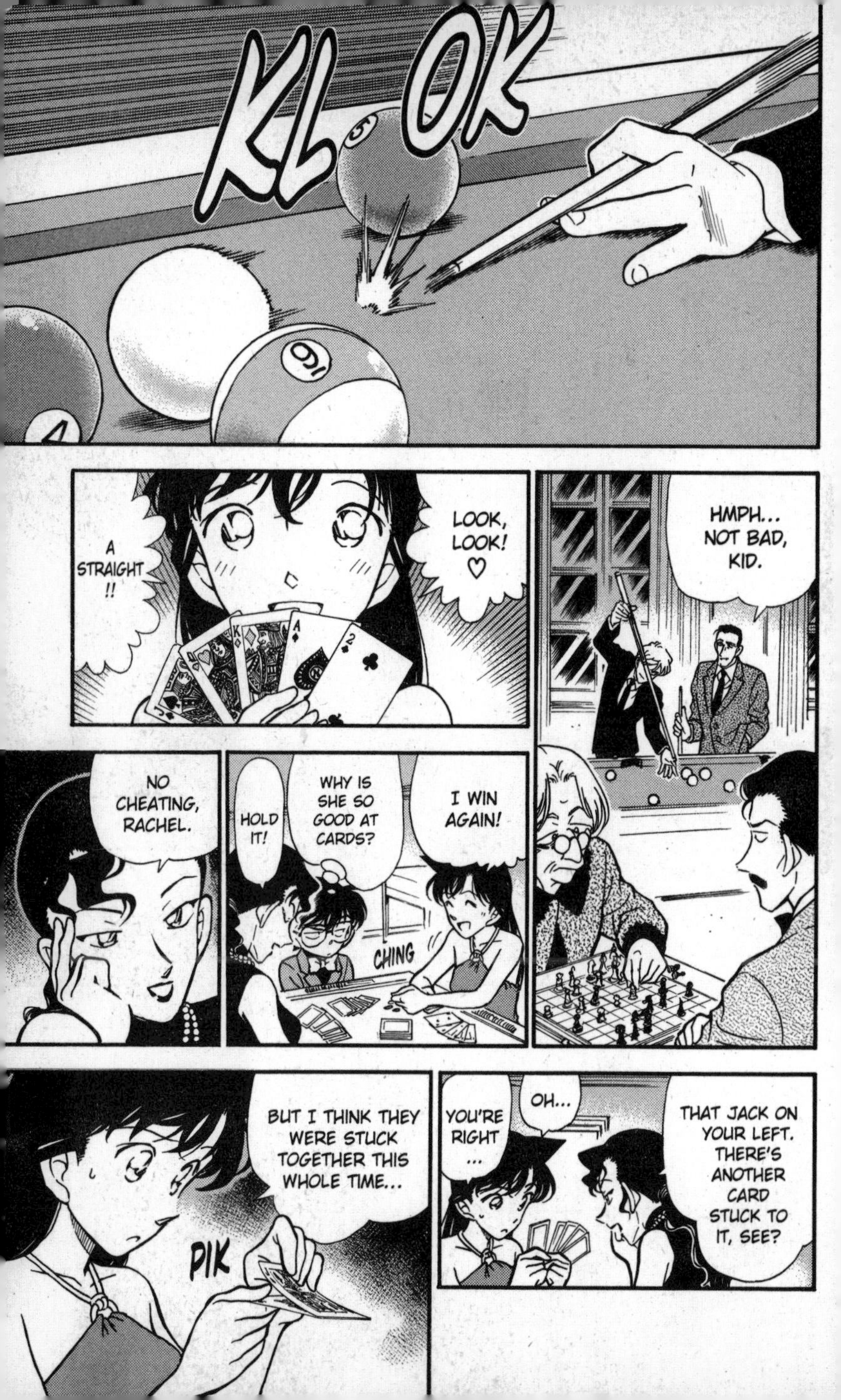
KLOK
HMPH... NOT BAD, KID.
LOOK, LOOK! ♡
A STRAIGHT !!
I WIN AGAIN!
CHING
WHY IS SHE SO GOOD AT CARDS?
HOLD IT!
NO CHEATING, RACHEL.
THAT JACK ON YOUR LEFT. THERE'S ANOTHER CARD STUCK TO IT, SEE?
OH...
YOU'RE RIGHT ...
BUT I THINK THEY WERE STUCK TOGETHER THIS WHOLE TIME...
PIK

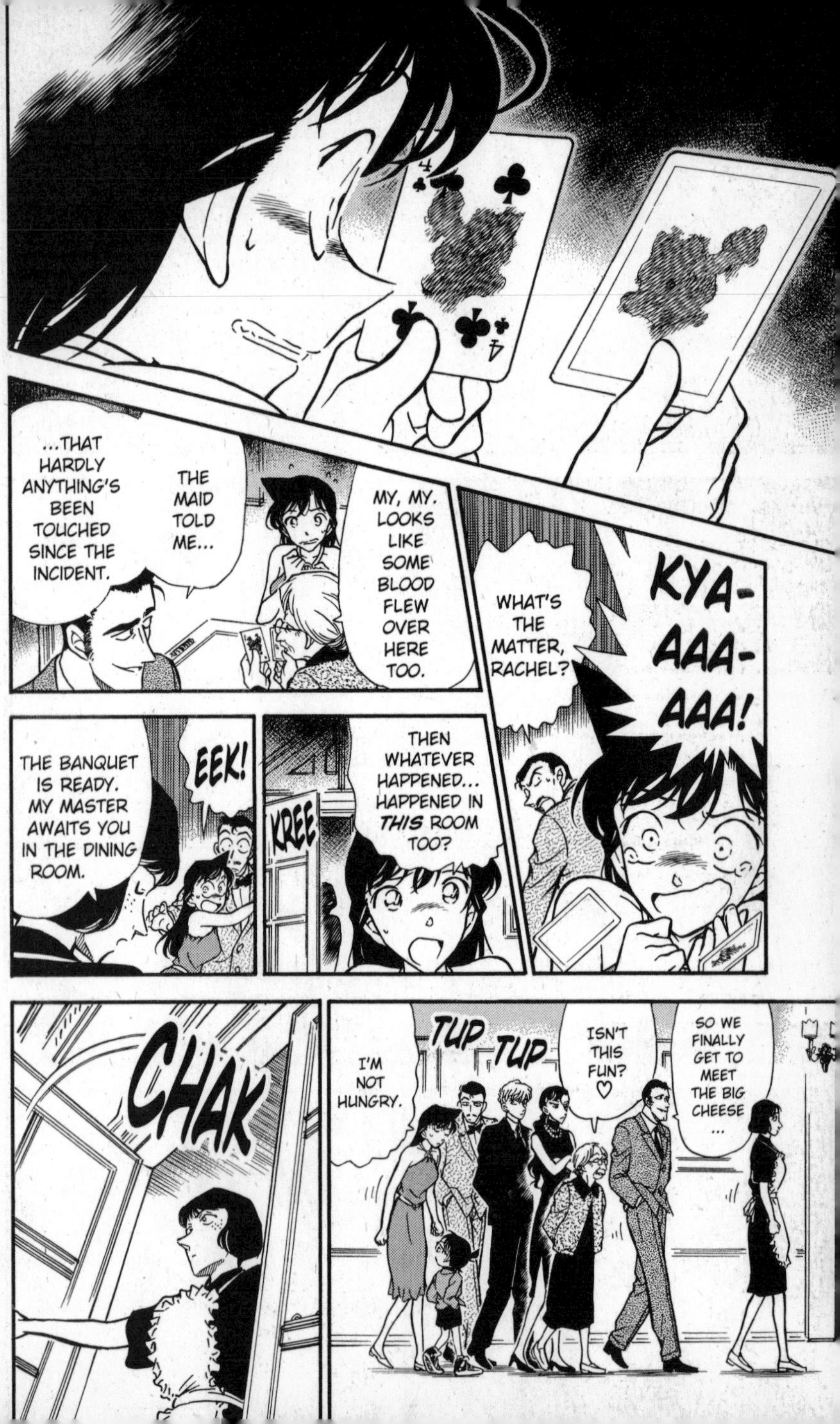
MY, MY. LOOKS LIKE SOME BLOOD FLEW OVER HERE TOO.
THE MAID TOLD ME...
...THAT HARDLY ANYTHING'S BEEN TOUCHED SINCE THE INCIDENT.
KYA-AAA-AAA!
WHAT'S THE MATTER, RACHEL?
THEN WHATEVER HAPPENED... HAPPENED IN *THIS* ROOM TOO?
KREE
EEK!
THE BANQUET IS READY. MY MASTER AWAITS YOU IN THE DINING ROOM.
SO WE FINALLY GET TO MEET THE BIG CHEESE ...
ISN'T THIS FUN? ♡
TUP
TUP
I'M NOT HUNGRY.
CHAK

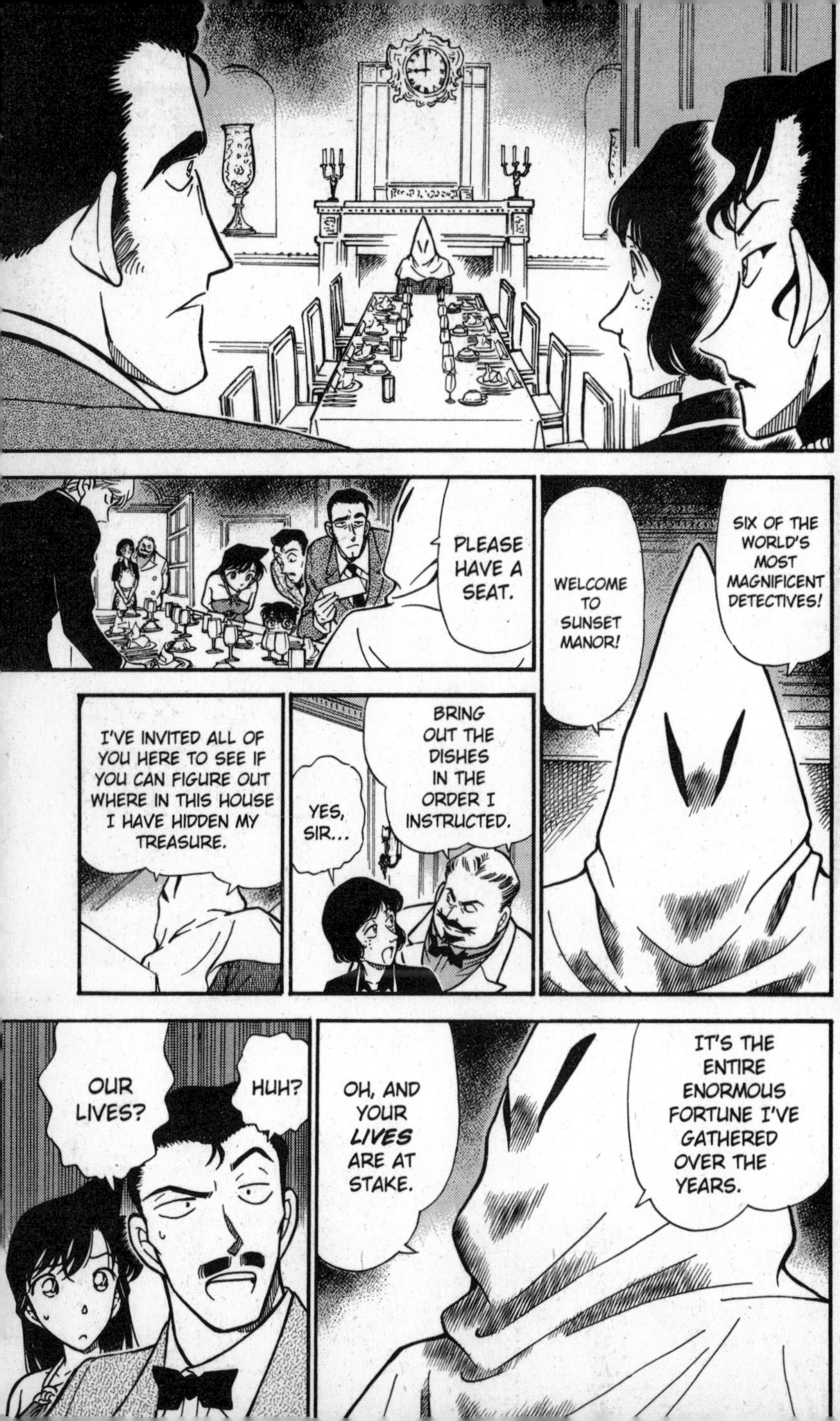

SIX OF THE WORLD'S MOST MAGNIFICENT DETECTIVES!
WELCOME TO SUNSET MANOR!
PLEASE HAVE A SEAT.
BRING OUT THE DISHES IN THE ORDER I INSTRUCTED.
YES, SIR...
I'VE INVITED ALL OF YOU HERE TO SEE IF YOU CAN FIGURE OUT WHERE IN THIS HOUSE I HAVE HIDDEN MY TREASURE.
IT'S THE ENTIRE ENORMOUS FORTUNE I'VE GATHERED OVER THE YEARS.
OH, AND YOUR *LIVES* ARE AT STAKE.
HUH?
OUR LIVES?

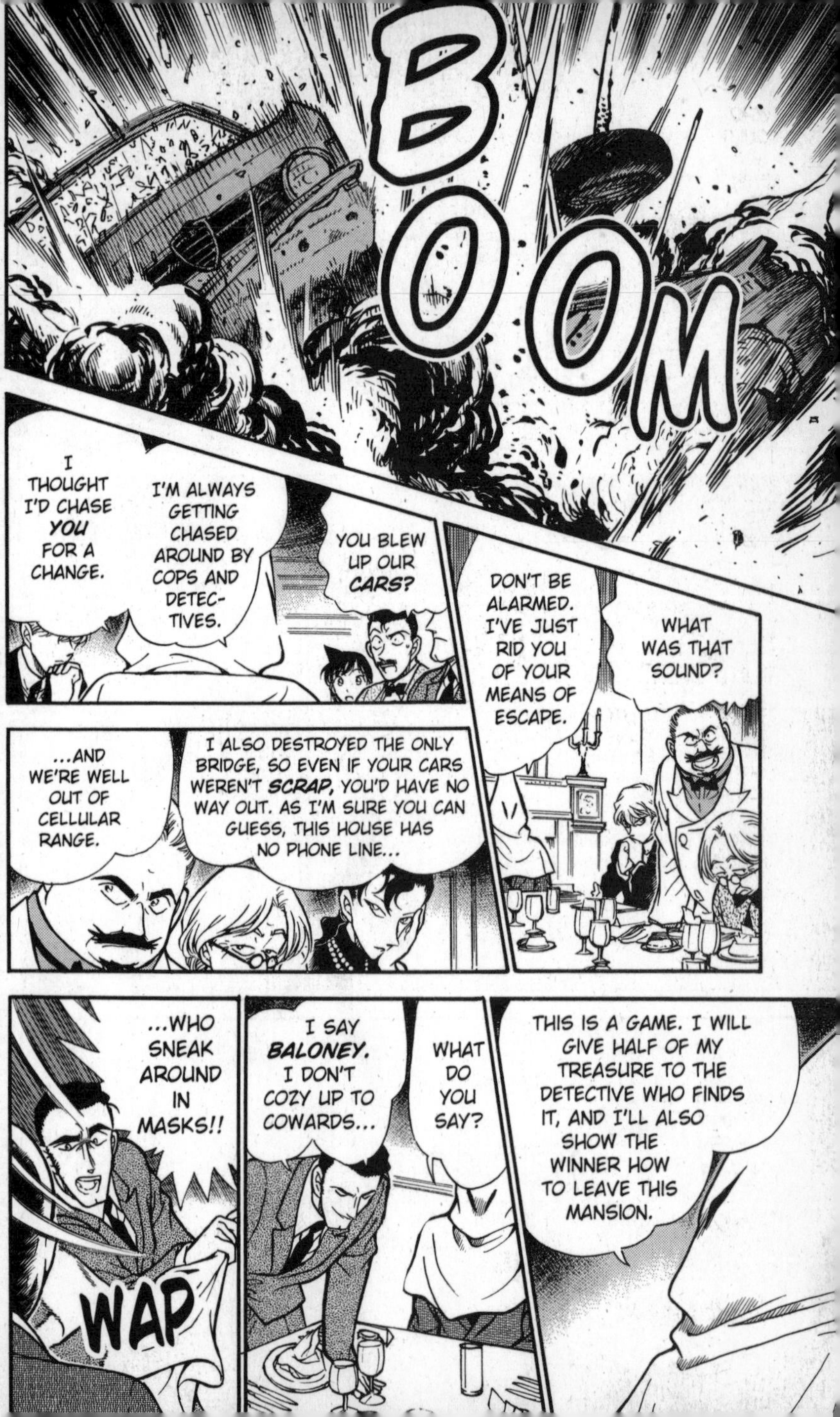
BOOOM
WHAT WAS THAT SOUND?
DON'T BE ALARMED. I'VE JUST RID YOU OF YOUR MEANS OF ESCAPE.
YOU BLEW UP OUR CARS?
I'M ALWAYS GETTING CHASED AROUND BY COPS AND DETEC-TIVES.
I THOUGHT I'D CHASE YOU FOR A CHANGE.
I ALSO DESTROYED THE ONLY BRIDGE, SO EVEN IF YOUR CARS WEREN'T SCRAP, YOU'D HAVE NO WAY OUT. AS I'M SURE YOU CAN GUESS, THIS HOUSE HAS NO PHONE LINE...
...AND WE'RE WELL OUT OF CELLULAR RANGE.
THIS IS A GAME. I WILL GIVE HALF OF MY TREASURE TO THE DETECTIVE WHO FINDS IT, AND I'LL ALSO SHOW THE WINNER HOW TO LEAVE THIS MANSION.
WHAT DO YOU SAY?
I SAY BALONEY. I DON'T COZY UP TO COWARDS...
...WHO SNEAK AROUND IN MASKS!!
WAP

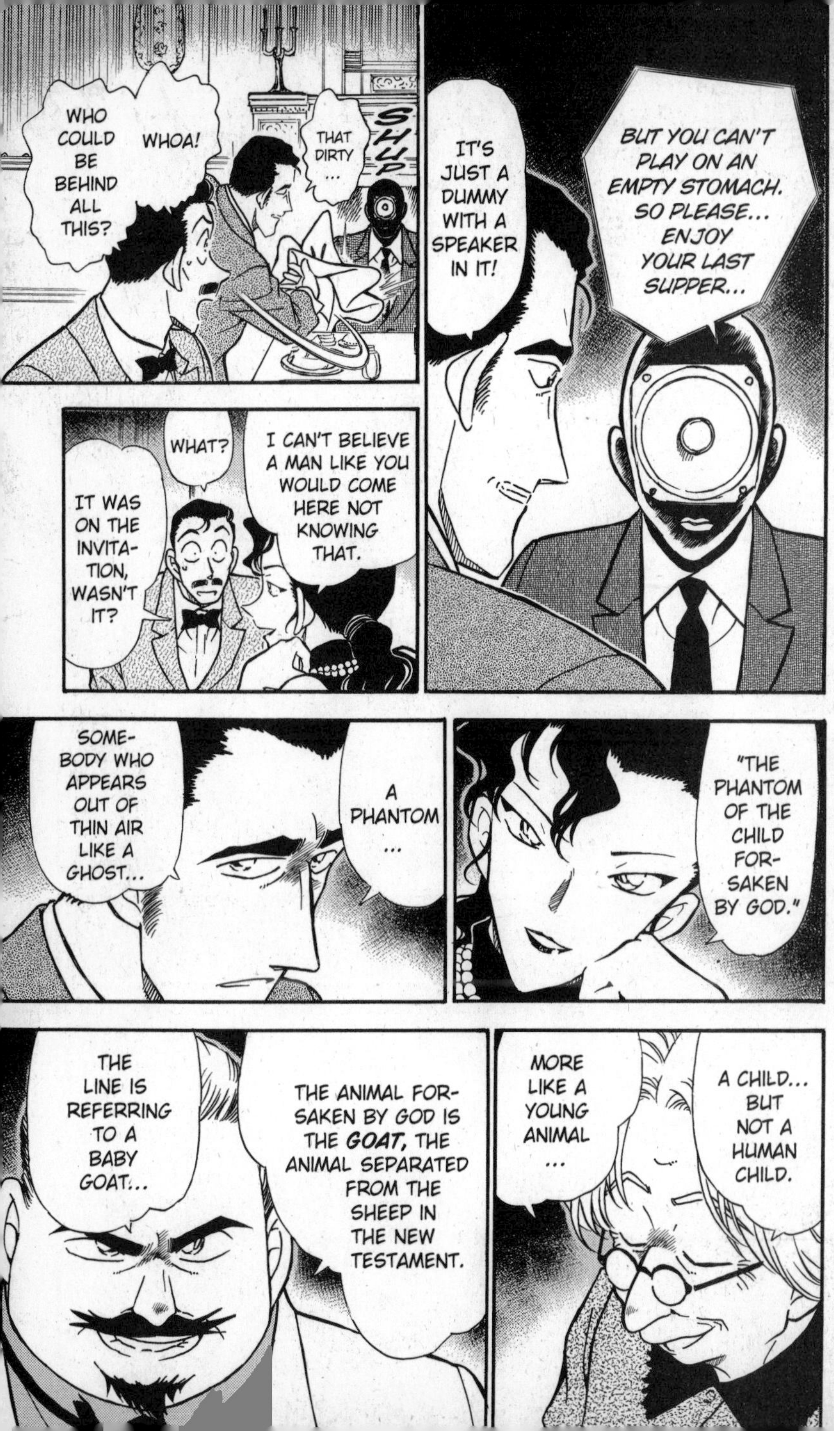
BUT YOU CAN'T PLAY ON AN EMPTY STOMACH. SO PLEASE... ENJOY YOUR LAST SUPPER...
IT'S JUST A DUMMY WITH A SPEAKER IN IT!
SHUP
THAT DIRTY ...
WHOA!
WHO COULD BE BEHIND ALL THIS?
I CAN'T BELIEVE A MAN LIKE YOU WOULD COME HERE NOT KNOWING THAT.
WHAT?
IT WAS ON THE INVITATION, WASN'T IT?
"THE PHANTOM OF THE CHILD FORSAKEN BY GOD."
A PHANTOM ...
SOMEBODY WHO APPEARS OUT OF THIN AIR LIKE A GHOST...
A CHILD... BUT NOT A HUMAN CHILD.
MORE LIKE A YOUNG ANIMAL ...
THE ANIMAL FORSAKEN BY GOD IS THE *GOAT,* THE ANIMAL SEPARATED FROM THE SHEEP IN THE NEW TESTAMENT.
THE LINE IS REFERRING TO A BABY GOAT...

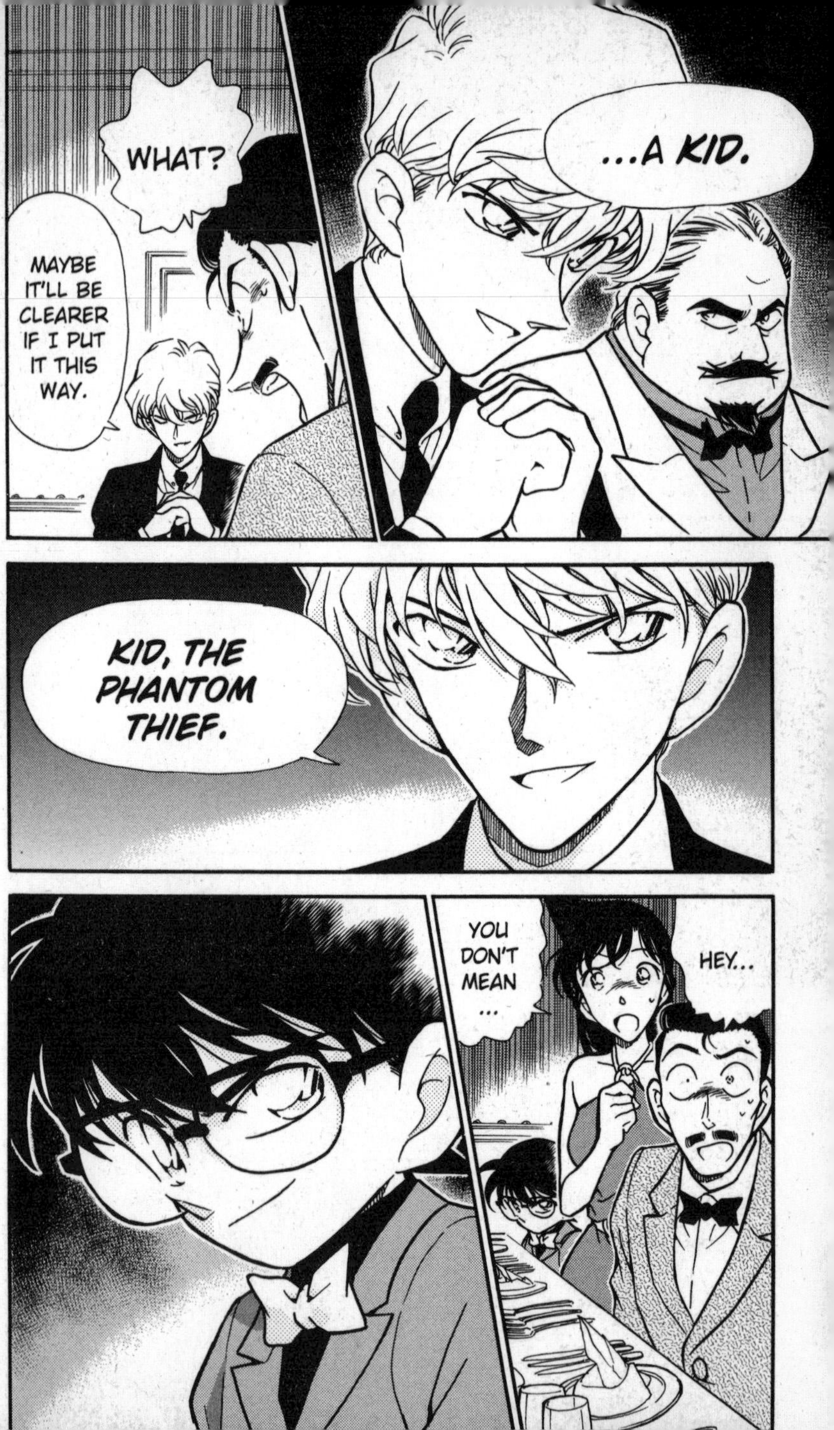
...A KID.
WHAT?
MAYBE IT'LL BE CLEARER IF I PUT IT THIS WAY.
KID, THE PHANTOM THIEF.
HEY...
YOU DON'T MEAN ...

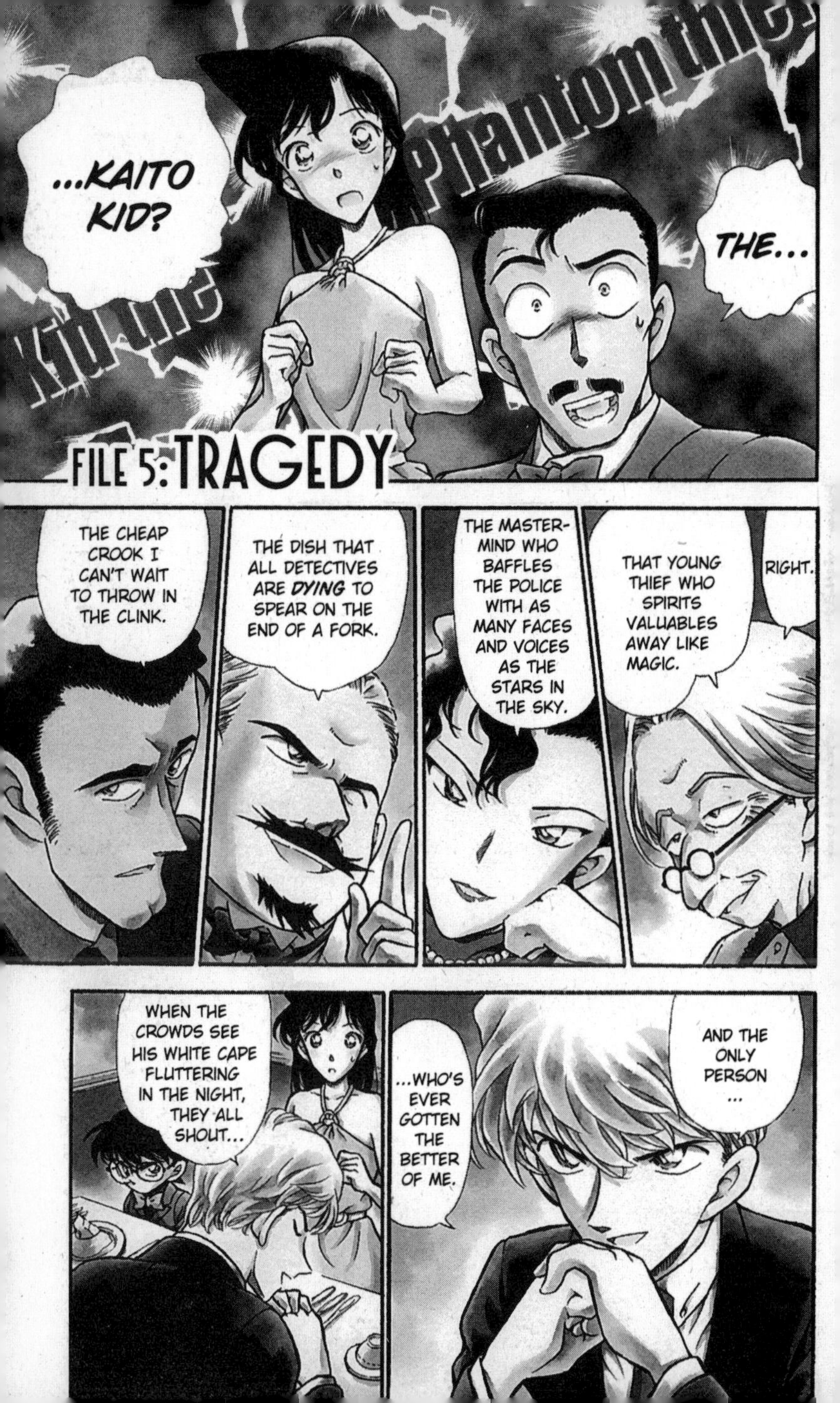
THE...
...KAITO KID?
FILE 5: TRAGEDY
RIGHT.
THAT YOUNG THIEF WHO SPIRITS VALUABLES AWAY LIKE MAGIC.
THE MASTER-MIND WHO BAFFLES THE POLICE WITH AS MANY FACES AND VOICES AS THE STARS IN THE SKY.
THE DISH THAT ALL DETECTIVES ARE *DYING* TO SPEAR ON THE END OF A FORK.
THE CHEAP CROOK I CAN'T WAIT TO THROW IN THE CLINK.
AND THE ONLY PERSON ...
...WHO'S EVER GOTTEN THE BETTER OF ME.
WHEN THE CROWDS SEE HIS WHITE CAPE FLUTTERING IN THE NIGHT, THEY ALL SHOUT...

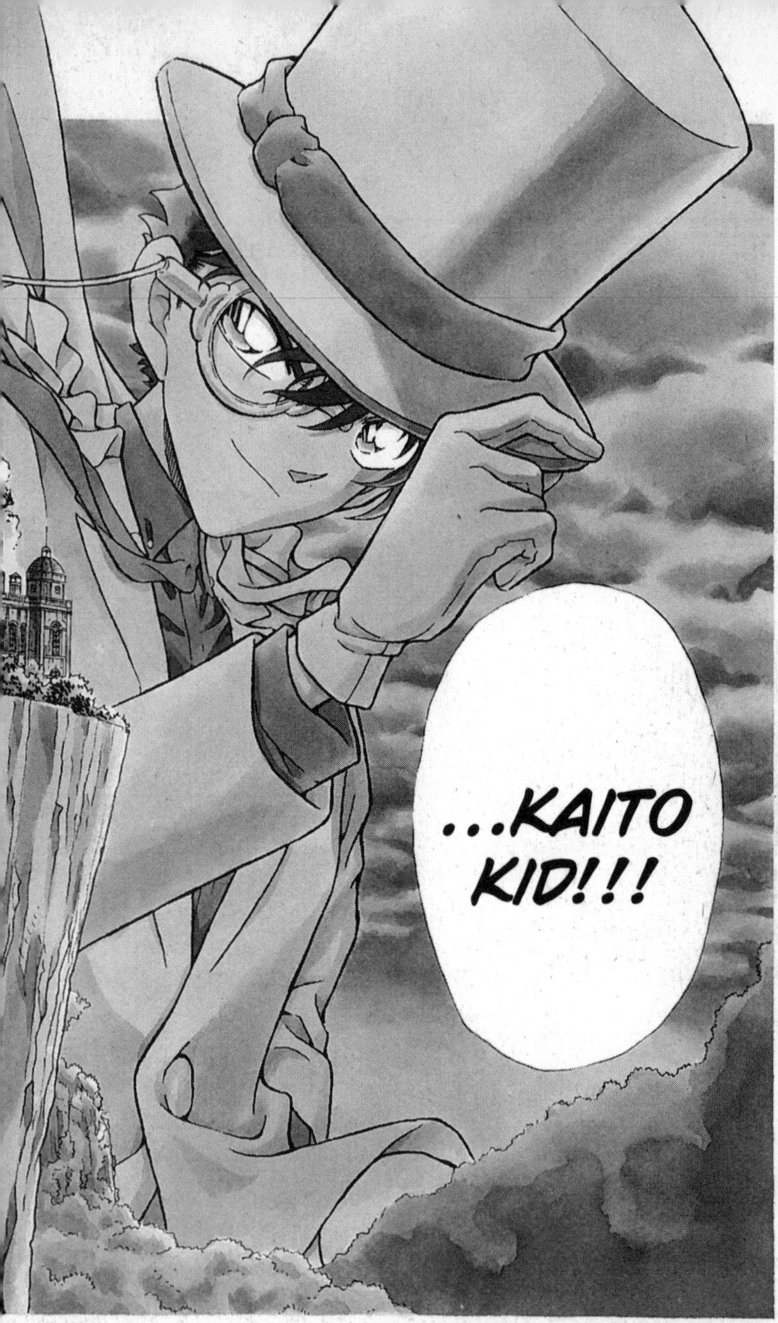
...KAITO KID!!!

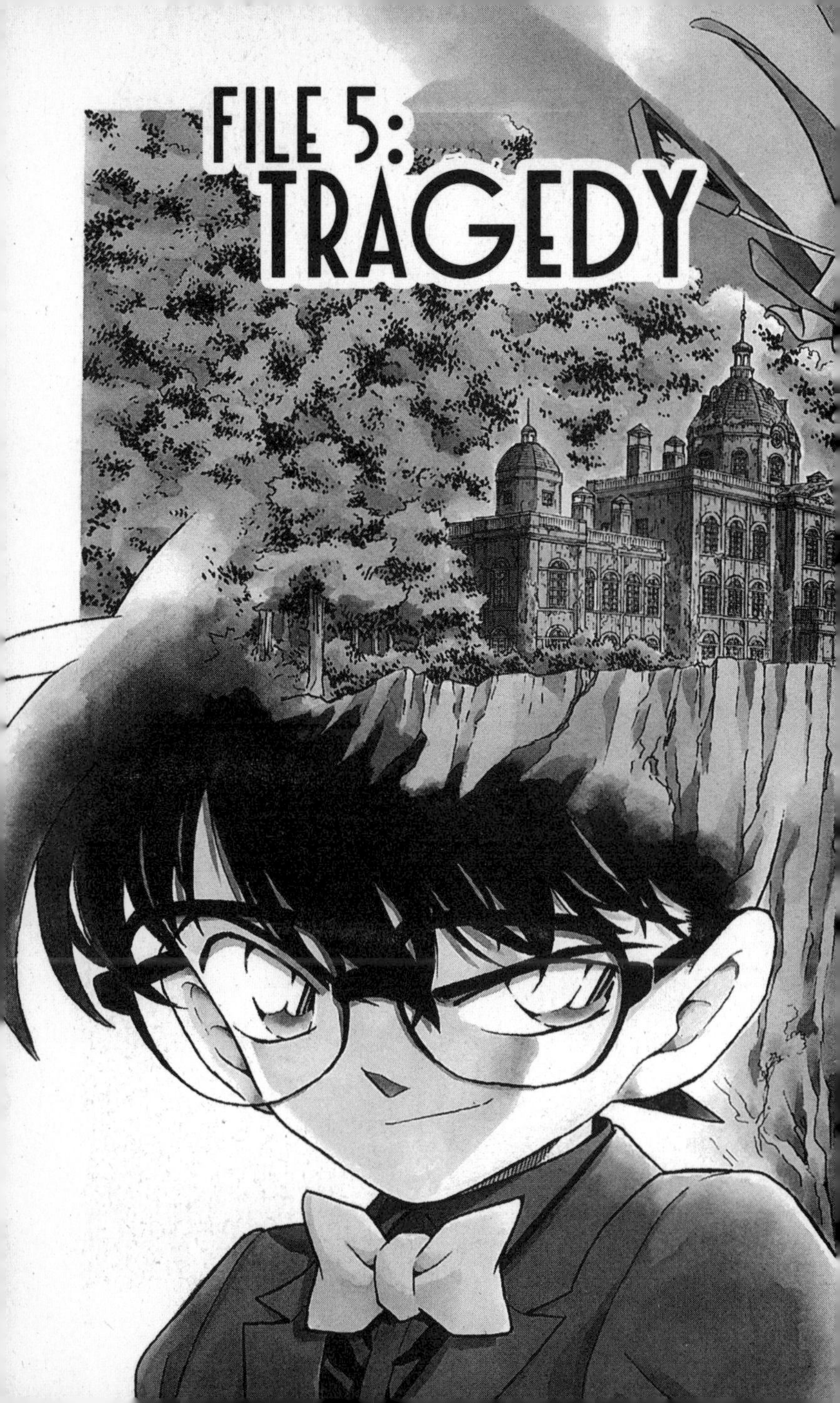
FILE 5:
TRAGEDY

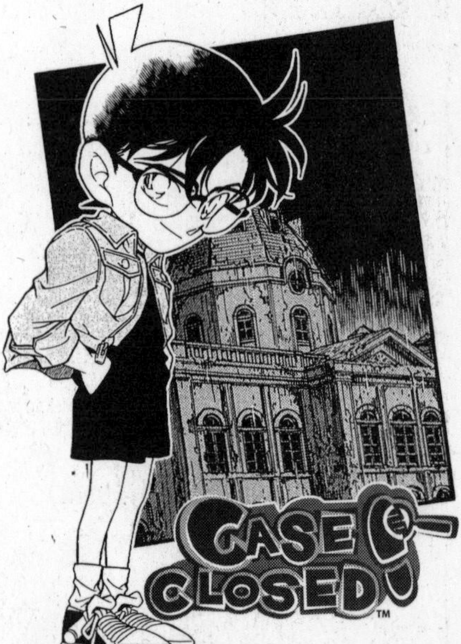
CASE CLOSED™

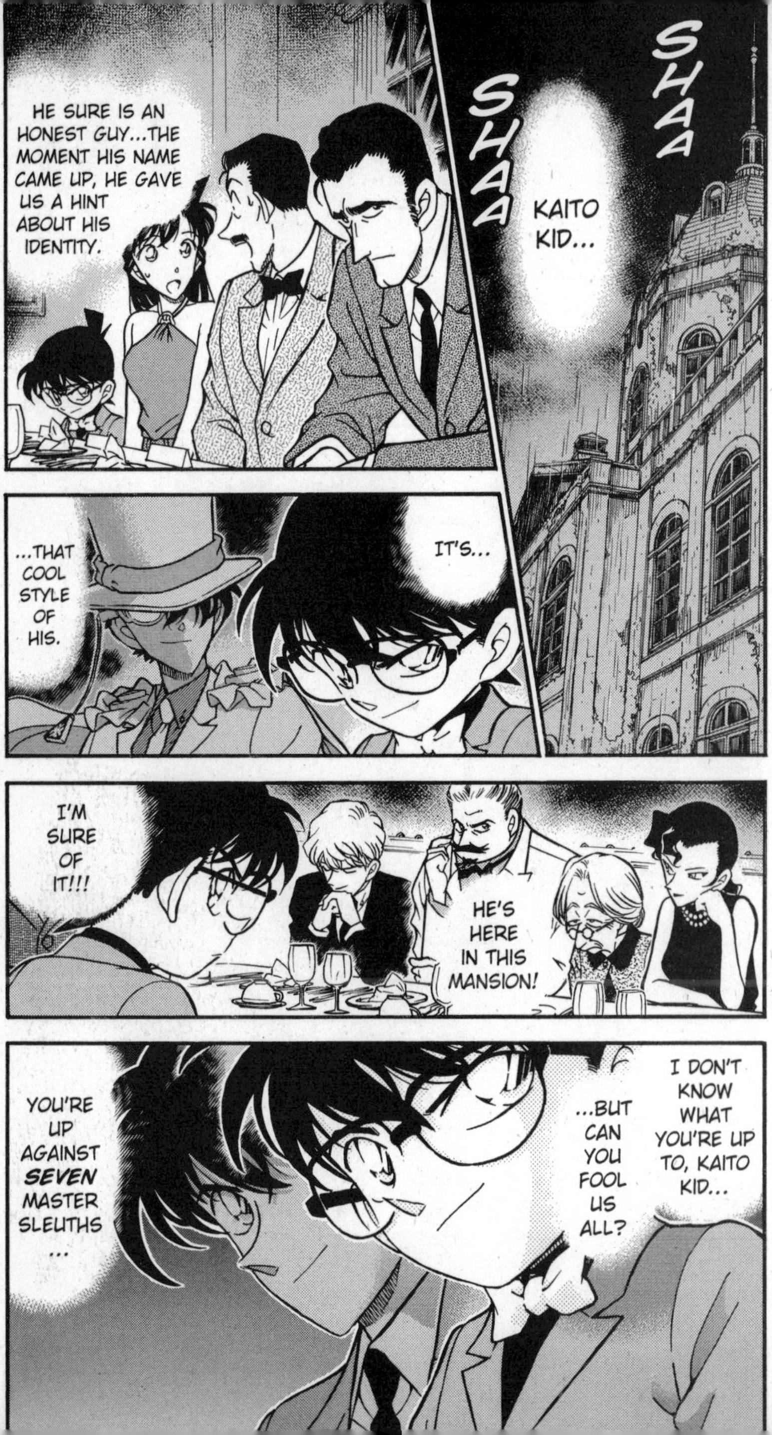

SHAA
SHAA
KAITO KID...
HE SURE IS AN HONEST GUY...THE MOMENT HIS NAME CAME UP, HE GAVE US A HINT ABOUT HIS IDENTITY.
IT'S...
...THAT COOL STYLE OF HIS.
HE'S HERE IN THIS MANSION!
I'M SURE OF IT!!!
I DON'T KNOW WHAT YOU'RE UP TO, KAITO KID...
...BUT CAN YOU FOOL US ALL?
YOU'RE UP AGAINST ***SEVEN*** MASTER SLEUTHS...

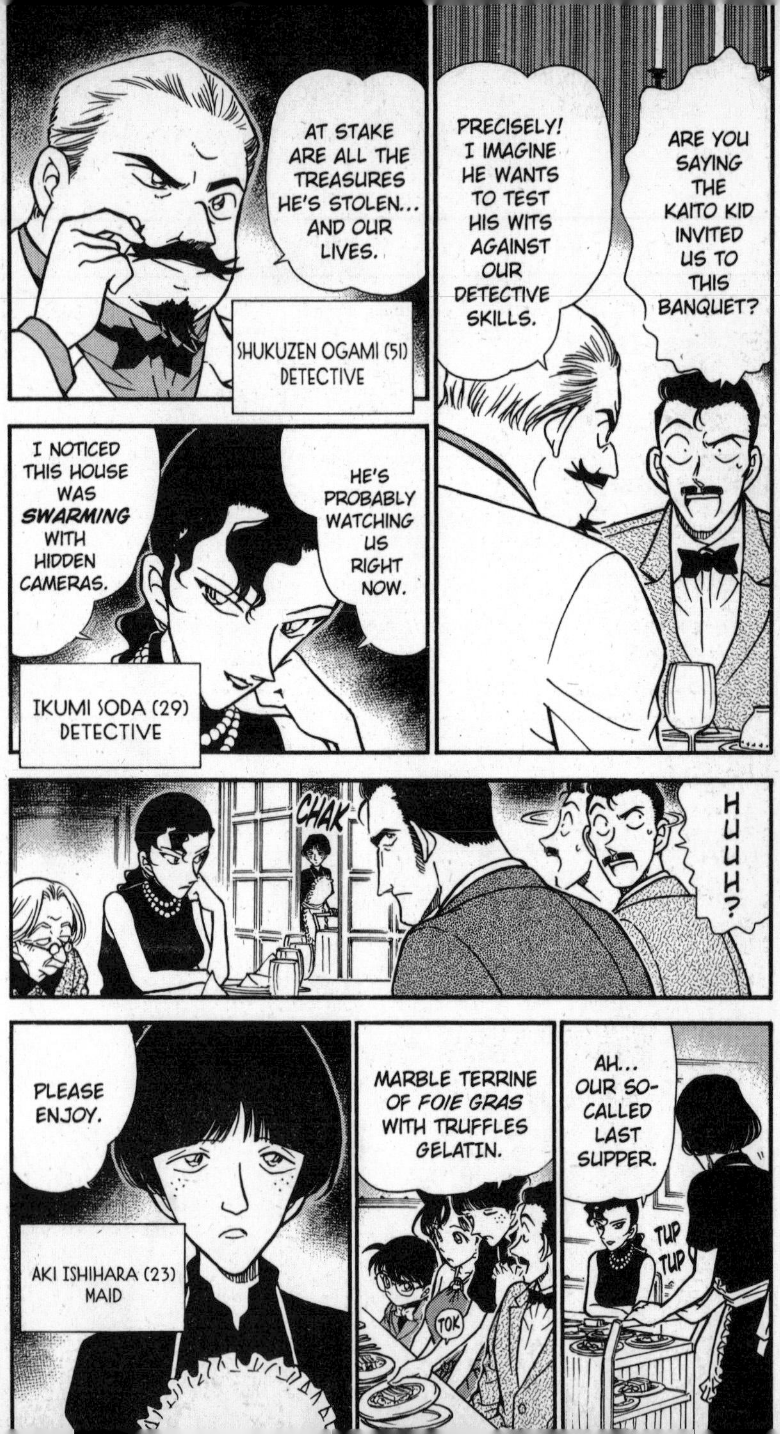
ARE YOU SAYING THE KAITO KID INVITED US TO THIS BANQUET?
PRECISELY! I IMAGINE HE WANTS TO TEST HIS WITS AGAINST OUR DETECTIVE SKILLS.
AT STAKE ARE ALL THE TREASURES HE'S STOLEN... AND OUR LIVES.
SHUKUZEN OGAMI (51) DETECTIVE
HE'S PROBABLY WATCHING US RIGHT NOW.
I NOTICED THIS HOUSE WAS SWARMING WITH HIDDEN CAMERAS.
IKUMI SODA (29) DETECTIVE
HUUH?
CHAK
AH... OUR SO-CALLED LAST SUPPER.
TUP TUP
MARBLE TERRINE OF FOIE GRAS WITH TRUFFLES GELATIN.
TOK
PLEASE ENJOY.
AKI ISHIHARA (23) MAID

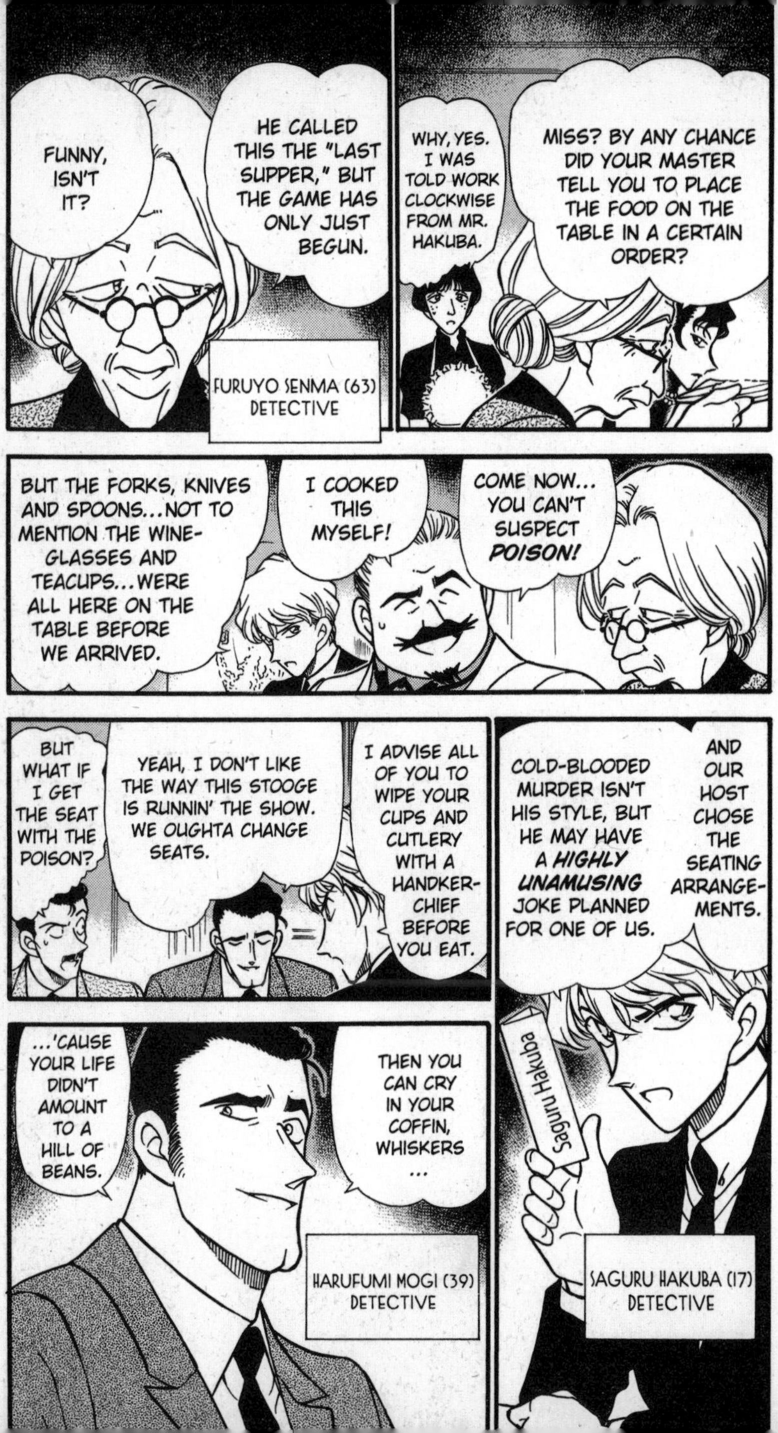
MISS? BY ANY CHANCE DID YOUR MASTER TELL YOU TO PLACE THE FOOD ON THE TABLE IN A CERTAIN ORDER?
WHY, YES. I WAS TOLD WORK CLOCKWISE FROM MR. HAKUBA.
HE CALLED THIS THE "LAST SUPPER," BUT THE GAME HAS ONLY JUST BEGUN.
FUNNY, ISN'T IT?
FURUYO SENMA (63) DETECTIVE
COME NOW... YOU CAN'T SUSPECT **POISON!**
I COOKED THIS MYSELF!
BUT THE FORKS, KNIVES AND SPOONS...NOT TO MENTION THE WINE-GLASSES AND TEACUPS...WERE ALL HERE ON THE TABLE BEFORE WE ARRIVED.
AND OUR HOST CHOSE THE SEATING ARRANGE-MENTS.
COLD-BLOODED MURDER ISN'T HIS STYLE, BUT HE MAY HAVE A ***HIGHLY UNAMUSING*** JOKE PLANNED FOR ONE OF US.
Saguru Hakuba
SAGURU HAKUBA (17) DETECTIVE
I ADVISE ALL OF YOU TO WIPE YOUR CUPS AND CUTLERY WITH A HANDKER-CHIEF BEFORE YOU EAT.
YEAH, I DON'T LIKE THE WAY THIS STOOGE IS RUNNIN' THE SHOW. WE OUGHTA CHANGE SEATS.
BUT WHAT IF I GET THE SEAT WITH THE POISON?
THEN YOU CAN CRY IN YOUR COFFIN, WHISKERS ...
...'CAUSE YOUR LIFE DIDN'T AMOUNT TO A HILL OF BEANS.
HARUFUMI MOGI (39) DETECTIVE

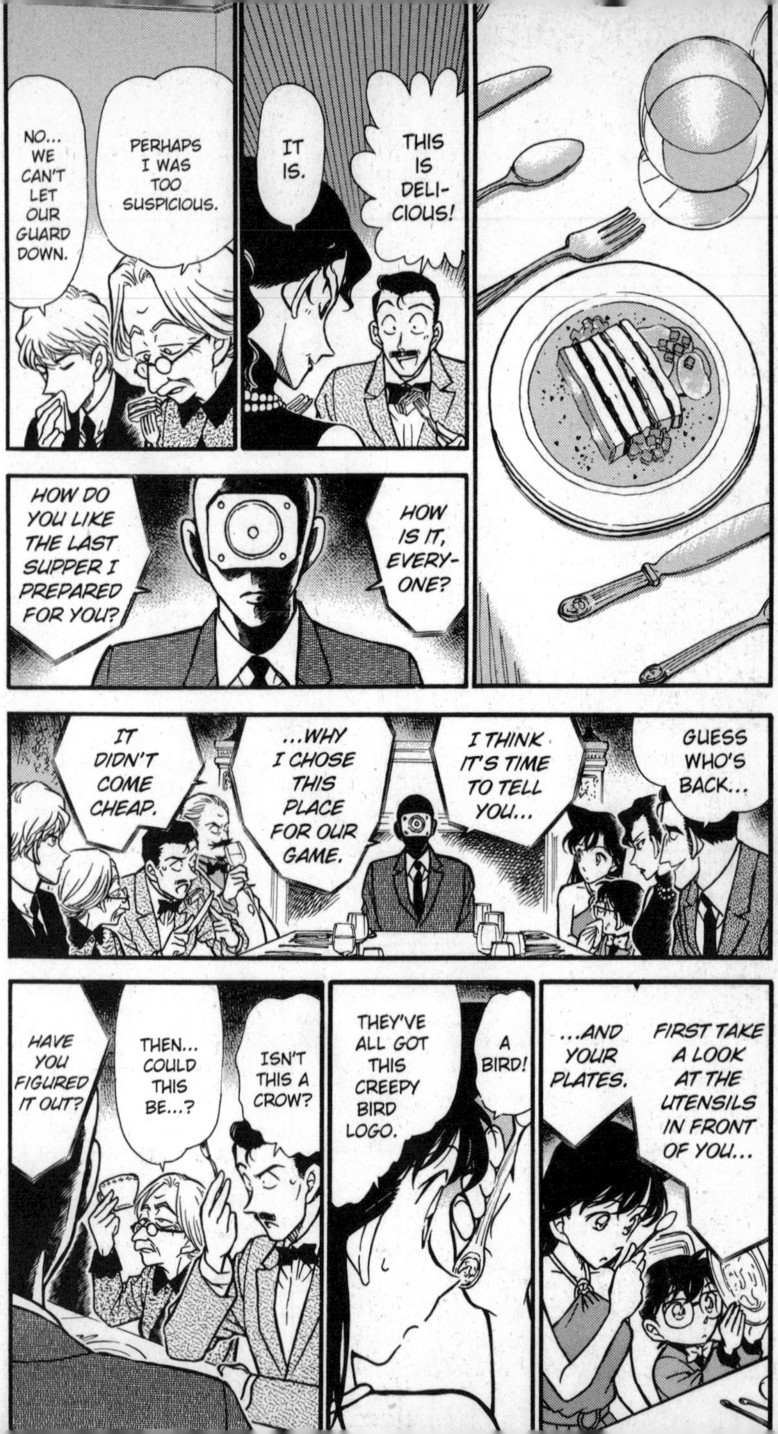
THIS IS DELICIOUS!
IT IS.
PERHAPS I WAS TOO SUSPICIOUS.
NO... WE CAN'T LET OUR GUARD DOWN.
HOW IS IT, EVERYONE?
HOW DO YOU LIKE THE LAST SUPPER I PREPARED FOR YOU?
GUESS WHO'S BACK...
I THINK IT'S TIME TO TELL YOU...
...WHY I CHOSE THIS PLACE FOR OUR GAME.
IT DIDN'T COME CHEAP.
FIRST TAKE A LOOK AT THE UTENSILS IN FRONT OF YOU...
...AND YOUR PLATES.
A BIRD!
THEY'VE ALL GOT THIS CREEPY BIRD LOGO.
ISN'T THIS A CROW?
THEN... COULD THIS BE...?
HAVE YOU FIGURED IT OUT?

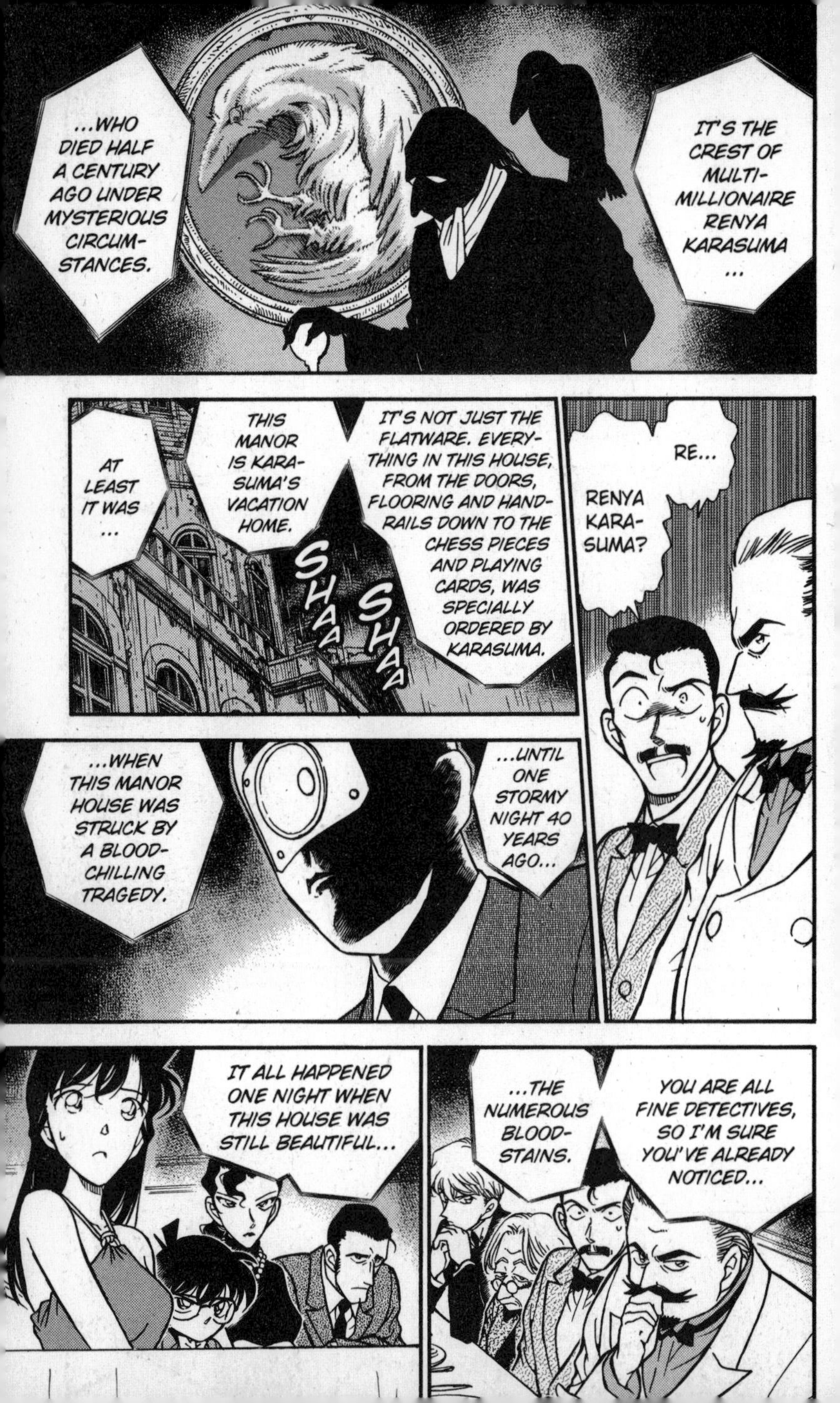
IT'S THE CREST OF MULTI-MILLIONAIRE RENYA KARASUMA ...
...WHO DIED HALF A CENTURY AGO UNDER MYSTERIOUS CIRCUM-STANCES.
RE...
RENYA KARA-SUMA?
IT'S NOT JUST THE FLATWARE. EVERY-THING IN THIS HOUSE, FROM THE DOORS, FLOORING AND HAND-RAILS DOWN TO THE CHESS PIECES AND PLAYING CARDS, WAS SPECIALLY ORDERED BY KARASUMA.
SHAA
SHAA
THIS MANOR IS KARA-SUMA'S VACATION HOME.
AT LEAST IT WAS ...
...UNTIL ONE STORMY NIGHT 40 YEARS AGO...
...WHEN THIS MANOR HOUSE WAS STRUCK BY A BLOOD-CHILLING TRAGEDY.
YOU ARE ALL FINE DETECTIVES, SO I'M SURE YOU'VE ALREADY NOTICED...
...THE NUMEROUS BLOOD-STAINS.
IT ALL HAPPENED ONE NIGHT WHEN THIS HOUSE WAS STILL BEAUTIFUL...

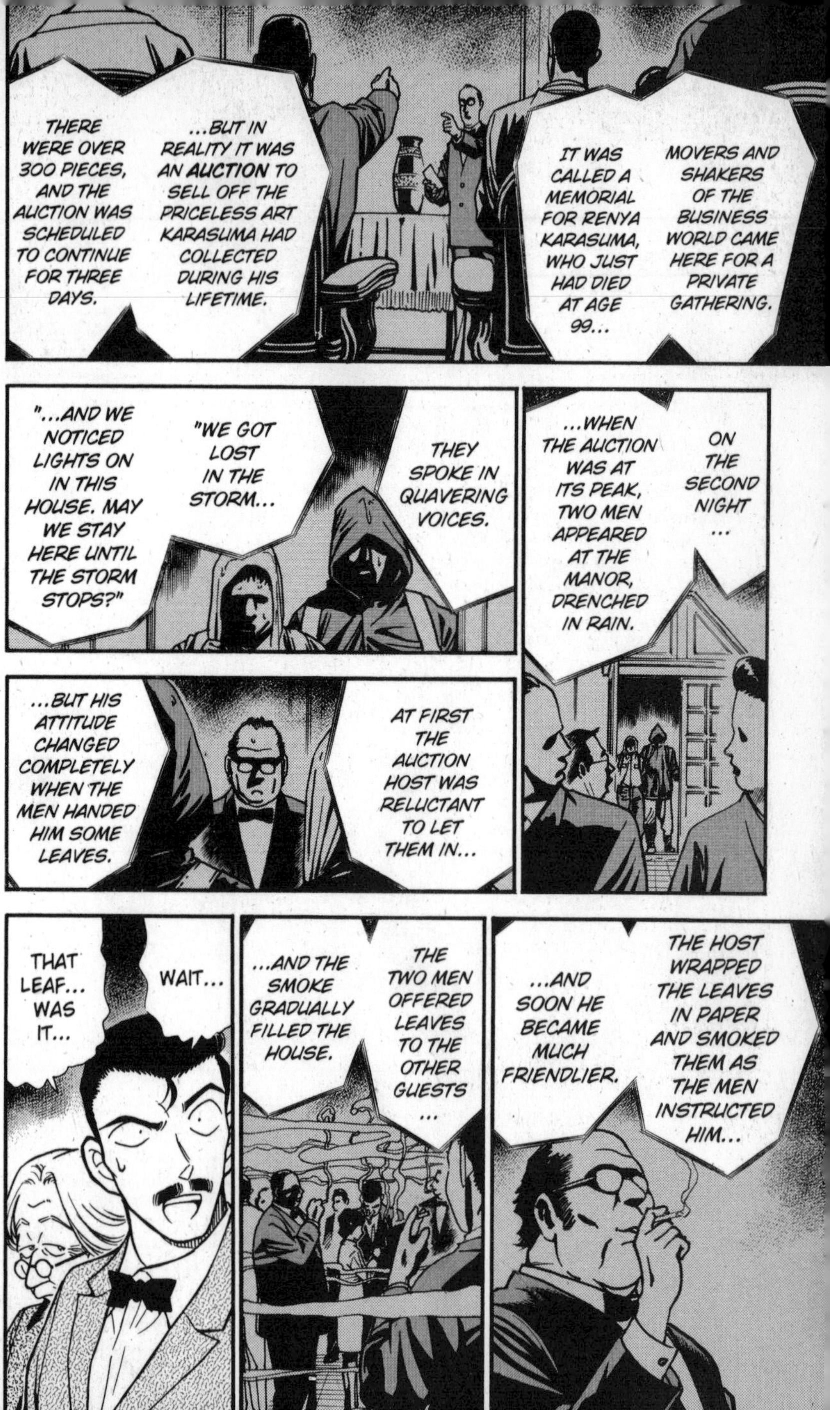
MOVERS AND SHAKERS OF THE BUSINESS WORLD CAME HERE FOR A PRIVATE GATHERING.
IT WAS CALLED A MEMORIAL FOR RENYA KARASUMA, WHO JUST HAD DIED AT AGE 99...
...BUT IN REALITY IT WAS AN **AUCTION** TO SELL OFF THE PRICELESS ART KARASUMA HAD COLLECTED DURING HIS LIFETIME.
THERE WERE OVER 300 PIECES, AND THE AUCTION WAS SCHEDULED TO CONTINUE FOR THREE DAYS.
ON THE SECOND NIGHT...
...WHEN THE AUCTION WAS AT ITS PEAK, TWO MEN APPEARED AT THE MANOR, DRENCHED IN RAIN.
THEY SPOKE IN QUAVERING VOICES.
"WE GOT LOST IN THE STORM...
"...AND WE NOTICED LIGHTS ON IN THIS HOUSE. MAY WE STAY HERE UNTIL THE STORM STOPS?"
AT FIRST THE AUCTION HOST WAS RELUCTANT TO LET THEM IN...
...BUT HIS ATTITUDE CHANGED COMPLETELY WHEN THE MEN HANDED HIM SOME LEAVES.
THE HOST WRAPPED THE LEAVES IN PAPER AND SMOKED THEM AS THE MEN INSTRUCTED HIM...
...AND SOON HE BECAME MUCH FRIENDLIER.
THE TWO MEN OFFERED LEAVES TO THE OTHER GUESTS...
...AND THE SMOKE GRADUALLY FILLED THE HOUSE.
WAIT...
THAT LEAF... WAS IT...

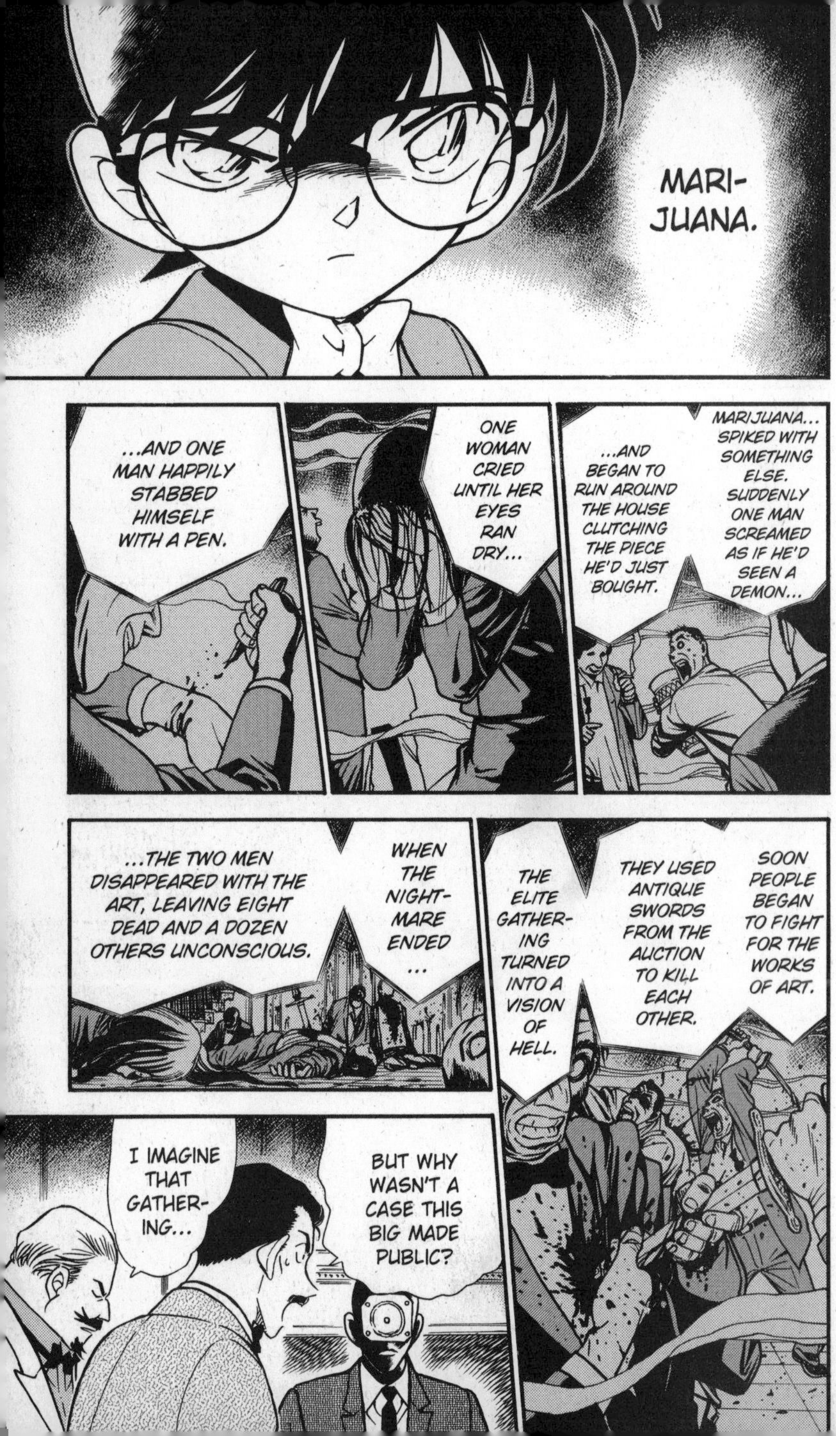
MARI-JUANA.
MARIJUANA... SPIKED WITH SOMETHING ELSE. SUDDENLY ONE MAN SCREAMED AS IF HE'D SEEN A DEMON...
...AND BEGAN TO RUN AROUND THE HOUSE CLUTCHING THE PIECE HE'D JUST BOUGHT.
ONE WOMAN CRIED UNTIL HER EYES RAN DRY...
...AND ONE MAN HAPPILY STABBED HIMSELF WITH A PEN.
SOON PEOPLE BEGAN TO FIGHT FOR THE WORKS OF ART.
THEY USED ANTIQUE SWORDS FROM THE AUCTION TO KILL EACH OTHER.
THE ELITE GATHER-ING TURNED INTO A VISION OF HELL.
WHEN THE NIGHT-MARE ENDED ...
...THE TWO MEN DISAPPEARED WITH THE ART, LEAVING EIGHT DEAD AND A DOZEN OTHERS UNCONSCIOUS.
BUT WHY WASN'T A CASE THIS BIG MADE PUBLIC?
I IMAGINE THAT GATHER-ING...

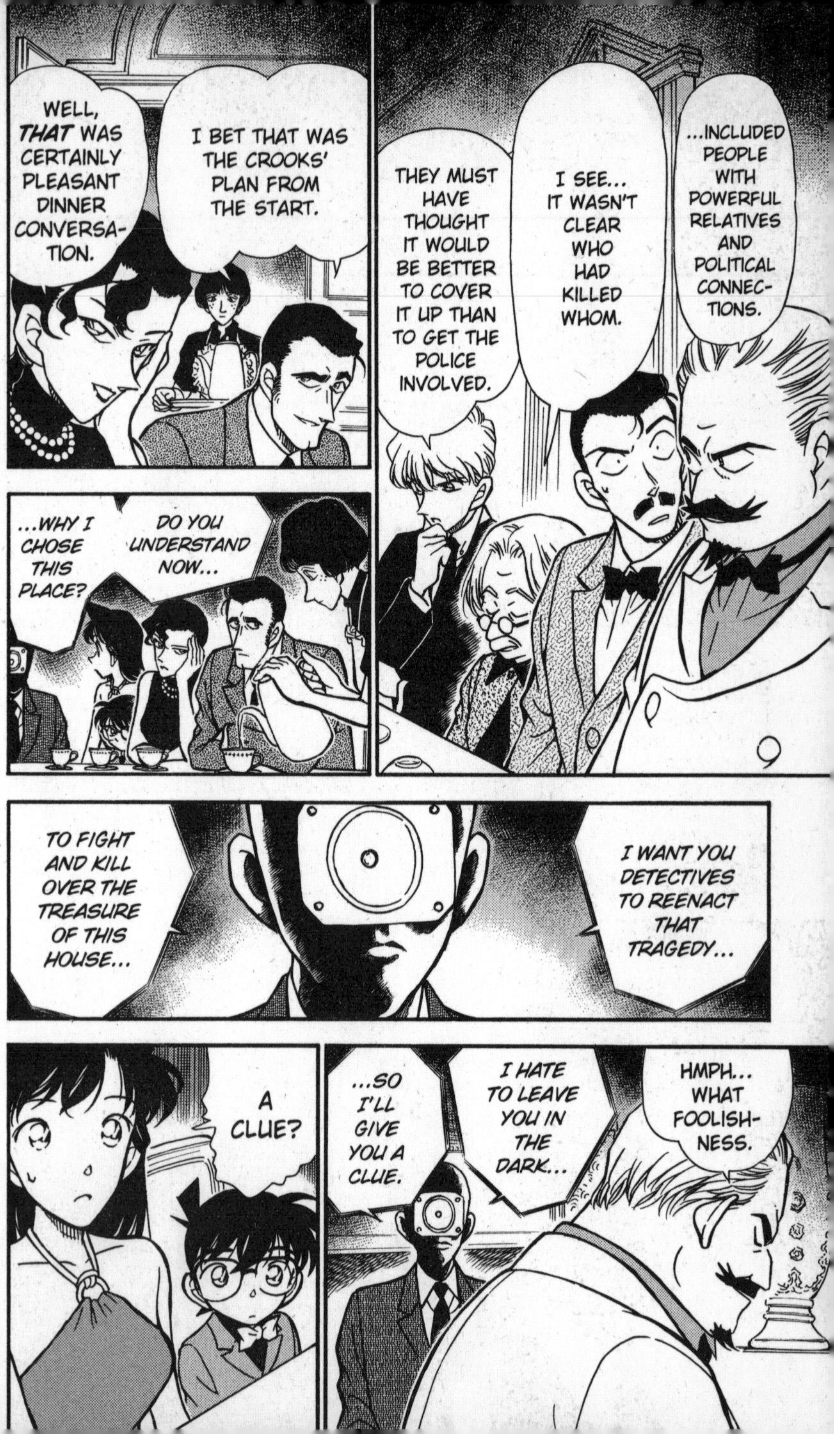
...INCLUDED PEOPLE WITH POWERFUL RELATIVES AND POLITICAL CONNEC-TIONS.
I SEE... IT WASN'T CLEAR WHO HAD KILLED WHOM.
THEY MUST HAVE THOUGHT IT WOULD BE BETTER TO COVER IT UP THAN TO GET THE POLICE INVOLVED.
I BET THAT WAS THE CROOKS' PLAN FROM THE START.
WELL, THAT WAS CERTAINLY PLEASANT DINNER CONVERSA-TION.
DO YOU UNDERSTAND NOW...
...WHY I CHOSE THIS PLACE?
I WANT YOU DETECTIVES TO REENACT THAT TRAGEDY...
TO FIGHT AND KILL OVER THE TREASURE OF THIS HOUSE...
HMPH... WHAT FOOLISH-NESS.
I HATE TO LEAVE YOU IN THE DARK...
...SO I'LL GIVE YOU A CLUE.
A CLUE?

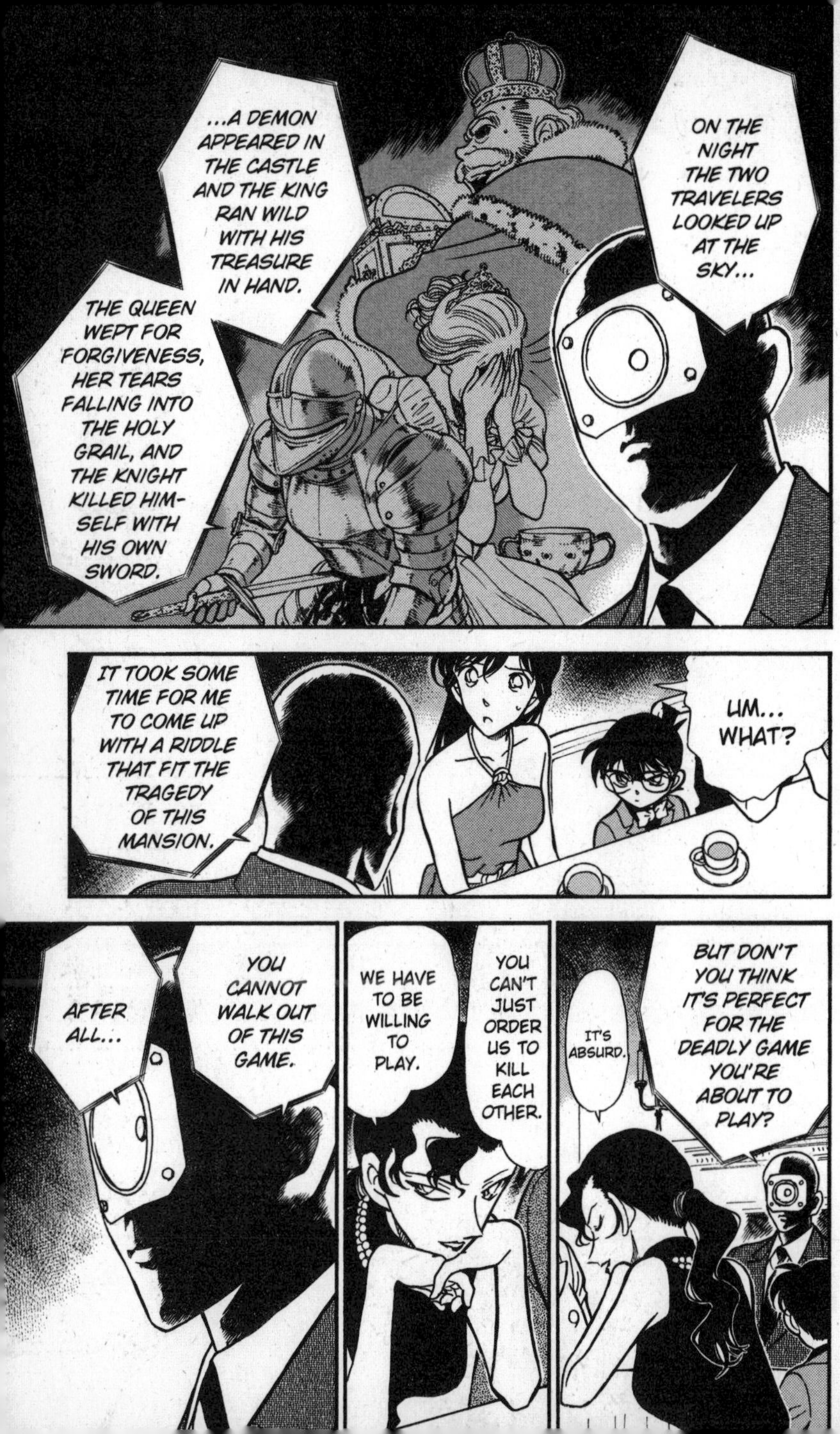
ON THE NIGHT THE TWO TRAVELERS LOOKED UP AT THE SKY...
...A DEMON APPEARED IN THE CASTLE AND THE KING RAN WILD WITH HIS TREASURE IN HAND.
THE QUEEN WEPT FOR FORGIVENESS, HER TEARS FALLING INTO THE HOLY GRAIL, AND THE KNIGHT KILLED HIM-SELF WITH HIS OWN SWORD.
UM... WHAT?
IT TOOK SOME TIME FOR ME TO COME UP WITH A RIDDLE THAT FIT THE TRAGEDY OF THIS MANSION.
BUT DON'T YOU THINK IT'S PERFECT FOR THE DEADLY GAME YOU'RE ABOUT TO PLAY?
IT'S ABSURD.
YOU CAN'T JUST ORDER US TO KILL EACH OTHER.
WE HAVE TO BE WILLING TO PLAY.
YOU CANNOT WALK OUT OF THIS GAME.
AFTER ALL...

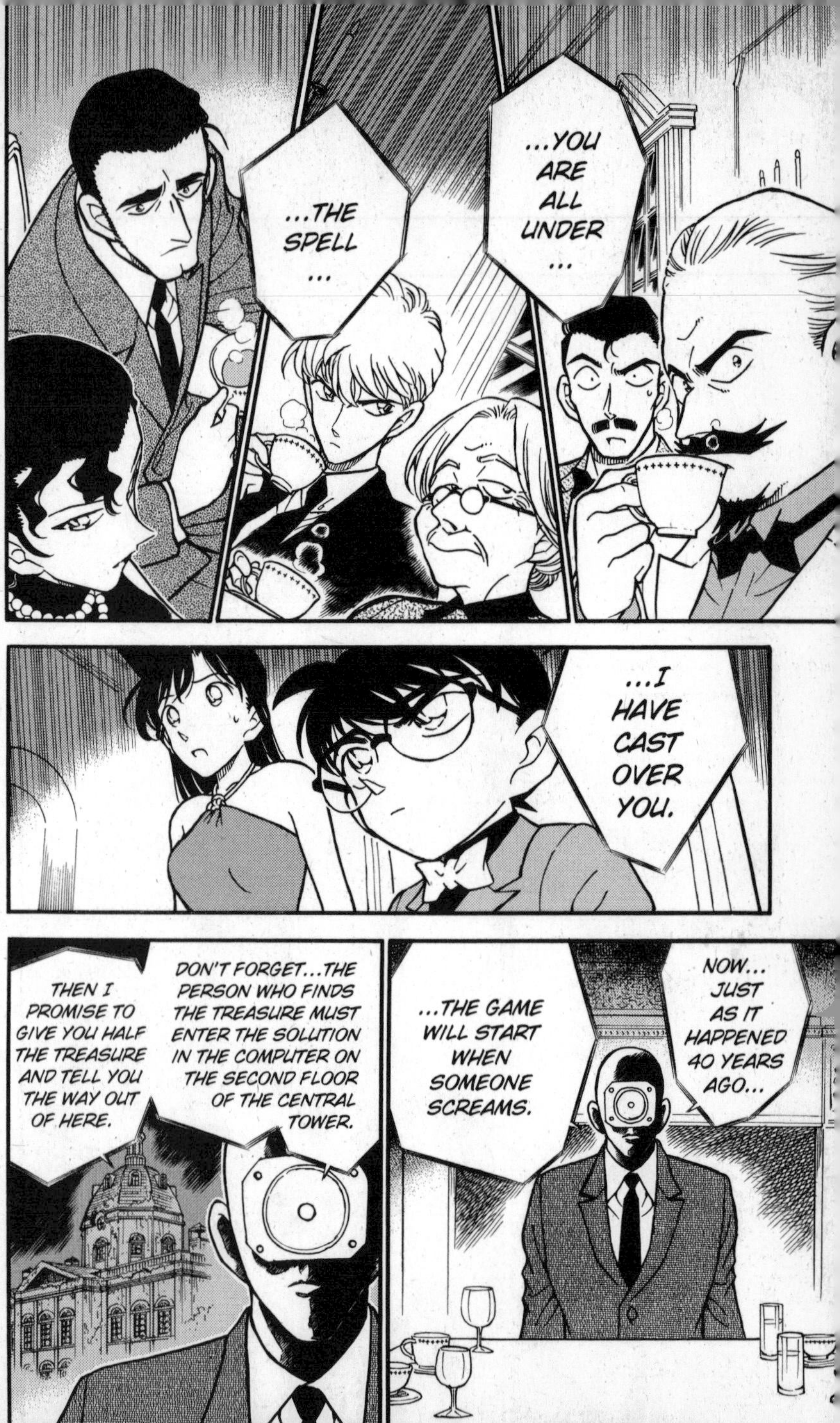
...YOU ARE ALL UNDER ...
...THE SPELL ...
...I HAVE CAST OVER YOU.
NOW... JUST AS IT HAPPENED 40 YEARS AGO...
...THE GAME WILL START WHEN SOMEONE SCREAMS.
DON'T FORGET...THE PERSON WHO FINDS THE TREASURE MUST ENTER THE SOLUTION IN THE COMPUTER ON THE SECOND FLOOR OF THE CENTRAL TOWER.
THEN I PROMISE TO GIVE YOU HALF THE TREASURE AND TELL YOU THE WAY OUT OF HERE.

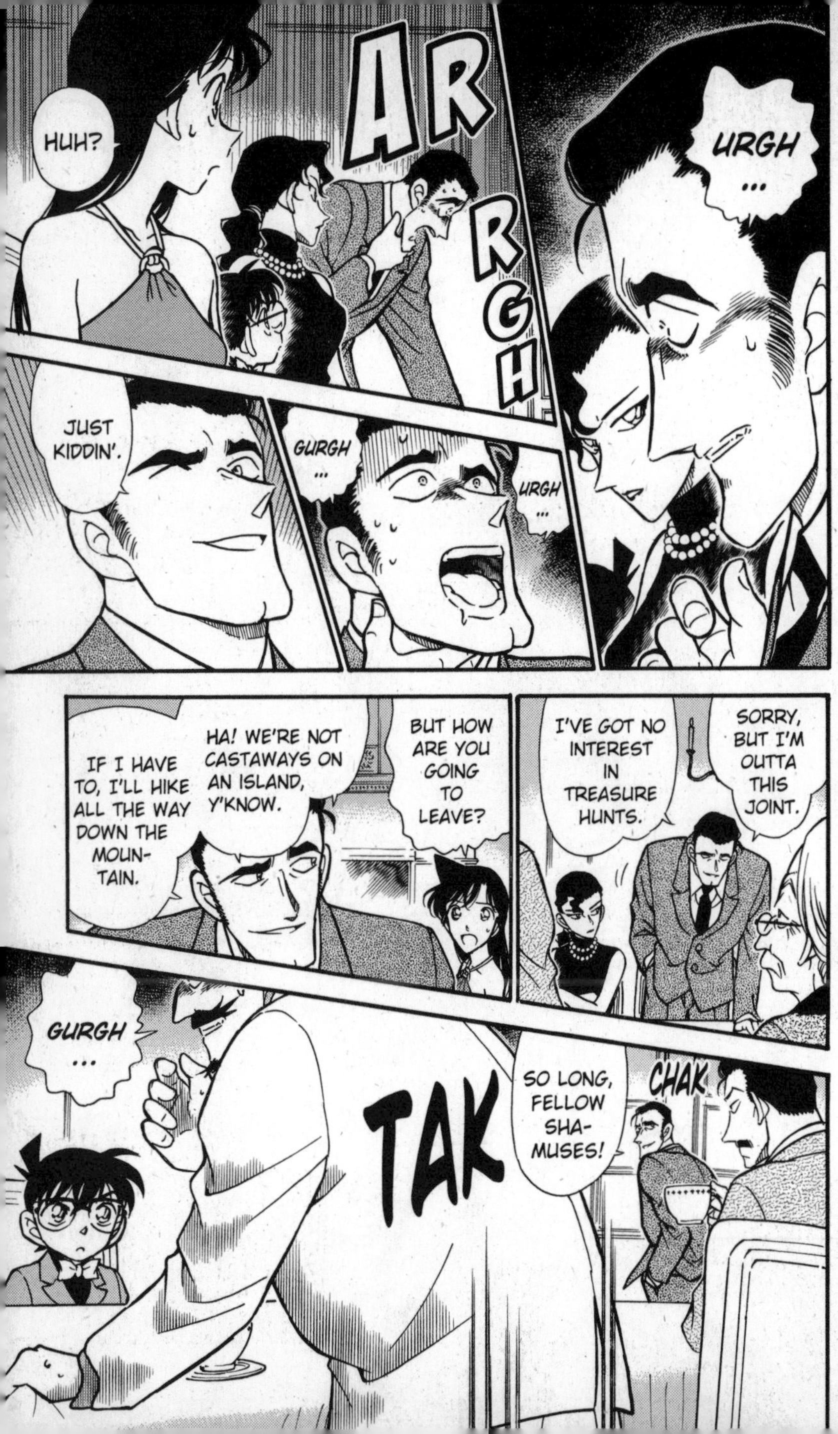
URGH ...
ARRGH
HUH?
URGH ...
GURGH ...
JUST KIDDIN'.
SORRY, BUT I'M OUTTA THIS JOINT.
I'VE GOT NO INTEREST IN TREASURE HUNTS.
BUT HOW ARE YOU GOING TO LEAVE?
HA! WE'RE NOT CASTAWAYS ON AN ISLAND, Y'KNOW.
IF I HAVE TO, I'LL HIKE ALL THE WAY DOWN THE MOUN-TAIN.
CHAK
SO LONG, FELLOW SHA-MUSES!
TAK
GURGH ...

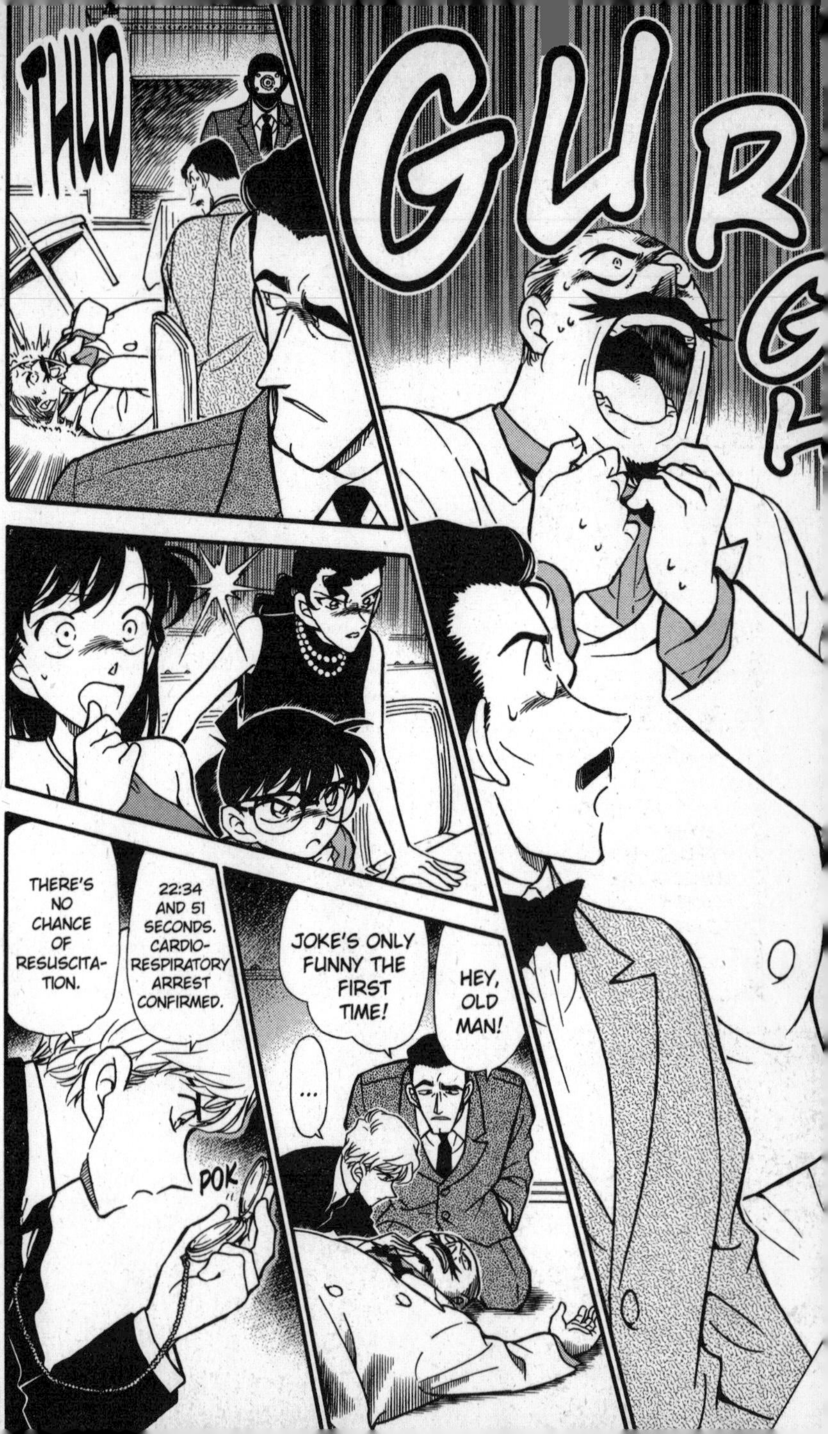

GURGL
THUD
HEY, OLD MAN!
JOKE'S ONLY FUNNY THE FIRST TIME!
...
22:34 AND 51 SECONDS. CARDIO-RESPIRATORY ARREST CONFIRMED.
THERE'S NO CHANCE OF RESUSCITATION.
POK

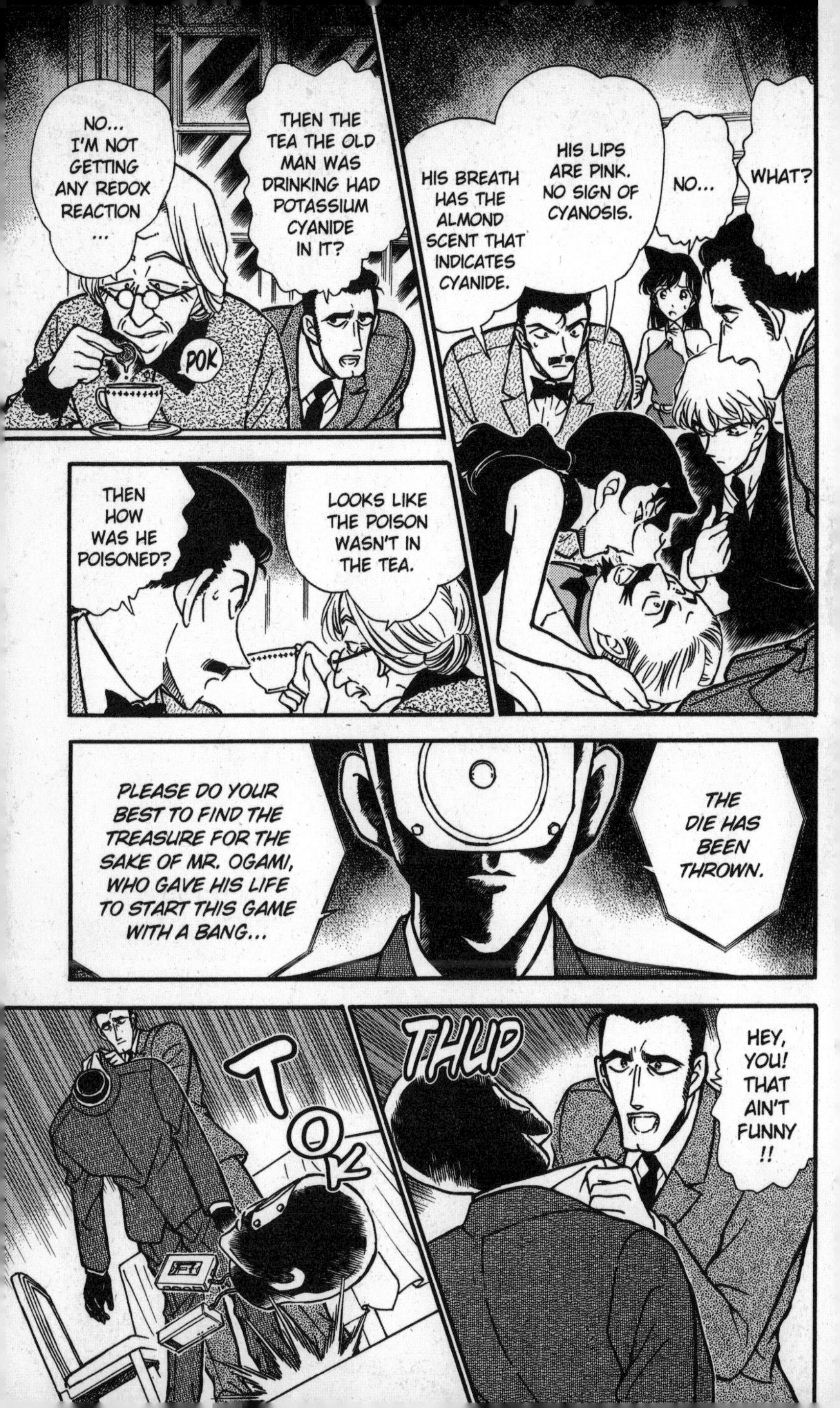
WHAT?
NO...
HIS LIPS ARE PINK. NO SIGN OF CYANOSIS.
HIS BREATH HAS THE ALMOND SCENT THAT INDICATES CYANIDE.
THEN THE TEA THE OLD MAN WAS DRINKING HAD POTASSIUM CYANIDE IN IT?
NO... I'M NOT GETTING ANY REDOX REACTION ...
POK
LOOKS LIKE THE POISON WASN'T IN THE TEA.
THEN HOW WAS HE POISONED?
THE DIE HAS BEEN THROWN.
PLEASE DO YOUR BEST TO FIND THE TREASURE FOR THE SAKE OF MR. OGAMI, WHO GAVE HIS LIFE TO START THIS GAME WITH A BANG...
HEY, YOU! THAT AIN'T FUNNY !!
THUP
TOK

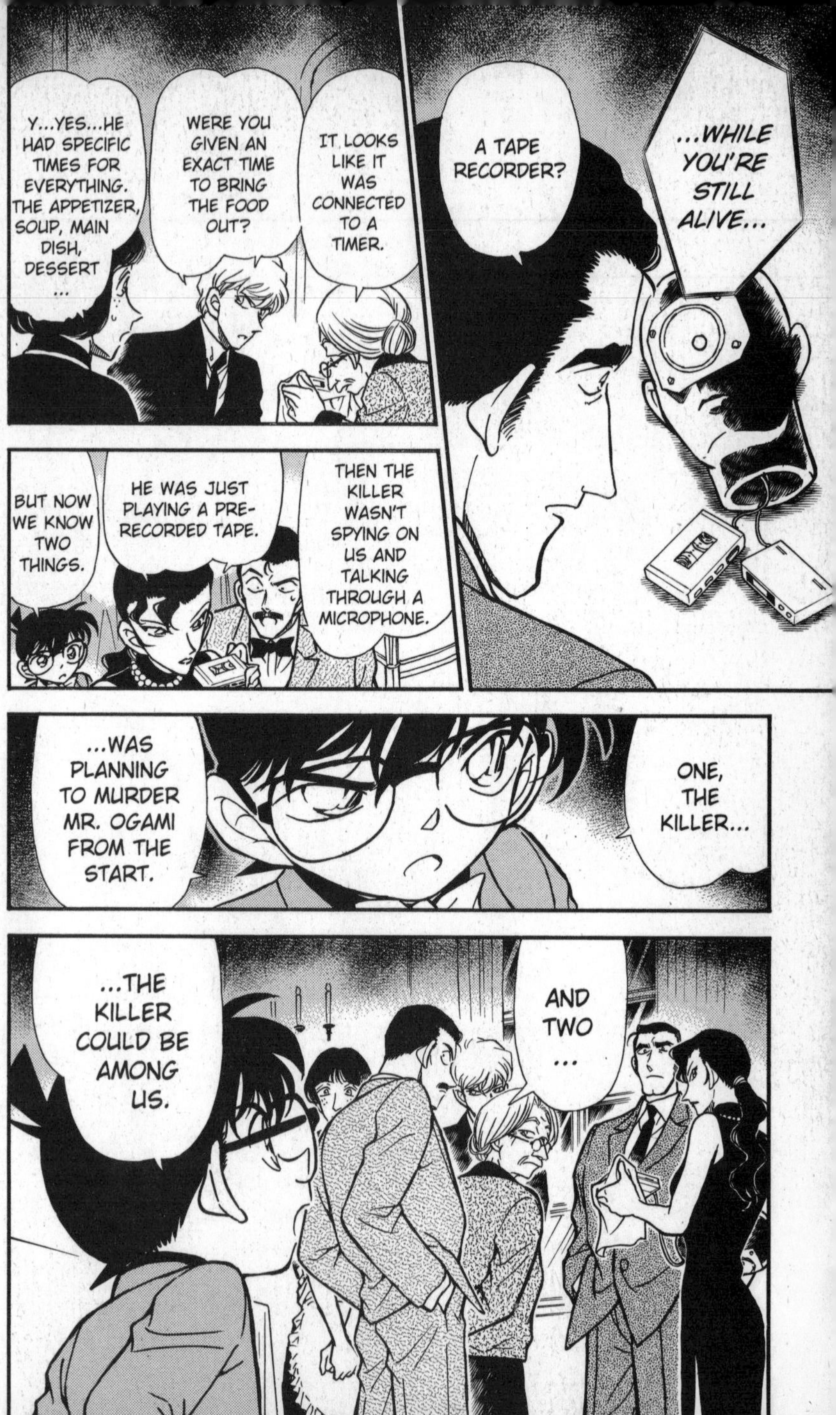
...WHILE YOU'RE STILL ALIVE...
A TAPE RECORDER?
IT LOOKS LIKE IT WAS CONNECTED TO A TIMER.
WERE YOU GIVEN AN EXACT TIME TO BRING THE FOOD OUT?
Y...YES...HE HAD SPECIFIC TIMES FOR EVERYTHING. THE APPETIZER, SOUP, MAIN DISH, DESSERT...
THEN THE KILLER WASN'T SPYING ON US AND TALKING THROUGH A MICROPHONE.
HE WAS JUST PLAYING A PRE-RECORDED TAPE.
BUT NOW WE KNOW TWO THINGS.
ONE, THE KILLER...
...WAS PLANNING TO MURDER MR. OGAMI FROM THE START.
AND TWO...
...THE KILLER COULD BE AMONG US.

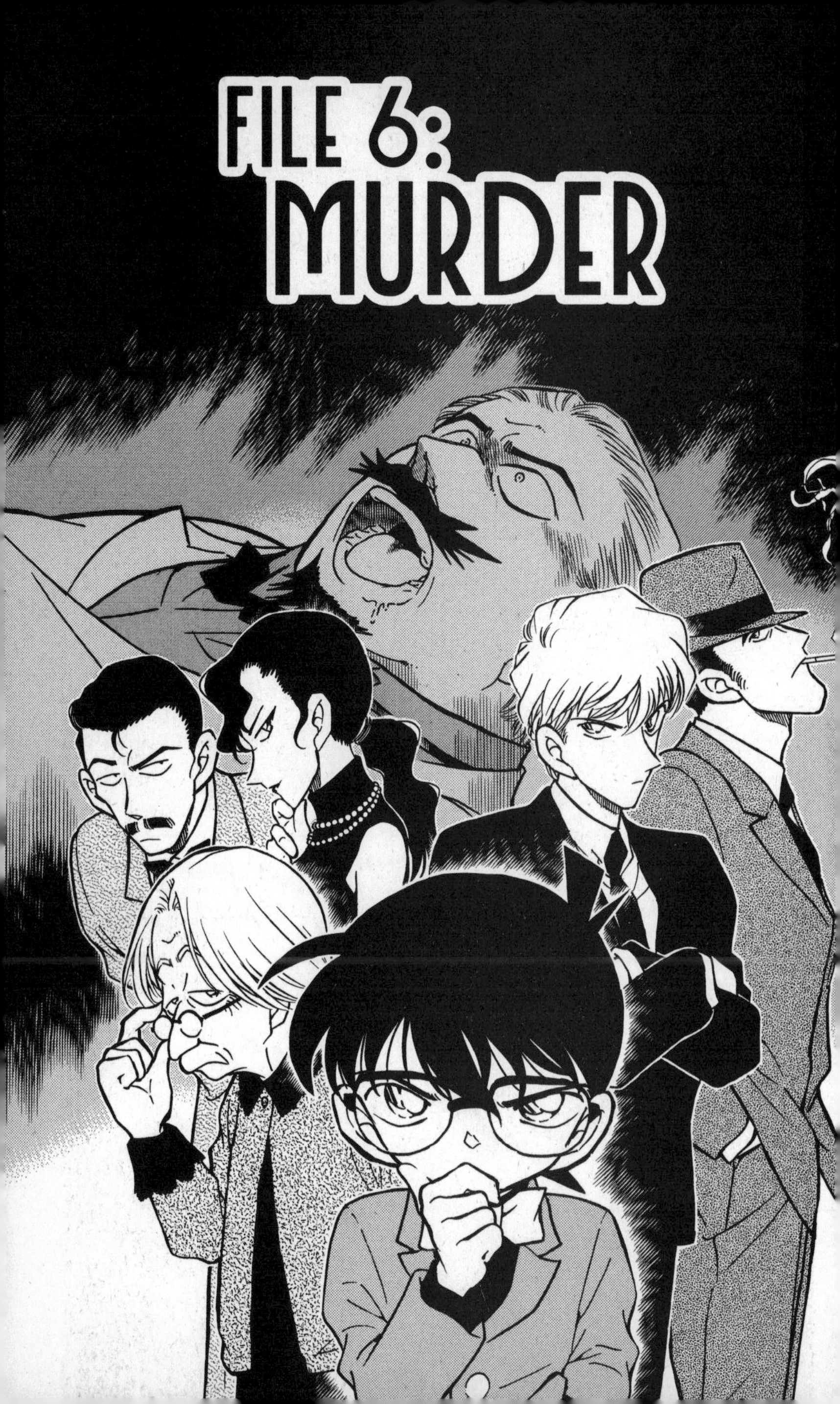
FILE 6:
MURDER

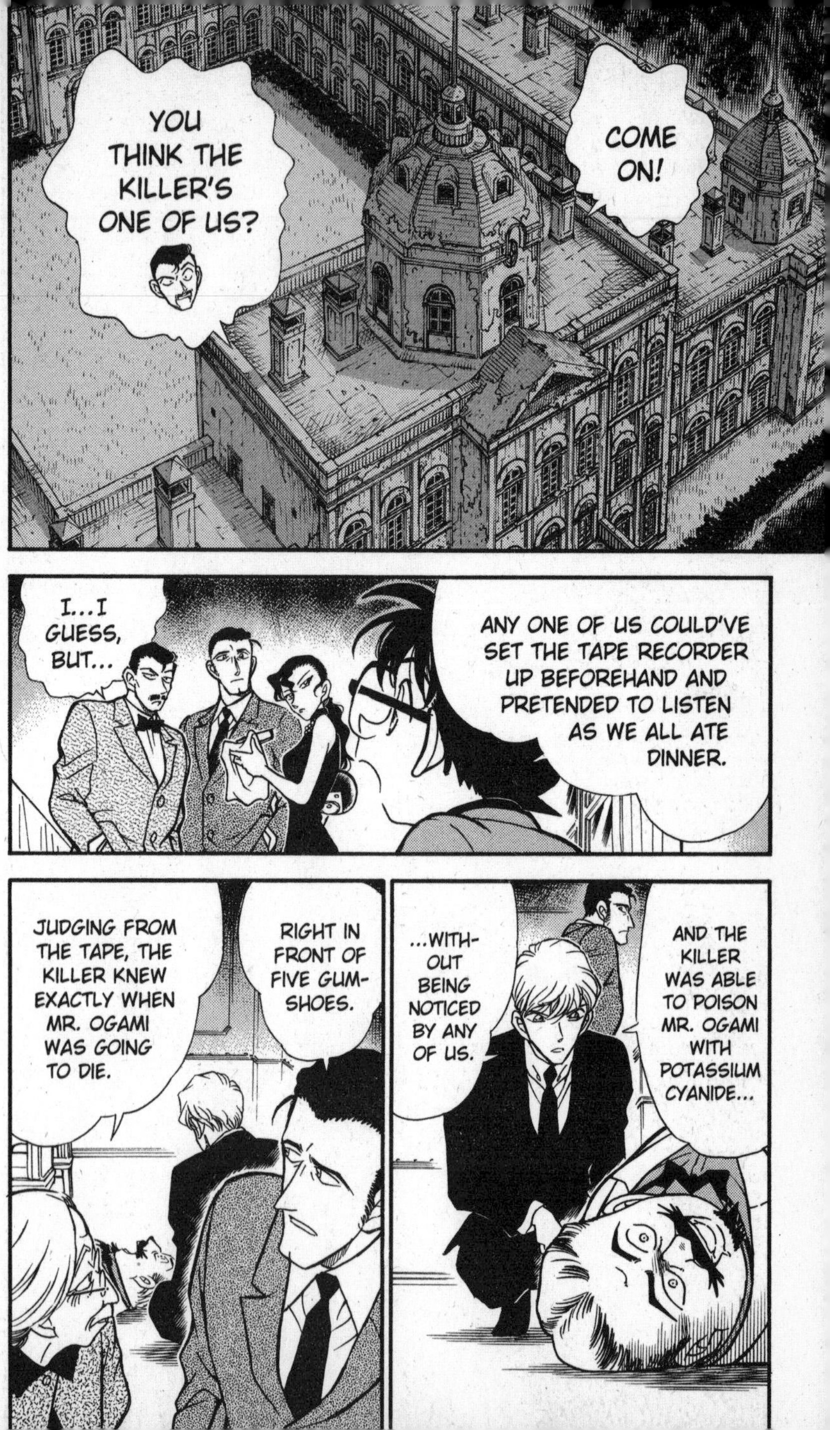
COME ON!
YOU THINK THE KILLER'S ONE OF US?
ANY ONE OF US COULD'VE SET THE TAPE RECORDER UP BEFOREHAND AND PRETENDED TO LISTEN AS WE ALL ATE DINNER.
I...I GUESS, BUT...
AND THE KILLER WAS ABLE TO POISON MR. OGAMI WITH POTASSIUM CYANIDE...
...WITH-OUT BEING NOTICED BY ANY OF US.
RIGHT IN FRONT OF FIVE GUM-SHOES.
JUDGING FROM THE TAPE, THE KILLER KNEW EXACTLY WHEN MR. OGAMI WAS GOING TO DIE.

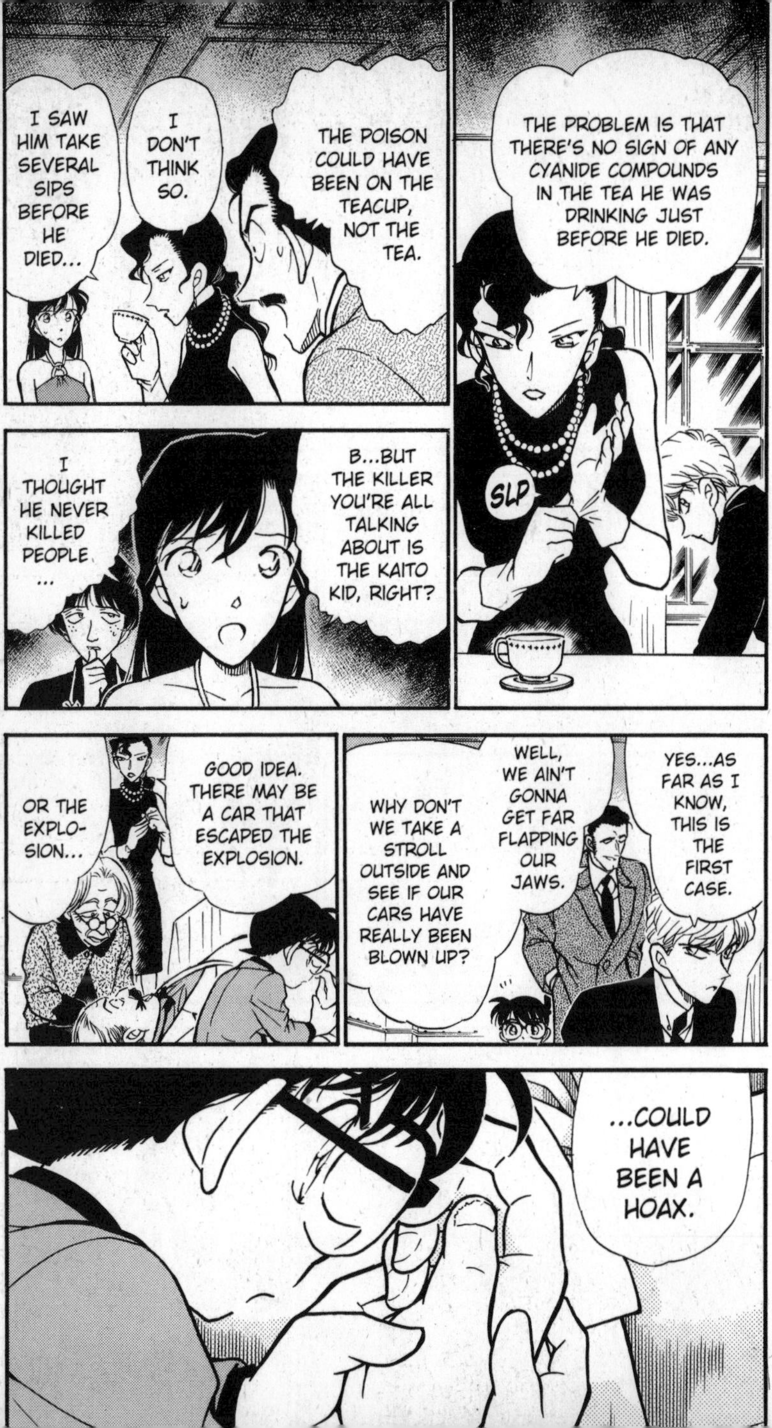
THE PROBLEM IS THAT THERE'S NO SIGN OF ANY CYANIDE COMPOUNDS IN THE TEA HE WAS DRINKING JUST BEFORE HE DIED.
SLP
THE POISON COULD HAVE BEEN ON THE TEACUP, NOT THE TEA.
I DON'T THINK SO.
I SAW HIM TAKE SEVERAL SIPS BEFORE HE DIED...
B...BUT THE KILLER YOU'RE ALL TALKING ABOUT IS THE KAITO KID, RIGHT?
I THOUGHT HE NEVER KILLED PEOPLE...
YES...AS FAR AS I KNOW, THIS IS THE FIRST CASE.
WELL, WE AIN'T GONNA GET FAR FLAPPING OUR JAWS.
WHY DON'T WE TAKE A STROLL OUTSIDE AND SEE IF OUR CARS HAVE REALLY BEEN BLOWN UP?
GOOD IDEA. THERE MAY BE A CAR THAT ESCAPED THE EXPLOSION.
OR THE EXPLOSION...
...COULD HAVE BEEN A HOAX.

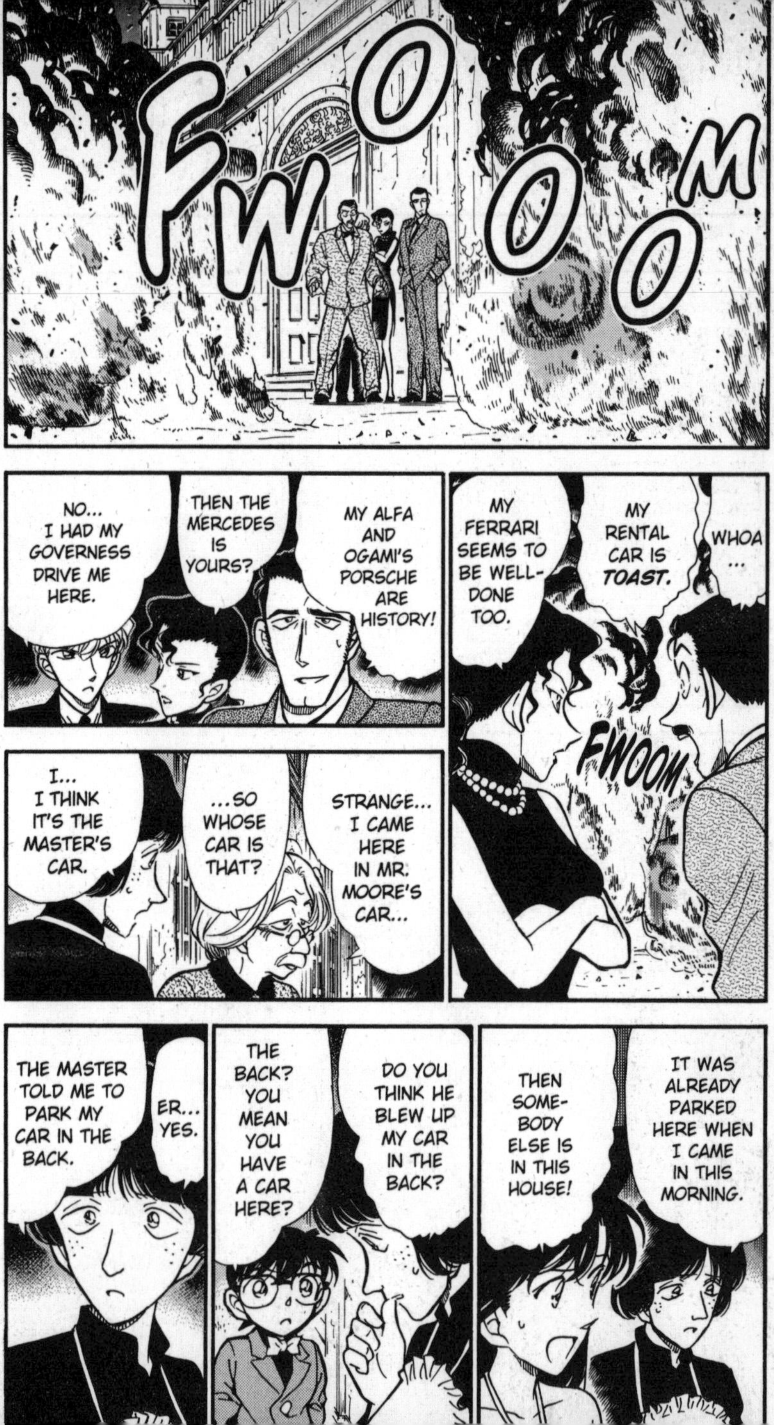
FWOOOOM
WHOA...
MY RENTAL CAR IS *TOAST.*
MY FERRARI SEEMS TO BE WELL-DONE TOO.
FWOOM
MY ALFA AND OGAMI'S PORSCHE ARE HISTORY!
THEN THE MERCEDES IS YOURS?
NO... I HAD MY GOVERNESS DRIVE ME HERE.
STRANGE... I CAME HERE IN MR. MOORE'S CAR...
...SO WHOSE CAR IS THAT?
I... I THINK IT'S THE MASTER'S CAR.
IT WAS ALREADY PARKED HERE WHEN I CAME IN THIS MORNING.
THEN SOME-BODY ELSE IS IN THIS HOUSE!
DO YOU THINK HE BLEW UP MY CAR IN THE BACK?
THE BACK? YOU MEAN YOU HAVE A CAR HERE?
ER... YES.
THE MASTER TOLD ME TO PARK MY CAR IN THE BACK.

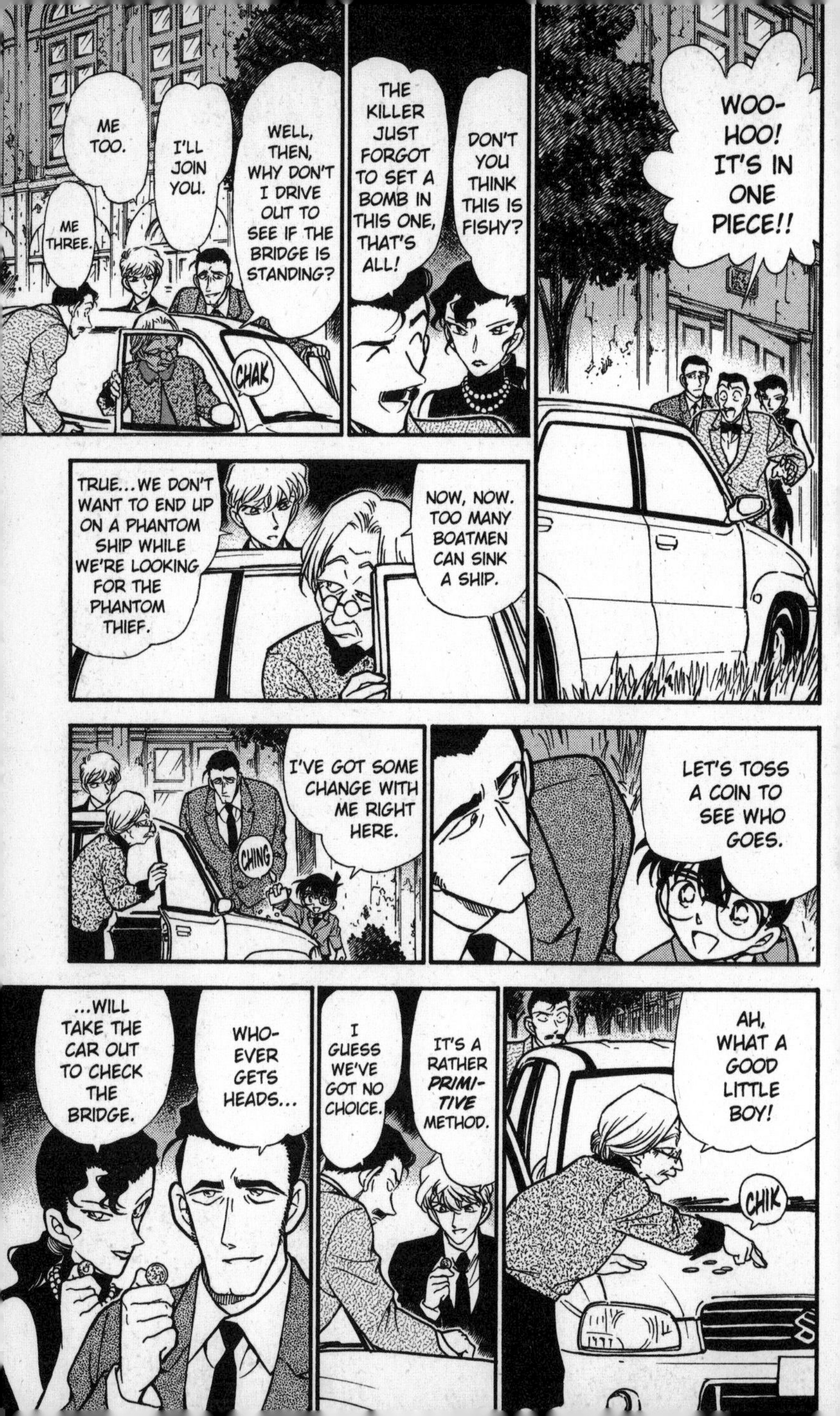
WOO-HOO! IT'S IN ONE PIECE!!
DON'T YOU THINK THIS IS FISHY?
THE KILLER JUST FORGOT TO SET A BOMB IN THIS ONE, THAT'S ALL!
WELL, THEN, WHY DON'T I DRIVE OUT TO SEE IF THE BRIDGE IS STANDING?
CHAK
I'LL JOIN YOU.
ME TOO.
ME THREE.
NOW, NOW. TOO MANY BOATMEN CAN SINK A SHIP.
TRUE...WE DON'T WANT TO END UP ON A PHANTOM SHIP WHILE WE'RE LOOKING FOR THE PHANTOM THIEF.
LET'S TOSS A COIN TO SEE WHO GOES.
I'VE GOT SOME CHANGE WITH ME RIGHT HERE.
CHING
AH, WHAT A GOOD LITTLE BOY!
CHIK
IT'S A RATHER *PRIMITIVE* METHOD.
I GUESS WE'VE GOT NO CHOICE.
WHO-EVER GETS HEADS...
...WILL TAKE THE CAR OUT TO CHECK THE BRIDGE.

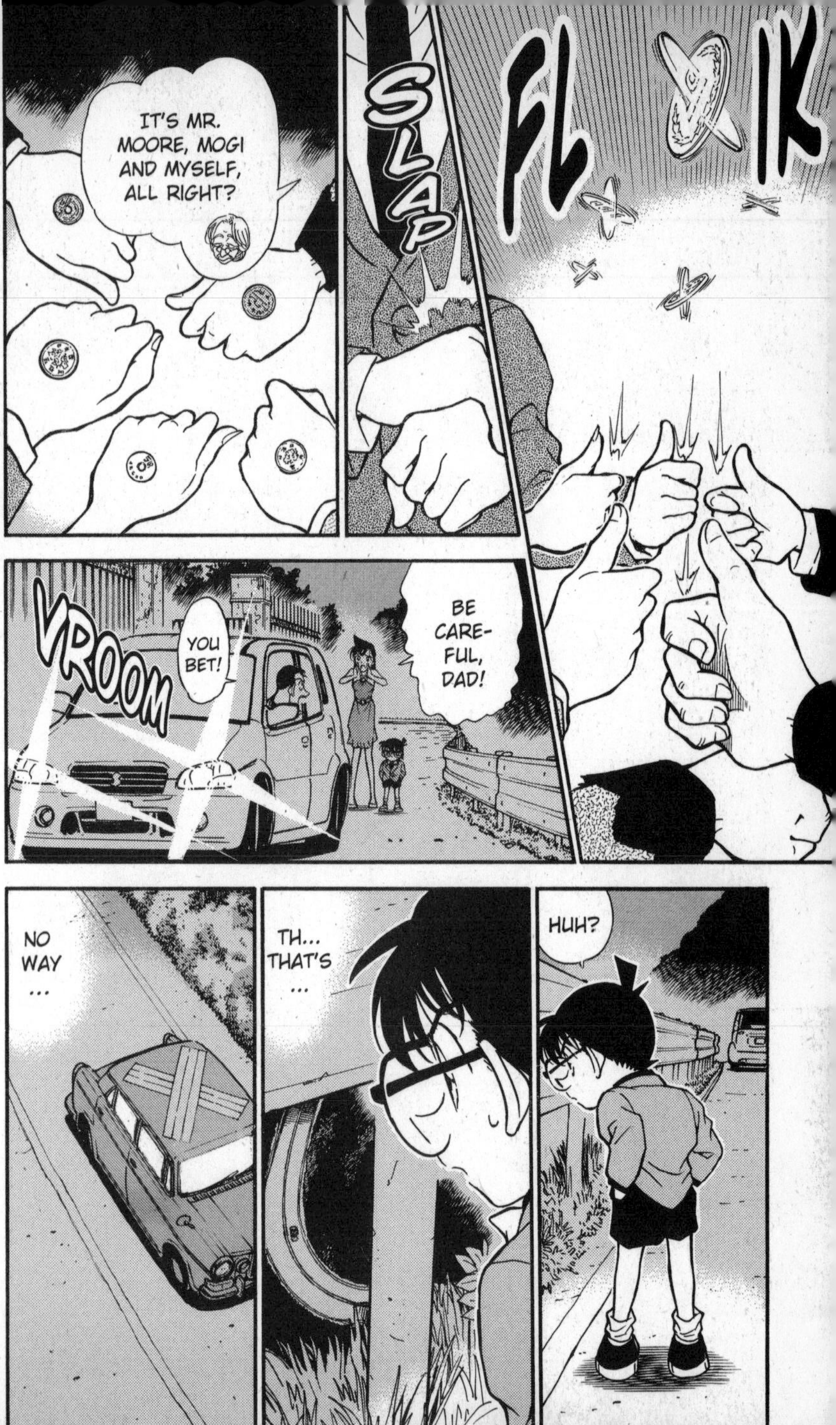

FL
K
SLAP
IT'S MR. MOORE, MOGI AND MYSELF, ALL RIGHT?
BE CARE-FUL, DAD!
YOU BET!
VROOM
HUH?
TH... THAT'S ...
NO WAY ...

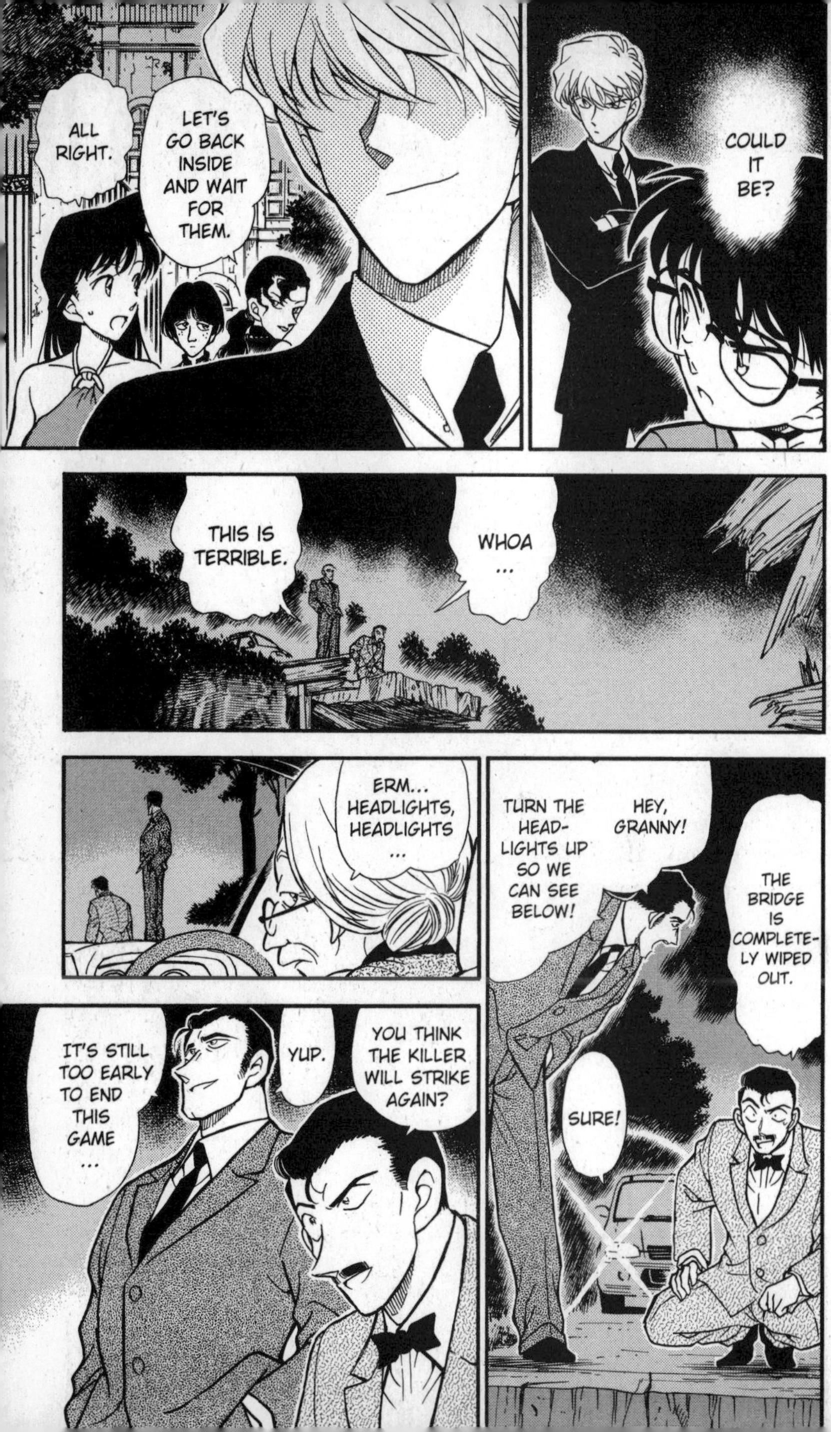
COULD IT BE?
LET'S GO BACK INSIDE AND WAIT FOR THEM.
ALL RIGHT.
WHOA ...
THIS IS TERRIBLE.
THE BRIDGE IS COMPLETELY WIPED OUT.
HEY, GRANNY!
TURN THE HEAD-LIGHTS UP SO WE CAN SEE BELOW!
SURE!
ERM... HEADLIGHTS, HEADLIGHTS ...
YOU THINK THE KILLER WILL STRIKE AGAIN?
YUP.
IT'S STILL TOO EARLY TO END THIS GAME ...

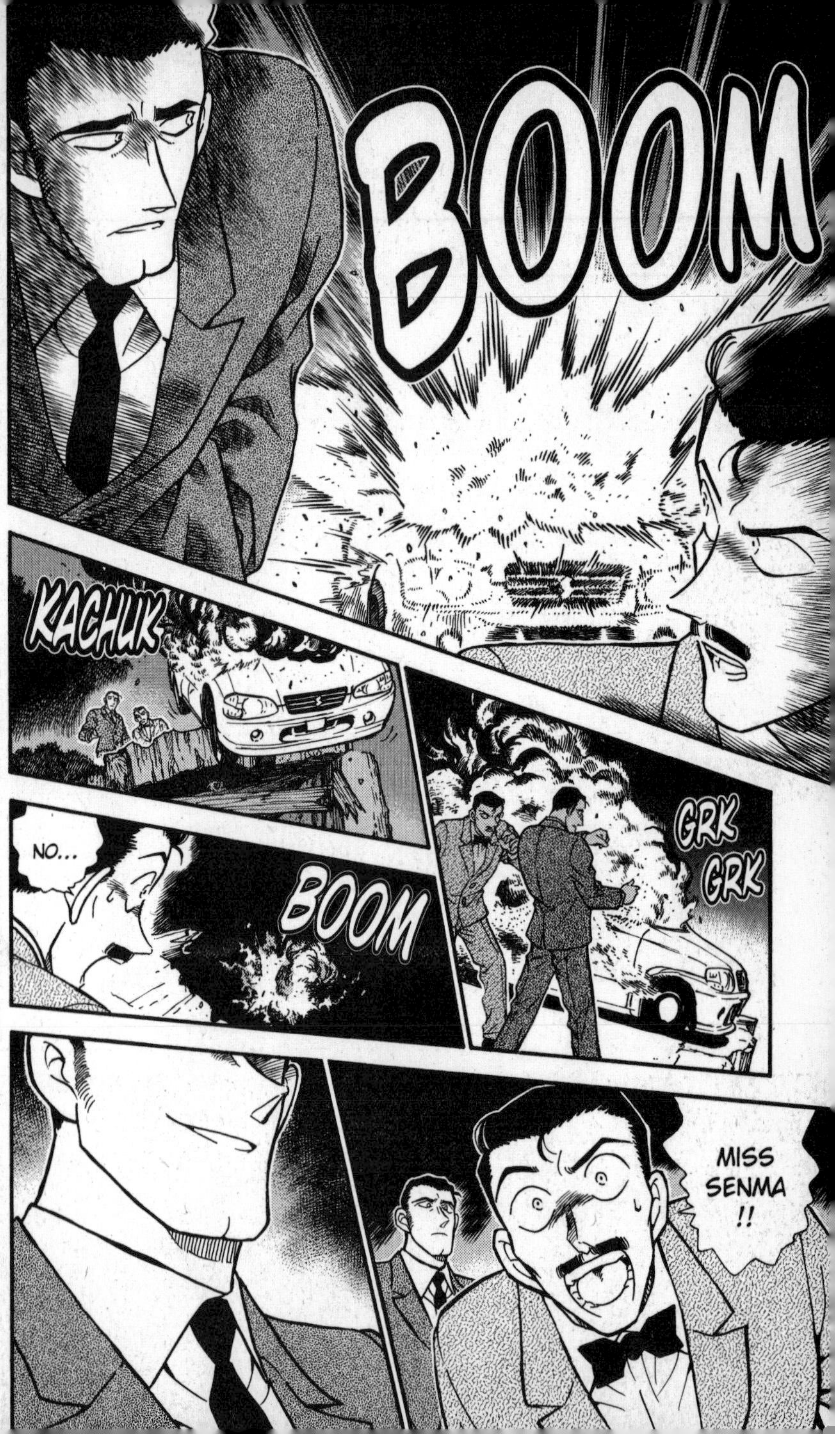
BOOM
GRK GRK
KACHUK
NO...
BOOM
MISS SENMA !!

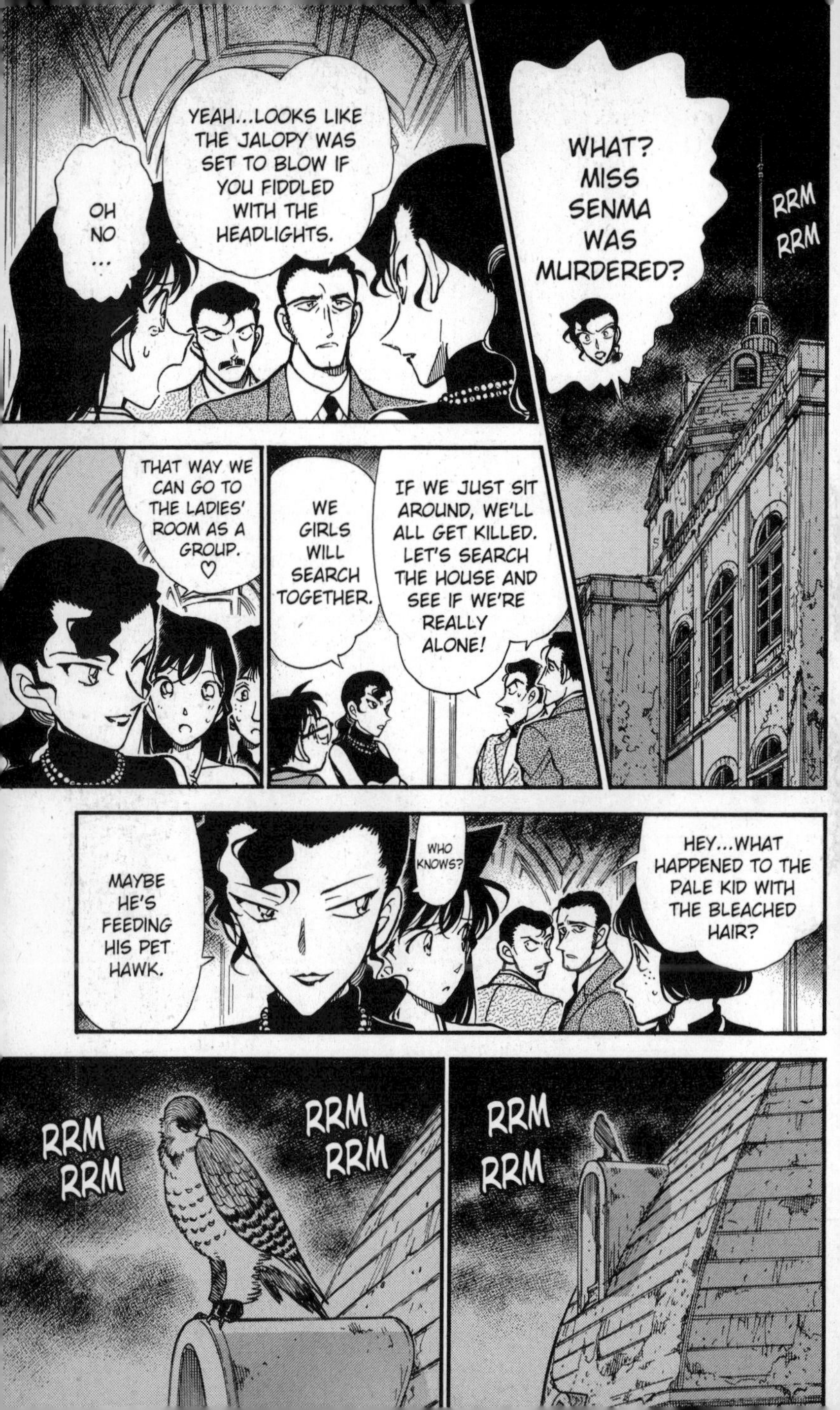
WHAT? MISS SENMA WAS MURDERED?
RRM RRM
YEAH...LOOKS LIKE THE JALOPY WAS SET TO BLOW IF YOU FIDDLED WITH THE HEADLIGHTS.
OH NO ...
IF WE JUST SIT AROUND, WE'LL ALL GET KILLED. LET'S SEARCH THE HOUSE AND SEE IF WE'RE REALLY ALONE!
WE GIRLS WILL SEARCH TOGETHER.
THAT WAY WE CAN GO TO THE LADIES' ROOM AS A GROUP. ♡
HEY...WHAT HAPPENED TO THE PALE KID WITH THE BLEACHED HAIR?
WHO KNOWS?
MAYBE HE'S FEEDING HIS PET HAWK.
RRM RRM
RRM RRM
RRM RRM

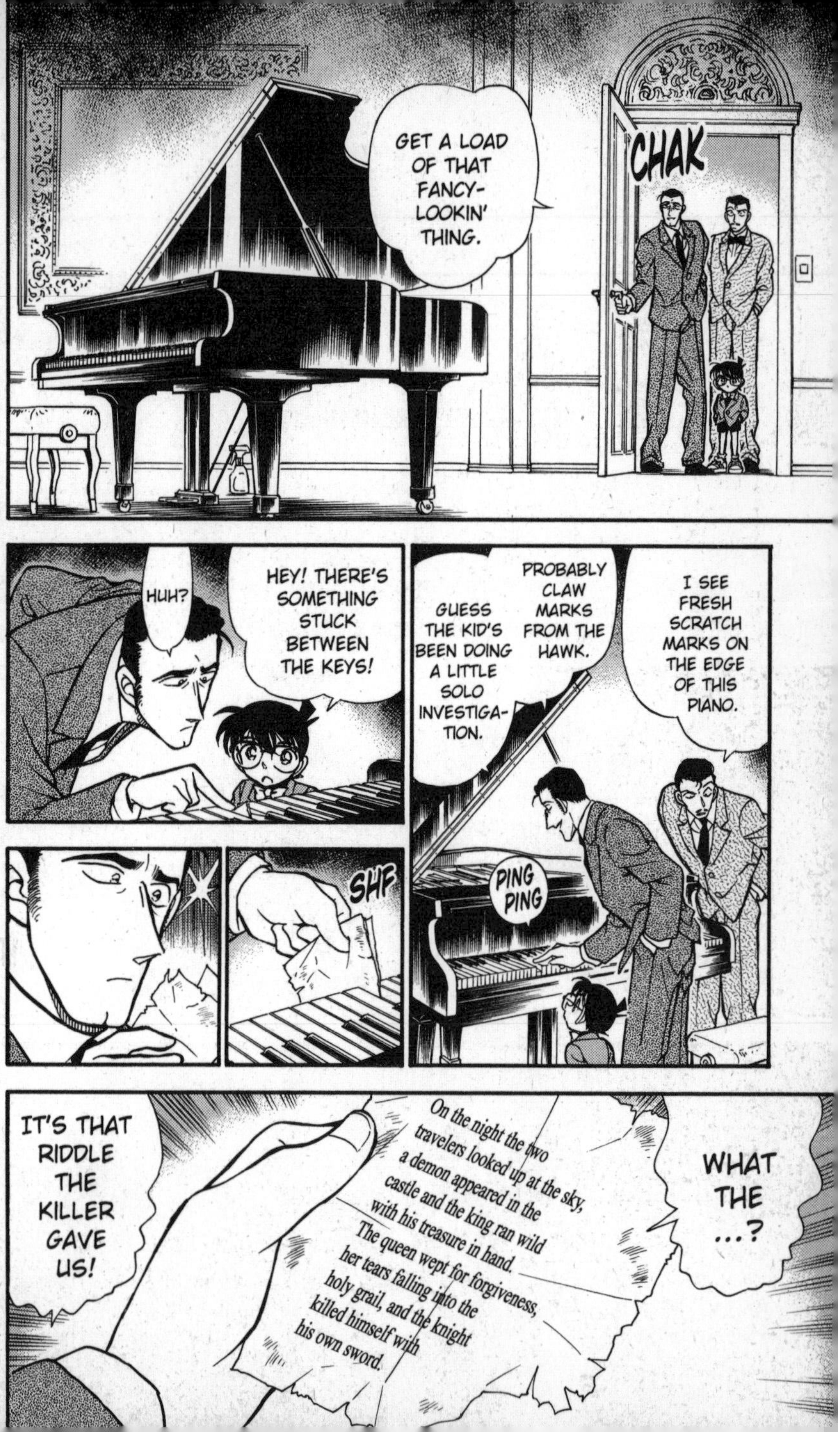
CHAK
GET A LOAD OF THAT FANCY-LOOKIN' THING.
I SEE FRESH SCRATCH MARKS ON THE EDGE OF THIS PIANO.
PROBABLY CLAW MARKS FROM THE HAWK.
GUESS THE KID'S BEEN DOING A LITTLE SOLO INVESTIGATION.
PING PING
HEY! THERE'S SOMETHING STUCK BETWEEN THE KEYS!
HUH?
SHF
WHAT THE ...?
On the night the two travelers looked up at the sky, a demon appeared in the castle and the king ran wild with his treasure in hand. The queen wept for forgiveness, her tears falling into the holy grail, and the knight killed himself with his own sword.
IT'S THAT RIDDLE THE KILLER GAVE US!

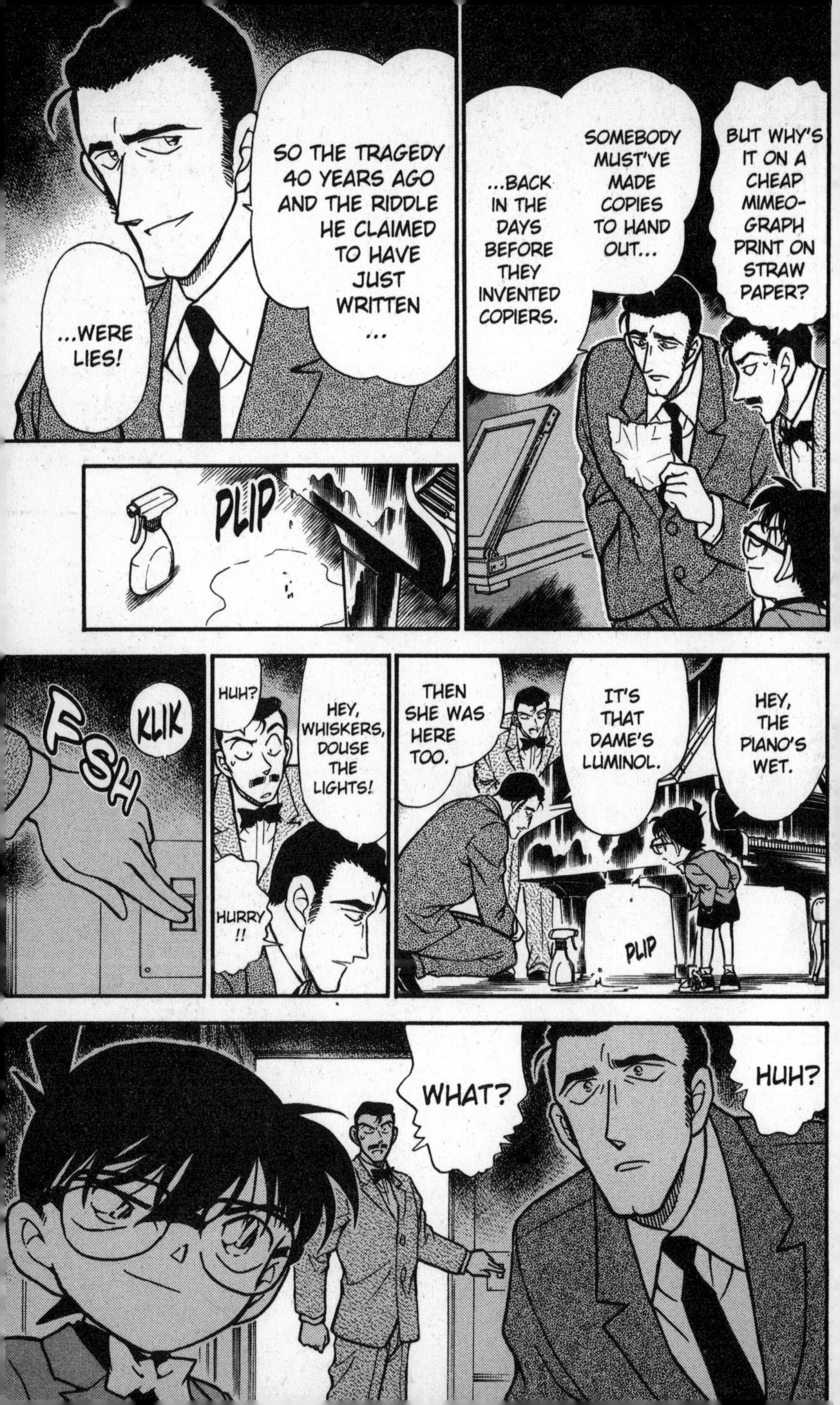
BUT WHY'S IT ON A CHEAP MIMEO-GRAPH PRINT ON STRAW PAPER?
SOMEBODY MUST'VE MADE COPIES TO HAND OUT...
...BACK IN THE DAYS BEFORE THEY INVENTED COPIERS.
SO THE TRAGEDY 40 YEARS AGO AND THE RIDDLE HE CLAIMED TO HAVE JUST WRITTEN ...
...WERE LIES!
PLIP
HEY, THE PIANO'S WET.
IT'S THAT DAME'S LUMINOL.
THEN SHE WAS HERE TOO.
PLIP
HEY, WHISKERS, DOUSE THE LIGHTS!
HUH?
HURRY !!
KLIK
FSH
HUH?
WHAT?

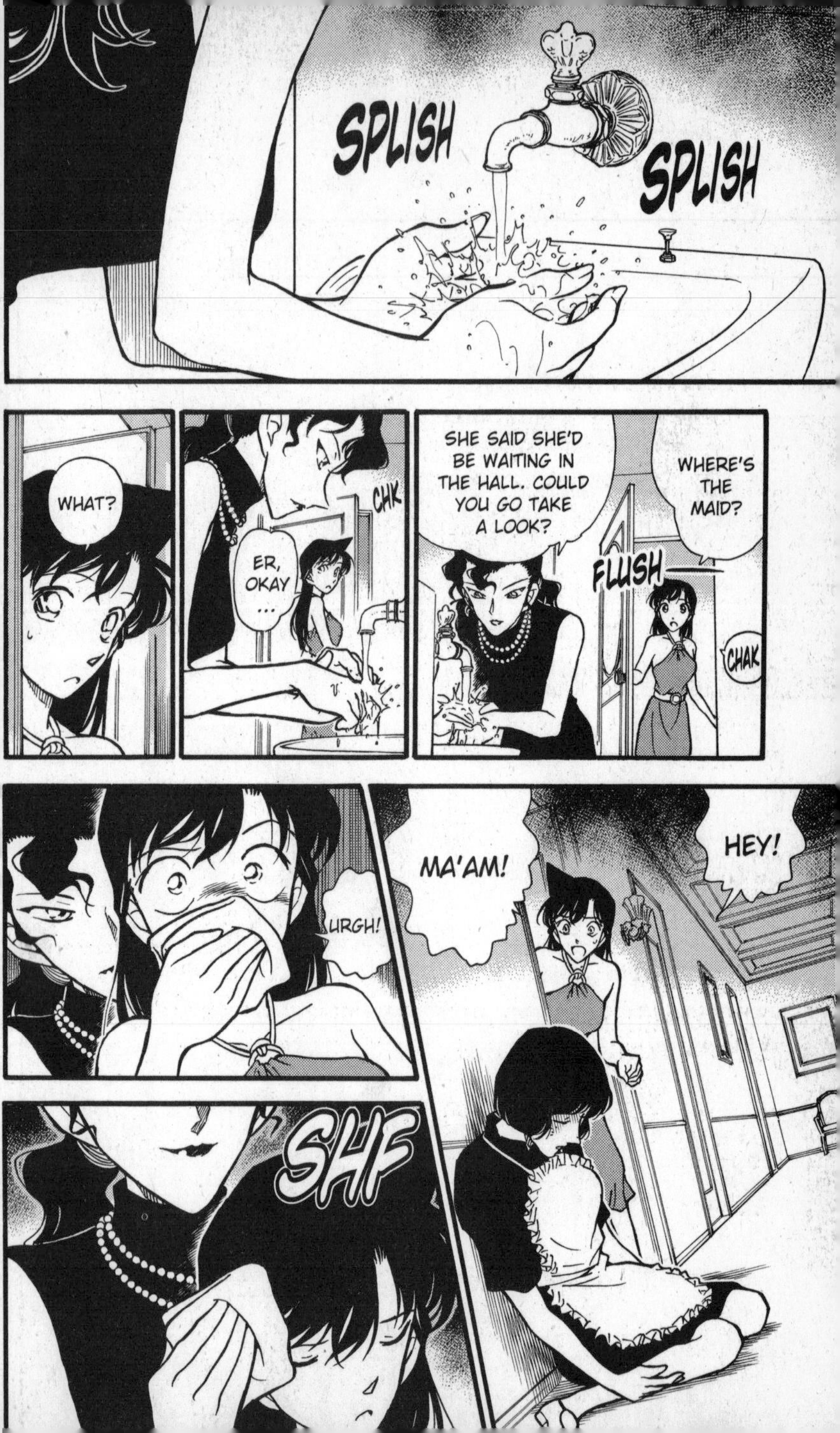
SPLISH
SPLISH
WHERE'S THE MAID?
CHAK
FLUSH
SHE SAID SHE'D BE WAITING IN THE HALL. COULD YOU GO TAKE A LOOK?
CHK
ER, OKAY ...
WHAT?
HEY!
MA'AM!
URGH!
SHF

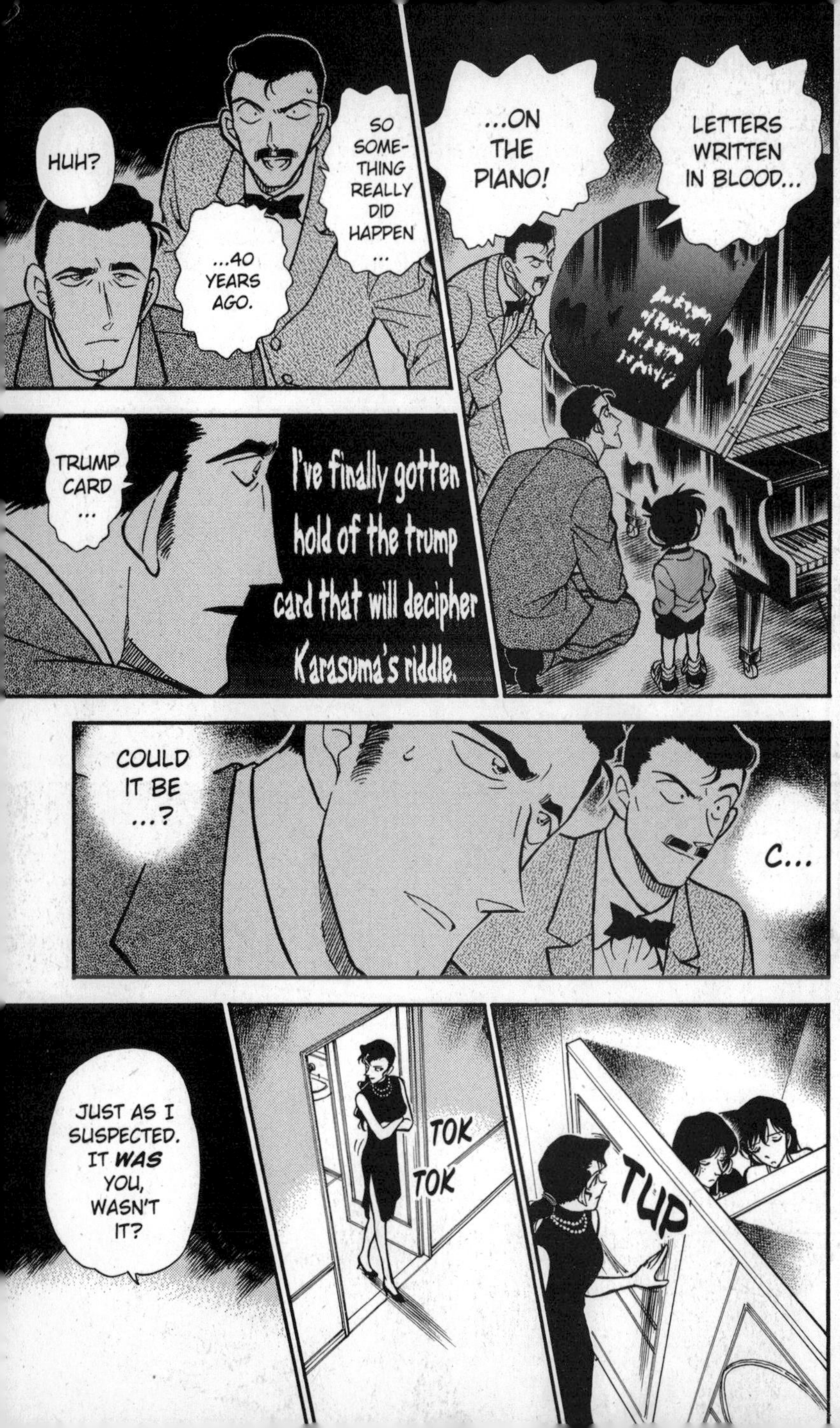
LETTERS WRITTEN IN BLOOD...
...ON THE PIANO!
SO SOMETHING REALLY DID HAPPEN...
...40 YEARS AGO.
HUH?
I've finally gotten hold of the trump card that will decipher Karasuma's riddle.
TRUMP CARD...
C...
COULD IT BE...?
TUP
TOK
TOK
JUST AS I SUSPECTED. IT *WAS* YOU, WASN'T IT?

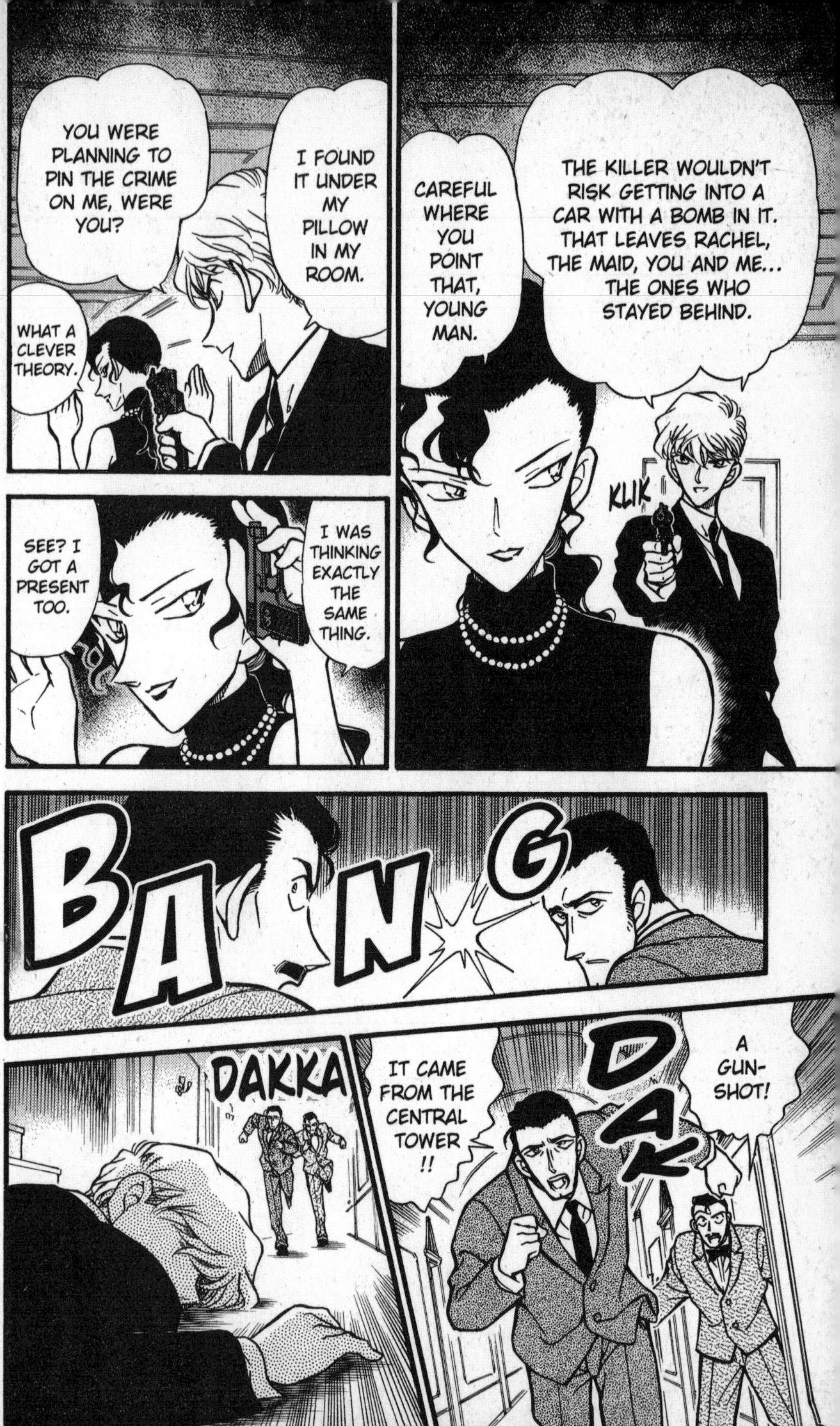
THE KILLER WOULDN'T RISK GETTING INTO A CAR WITH A BOMB IN IT. THAT LEAVES RACHEL, THE MAID, YOU AND ME... THE ONES WHO STAYED BEHIND.
CAREFUL WHERE YOU POINT THAT, YOUNG MAN.
KLIK
I FOUND IT UNDER MY PILLOW IN MY ROOM.
YOU WERE PLANNING TO PIN THE CRIME ON ME, WERE YOU?
WHAT A CLEVER THEORY.
I WAS THINKING EXACTLY THE SAME THING.
SEE? I GOT A PRESENT TOO.
BANG
A GUN-SHOT!
DAK
IT CAME FROM THE CENTRAL TOWER !!
DAKKA

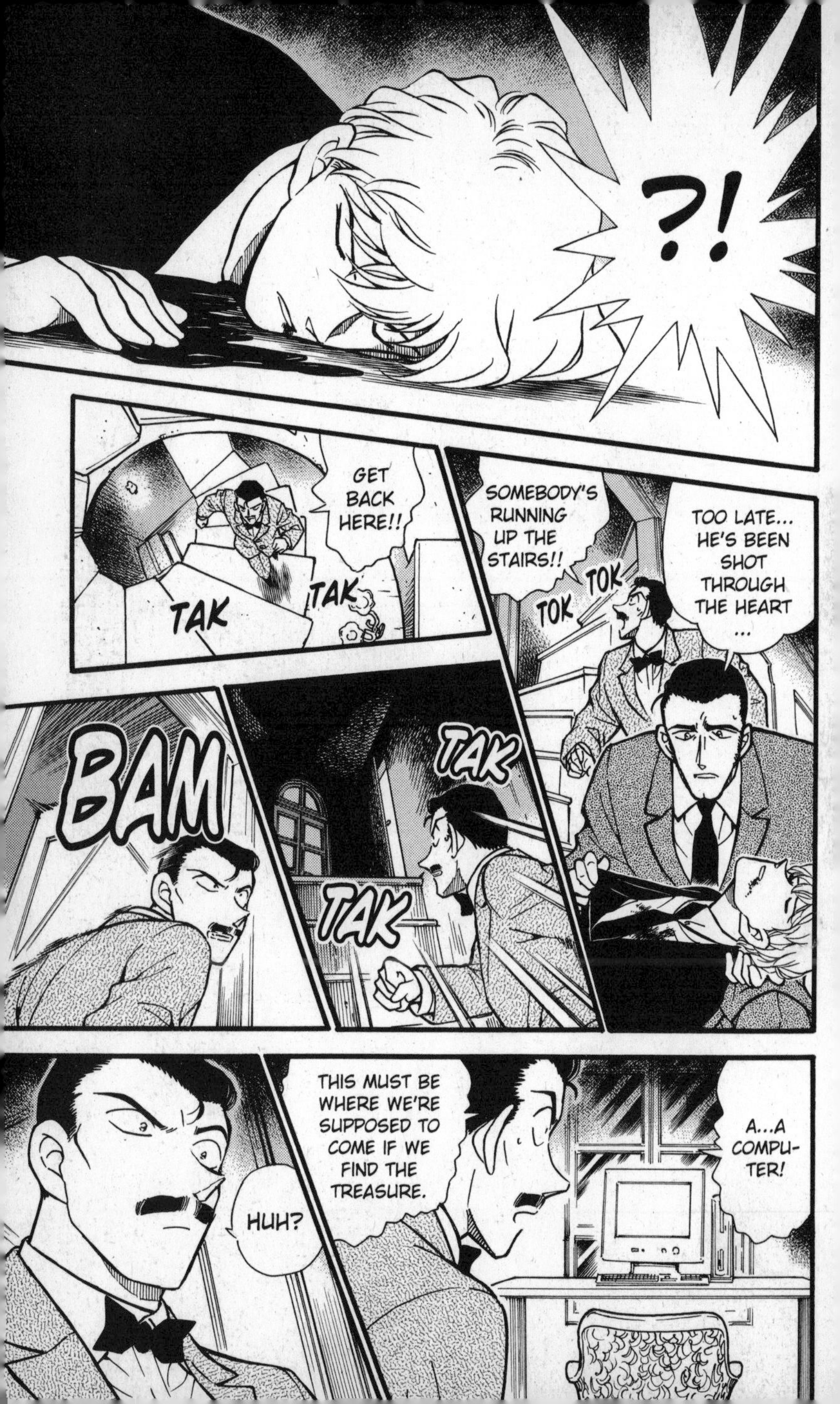
?!
TOO LATE... HE'S BEEN SHOT THROUGH THE HEART ...
SOMEBODY'S RUNNING UP THE STAIRS!!
TOK TOK
GET BACK HERE!!
TAK TAK
TAK TAK
BAM
A...A COMPUTER!
THIS MUST BE WHERE WE'RE SUPPOSED TO COME IF WE FIND THE TREASURE.
HUH?

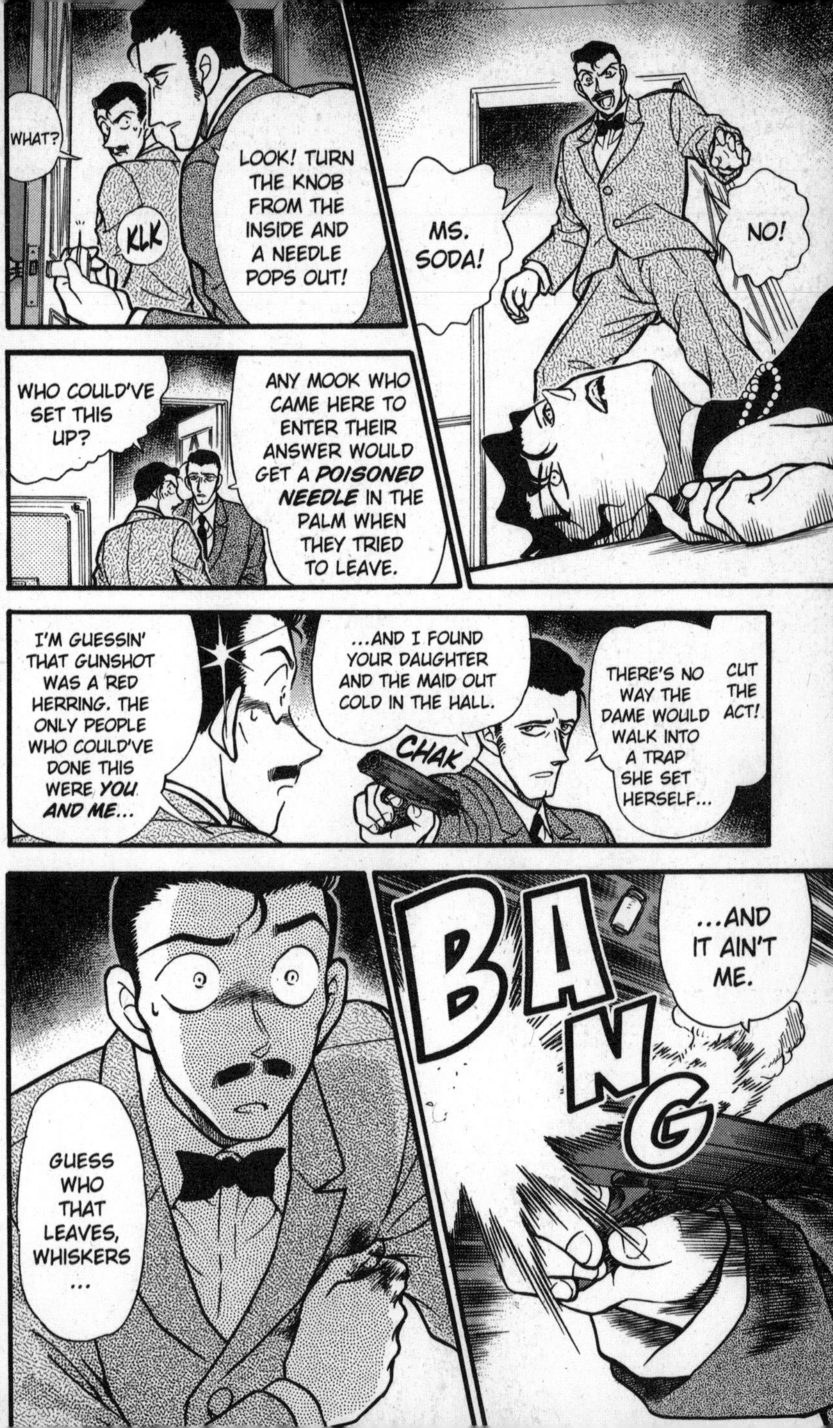
NO!
MS. SODA!
LOOK! TURN THE KNOB FROM THE INSIDE AND A NEEDLE POPS OUT!
KLK
WHAT?
ANY MOOK WHO CAME HERE TO ENTER THEIR ANSWER WOULD GET A POISONED NEEDLE IN THE PALM WHEN THEY TRIED TO LEAVE.
WHO COULD'VE SET THIS UP?
CUT THE ACT!
THERE'S NO WAY THE DAME WOULD WALK INTO A TRAP SHE SET HERSELF...
CHAK
...AND I FOUND YOUR DAUGHTER AND THE MAID OUT COLD IN THE HALL.
I'M GUESSIN' THAT GUNSHOT WAS A RED HERRING. THE ONLY PEOPLE WHO COULD'VE DONE THIS WERE YOU AND ME...
...AND IT AIN'T ME.
BANG
GUESS WHO THAT LEAVES, WHISKERS ...

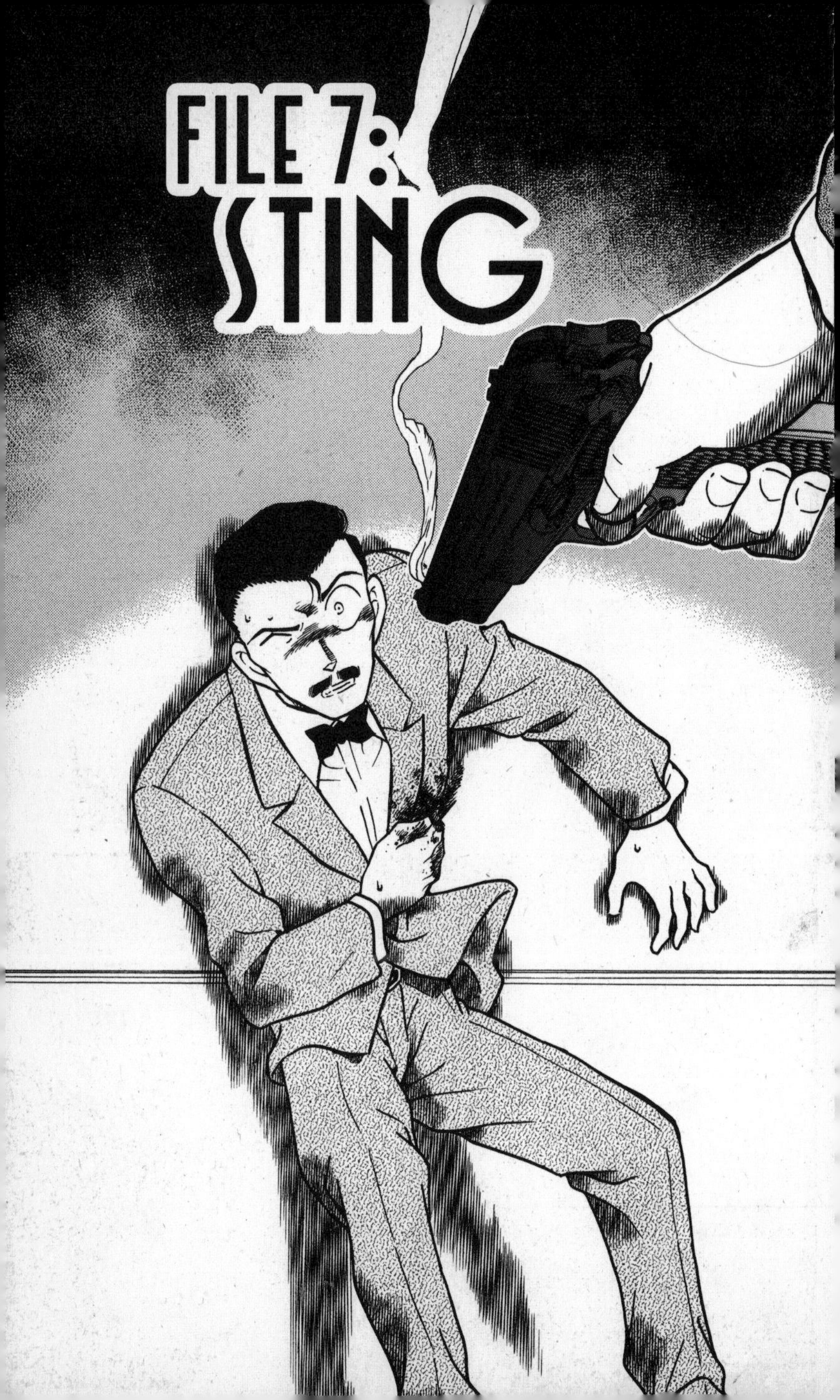
FILE 7:
STING

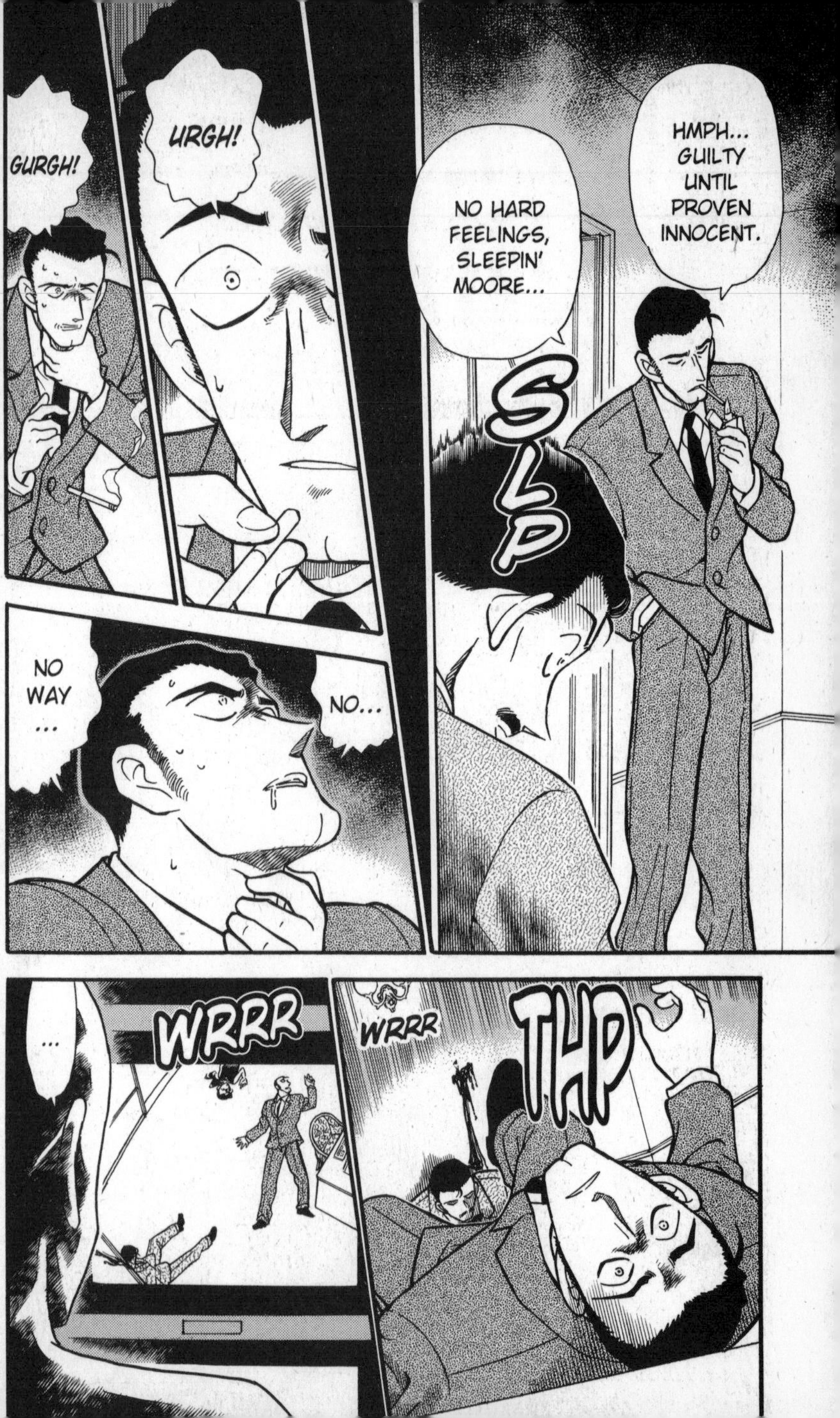
HMPH... GUILTY UNTIL PROVEN INNOCENT.
NO HARD FEELINGS, SLEEPIN' MOORE...
SLP
URGH!
GURGH!
NO...
NO WAY ...
THP
WRRR
WRRR
...

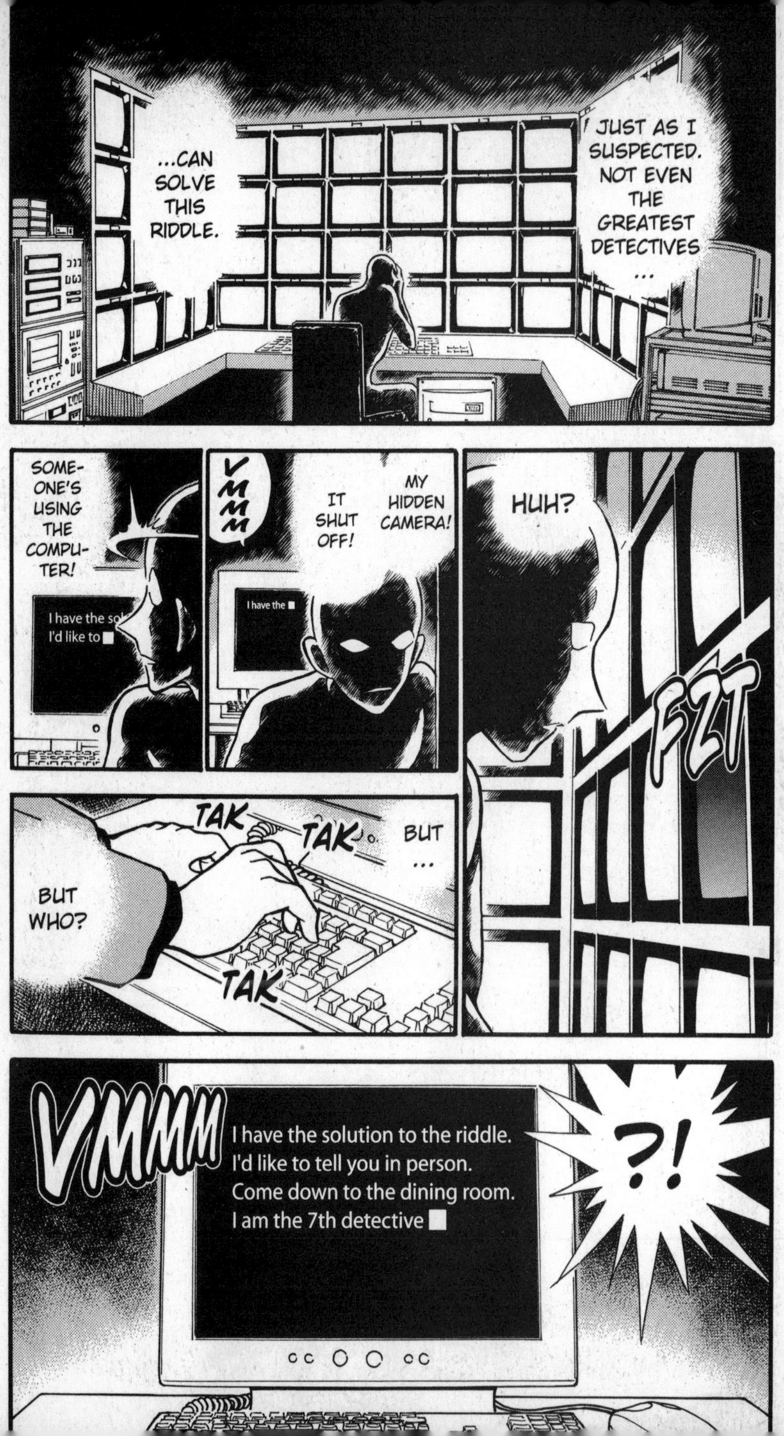
JUST AS I SUSPECTED. NOT EVEN THE GREATEST DETECTIVES...
...CAN SOLVE THIS RIDDLE.
HUH?
FZT
VMMM
MY HIDDEN CAMERA!
IT SHUT OFF!
I have the
SOME-ONE'S USING THE COMPU-TER!
I'd like to
BUT...
TAK
TAK
BUT WHO?
TAK
?!
I have the solution to the riddle.
I'd like to tell you in person.
Come down to the dining room.
I am the 7th detective
VMMM

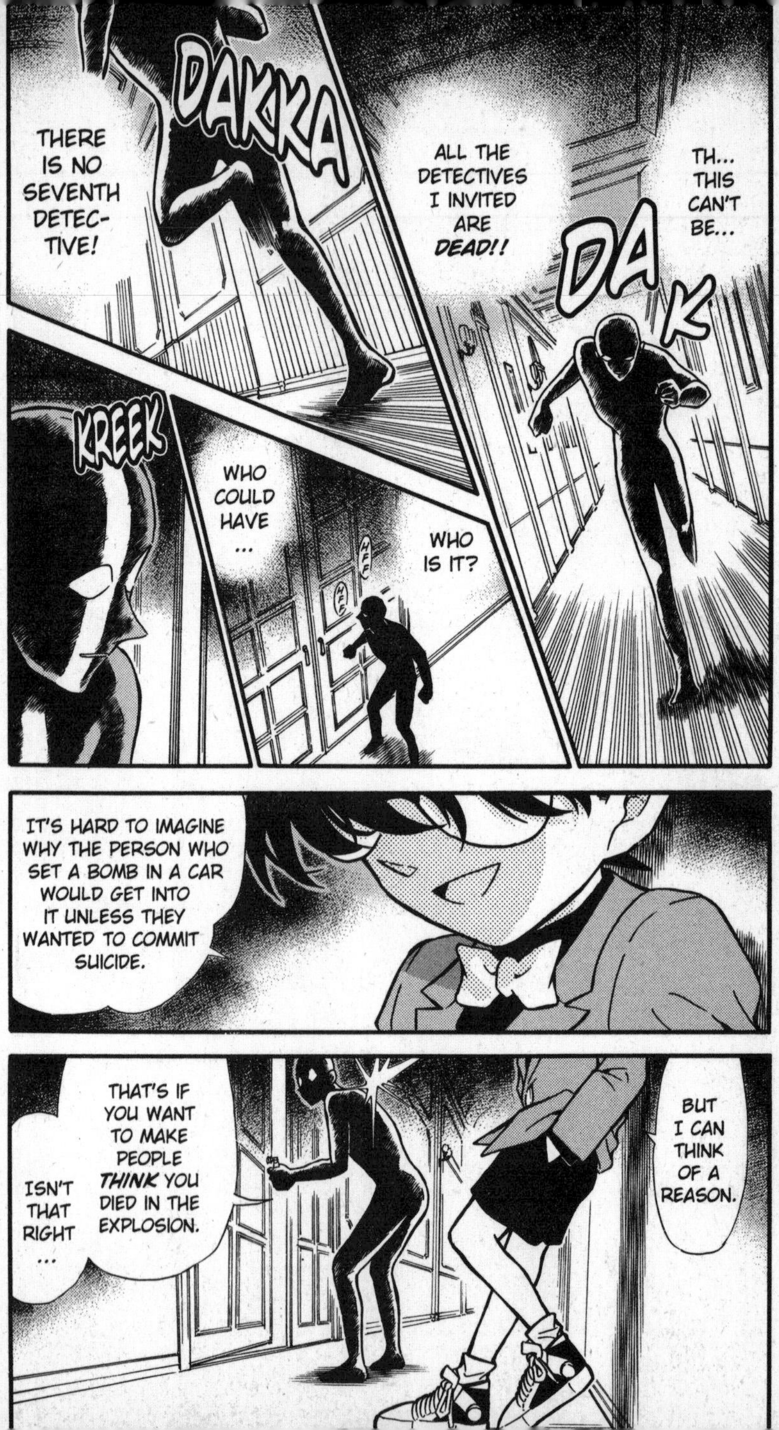

TH... THIS CAN'T BE...
DA K
ALL THE DETECTIVES I INVITED ARE *DEAD!!*
DAKKA
THERE IS NO SEVENTH DETEC-TIVE!
WHO IS IT?
HFF HFF
WHO COULD HAVE ...
KREEK
IT'S HARD TO IMAGINE WHY THE PERSON WHO SET A BOMB IN A CAR WOULD GET INTO IT UNLESS THEY WANTED TO COMMIT SUICIDE.
BUT I CAN THINK OF A REASON.
THAT'S IF YOU WANT TO MAKE PEOPLE ***THINK*** YOU DIED IN THE EXPLOSION.
ISN'T THAT RIGHT ...

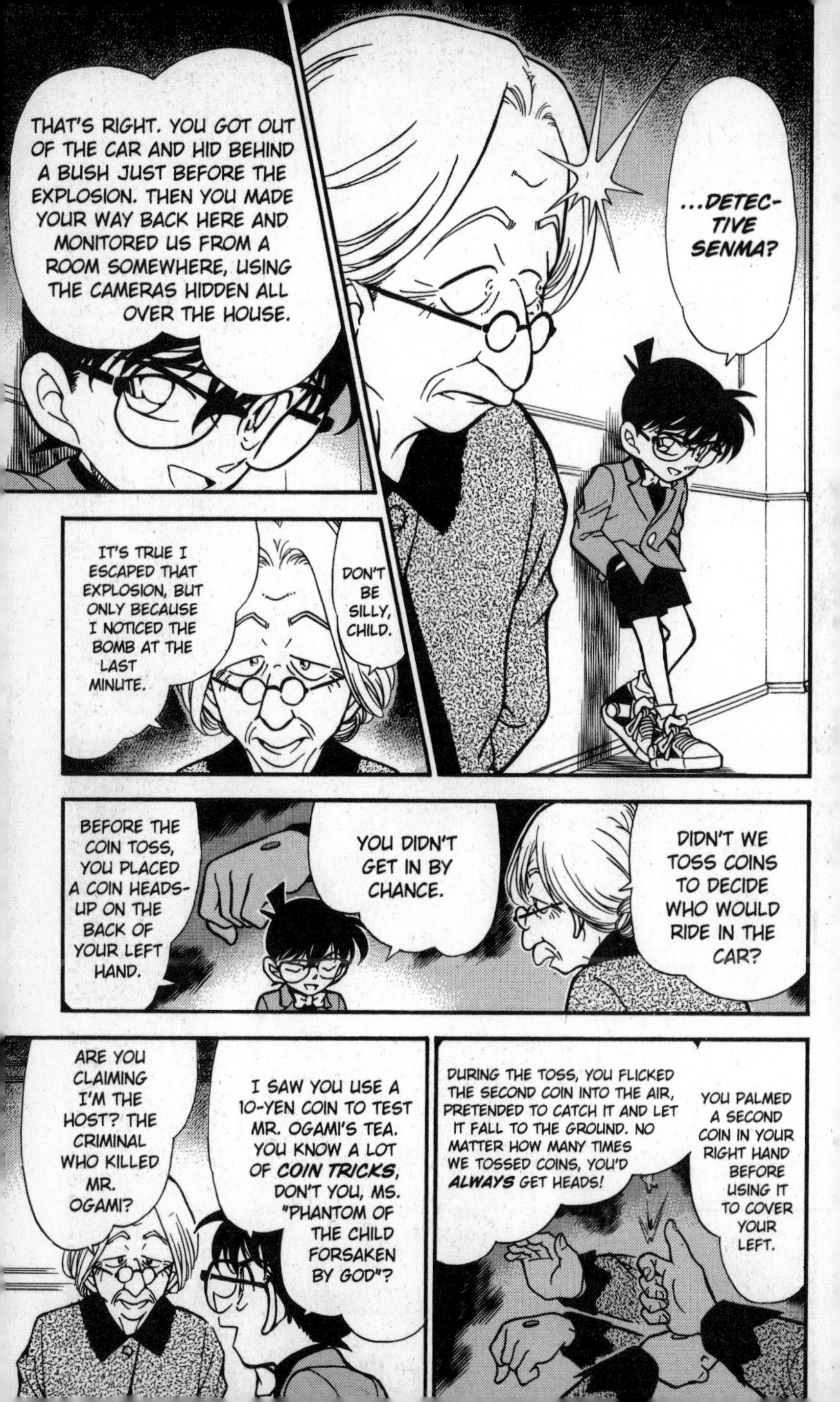
...DETECTIVE SENMA?
THAT'S RIGHT. YOU GOT OUT OF THE CAR AND HID BEHIND A BUSH JUST BEFORE THE EXPLOSION. THEN YOU MADE YOUR WAY BACK HERE AND MONITORED US FROM A ROOM SOMEWHERE, USING THE CAMERAS HIDDEN ALL OVER THE HOUSE.
DON'T BE SILLY, CHILD.
IT'S TRUE I ESCAPED THAT EXPLOSION, BUT ONLY BECAUSE I NOTICED THE BOMB AT THE LAST MINUTE.
DIDN'T WE TOSS COINS TO DECIDE WHO WOULD RIDE IN THE CAR?
YOU DIDN'T GET IN BY CHANCE.
BEFORE THE COIN TOSS, YOU PLACED A COIN HEADS-UP ON THE BACK OF YOUR LEFT HAND.
YOU PALMED A SECOND COIN IN YOUR RIGHT HAND BEFORE USING IT TO COVER YOUR LEFT.
DURING THE TOSS, YOU FLICKED THE SECOND COIN INTO THE AIR, PRETENDED TO CATCH IT AND LET IT FALL TO THE GROUND. NO MATTER HOW MANY TIMES WE TOSSED COINS, YOU'D ***ALWAYS*** GET HEADS!
I SAW YOU USE A 10-YEN COIN TO TEST MR. OGAMI'S TEA. YOU KNOW A LOT OF ***COIN TRICKS***, DON'T YOU, MS. "PHANTOM OF THE CHILD FORSAKEN BY GOD"?
ARE YOU CLAIMING I'M THE HOST? THE CRIMINAL WHO KILLED MR. OGAMI?

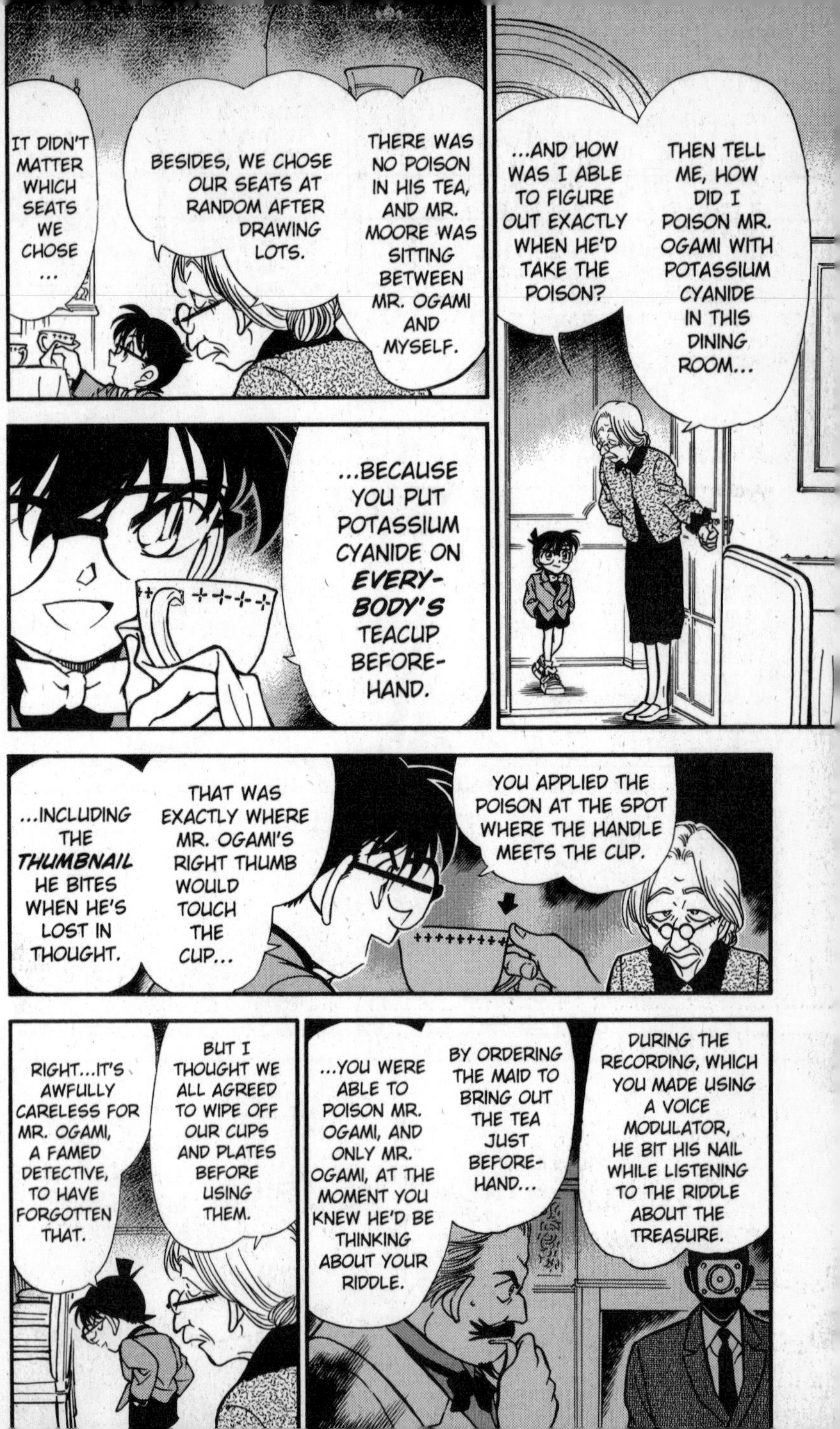
THEN TELL ME, HOW DID I POISON MR. OGAMI WITH POTASSIUM CYANIDE IN THIS DINING ROOM...
...AND HOW WAS I ABLE TO FIGURE OUT EXACTLY WHEN HE'D TAKE THE POISON?
THERE WAS NO POISON IN HIS TEA, AND MR. MOORE WAS SITTING BETWEEN MR. OGAMI AND MYSELF.
BESIDES, WE CHOSE OUR SEATS AT RANDOM AFTER DRAWING LOTS.
IT DIDN'T MATTER WHICH SEATS WE CHOSE ...
...BECAUSE YOU PUT POTASSIUM CYANIDE ON ***EVERYBODY'S*** TEACUP BEFOREHAND.
YOU APPLIED THE POISON AT THE SPOT WHERE THE HANDLE MEETS THE CUP.
THAT WAS EXACTLY WHERE MR. OGAMI'S RIGHT THUMB WOULD TOUCH THE CUP...
...INCLUDING THE ***THUMBNAIL*** HE BITES WHEN HE'S LOST IN THOUGHT.
DURING THE RECORDING, WHICH YOU MADE USING A VOICE MODULATOR, HE BIT HIS NAIL WHILE LISTENING TO THE RIDDLE ABOUT THE TREASURE.
BY ORDERING THE MAID TO BRING OUT THE TEA JUST BEFOREHAND...
...YOU WERE ABLE TO POISON MR. OGAMI, AND ONLY MR. OGAMI, AT THE MOMENT YOU KNEW HE'D BE THINKING ABOUT YOUR RIDDLE.
BUT I THOUGHT WE ALL AGREED TO WIPE OFF OUR CUPS AND PLATES BEFORE USING THEM.
RIGHT...IT'S AWFULLY CARELESS FOR MR. OGAMI, A FAMED DETECTIVE, TO HAVE FORGOTTEN THAT.

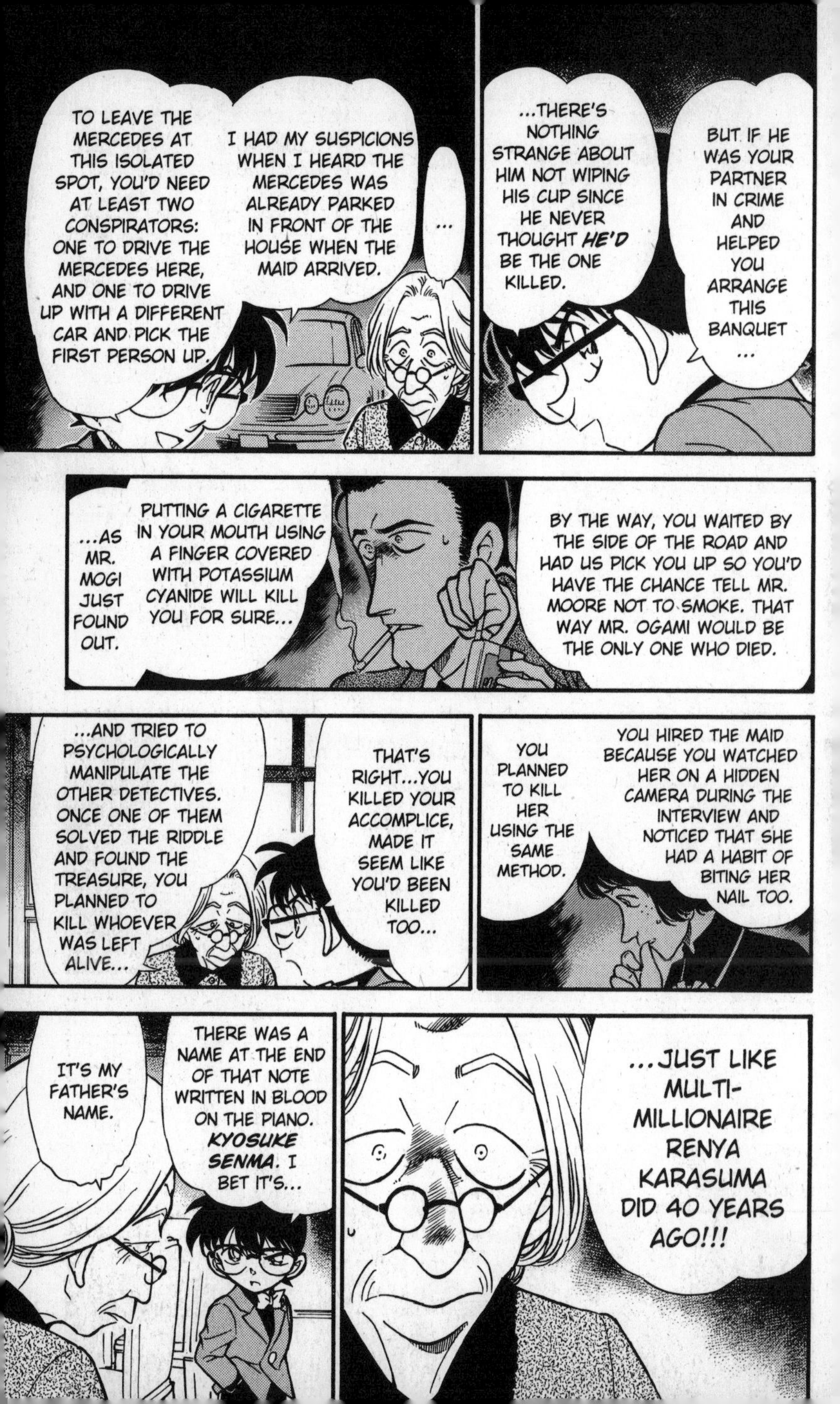
BUT IF HE WAS YOUR PARTNER IN CRIME AND HELPED YOU ARRANGE THIS BANQUET...
...THERE'S NOTHING STRANGE ABOUT HIM NOT WIPING HIS CUP SINCE HE NEVER THOUGHT *HE'D* BE THE ONE KILLED.
...
I HAD MY SUSPICIONS WHEN I HEARD THE MERCEDES WAS ALREADY PARKED IN FRONT OF THE HOUSE WHEN THE MAID ARRIVED.
TO LEAVE THE MERCEDES AT THIS ISOLATED SPOT, YOU'D NEED AT LEAST TWO CONSPIRATORS: ONE TO DRIVE THE MERCEDES HERE, AND ONE TO DRIVE UP WITH A DIFFERENT CAR AND PICK THE FIRST PERSON UP.
BY THE WAY, YOU WAITED BY THE SIDE OF THE ROAD AND HAD US PICK YOU UP SO YOU'D HAVE THE CHANCE TELL MR. MOORE NOT TO SMOKE. THAT WAY MR. OGAMI WOULD BE THE ONLY ONE WHO DIED.
PUTTING A CIGARETTE IN YOUR MOUTH USING A FINGER COVERED WITH POTASSIUM CYANIDE WILL KILL YOU FOR SURE...
...AS MR. MOGI JUST FOUND OUT.
YOU HIRED THE MAID BECAUSE YOU WATCHED HER ON A HIDDEN CAMERA DURING THE INTERVIEW AND NOTICED THAT SHE HAD A HABIT OF BITING HER NAIL TOO.
YOU PLANNED TO KILL HER USING THE SAME METHOD.
THAT'S RIGHT...YOU KILLED YOUR ACCOMPLICE, MADE IT SEEM LIKE YOU'D BEEN KILLED TOO...
...AND TRIED TO PSYCHOLOGICALLY MANIPULATE THE OTHER DETECTIVES. ONCE ONE OF THEM SOLVED THE RIDDLE AND FOUND THE TREASURE, YOU PLANNED TO KILL WHOEVER WAS LEFT ALIVE...
...JUST LIKE MULTI-MILLIONAIRE RENYA KARASUMA DID 40 YEARS AGO!!!
THERE WAS A NAME AT THE END OF THAT NOTE WRITTEN IN BLOOD ON THE PIANO. *KYOSUKE SENMA*. I BET IT'S...
IT'S MY FATHER'S NAME.

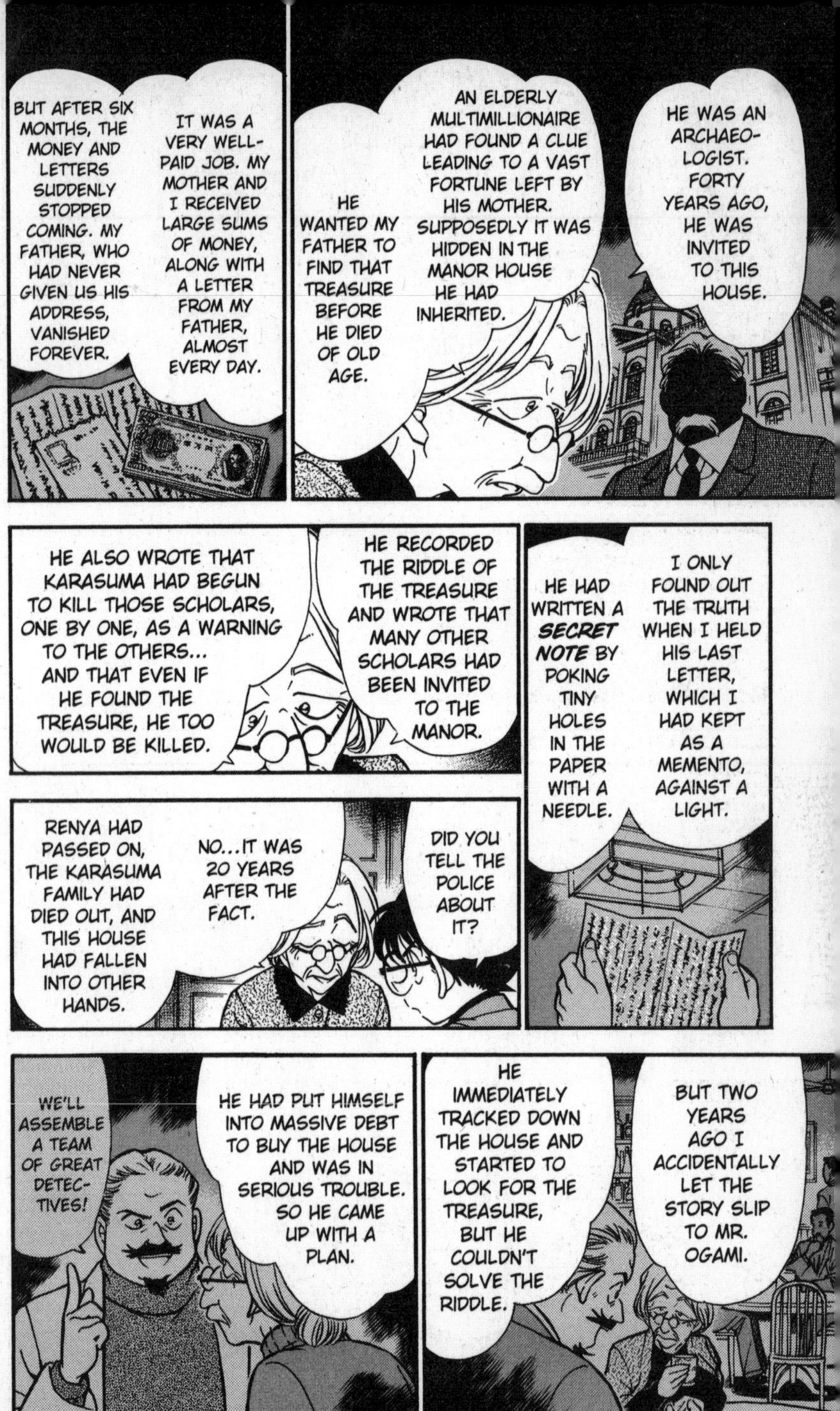
HE WAS AN ARCHAEO-LOGIST. FORTY YEARS AGO, HE WAS INVITED TO THIS HOUSE.
AN ELDERLY MULTIMILLIONAIRE HAD FOUND A CLUE LEADING TO A VAST FORTUNE LEFT BY HIS MOTHER. SUPPOSEDLY IT WAS HIDDEN IN THE MANOR HOUSE HE HAD INHERITED.
HE WANTED MY FATHER TO FIND THAT TREASURE BEFORE HE DIED OF OLD AGE.
IT WAS A VERY WELL-PAID JOB. MY MOTHER AND I RECEIVED LARGE SUMS OF MONEY, ALONG WITH A LETTER FROM MY FATHER, ALMOST EVERY DAY.
BUT AFTER SIX MONTHS, THE MONEY AND LETTERS SUDDENLY STOPPED COMING. MY FATHER, WHO HAD NEVER GIVEN US HIS ADDRESS, VANISHED FOREVER.
I ONLY FOUND OUT THE TRUTH WHEN I HELD HIS LAST LETTER, WHICH I HAD KEPT AS A MEMENTO, AGAINST A LIGHT.
HE HAD WRITTEN A ***SECRET NOTE*** BY POKING TINY HOLES IN THE PAPER WITH A NEEDLE.
HE RECORDED THE RIDDLE OF THE TREASURE AND WROTE THAT MANY OTHER SCHOLARS HAD BEEN INVITED TO THE MANOR.
HE ALSO WROTE THAT KARASUMA HAD BEGUN TO KILL THOSE SCHOLARS, ONE BY ONE, AS A WARNING TO THE OTHERS... AND THAT EVEN IF HE FOUND THE TREASURE, HE TOO WOULD BE KILLED.
DID YOU TELL THE POLICE ABOUT IT?
NO...IT WAS 20 YEARS AFTER THE FACT.
RENYA HAD PASSED ON, THE KARASUMA FAMILY HAD DIED OUT, AND THIS HOUSE HAD FALLEN INTO OTHER HANDS.
BUT TWO YEARS AGO I ACCIDENTALLY LET THE STORY SLIP TO MR. OGAMI.
HE IMMEDIATELY TRACKED DOWN THE HOUSE AND STARTED TO LOOK FOR THE TREASURE, BUT HE COULDN'T SOLVE THE RIDDLE.
HE HAD PUT HIMSELF INTO MASSIVE DEBT TO BUY THE HOUSE AND WAS IN SERIOUS TROUBLE. SO HE CAME UP WITH A PLAN.
WE'LL ASSEMBLE A TEAM OF GREAT DETEC-TIVES!

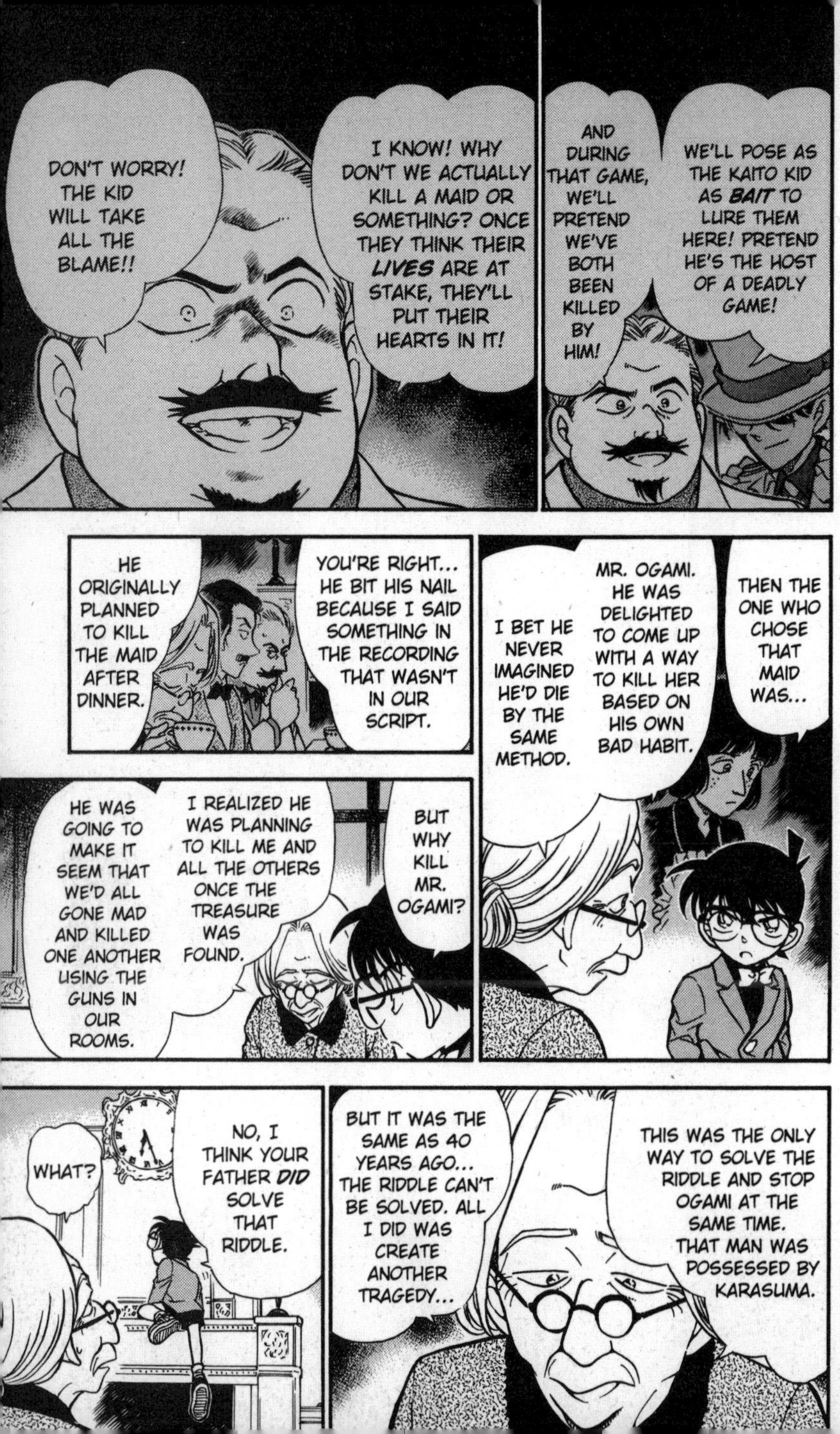
WE'LL POSE AS THE KAITO KID AS *BAIT* TO LURE THEM HERE! PRETEND HE'S THE HOST OF A DEADLY GAME!
AND DURING THAT GAME, WE'LL PRETEND WE'VE BOTH BEEN KILLED BY HIM!
I KNOW! WHY DON'T WE ACTUALLY KILL A MAID OR SOMETHING? ONCE THEY THINK THEIR *LIVES* ARE AT STAKE, THEY'LL PUT THEIR HEARTS IN IT!
DON'T WORRY! THE KID WILL TAKE ALL THE BLAME!!
THEN THE ONE WHO CHOSE THAT MAID WAS...
MR. OGAMI. HE WAS DELIGHTED TO COME UP WITH A WAY TO KILL HER BASED ON HIS OWN BAD HABIT.
I BET HE NEVER IMAGINED HE'D DIE BY THE SAME METHOD.
YOU'RE RIGHT... HE BIT HIS NAIL BECAUSE I SAID SOMETHING IN THE RECORDING THAT WASN'T IN OUR SCRIPT.
HE ORIGINALLY PLANNED TO KILL THE MAID AFTER DINNER.
BUT WHY KILL MR. OGAMI?
I REALIZED HE WAS PLANNING TO KILL ME AND ALL THE OTHERS ONCE THE TREASURE WAS FOUND.
HE WAS GOING TO MAKE IT SEEM THAT WE'D ALL GONE MAD AND KILLED ONE ANOTHER USING THE GUNS IN OUR ROOMS.
THIS WAS THE ONLY WAY TO SOLVE THE RIDDLE AND STOP OGAMI AT THE SAME TIME. THAT MAN WAS POSSESSED BY KARASUMA.
BUT IT WAS THE SAME AS 40 YEARS AGO... THE RIDDLE CAN'T BE SOLVED. ALL I DID WAS CREATE ANOTHER TRAGEDY...
NO, I THINK YOUR FATHER *DID* SOLVE THAT RIDDLE.
WHAT?

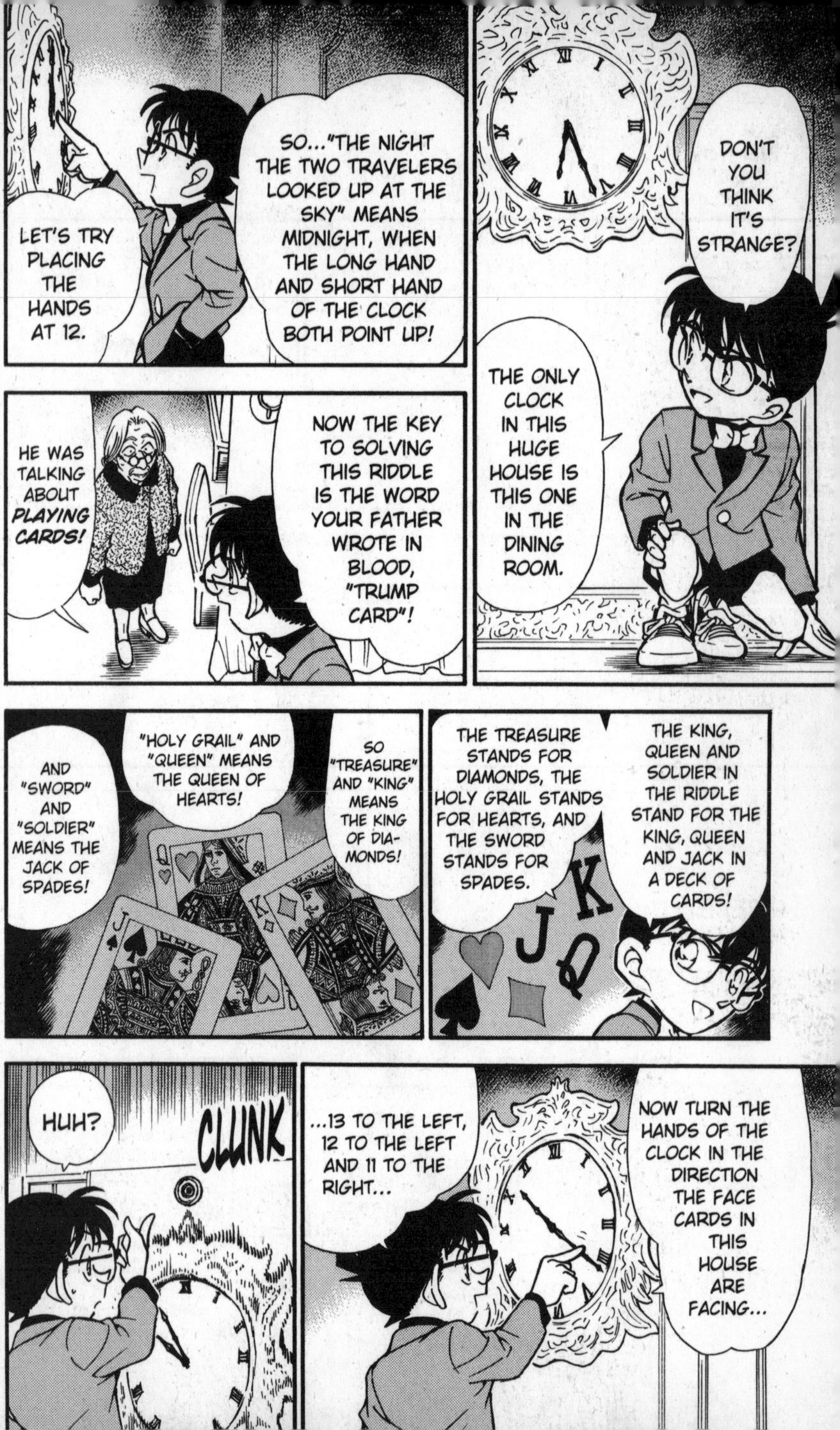
DON'T YOU THINK IT'S STRANGE?
THE ONLY CLOCK IN THIS HUGE HOUSE IS THIS ONE IN THE DINING ROOM.
SO..."THE NIGHT THE TWO TRAVELERS LOOKED UP AT THE SKY" MEANS MIDNIGHT, WHEN THE LONG HAND AND SHORT HAND OF THE CLOCK BOTH POINT UP!
LET'S TRY PLACING THE HANDS AT 12.
NOW THE KEY TO SOLVING THIS RIDDLE IS THE WORD YOUR FATHER WROTE IN BLOOD, "TRUMP CARD"!
HE WAS TALKING ABOUT *PLAYING CARDS!*
THE KING, QUEEN AND SOLDIER IN THE RIDDLE STAND FOR THE KING, QUEEN AND JACK IN A DECK OF CARDS!
THE TREASURE STANDS FOR DIAMONDS, THE HOLY GRAIL STANDS FOR HEARTS, AND THE SWORD STANDS FOR SPADES.
SO "TREASURE" AND "KING" MEANS THE KING OF DIAMONDS!
"HOLY GRAIL" AND "QUEEN" MEANS THE QUEEN OF HEARTS!
AND "SWORD" AND "SOLDIER" MEANS THE JACK OF SPADES!
NOW TURN THE HANDS OF THE CLOCK IN THE DIRECTION THE FACE CARDS IN THIS HOUSE ARE FACING...
...13 TO THE LEFT, 12 TO THE LEFT AND 11 TO THE RIGHT...
CLUNK
HUH?

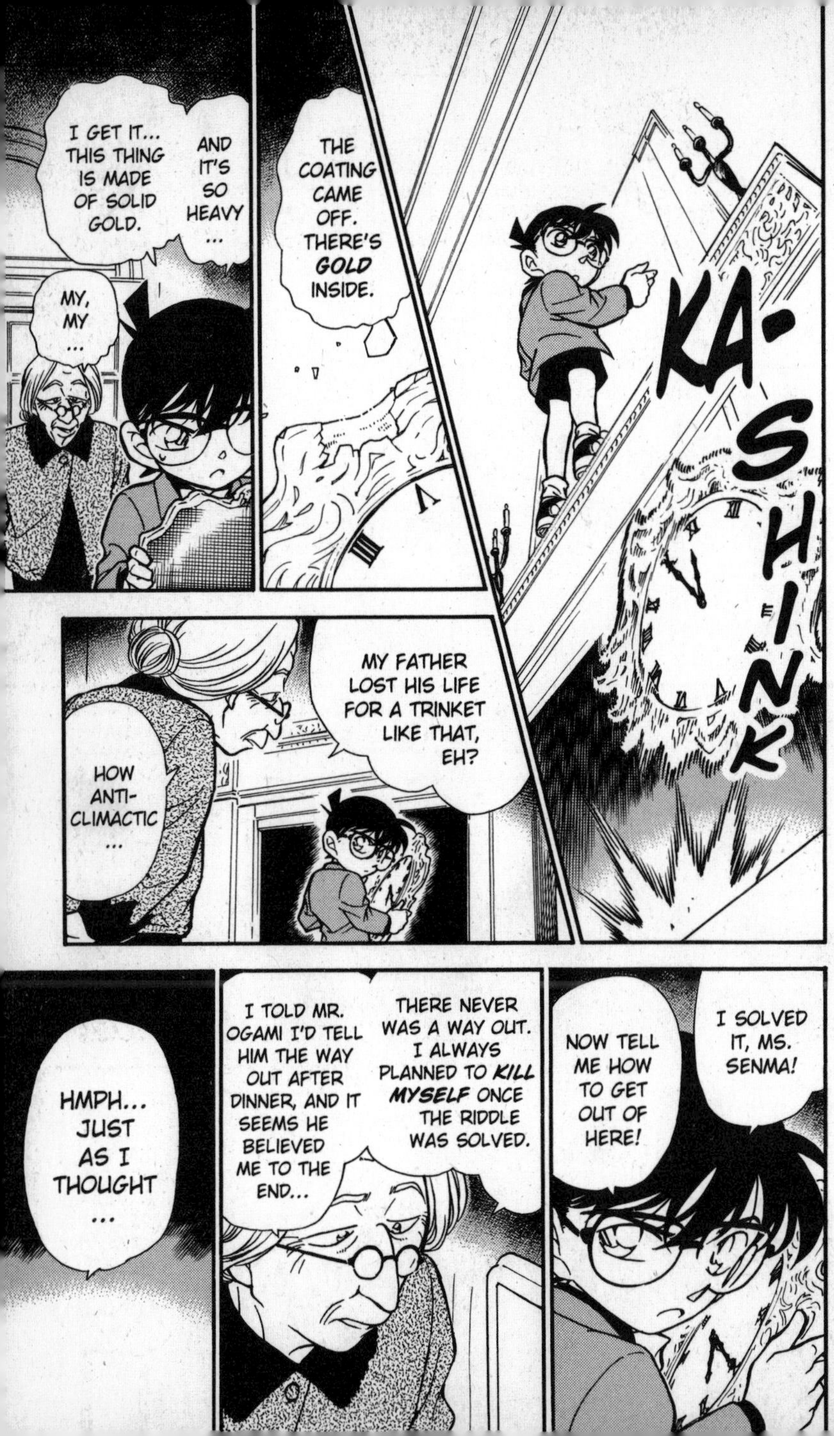

KA-SHINK
THE COATING CAME OFF. THERE'S GOLD INSIDE.
I GET IT... THIS THING IS MADE OF SOLID GOLD.
AND IT'S SO HEAVY...
MY, MY...
MY FATHER LOST HIS LIFE FOR A TRINKET LIKE THAT, EH?
HOW ANTI-CLIMACTIC...
I SOLVED IT, MS. SENMA!
NOW TELL ME HOW TO GET OUT OF HERE!
THERE NEVER WAS A WAY OUT. I ALWAYS PLANNED TO KILL MYSELF ONCE THE RIDDLE WAS SOLVED.
I TOLD MR. OGAMI I'D TELL HIM THE WAY OUT AFTER DINNER, AND IT SEEMS HE BELIEVED ME TO THE END...
HMPH... JUST AS I THOUGHT...

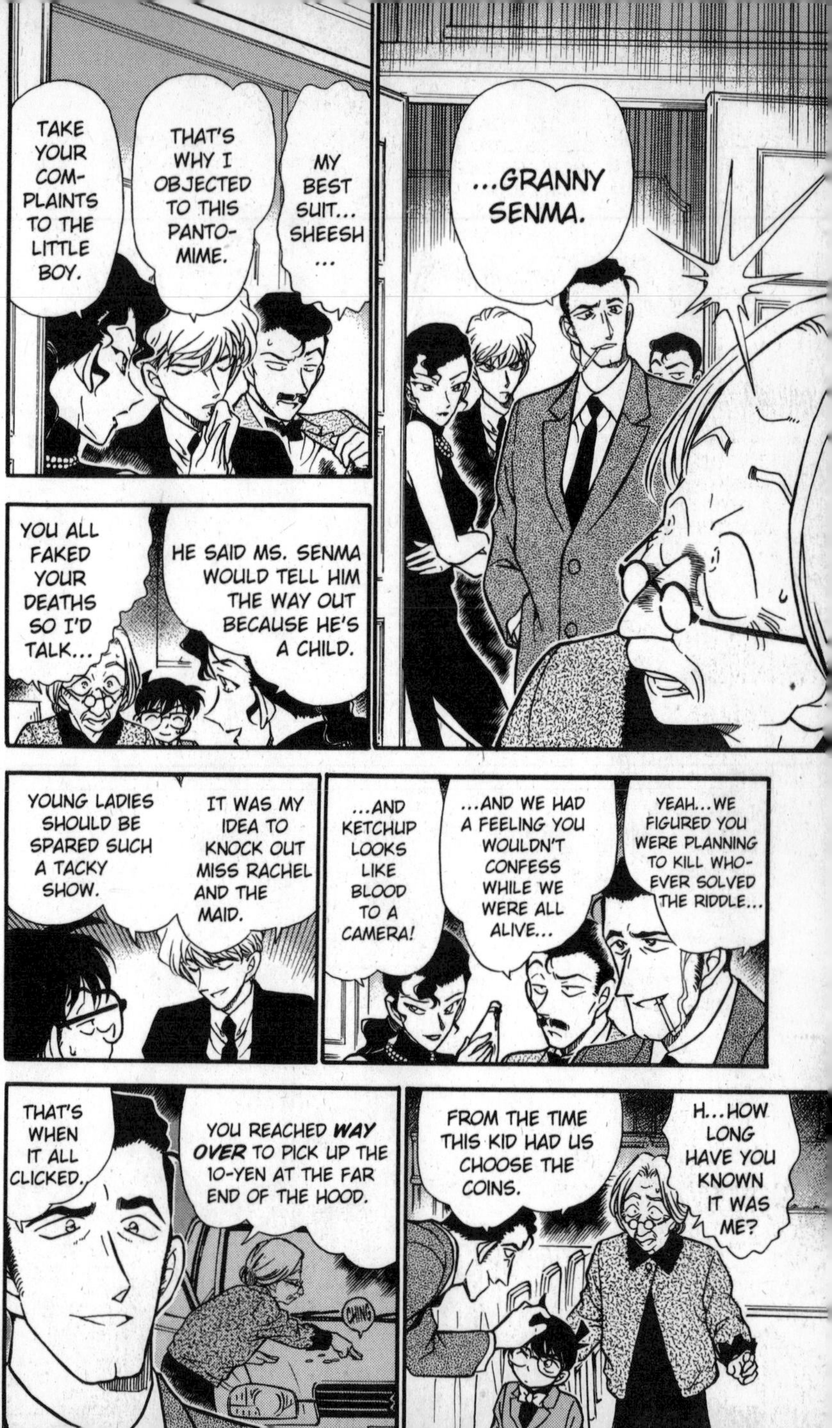
...GRANNY SENMA.
MY BEST SUIT... SHEESH...
THAT'S WHY I OBJECTED TO THIS PANTOMIME.
TAKE YOUR COMPLAINTS TO THE LITTLE BOY.
HE SAID MS. SENMA WOULD TELL HIM THE WAY OUT BECAUSE HE'S A CHILD.
YOU ALL FAKED YOUR DEATHS SO I'D TALK...
YEAH...WE FIGURED YOU WERE PLANNING TO KILL WHOEVER SOLVED THE RIDDLE...
...AND WE HAD A FEELING YOU WOULDN'T CONFESS WHILE WE WERE ALL ALIVE...
...AND KETCHUP LOOKS LIKE BLOOD TO A CAMERA!
IT WAS MY IDEA TO KNOCK OUT MISS RACHEL AND THE MAID.
YOUNG LADIES SHOULD BE SPARED SUCH A TACKY SHOW.
H...HOW LONG HAVE YOU KNOWN IT WAS ME?
FROM THE TIME THIS KID HAD US CHOOSE THE COINS.
YOU REACHED ***WAY OVER*** TO PICK UP THE 10-YEN AT THE FAR END OF THE HOOD.
CHING
THAT'S WHEN IT ALL CLICKED.

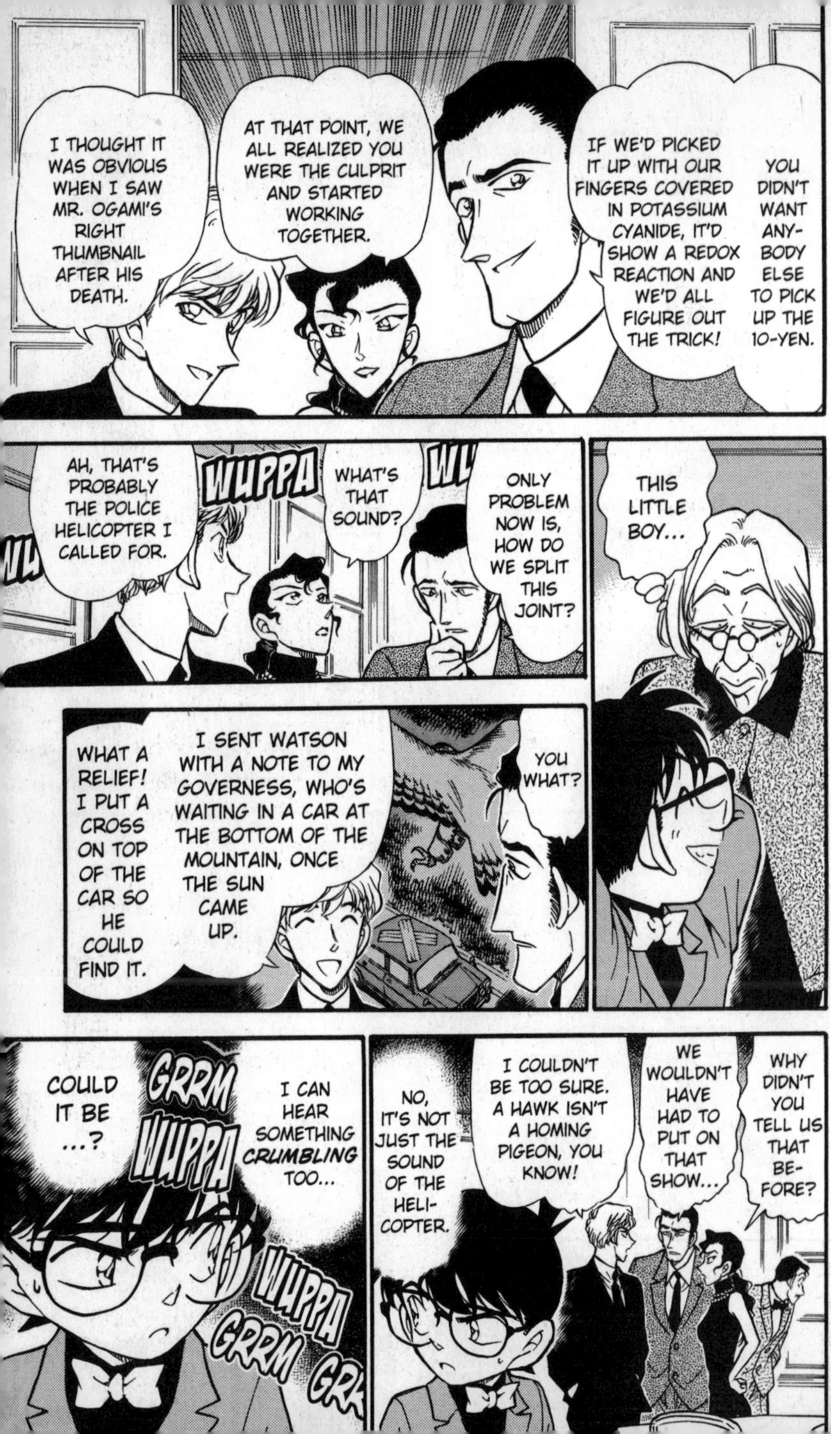
YOU DIDN'T WANT ANYBODY ELSE TO PICK UP THE 10-YEN.
IF WE'D PICKED IT UP WITH OUR FINGERS COVERED IN POTASSIUM CYANIDE, IT'D SHOW A REDOX REACTION AND WE'D ALL FIGURE OUT THE TRICK!
AT THAT POINT, WE ALL REALIZED YOU WERE THE CULPRIT AND STARTED WORKING TOGETHER.
I THOUGHT IT WAS OBVIOUS WHEN I SAW MR. OGAMI'S RIGHT THUMBNAIL AFTER HIS DEATH.
THIS LITTLE BOY...
WU
ONLY PROBLEM NOW IS, HOW DO WE SPLIT THIS JOINT?
WHAT'S THAT SOUND?
WUPPA
AH, THAT'S PROBABLY THE POLICE HELICOPTER I CALLED FOR.
WU
YOU WHAT?
I SENT WATSON WITH A NOTE TO MY GOVERNESS, WHO'S WAITING IN A CAR AT THE BOTTOM OF THE MOUNTAIN, ONCE THE SUN CAME UP.
WHAT A RELIEF! I PUT A CROSS ON TOP OF THE CAR SO HE COULD FIND IT.
WHY DIDN'T YOU TELL US THAT BEFORE?
WE WOULDN'T HAVE HAD TO PUT ON THAT SHOW...
I COULDN'T BE TOO SURE. A HAWK ISN'T A HOMING PIGEON, YOU KNOW!
NO, IT'S NOT JUST THE SOUND OF THE HELICOPTER.
I CAN HEAR SOMETHING CRUMBLING TOO...
GRRM
WUPPA
COULD IT BE ...?
WUPPA
GRRM
GRR

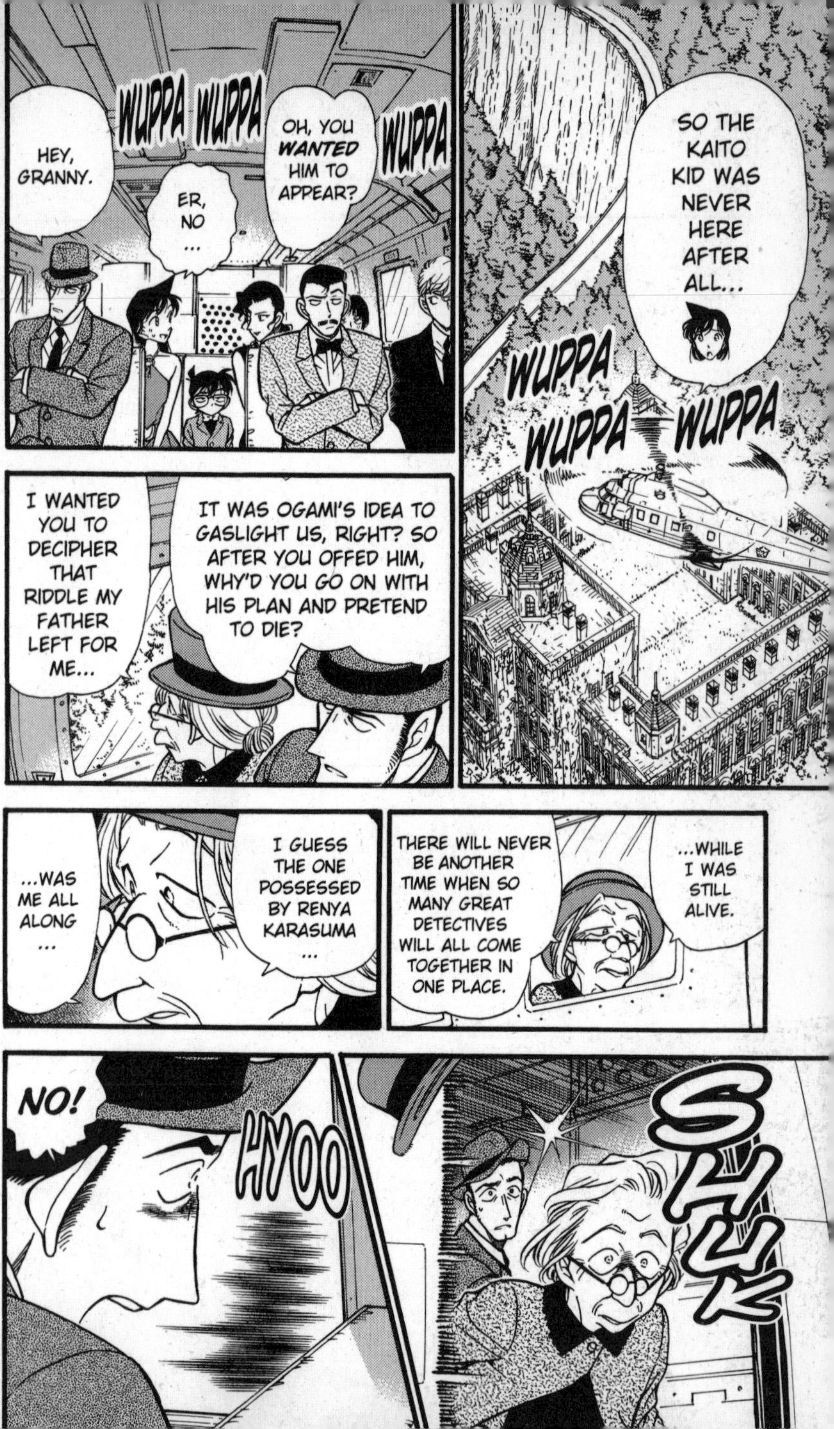
SO THE KAITO KID WAS NEVER HERE AFTER ALL...
WUPPA
WUPPA
WUPPA
WUPPA
OH, YOU WANTED HIM TO APPEAR?
WUPPA WUPPA
ER, NO ...
HEY, GRANNY.
IT WAS OGAMI'S IDEA TO GASLIGHT US, RIGHT? SO AFTER YOU OFFED HIM, WHY'D YOU GO ON WITH HIS PLAN AND PRETEND TO DIE?
I WANTED YOU TO DECIPHER THAT RIDDLE MY FATHER LEFT FOR ME...
...WHILE I WAS STILL ALIVE.
THERE WILL NEVER BE ANOTHER TIME WHEN SO MANY GREAT DETECTIVES WILL ALL COME TOGETHER IN ONE PLACE.
I GUESS THE ONE POSSESSED BY RENYA KARASUMA ...
...WAS ME ALL ALONG ...
SHUK
HYOO
NO!

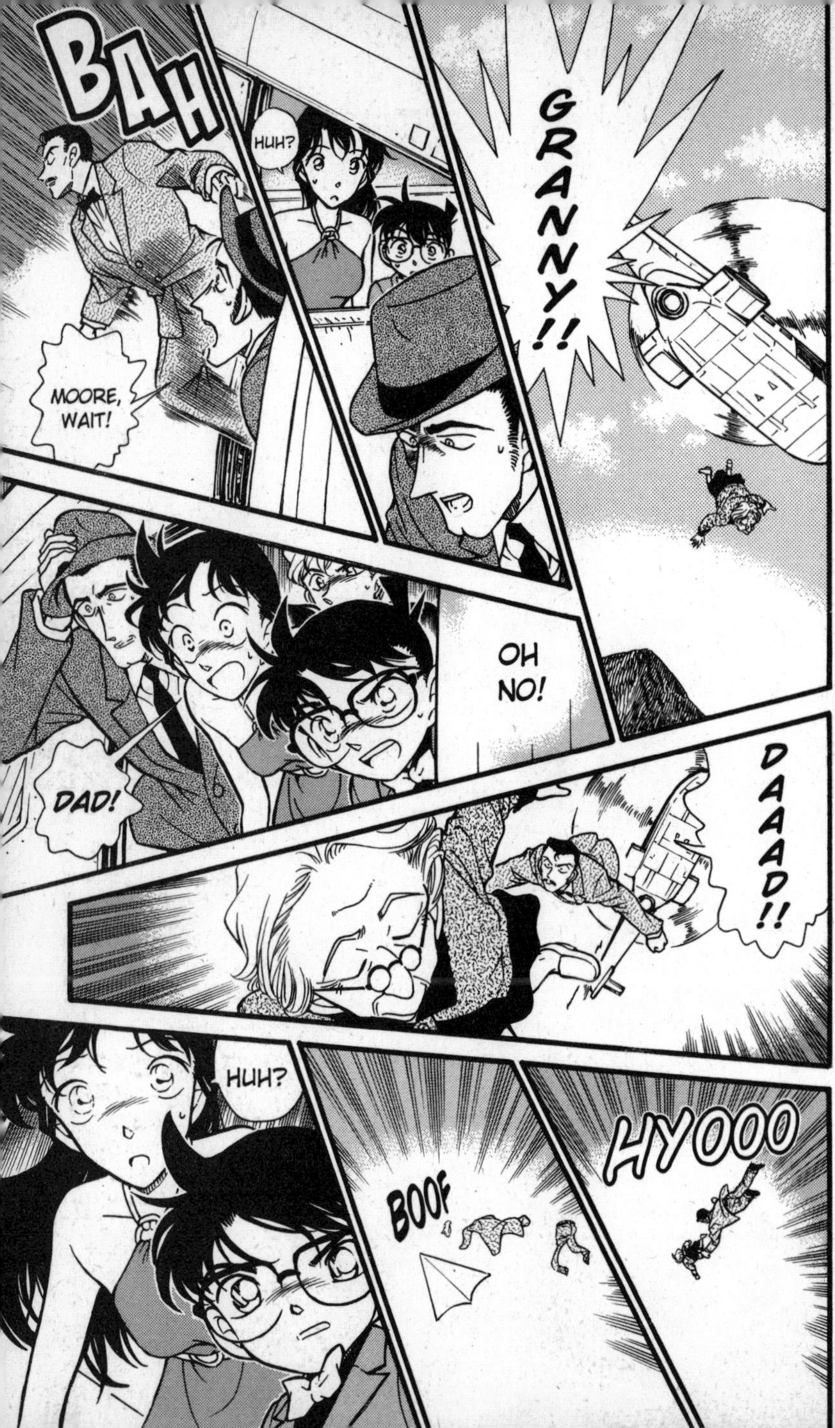
GRANNY!!
HUH?
BAH
MOORE, WAIT!
OH NO!
DAD!
DAAAAD!!
HYOOO
BOOF
HUH?

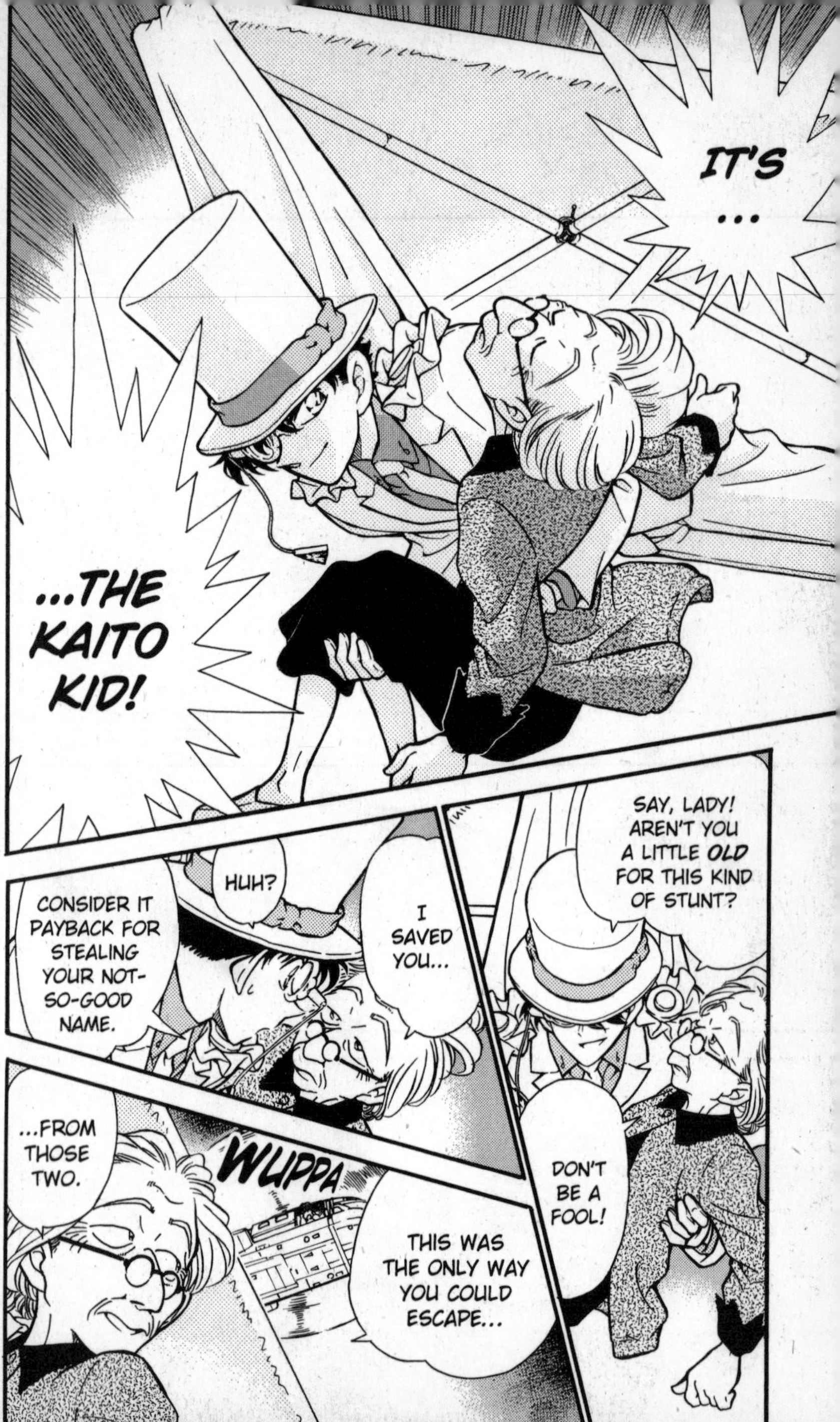
IT'S ...
...THE KAITO KID!
SAY, LADY! AREN'T YOU A LITTLE OLD FOR THIS KIND OF STUNT?
DON'T BE A FOOL!
HUH?
I SAVED YOU...
CONSIDER IT PAYBACK FOR STEALING YOUR NOT-SO-GOOD NAME.
WUPPA
THIS WAS THE ONLY WAY YOU COULD ESCAPE...
...FROM THOSE TWO.

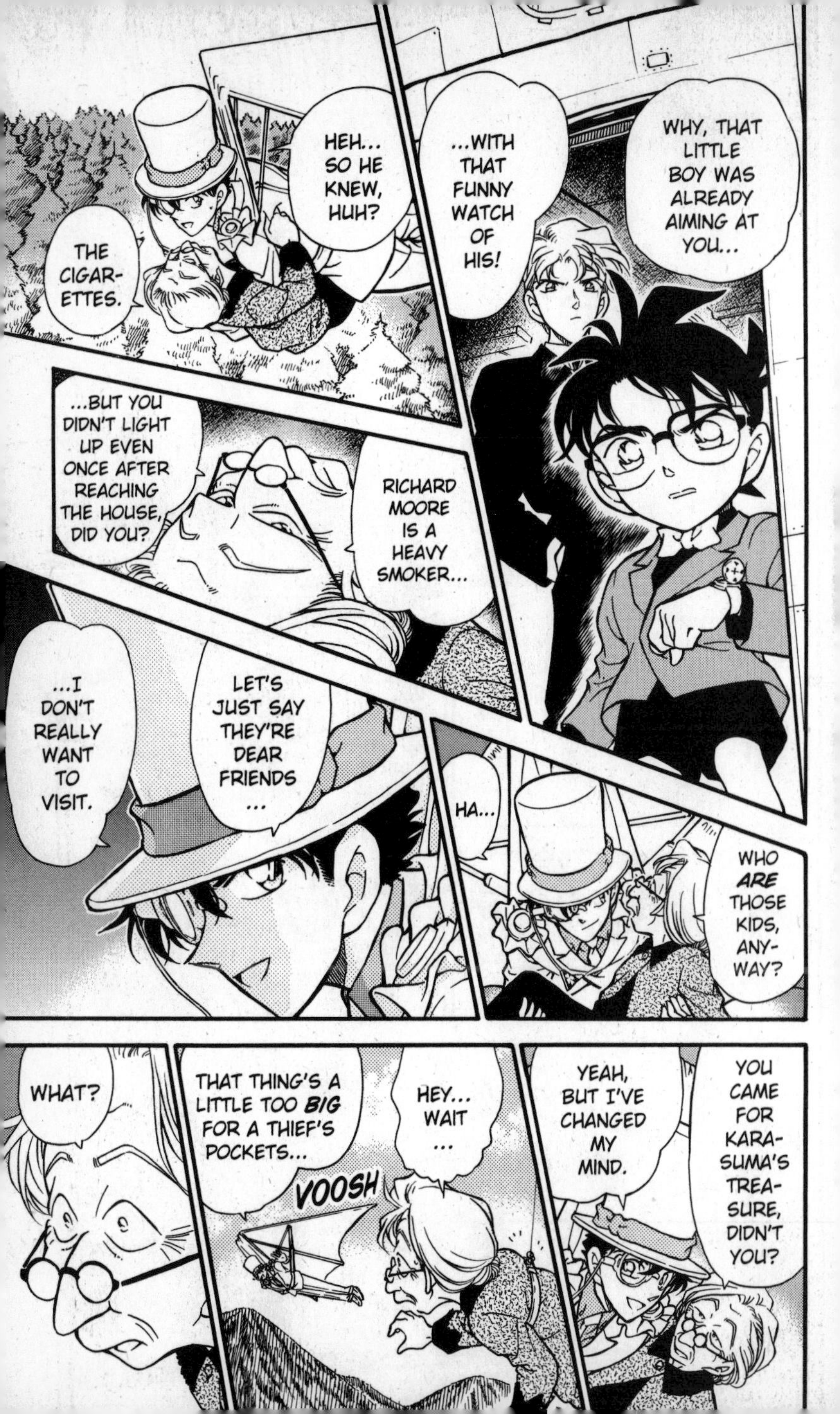
WHY, THAT LITTLE BOY WAS ALREADY AIMING AT YOU...
...WITH THAT FUNNY WATCH OF HIS!
HEH... SO HE KNEW, HUH?
THE CIGARETTES.
RICHARD MOORE IS A HEAVY SMOKER...
...BUT YOU DIDN'T LIGHT UP EVEN ONCE AFTER REACHING THE HOUSE, DID YOU?
WHO *ARE* THOSE KIDS, ANYWAY?
HA...
LET'S JUST SAY THEY'RE DEAR FRIENDS...
...I DON'T REALLY WANT TO VISIT.
YOU CAME FOR KARASUMA'S TREASURE, DIDN'T YOU?
YEAH, BUT I'VE CHANGED MY MIND.
HEY... WAIT...
VOOSH
THAT THING'S A LITTLE TOO *BIG* FOR A THIEF'S POCKETS...
WHAT?

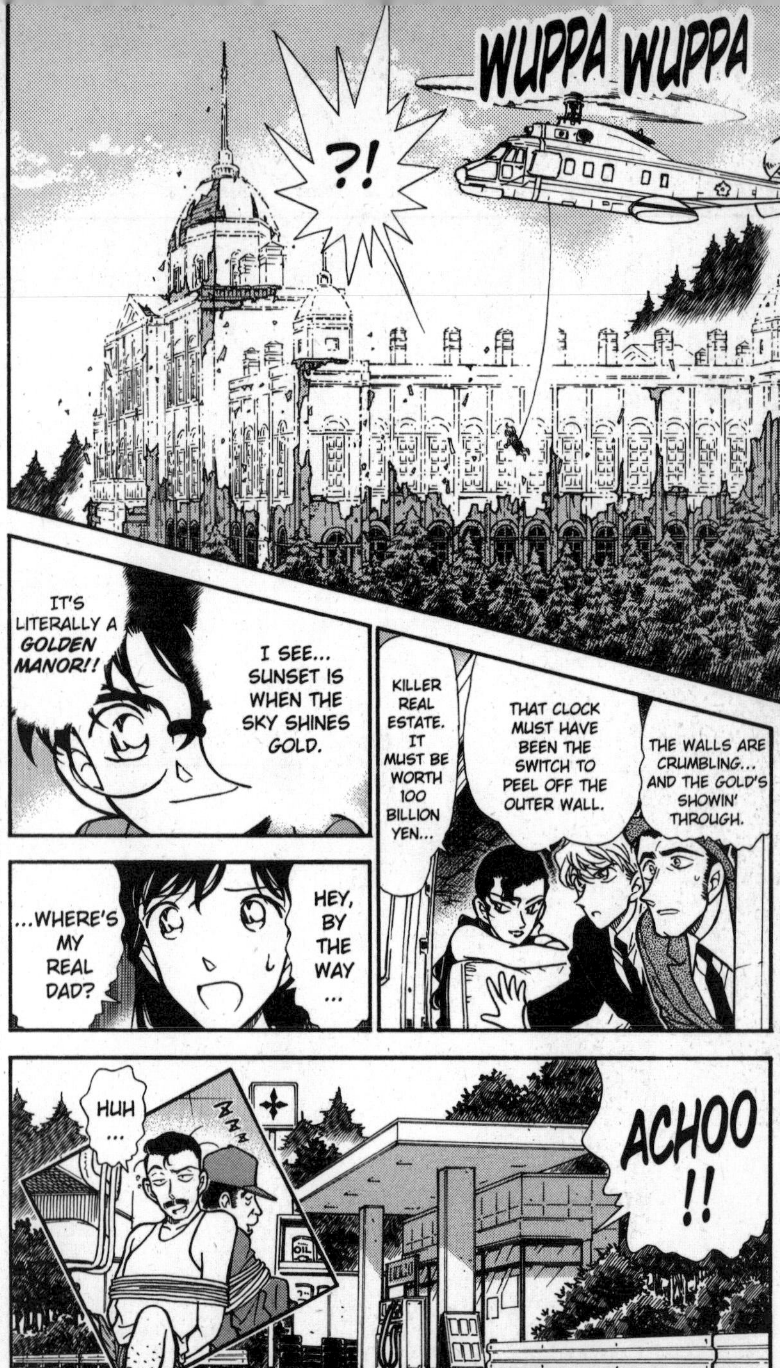
WUPPA WUPPA
?!
THE WALLS ARE CRUMBLING... AND THE GOLD'S SHOWIN' THROUGH.
THAT CLOCK MUST HAVE BEEN THE SWITCH TO PEEL OFF THE OUTER WALL.
KILLER REAL ESTATE. IT MUST BE WORTH 100 BILLION YEN...
I SEE... SUNSET IS WHEN THE SKY SHINES GOLD.
IT'S LITERALLY A GOLDEN MANOR!!
HEY, BY THE WAY...
...WHERE'S MY REAL DAD?
ACHOO!!
HUH...

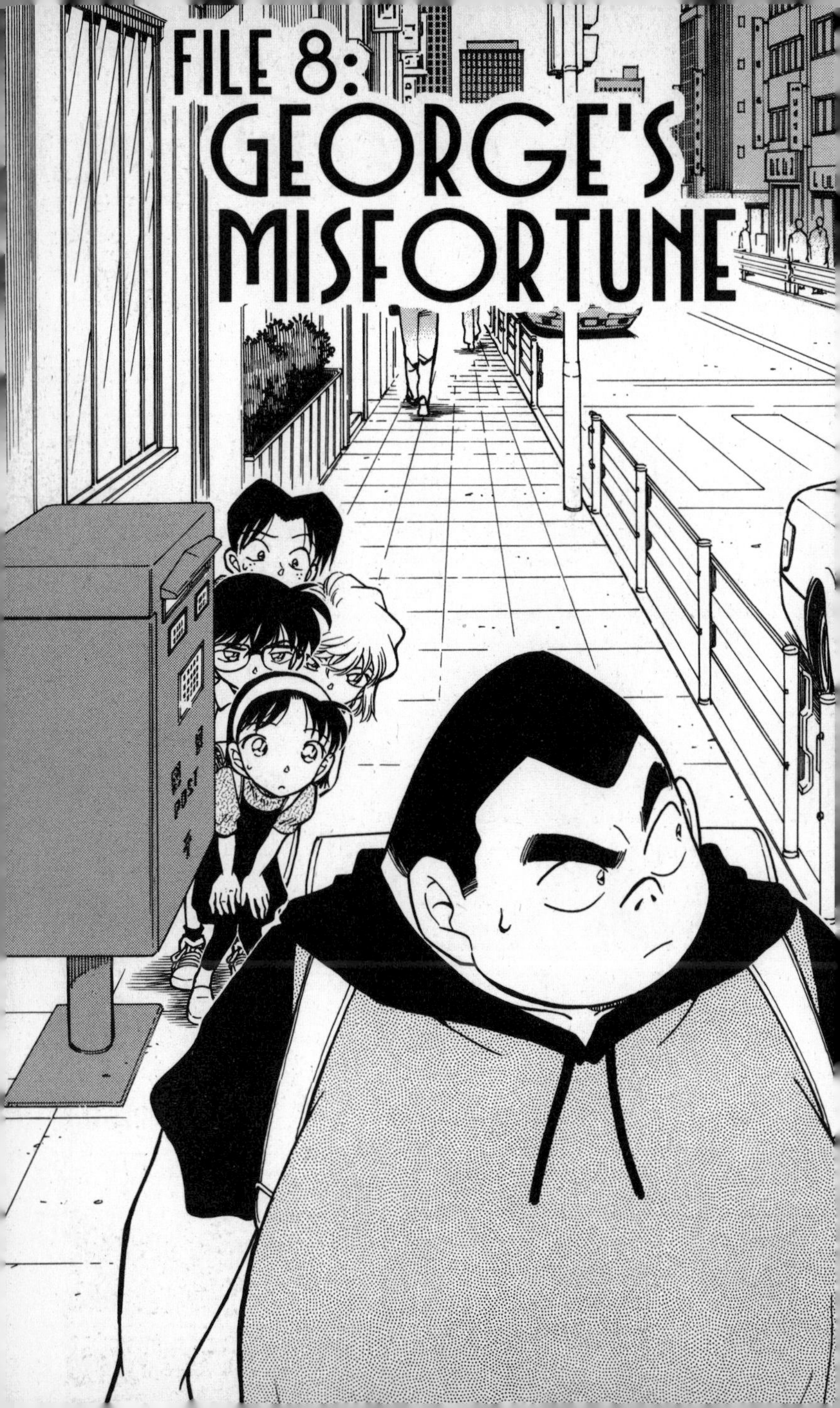
FILE 8:
GEORGE'S MISFORTUNE
POST

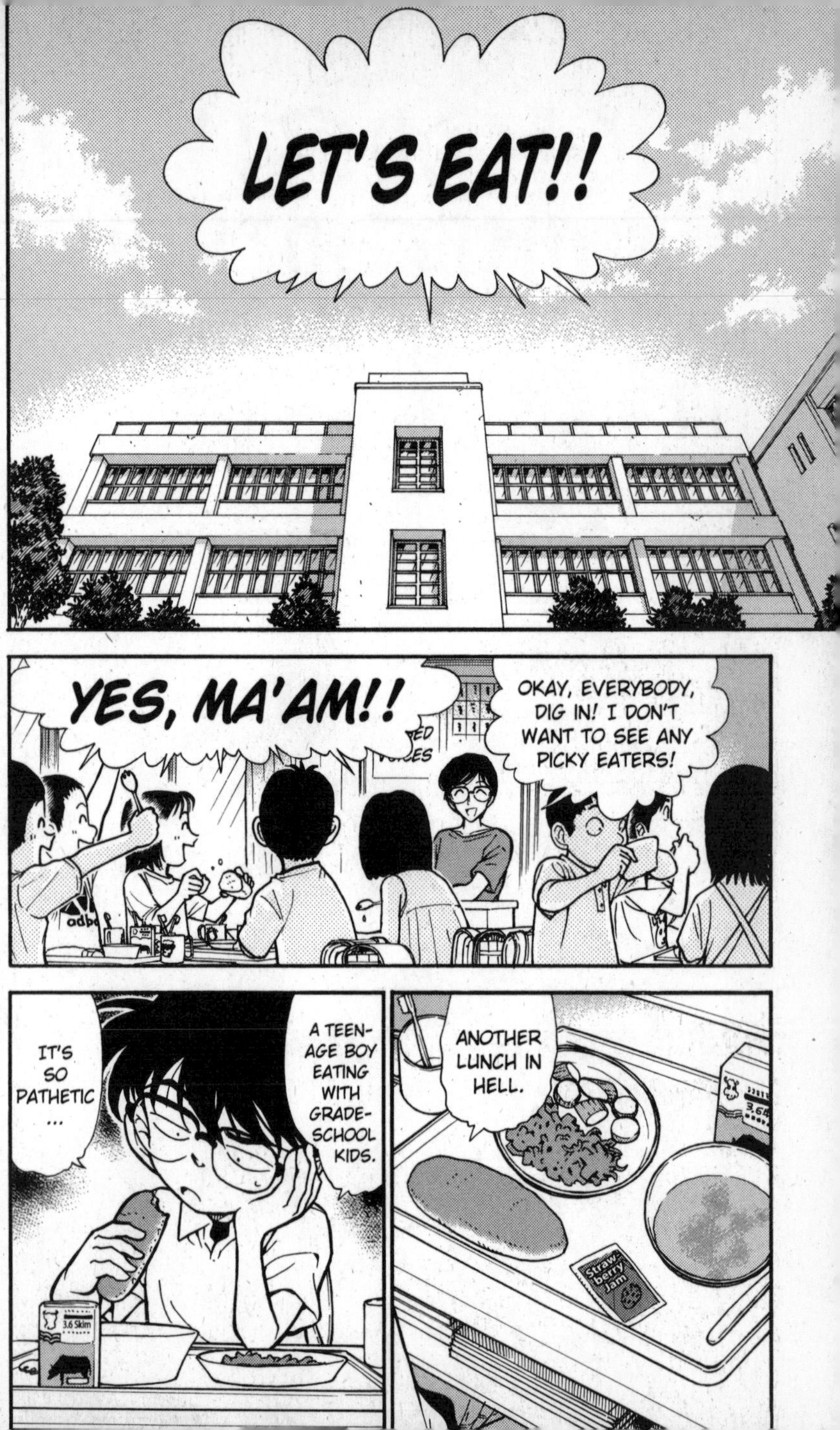
LET'S EAT!!
OKAY, EVERYBODY, DIG IN! I DON'T WANT TO SEE ANY PICKY EATERS!
YES, MA'AM!!
ANOTHER LUNCH IN HELL.
Straw-berry Jam
A TEEN-AGE BOY EATING WITH GRADE-SCHOOL KIDS.
IT'S SO PATHETIC ...
3.6 Skim

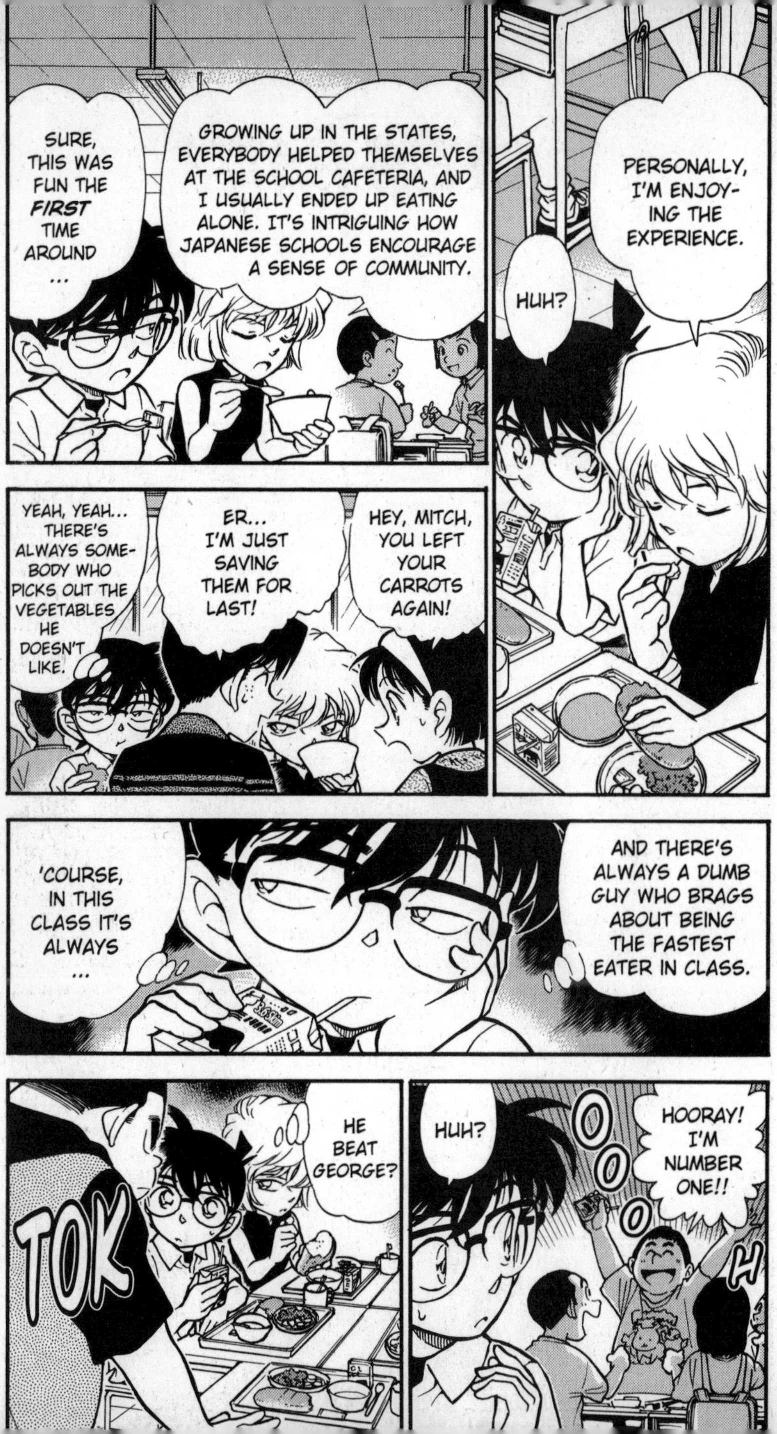
PERSONALLY, I'M ENJOYING THE EXPERIENCE.
HUH?
GROWING UP IN THE STATES, EVERYBODY HELPED THEMSELVES AT THE SCHOOL CAFETERIA, AND I USUALLY ENDED UP EATING ALONE. IT'S INTRIGUING HOW JAPANESE SCHOOLS ENCOURAGE A SENSE OF COMMUNITY.
SURE, THIS WAS FUN THE *FIRST* TIME AROUND ...
HEY, MITCH, YOU LEFT YOUR CARROTS AGAIN!
ER... I'M JUST SAVING THEM FOR LAST!
YEAH, YEAH... THERE'S ALWAYS SOMEBODY WHO PICKS OUT THE VEGETABLES HE DOESN'T LIKE.
AND THERE'S ALWAYS A DUMB GUY WHO BRAGS ABOUT BEING THE FASTEST EATER IN CLASS.
'COURSE, IN THIS CLASS IT'S ALWAYS ...
HOORAY! I'M NUMBER ONE!!
OOOOH
HUH?
HE BEAT GEORGE?
TOK

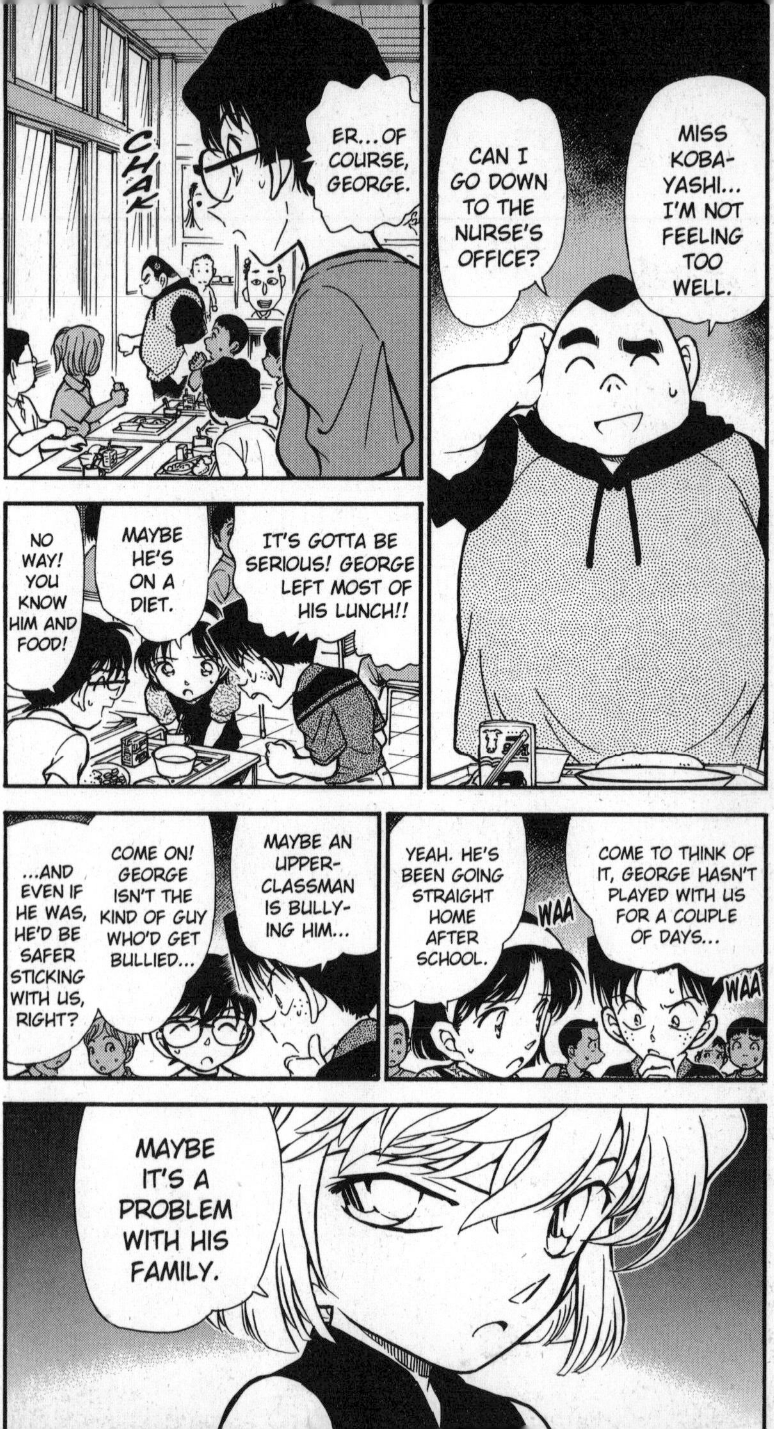
MISS KOBA-YASHI... I'M NOT FEELING TOO WELL.
CAN I GO DOWN TO THE NURSE'S OFFICE?
CHAK
ER...OF COURSE, GEORGE.
IT'S GOTTA BE SERIOUS! GEORGE LEFT MOST OF HIS LUNCH!!
MAYBE HE'S ON A DIET.
NO WAY! YOU KNOW HIM AND FOOD!
COME TO THINK OF IT, GEORGE HASN'T PLAYED WITH US FOR A COUPLE OF DAYS...
WAA
YEAH. HE'S BEEN GOING STRAIGHT HOME AFTER SCHOOL.
WAA
MAYBE AN UPPER-CLASSMAN IS BULLY-ING HIM...
COME ON! GEORGE ISN'T THE KIND OF GUY WHO'D GET BULLIED...
...AND EVEN IF HE WAS, HE'D BE SAFER STICKING WITH US, RIGHT?
MAYBE IT'S A PROBLEM WITH HIS FAMILY.

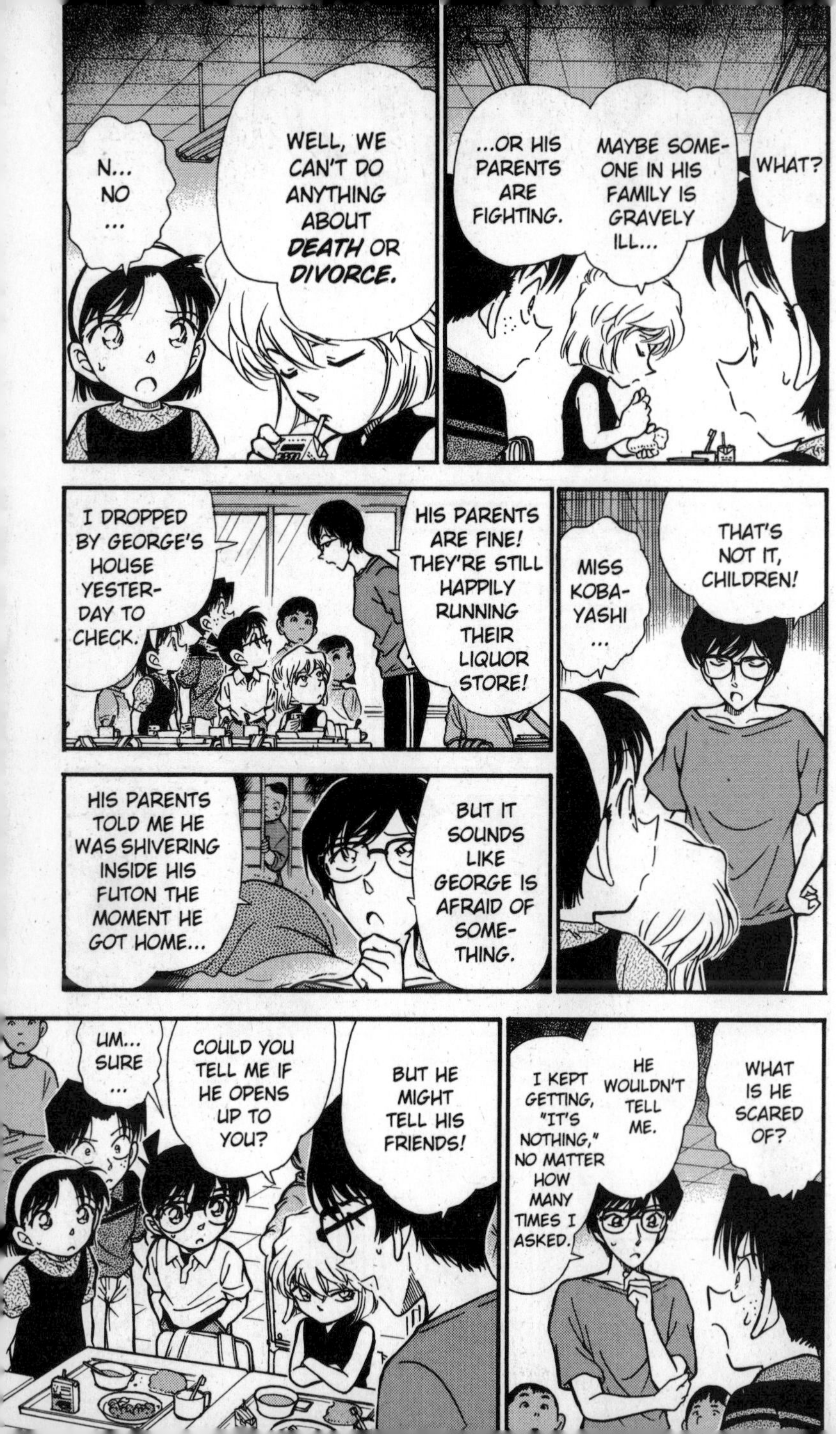
WHAT?
MAYBE SOME-ONE IN HIS FAMILY IS GRAVELY ILL...
...OR HIS PARENTS ARE FIGHTING.
WELL, WE CAN'T DO ANYTHING ABOUT *DEATH* OR *DIVORCE.*
N... NO ...
THAT'S NOT IT, CHILDREN!
MISS KOBA-YASHI ...
HIS PARENTS ARE FINE! THEY'RE STILL HAPPILY RUNNING THEIR LIQUOR STORE!
I DROPPED BY GEORGE'S HOUSE YESTER-DAY TO CHECK.
BUT IT SOUNDS LIKE GEORGE IS AFRAID OF SOME-THING.
HIS PARENTS TOLD ME HE WAS SHIVERING INSIDE HIS FUTON THE MOMENT HE GOT HOME...
WHAT IS HE SCARED OF?
HE WOULDN'T TELL ME.
I KEPT GETTING, "IT'S NOTHING," NO MATTER HOW MANY TIMES I ASKED.
BUT HE MIGHT TELL HIS FRIENDS!
COULD YOU TELL ME IF HE OPENS UP TO YOU?
UM... SURE ...

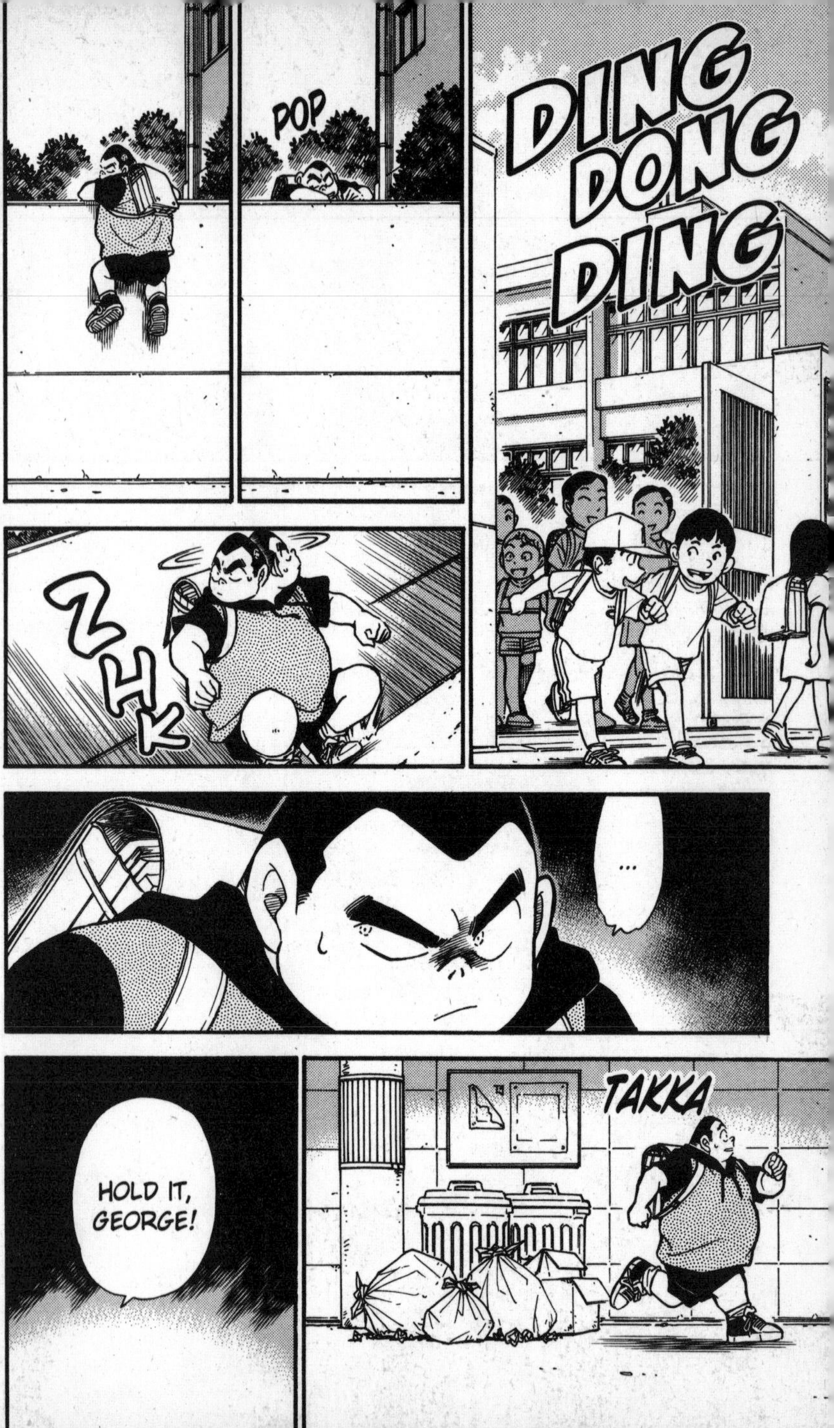
DING DONG DING
POP
ZHK
...
TAKKA
HOLD IT, GEORGE!

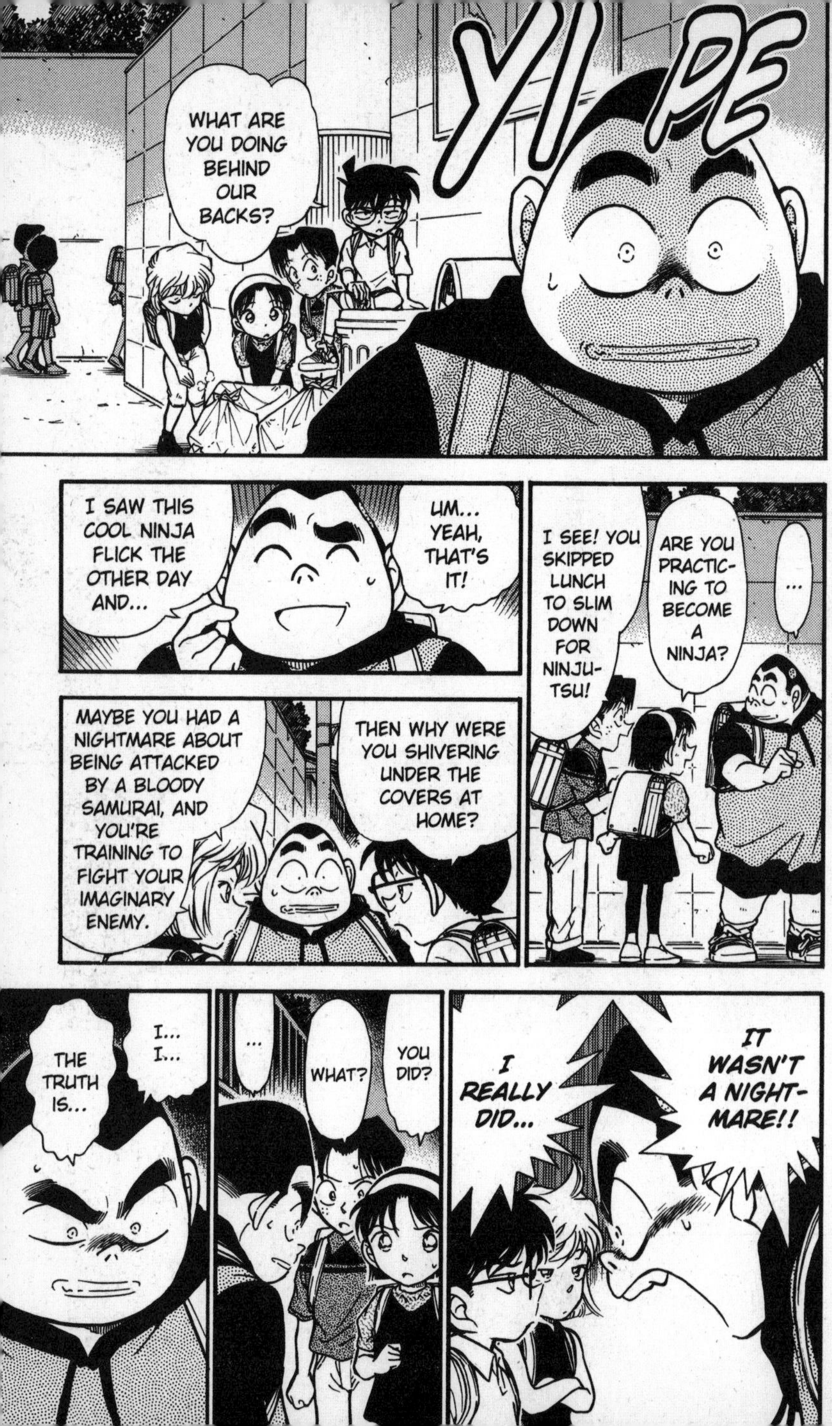
YIPE
WHAT ARE YOU DOING BEHIND OUR BACKS?
...
ARE YOU PRACTIC-ING TO BECOME A NINJA?
I SEE! YOU SKIPPED LUNCH TO SLIM DOWN FOR NINJU-TSU!
UM... YEAH, THAT'S IT!
I SAW THIS COOL NINJA FLICK THE OTHER DAY AND...
THEN WHY WERE YOU SHIVERING UNDER THE COVERS AT HOME?
MAYBE YOU HAD A NIGHTMARE ABOUT BEING ATTACKED BY A BLOODY SAMURAI, AND YOU'RE TRAINING TO FIGHT YOUR IMAGINARY ENEMY.
IT WASN'T A NIGHT-MARE!!
I REALLY DID...
YOU DID?
WHAT?
...
I... I...
THE TRUTH IS...

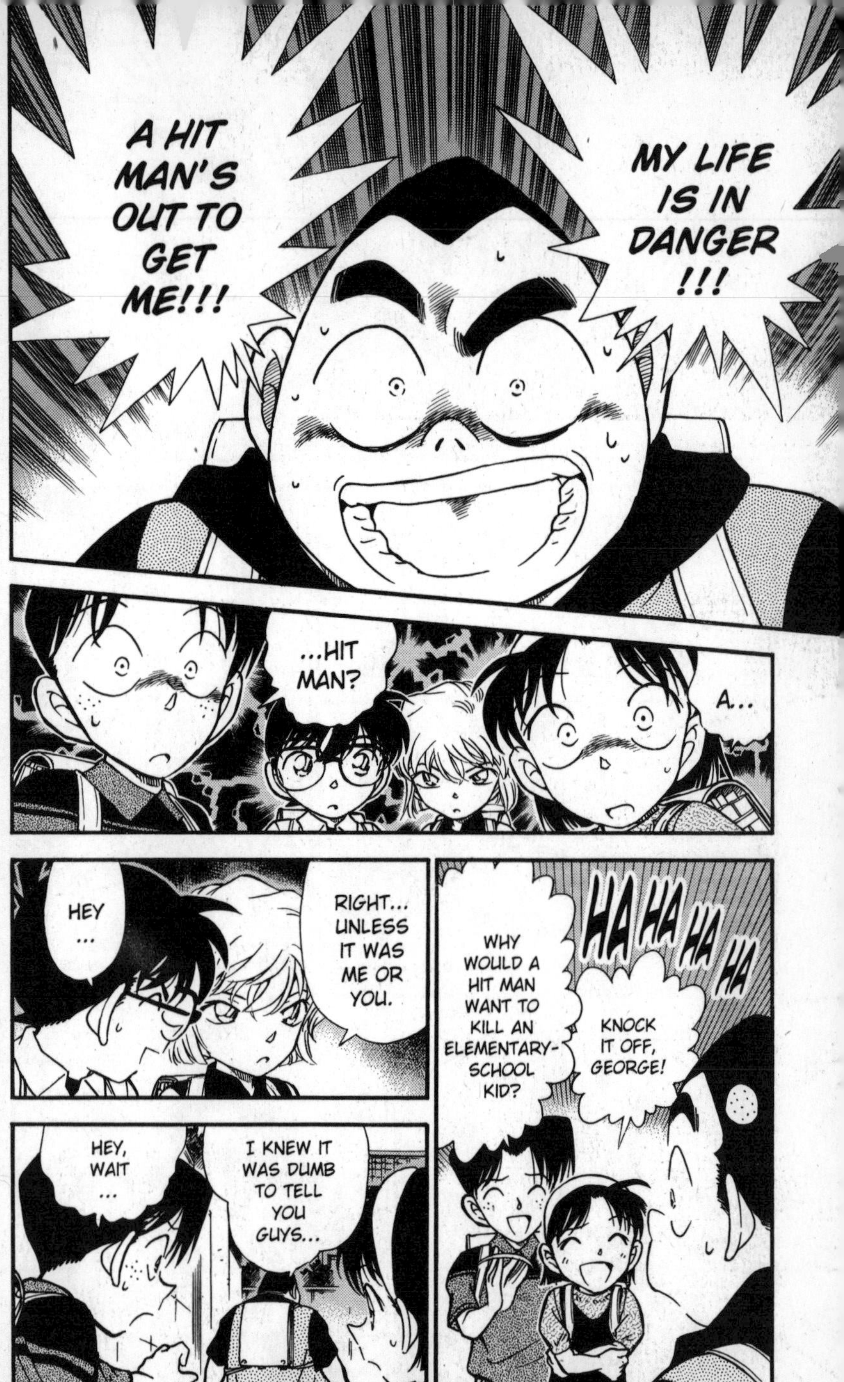
MY LIFE IS IN DANGER!!!
A HIT MAN'S OUT TO GET ME!!!
A...
...HIT MAN?
HA HA HA HA HA
WHY WOULD A HIT MAN WANT TO KILL AN ELEMENTARY-SCHOOL KID?
KNOCK IT OFF, GEORGE!
RIGHT... UNLESS IT WAS ME OR YOU.
HEY ...
I KNEW IT WAS DUMB TO TELL YOU GUYS...
HEY, WAIT ...

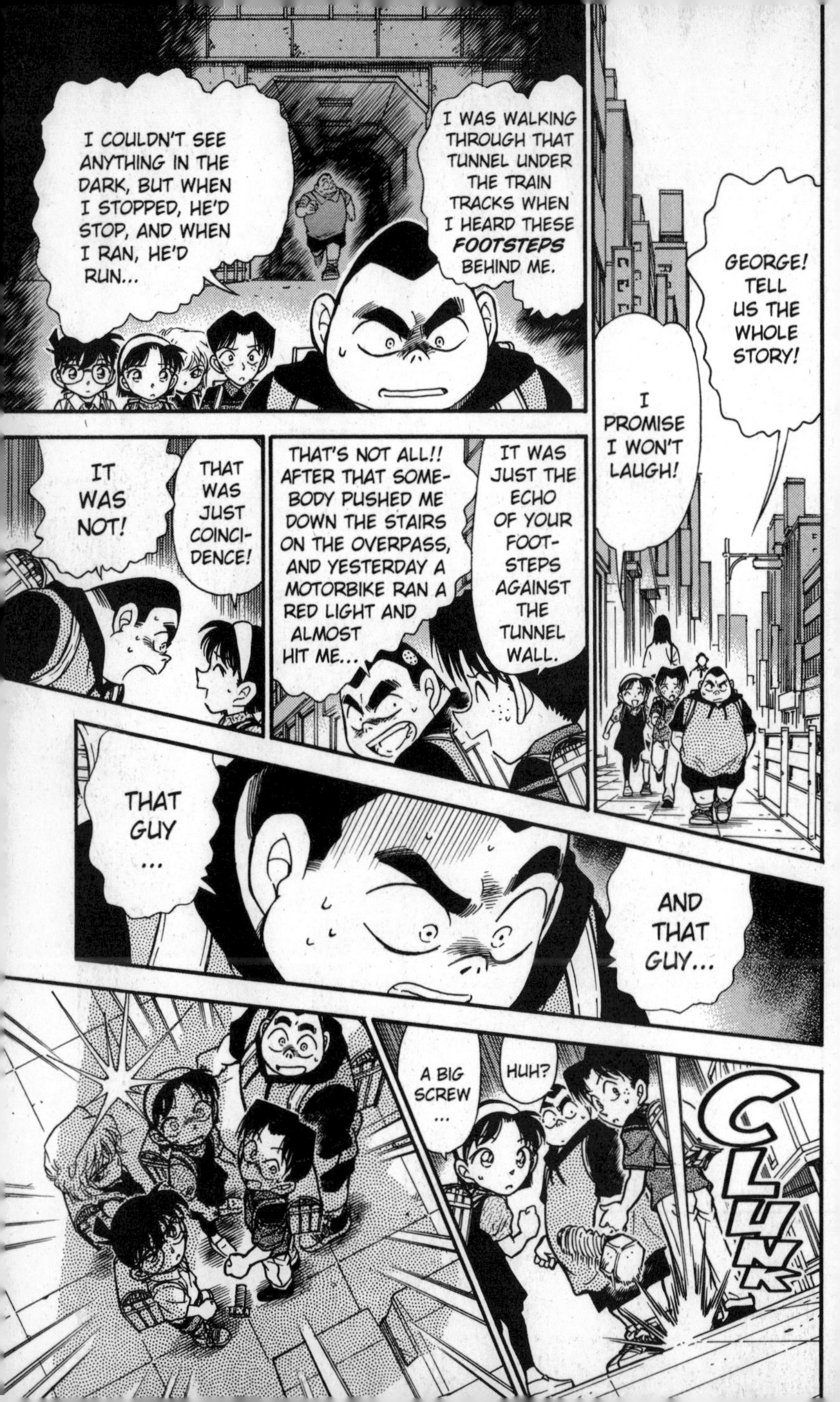
GEORGE! TELL US THE WHOLE STORY!
I PROMISE I WON'T LAUGH!
I WAS WALKING THROUGH THAT TUNNEL UNDER THE TRAIN TRACKS WHEN I HEARD THESE ***FOOTSTEPS*** BEHIND ME.
I COULDN'T SEE ANYTHING IN THE DARK, BUT WHEN I STOPPED, HE'D STOP, AND WHEN I RAN, HE'D RUN...
IT WAS JUST THE ECHO OF YOUR FOOT-STEPS AGAINST THE TUNNEL WALL.
THAT'S NOT ALL!! AFTER THAT SOME-BODY PUSHED ME DOWN THE STAIRS ON THE OVERPASS, AND YESTERDAY A MOTORBIKE RAN A RED LIGHT AND ALMOST HIT ME...
THAT WAS JUST COINCI-DENCE!
IT WAS NOT!
THAT GUY ...
AND THAT GUY...
CLUNK
HUH?
A BIG SCREW ...

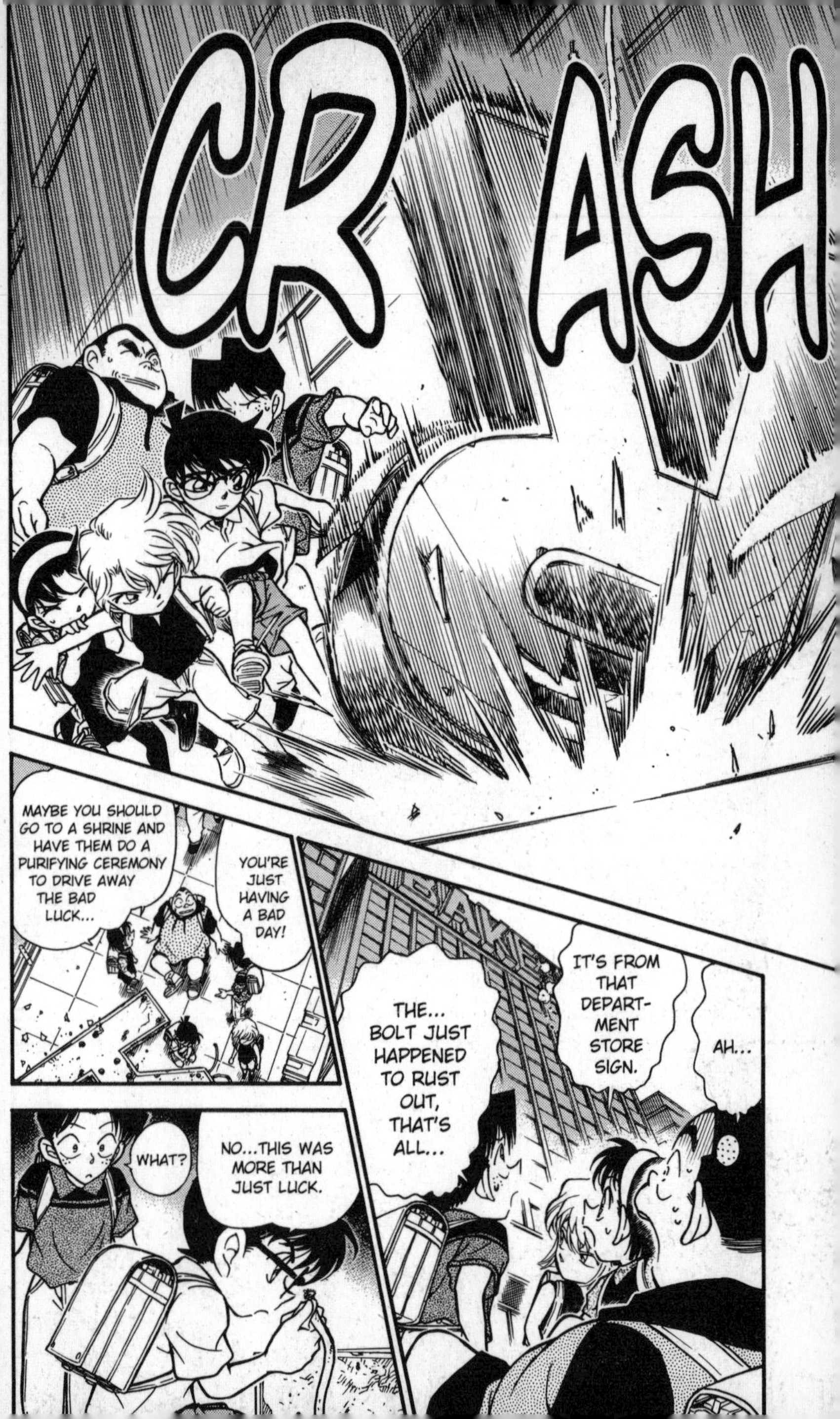
CRASH
AH...
IT'S FROM THAT DEPARTMENT STORE SIGN.
THE... BOLT JUST HAPPENED TO RUST OUT, THAT'S ALL...
YOU'RE JUST HAVING A BAD DAY!
MAYBE YOU SHOULD GO TO A SHRINE AND HAVE THEM DO A PURIFYING CEREMONY TO DRIVE AWAY THE BAD LUCK...
NO...THIS WAS MORE THAN JUST LUCK.
WHAT?

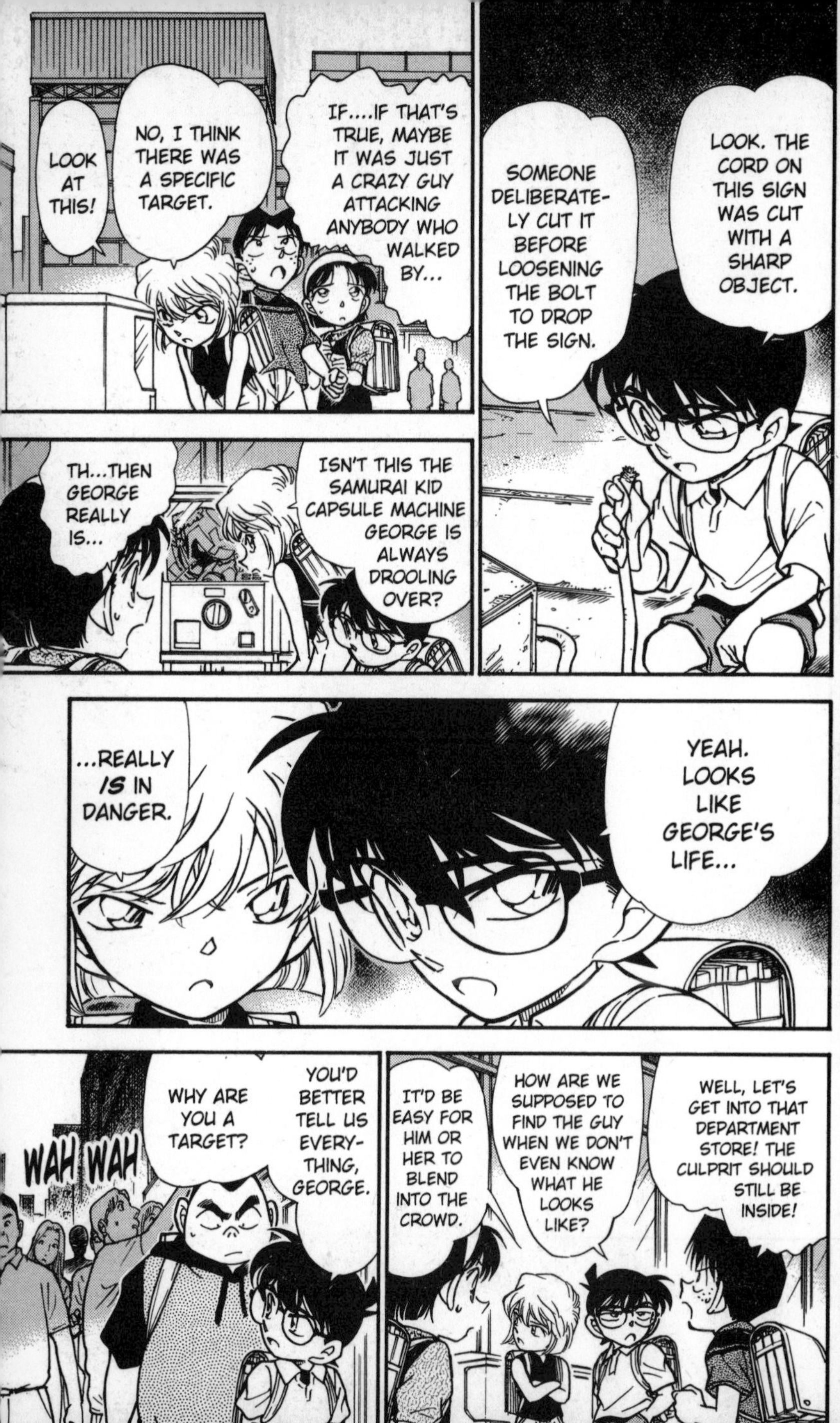
LOOK. THE CORD ON THIS SIGN WAS CUT WITH A SHARP OBJECT.
SOMEONE DELIBERATE-LY CUT IT BEFORE LOOSENING THE BOLT TO DROP THE SIGN.
IF....IF THAT'S TRUE, MAYBE IT WAS JUST A CRAZY GUY ATTACKING ANYBODY WHO WALKED BY...
NO, I THINK THERE WAS A SPECIFIC TARGET.
LOOK AT THIS!
ISN'T THIS THE SAMURAI KID CAPSULE MACHINE GEORGE IS ALWAYS DROOLING OVER?
TH...THEN GEORGE REALLY IS...
YEAH. LOOKS LIKE GEORGE'S LIFE...
...REALLY *IS* IN DANGER.
WELL, LET'S GET INTO THAT DEPARTMENT STORE! THE CULPRIT SHOULD STILL BE INSIDE!
HOW ARE WE SUPPOSED TO FIND THE GUY WHEN WE DON'T EVEN KNOW WHAT HE LOOKS LIKE?
IT'D BE EASY FOR HIM OR HER TO BLEND INTO THE CROWD.
YOU'D BETTER TELL US EVERY-THING, GEORGE.
WHY ARE YOU A TARGET?
WAH WAH

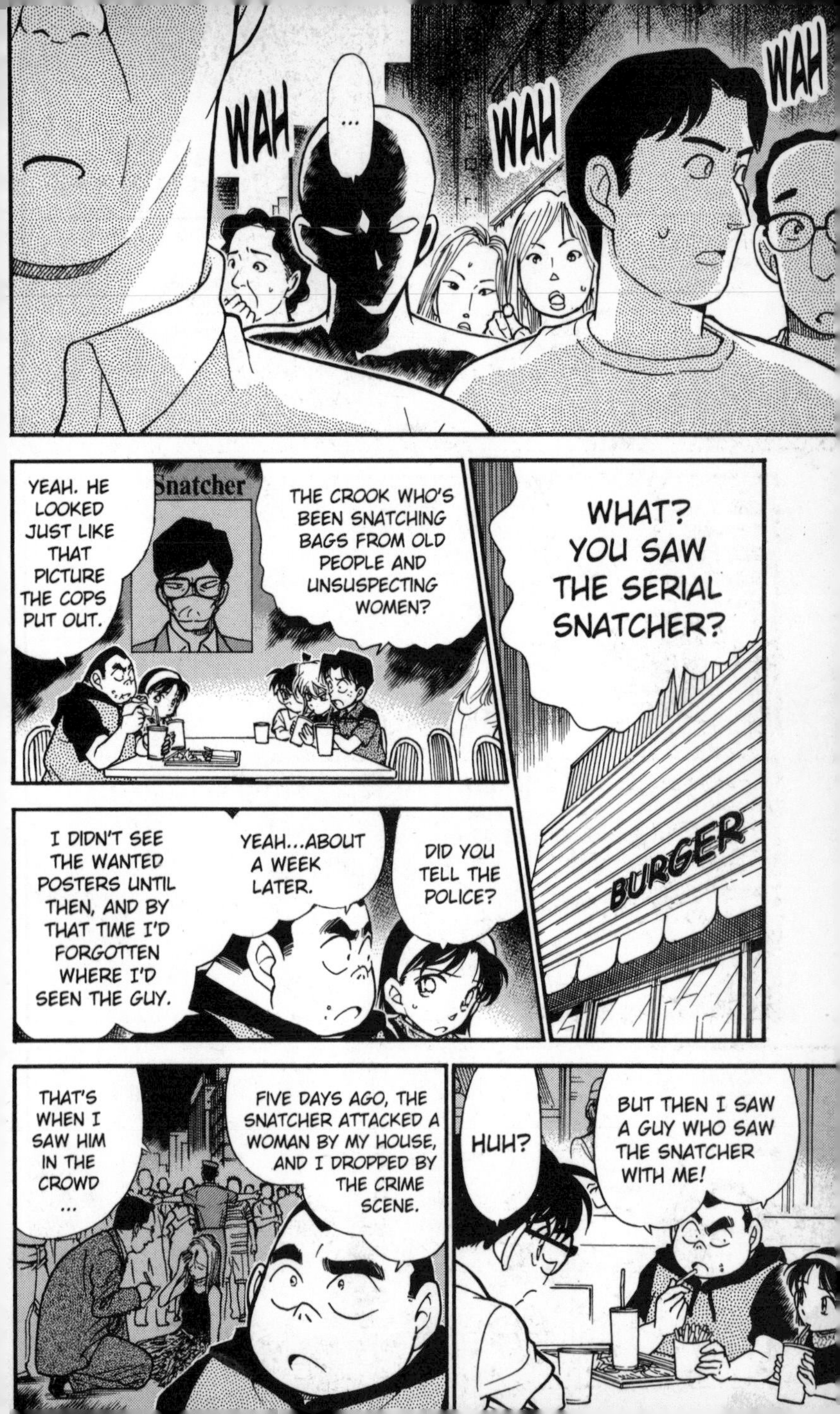
WAH
WAH
...
WAH
WHAT? YOU SAW THE SERIAL SNATCHER?
BURGER
THE CROOK WHO'S BEEN SNATCHING BAGS FROM OLD PEOPLE AND UNSUSPECTING WOMEN?
Snatcher
YEAH. HE LOOKED JUST LIKE THAT PICTURE THE COPS PUT OUT.
DID YOU TELL THE POLICE?
YEAH...ABOUT A WEEK LATER.
I DIDN'T SEE THE WANTED POSTERS UNTIL THEN, AND BY THAT TIME I'D FORGOTTEN WHERE I'D SEEN THE GUY.
BUT THEN I SAW A GUY WHO SAW THE SNATCHER WITH ME!
HUH?
FIVE DAYS AGO, THE SNATCHER ATTACKED A WOMAN BY MY HOUSE, AND I DROPPED BY THE CRIME SCENE.
THAT'S WHEN I SAW HIM IN THE CROWD ...

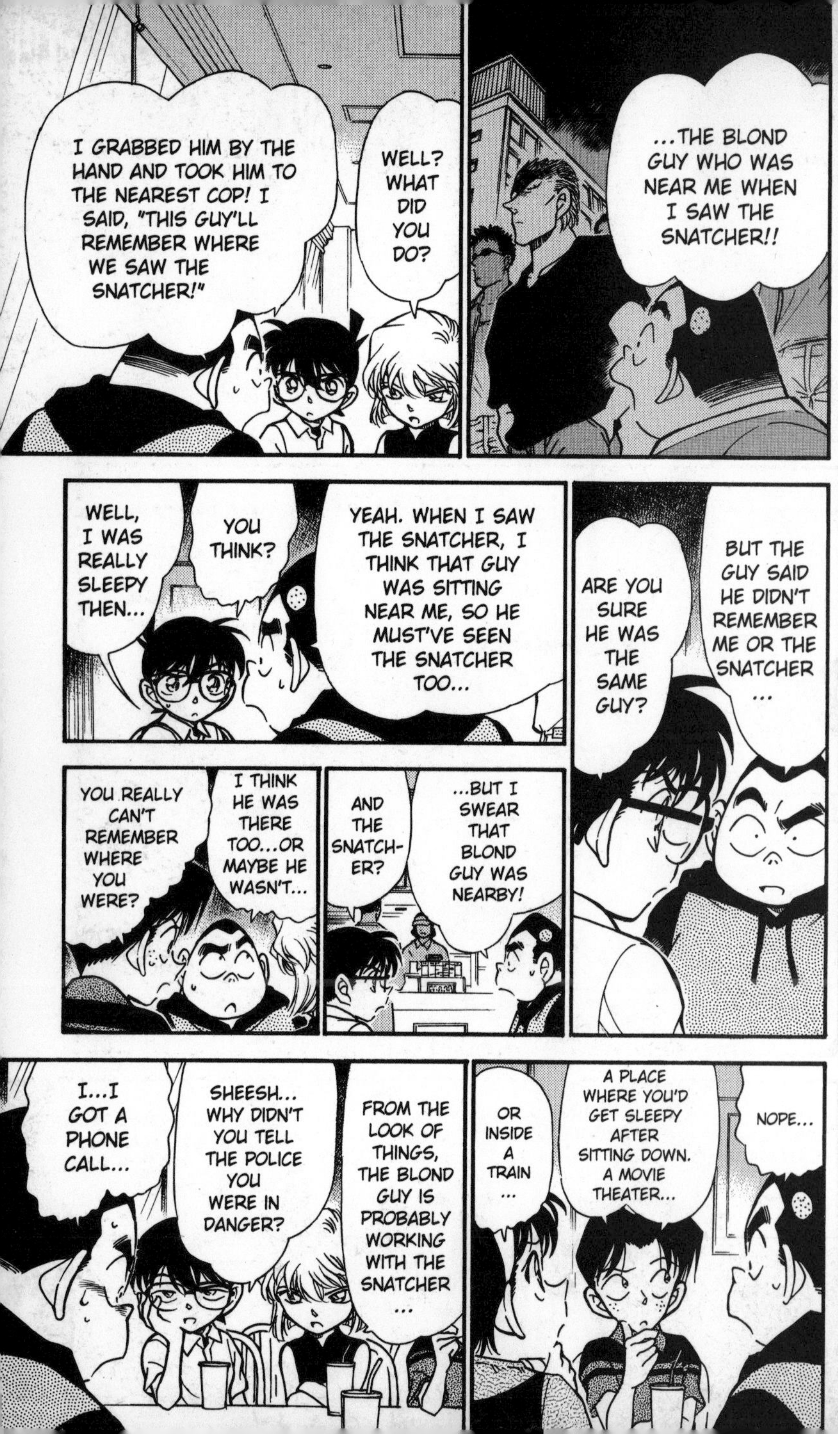
...THE BLOND GUY WHO WAS NEAR ME WHEN I SAW THE SNATCHER!!
WELL? WHAT DID YOU DO?
I GRABBED HIM BY THE HAND AND TOOK HIM TO THE NEAREST COP! I SAID, "THIS GUY'LL REMEMBER WHERE WE SAW THE SNATCHER!"
BUT THE GUY SAID HE DIDN'T REMEMBER ME OR THE SNATCHER...
ARE YOU SURE HE WAS THE SAME GUY?
YEAH. WHEN I SAW THE SNATCHER, I THINK THAT GUY WAS SITTING NEAR ME, SO HE MUST'VE SEEN THE SNATCHER TOO...
YOU THINK?
WELL, I WAS REALLY SLEEPY THEN...
...BUT I SWEAR THAT BLOND GUY WAS NEARBY!
AND THE SNATCH-ER?
I THINK HE WAS THERE TOO...OR MAYBE HE WASN'T...
YOU REALLY CAN'T REMEMBER WHERE YOU WERE?
NOPE...
A PLACE WHERE YOU'D GET SLEEPY AFTER SITTING DOWN. A MOVIE THEATER...
OR INSIDE A TRAIN...
FROM THE LOOK OF THINGS, THE BLOND GUY IS PROBABLY WORKING WITH THE SNATCHER...
SHEESH... WHY DIDN'T YOU TELL THE POLICE YOU WERE IN DANGER?
I...I GOT A PHONE CALL...

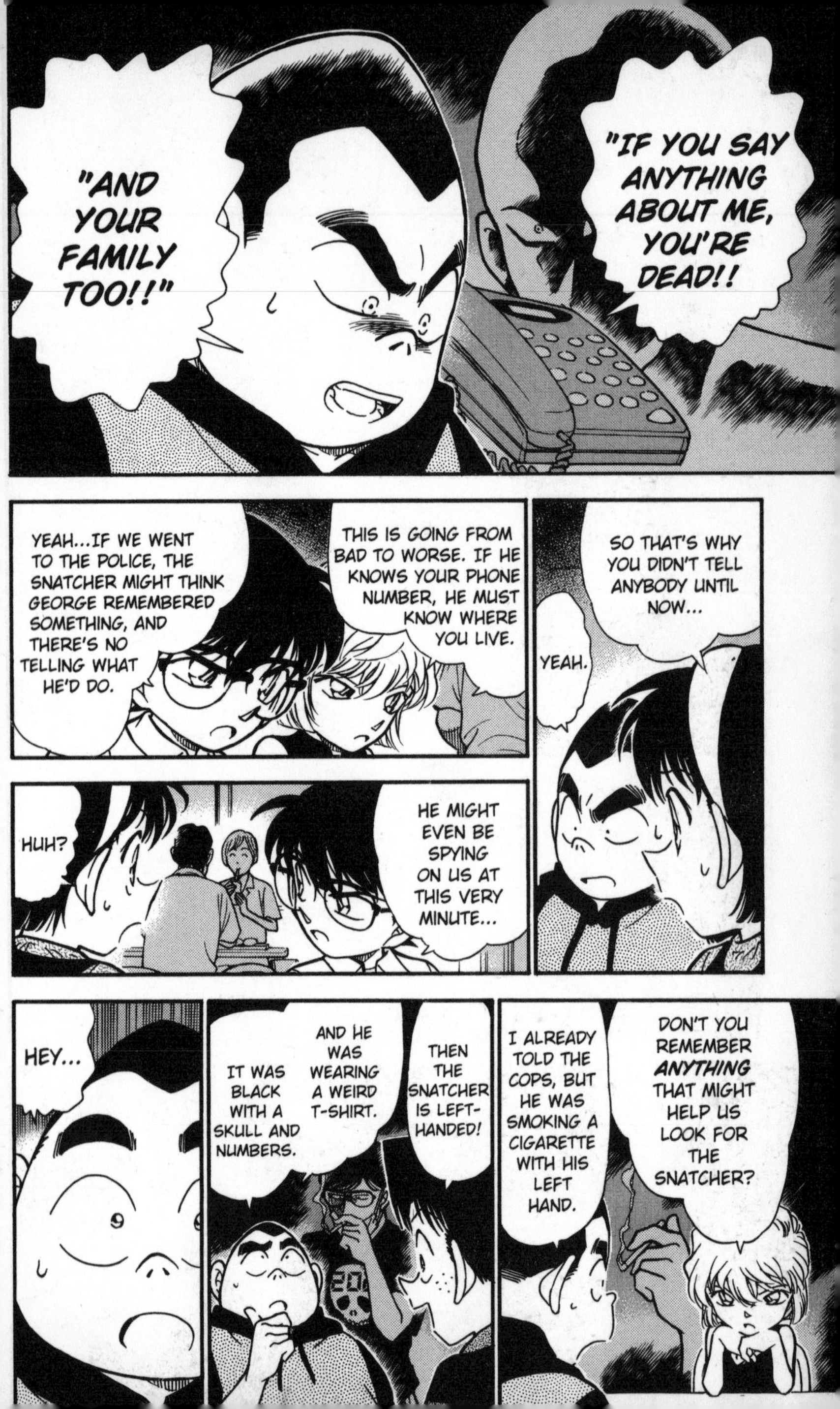
"IF YOU SAY ANYTHING ABOUT ME, YOU'RE DEAD!!
"AND YOUR FAMILY TOO!!"
SO THAT'S WHY YOU DIDN'T TELL ANYBODY UNTIL NOW...
YEAH.
THIS IS GOING FROM BAD TO WORSE. IF HE KNOWS YOUR PHONE NUMBER, HE MUST KNOW WHERE YOU LIVE.
YEAH...IF WE WENT TO THE POLICE, THE SNATCHER MIGHT THINK GEORGE REMEMBERED SOMETHING, AND THERE'S NO TELLING WHAT HE'D DO.
HE MIGHT EVEN BE SPYING ON US AT THIS VERY MINUTE...
HUH?
DON'T YOU REMEMBER *ANYTHING* THAT MIGHT HELP US LOOK FOR THE SNATCHER?
I ALREADY TOLD THE COPS, BUT HE WAS SMOKING A CIGARETTE WITH HIS LEFT HAND.
THEN THE SNATCHER IS LEFT-HANDED!
AND HE WAS WEARING A WEIRD T-SHIRT.
IT WAS BLACK WITH A SKULL AND NUMBERS.
HEY...

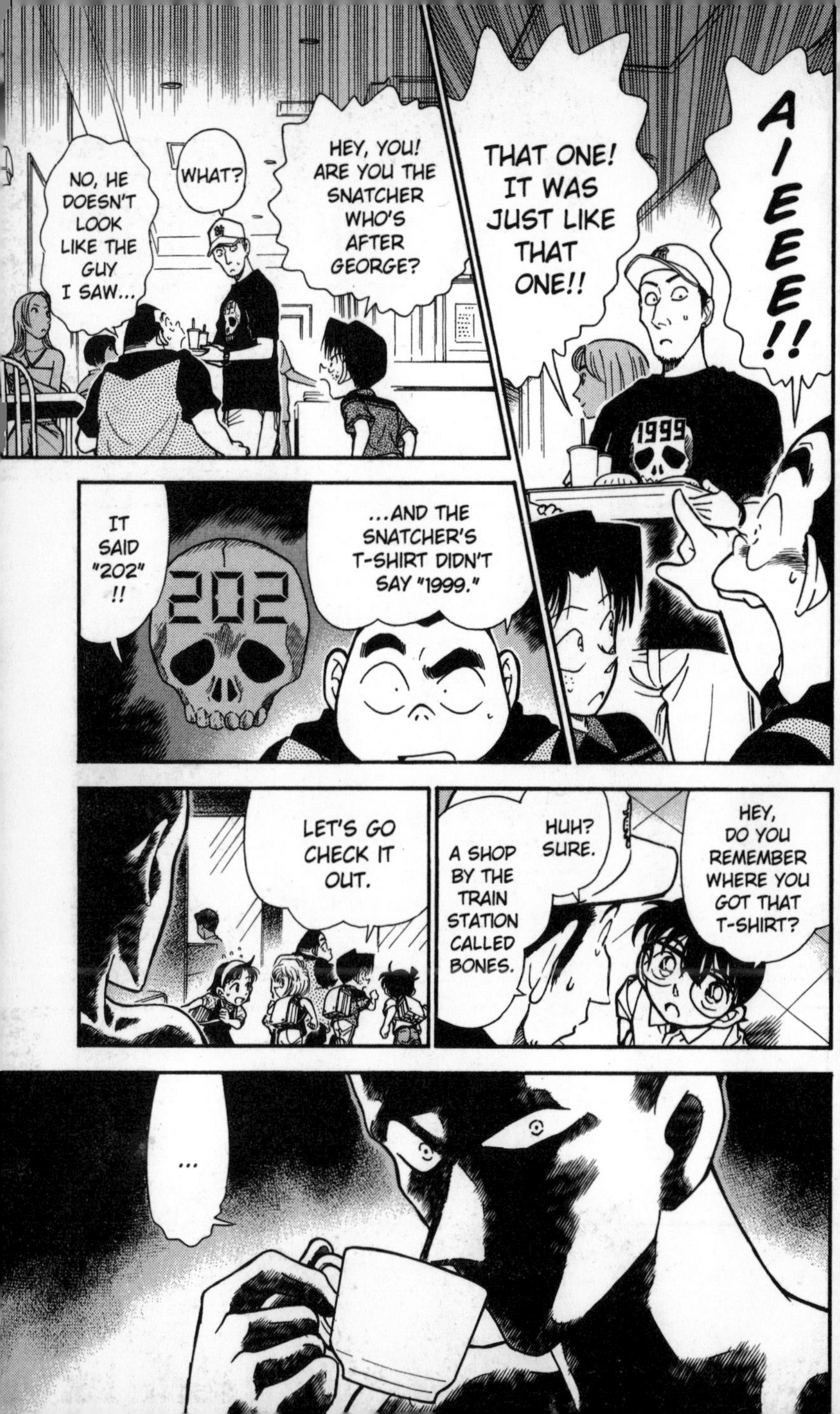
AIEEE!!
THAT ONE! IT WAS JUST LIKE THAT ONE!!
1999
HEY, YOU! ARE YOU THE SNATCHER WHO'S AFTER GEORGE?
WHAT?
NO, HE DOESN'T LOOK LIKE THE GUY I SAW...
...AND THE SNATCHER'S T-SHIRT DIDN'T SAY "1999."
IT SAID "202" !!
202
HEY, DO YOU REMEMBER WHERE YOU GOT THAT T-SHIRT?
HUH? SURE.
A SHOP BY THE TRAIN STATION CALLED BONES.
LET'S GO CHECK IT OUT.
...

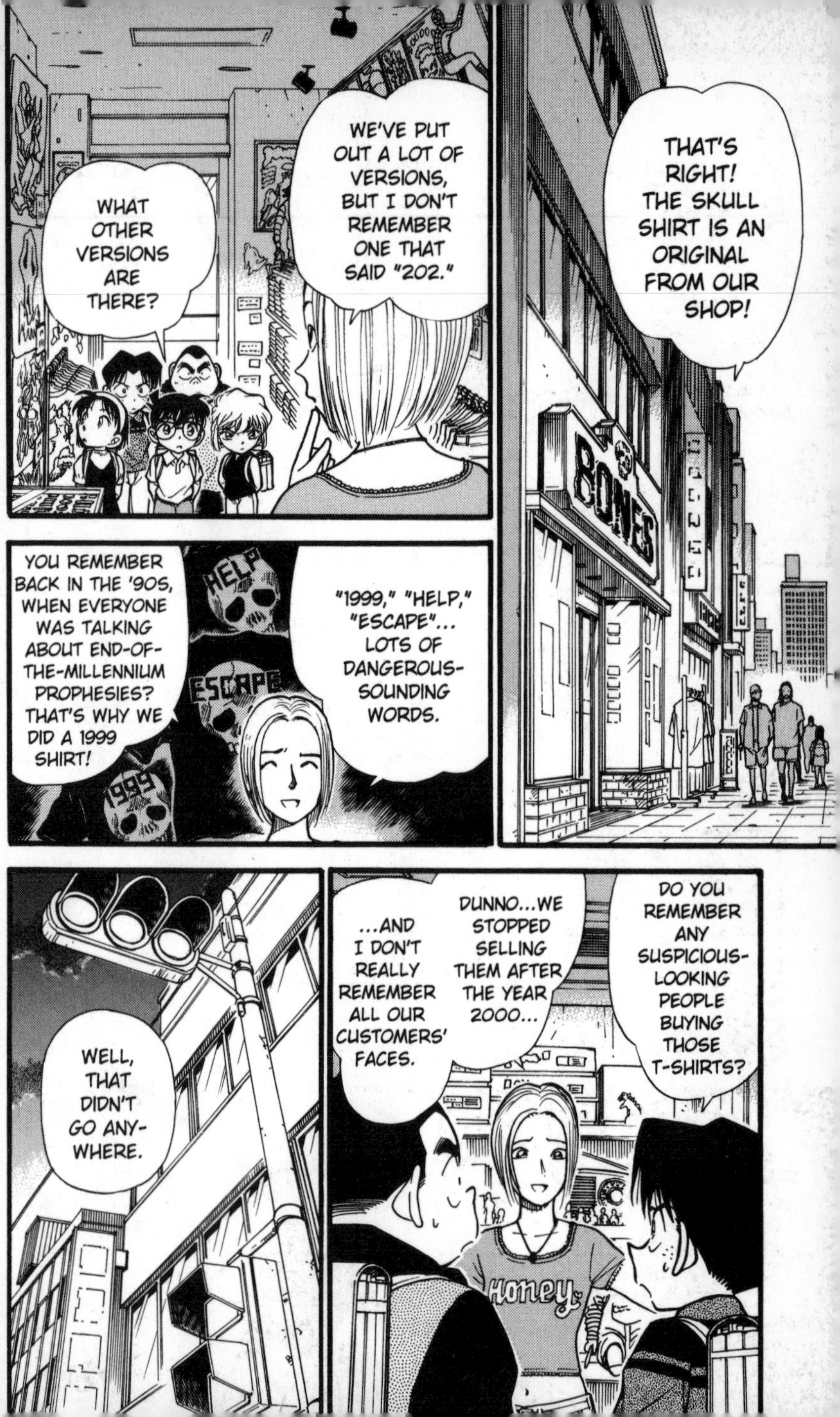
THAT'S RIGHT! THE SKULL SHIRT IS AN ORIGINAL FROM OUR SHOP!
BONES
WE'VE PUT OUT A LOT OF VERSIONS, BUT I DON'T REMEMBER ONE THAT SAID "202."
WHAT OTHER VERSIONS ARE THERE?
"1999," "HELP," "ESCAPE"... LOTS OF DANGEROUS-SOUNDING WORDS.
HELP
ESCAPE
1999
YOU REMEMBER BACK IN THE '90S, WHEN EVERYONE WAS TALKING ABOUT END-OF-THE-MILLENNIUM PROPHESIES? THAT'S WHY WE DID A 1999 SHIRT!
DO YOU REMEMBER ANY SUSPICIOUS-LOOKING PEOPLE BUYING THOSE T-SHIRTS?
DUNNO...WE STOPPED SELLING THEM AFTER THE YEAR 2000...
...AND I DON'T REALLY REMEMBER ALL OUR CUSTOMERS' FACES.
Honey
WELL, THAT DIDN'T GO ANY-WHERE.

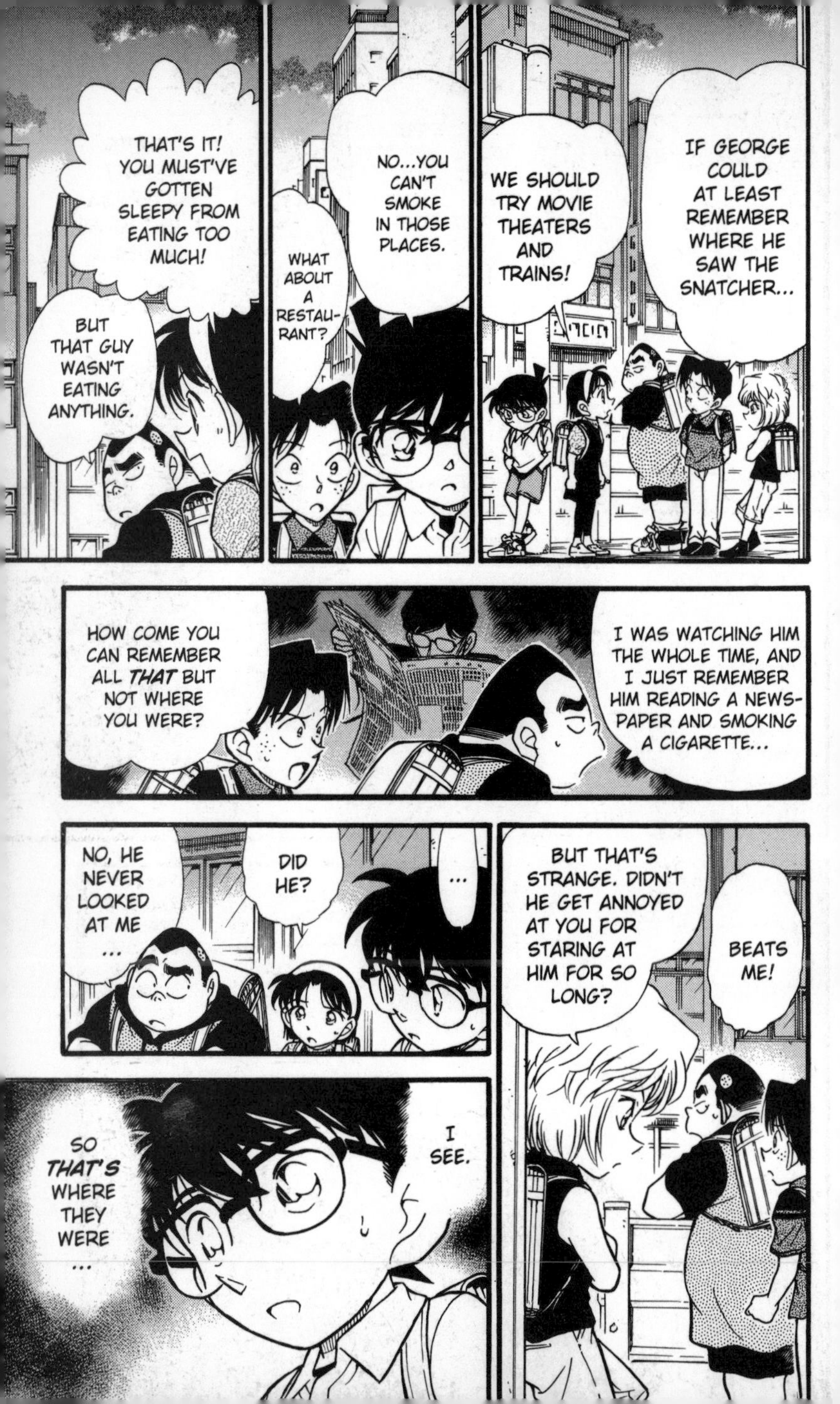
IF GEORGE COULD AT LEAST REMEMBER WHERE HE SAW THE SNATCHER...
WE SHOULD TRY MOVIE THEATERS AND TRAINS!
NO...YOU CAN'T SMOKE IN THOSE PLACES.
WHAT ABOUT A RESTAU-RANT?
THAT'S IT! YOU MUST'VE GOTTEN SLEEPY FROM EATING TOO MUCH!
BUT THAT GUY WASN'T EATING ANYTHING.
I WAS WATCHING HIM THE WHOLE TIME, AND I JUST REMEMBER HIM READING A NEWS-PAPER AND SMOKING A CIGARETTE...
HOW COME YOU CAN REMEMBER ALL *THAT* BUT NOT WHERE YOU WERE?
BUT THAT'S STRANGE. DIDN'T HE GET ANNOYED AT YOU FOR STARING AT HIM FOR SO LONG?
BEATS ME!
...
DID HE?
NO, HE NEVER LOOKED AT ME ...
I SEE.
SO *THAT'S* WHERE THEY WERE ...

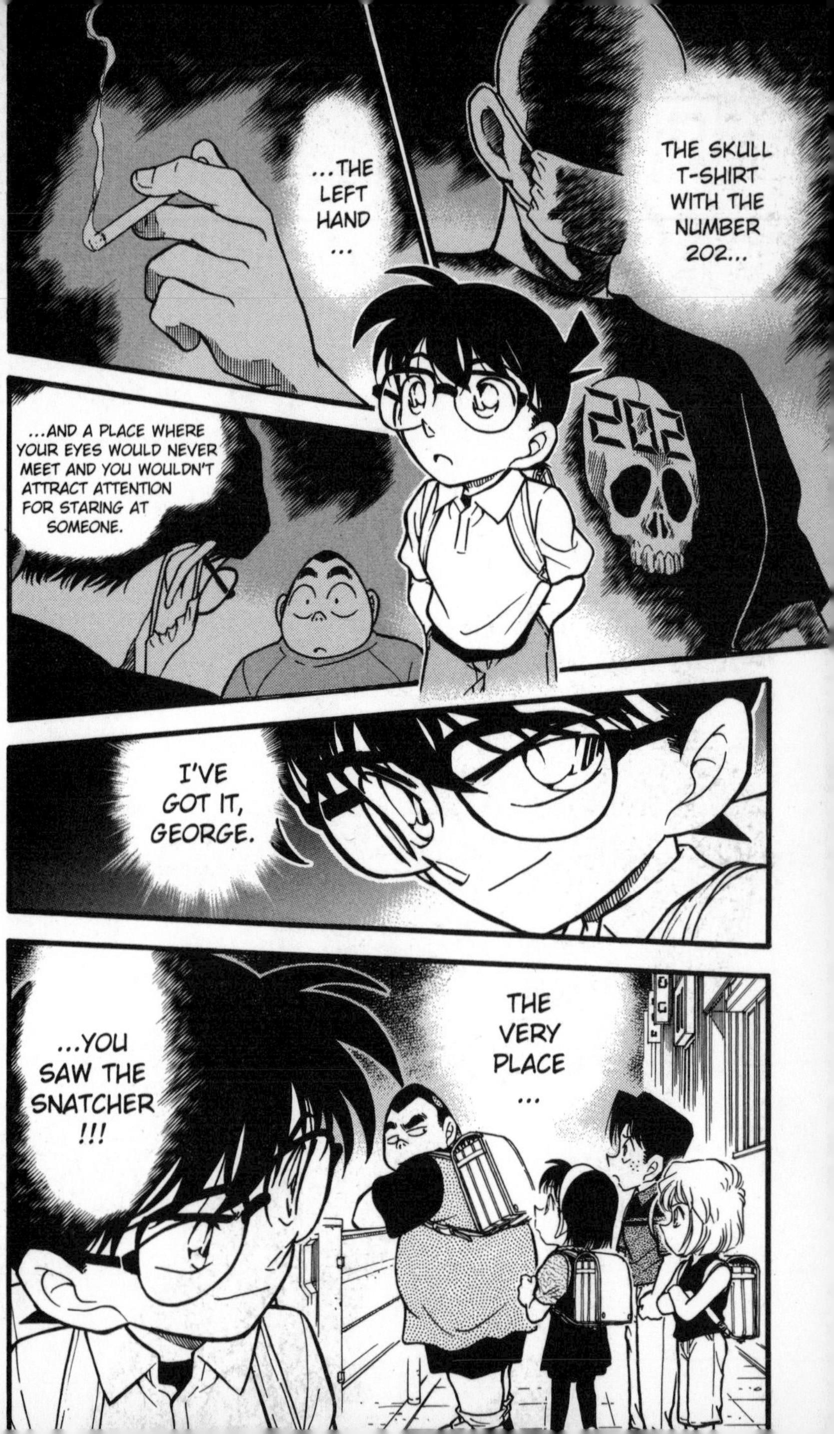
THE SKULL T-SHIRT WITH THE NUMBER 202...
...THE LEFT HAND ...
202
...AND A PLACE WHERE YOUR EYES WOULD NEVER MEET AND YOU WOULDN'T ATTRACT ATTENTION FOR STARING AT SOMEONE.
I'VE GOT IT, GEORGE.
THE VERY PLACE ...
...YOU SAW THE SNATCHER !!!

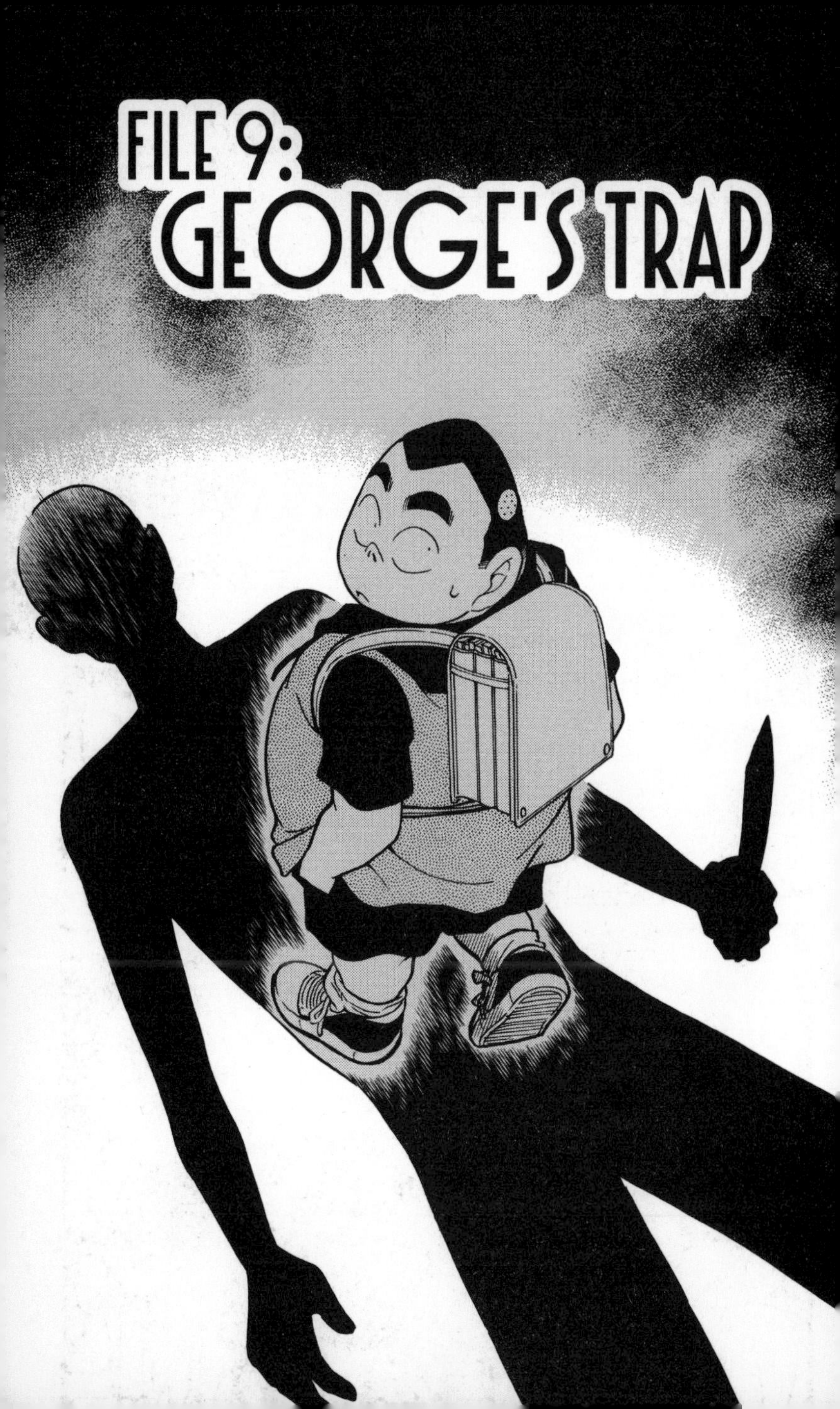
FILE 9:
GEORGE'S TRAP

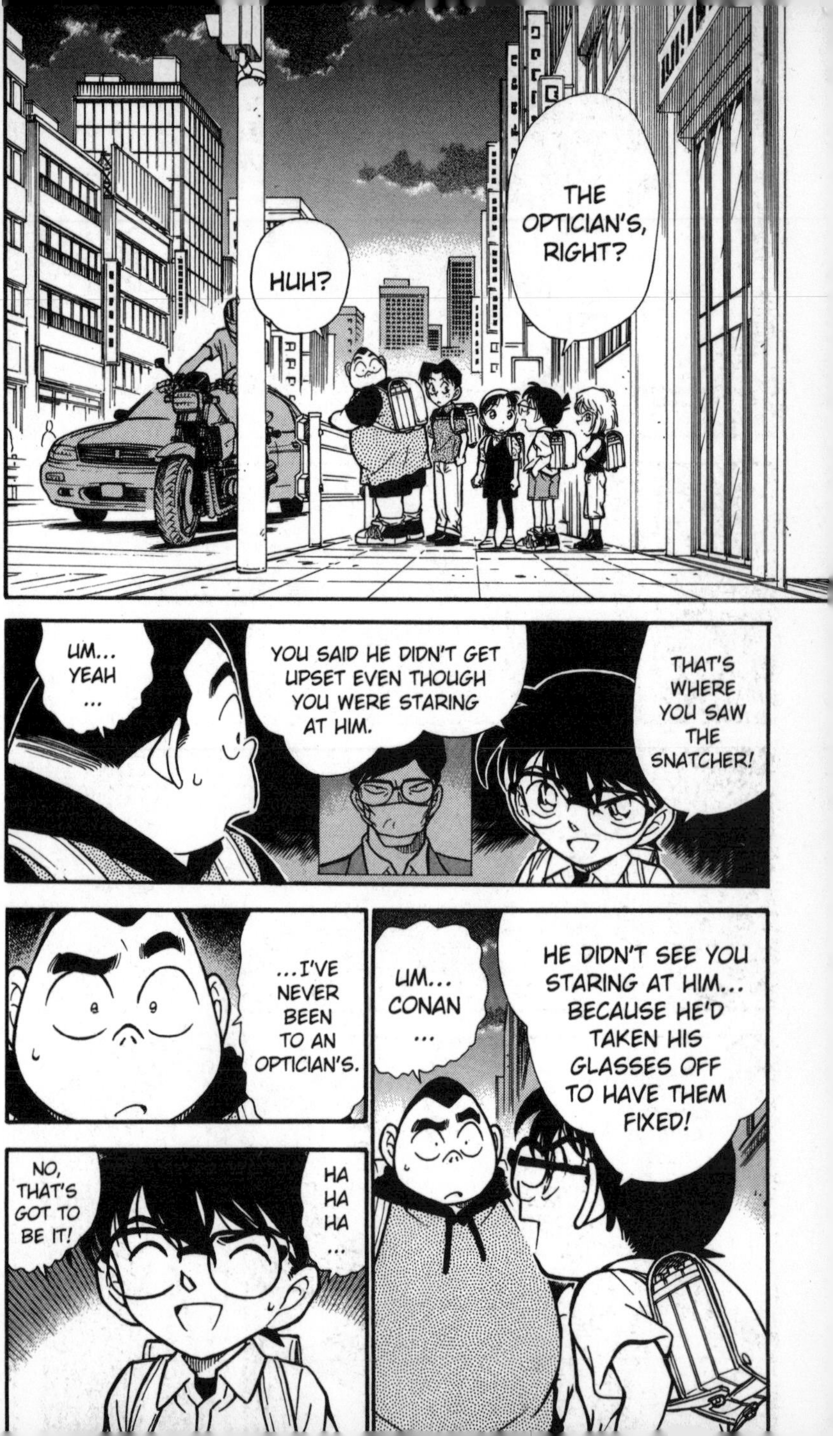

THE OPTICIAN'S, RIGHT?
HUH?
THAT'S WHERE YOU SAW THE SNATCHER!
YOU SAID HE DIDN'T GET UPSET EVEN THOUGH YOU WERE STARING AT HIM.
UM... YEAH ...
HE DIDN'T SEE YOU STARING AT HIM... BECAUSE HE'D TAKEN HIS GLASSES OFF TO HAVE THEM FIXED!
UM... CONAN ...
...I'VE NEVER BEEN TO AN OPTICIAN'S.
HA HA HA ...
NO, THAT'S GOT TO BE IT!

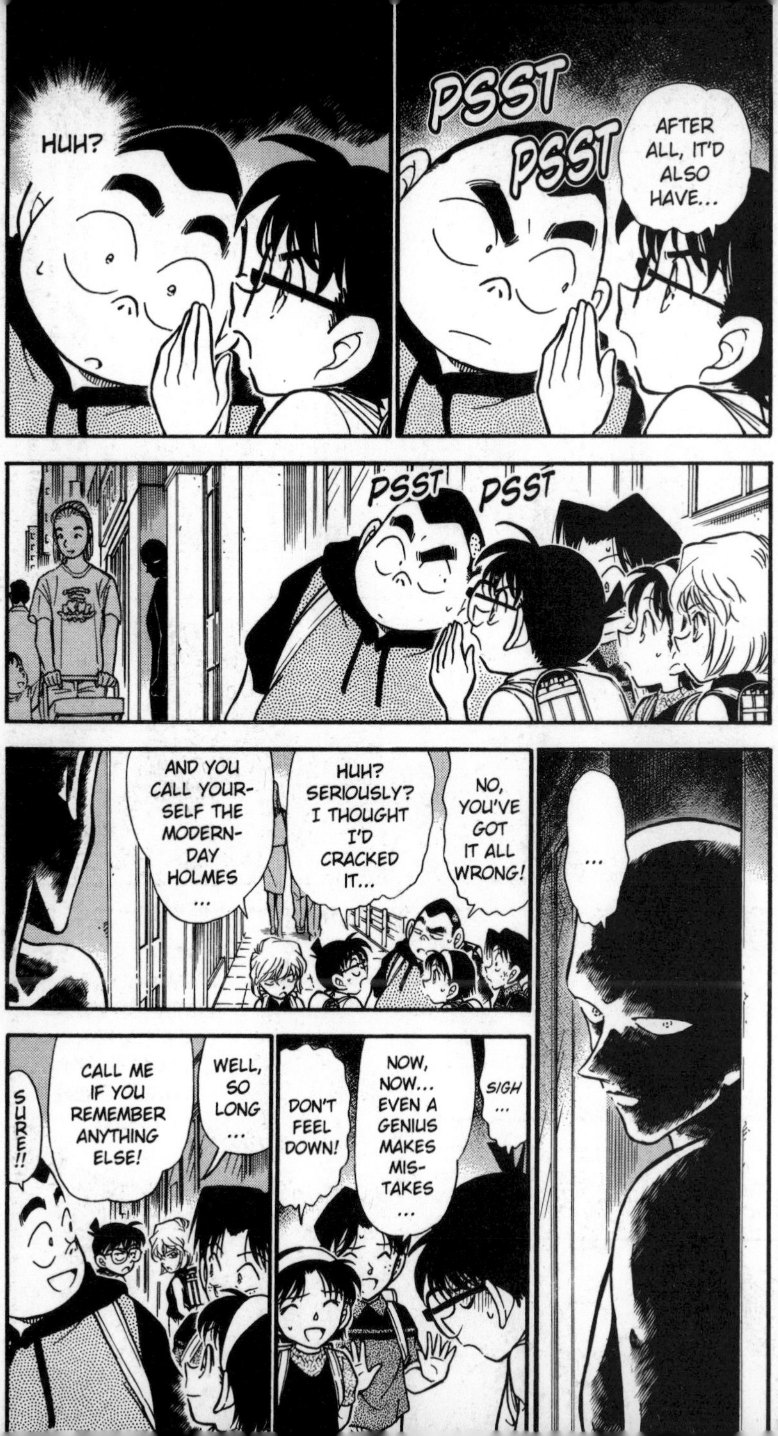
PSST
PSST
AFTER ALL, IT'D ALSO HAVE...
HUH?
PSST
PSST
...
NO, YOU'VE GOT IT ALL WRONG!
HUH? SERIOUSLY? I THOUGHT I'D CRACKED IT...
AND YOU CALL YOURSELF THE MODERN-DAY HOLMES...
SIGH...
NOW, NOW... EVEN A GENIUS MAKES MISTAKES...
DON'T FEEL DOWN!
WELL, SO LONG...
CALL ME IF YOU REMEMBER ANYTHING ELSE!
SURE!!

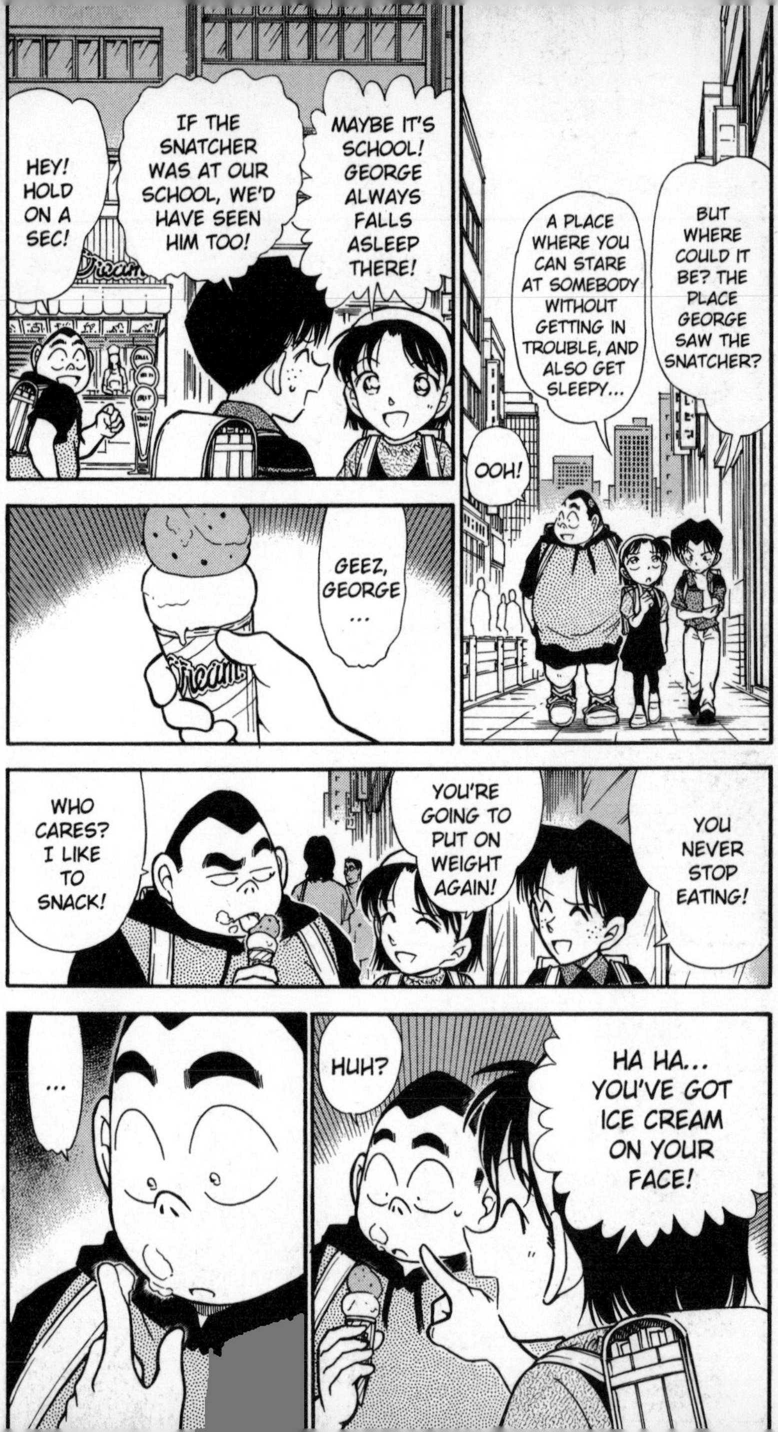
BUT WHERE COULD IT BE? THE PLACE GEORGE SAW THE SNATCHER?
A PLACE WHERE YOU CAN STARE AT SOMEBODY WITHOUT GETTING IN TROUBLE, AND ALSO GET SLEEPY...
OOH!
MAYBE IT'S SCHOOL! GEORGE ALWAYS FALLS ASLEEP THERE!
IF THE SNATCHER WAS AT OUR SCHOOL, WE'D HAVE SEEN HIM TOO!
HEY! HOLD ON A SEC!
GEEZ, GEORGE...
YOU NEVER STOP EATING!
YOU'RE GOING TO PUT ON WEIGHT AGAIN!
WHO CARES? I LIKE TO SNACK!
HA HA... YOU'VE GOT ICE CREAM ON YOUR FACE!
HUH?
...

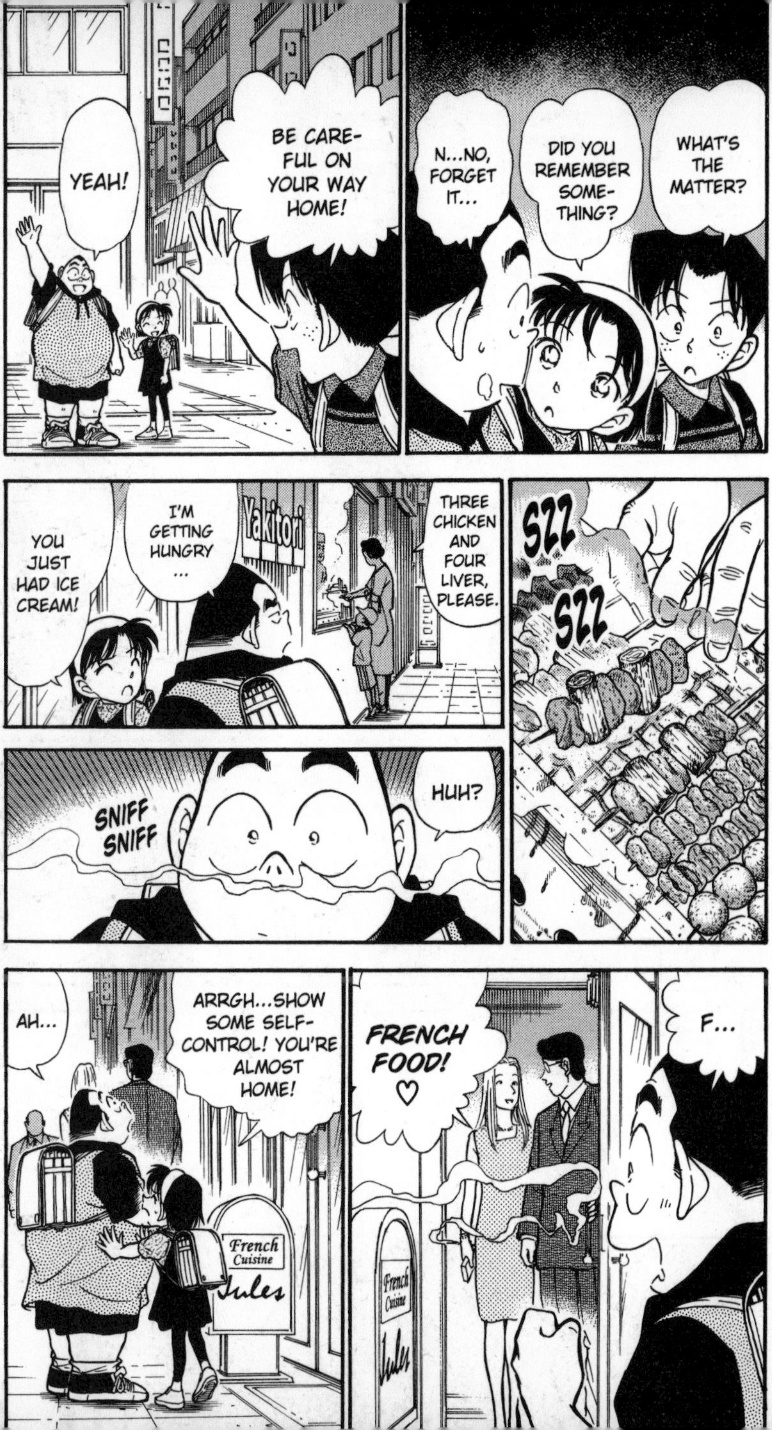
WHAT'S THE MATTER?
DID YOU REMEMBER SOME-THING?
N...NO, FORGET IT...
BE CARE-FUL ON YOUR WAY HOME!
YEAH!
SZZ
SZZ
THREE CHICKEN AND FOUR LIVER, PLEASE.
Yakitori
I'M GETTING HUNGRY ...
YOU JUST HAD ICE CREAM!
HUH?
SNIFF SNIFF
F...
FRENCH FOOD! ♡
French Cuisine
Jules
ARRGH...SHOW SOME SELF-CONTROL! YOU'RE ALMOST HOME!
AH...
French Cuisine
Jules

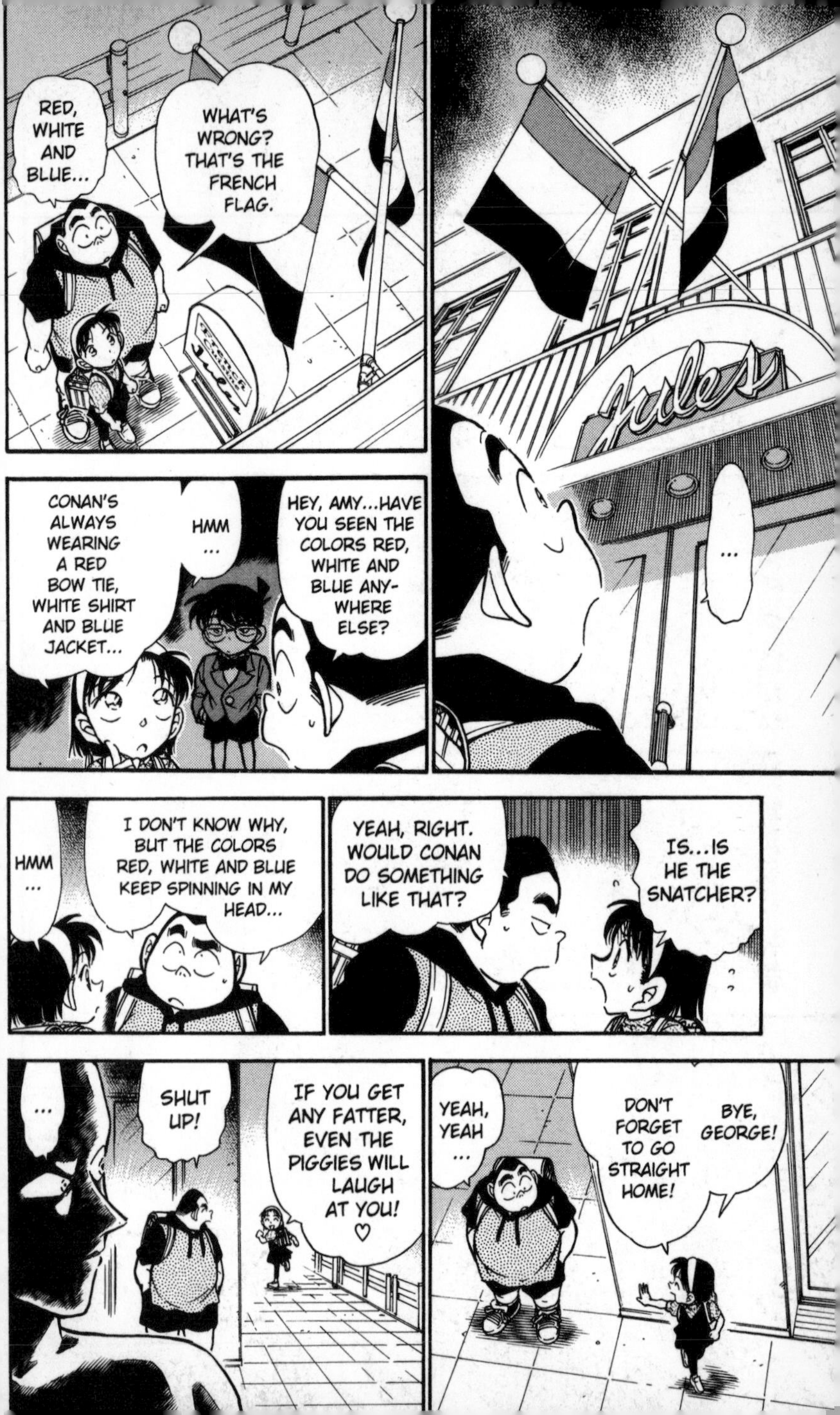
...
WHAT'S WRONG? THAT'S THE FRENCH FLAG.
RED, WHITE AND BLUE...
HEY, AMY...HAVE YOU SEEN THE COLORS RED, WHITE AND BLUE ANYWHERE ELSE?
HMM ...
CONAN'S ALWAYS WEARING A RED BOW TIE, WHITE SHIRT AND BLUE JACKET...
IS...IS HE THE SNATCHER?
YEAH, RIGHT. WOULD CONAN DO SOMETHING LIKE THAT?
I DON'T KNOW WHY, BUT THE COLORS RED, WHITE AND BLUE KEEP SPINNING IN MY HEAD...
HMM ...
BYE, GEORGE!
DON'T FORGET TO GO STRAIGHT HOME!
YEAH, YEAH ...
IF YOU GET ANY FATTER, EVEN THE PIGGIES WILL LAUGH AT YOU! ♡
SHUT UP!
...

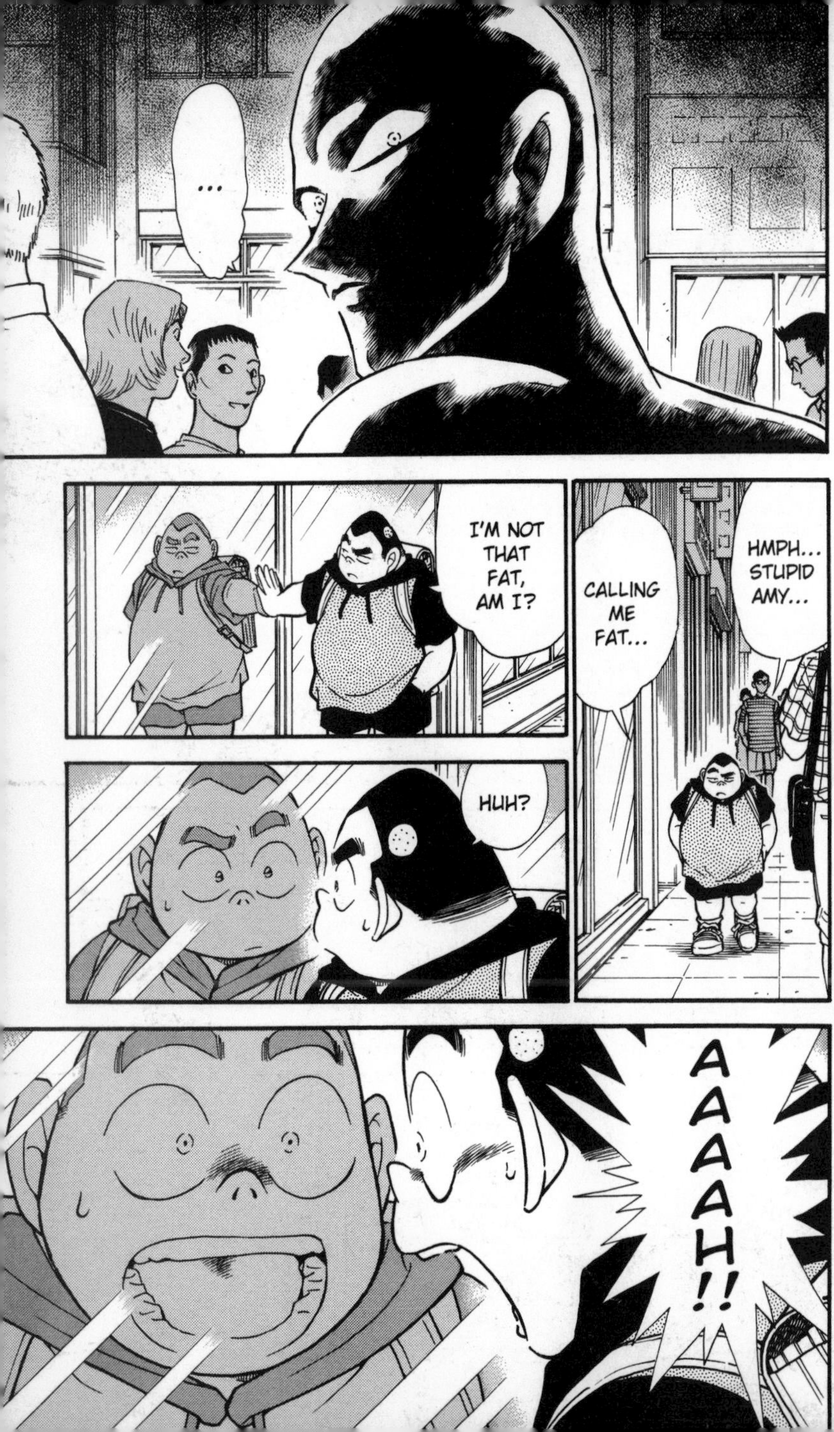
...
HMPH... STUPID AMY...
CALLING ME FAT...
I'M NOT THAT FAT, AM I?
HUH?
AAAAAH!!

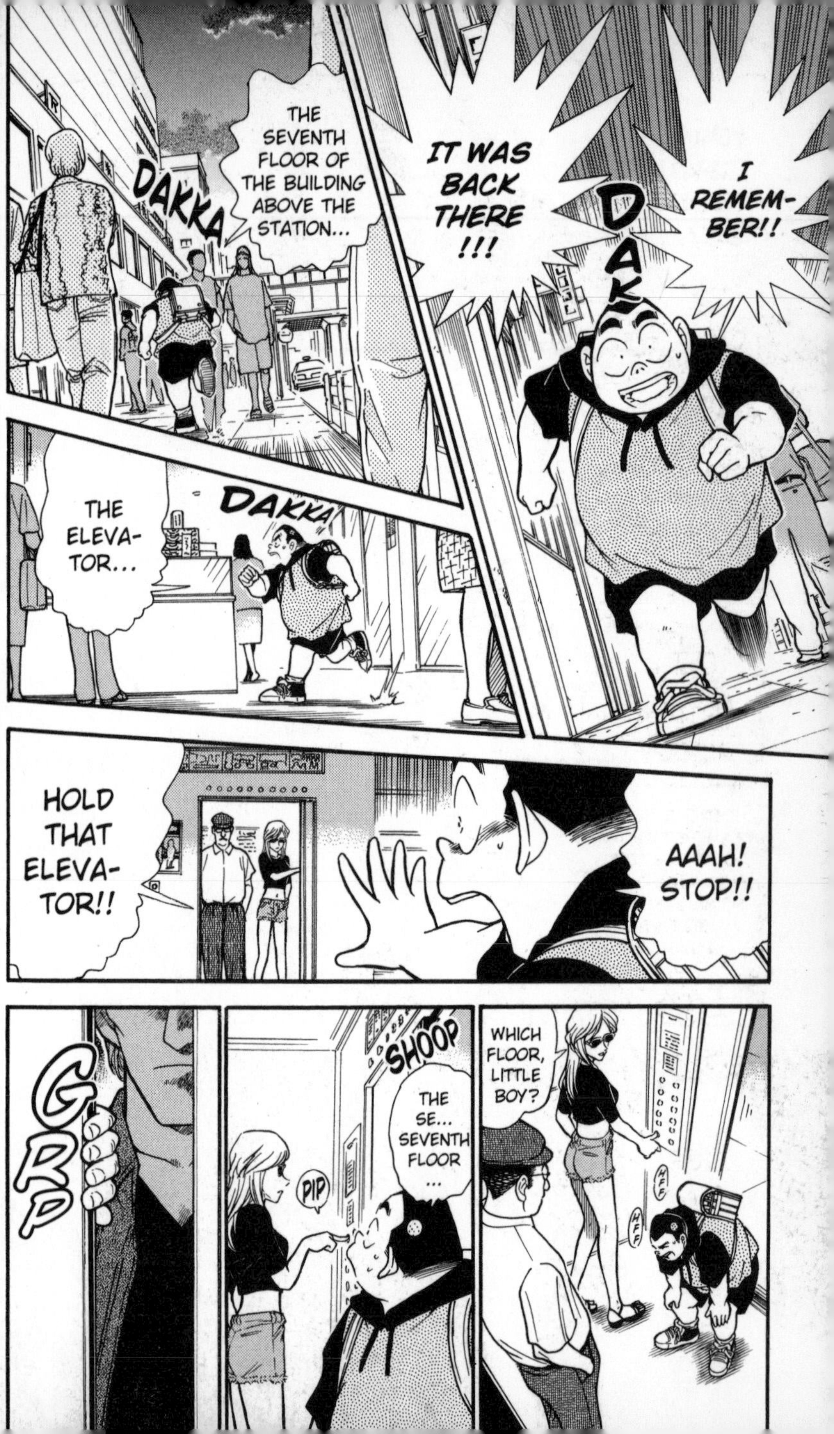
I REMEMBER!!
DAK
IT WAS BACK THERE!!!
THE SEVENTH FLOOR OF THE BUILDING ABOVE THE STATION...
DAKKA
DAKKA
THE ELEVATOR...
AAAH! STOP!!
HOLD THAT ELEVATOR!!
WHICH FLOOR, LITTLE BOY?
HFF
HFF
SHOOP
THE SE... SEVENTH FLOOR ...
PIP
GRP

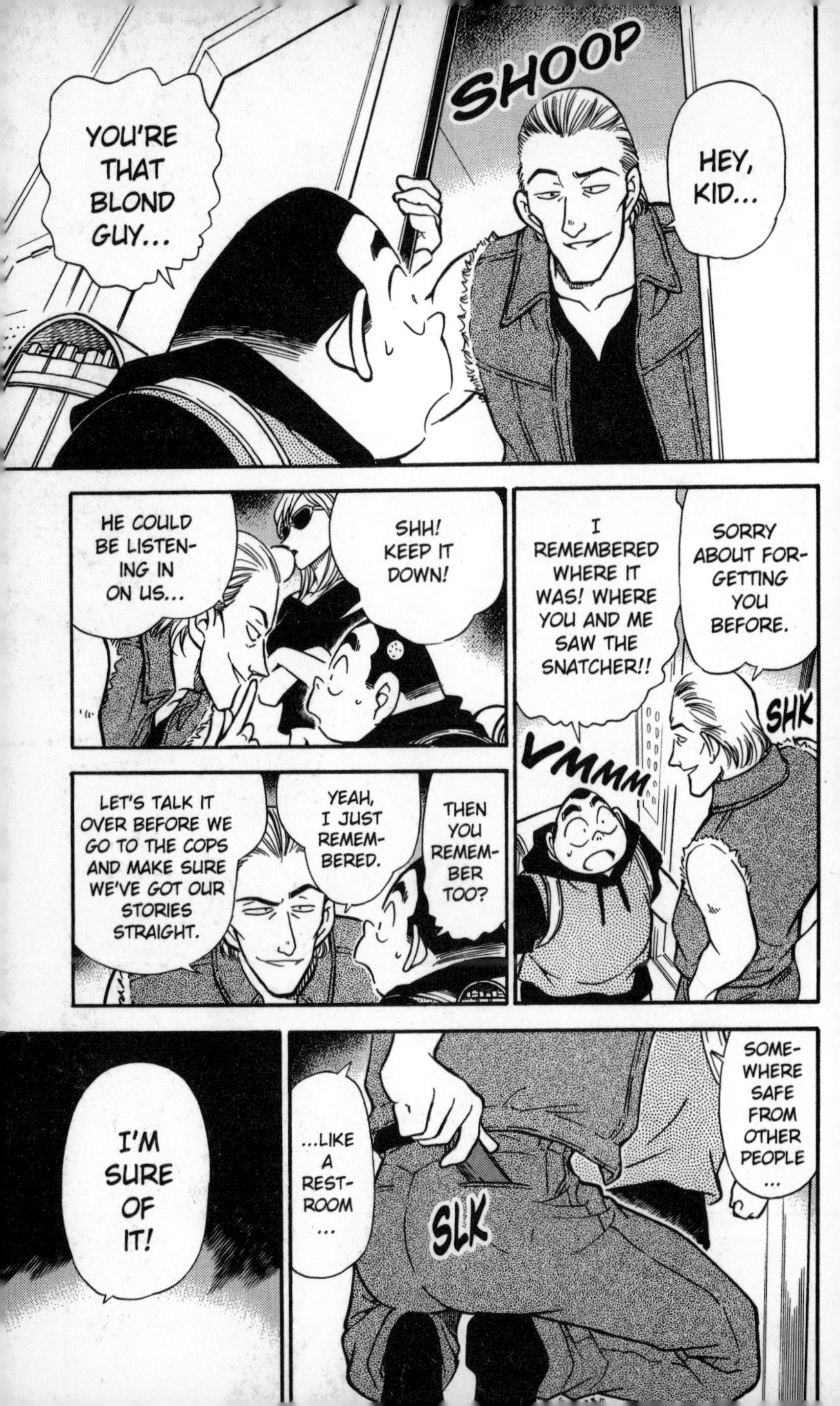
HEY, KID...
SHOOP
YOU'RE THAT BLOND GUY...
SORRY ABOUT FORGETTING YOU BEFORE.
I REMEMBERED WHERE IT WAS! WHERE YOU AND ME SAW THE SNATCHER!!
SHK
VMMM
SHH! KEEP IT DOWN!
HE COULD BE LISTENING IN ON US...
THEN YOU REMEMBER TOO?
YEAH, I JUST REMEMBERED.
LET'S TALK IT OVER BEFORE WE GO TO THE COPS AND MAKE SURE WE'VE GOT OUR STORIES STRAIGHT.
SOMEWHERE SAFE FROM OTHER PEOPLE...
...LIKE A RESTROOM...
SLK
I'M SURE OF IT!

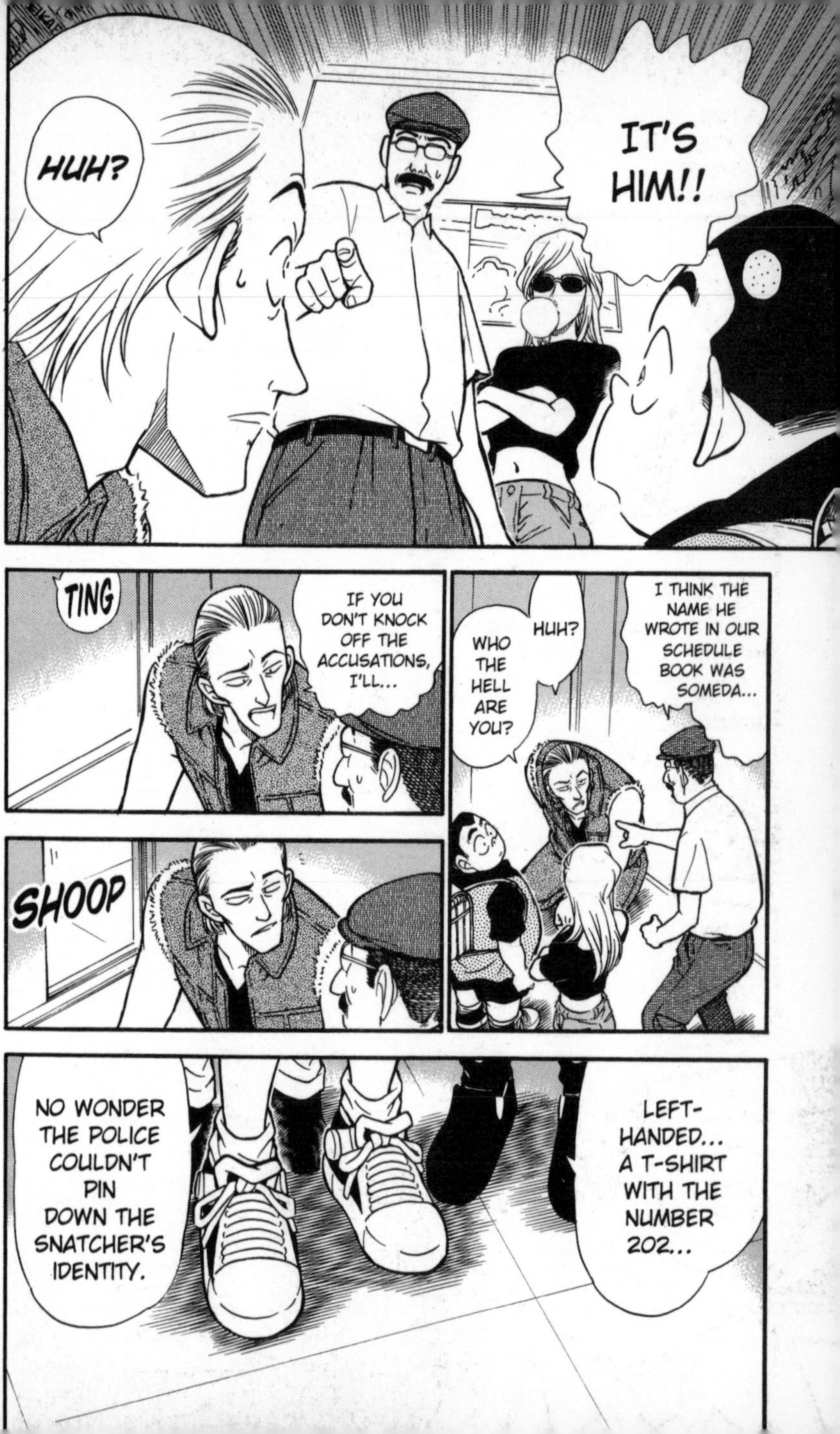
IT'S HIM!!
HUH?
I THINK THE NAME HE WROTE IN OUR SCHEDULE BOOK WAS SOMEDA...
HUH?
WHO THE HELL ARE YOU?
IF YOU DON'T KNOCK OFF THE ACCUSATIONS, I'LL...
TING
SHOOP
LEFT-HANDED... A T-SHIRT WITH THE NUMBER 202...
NO WONDER THE POLICE COULDN'T PIN DOWN THE SNATCHER'S IDENTITY.

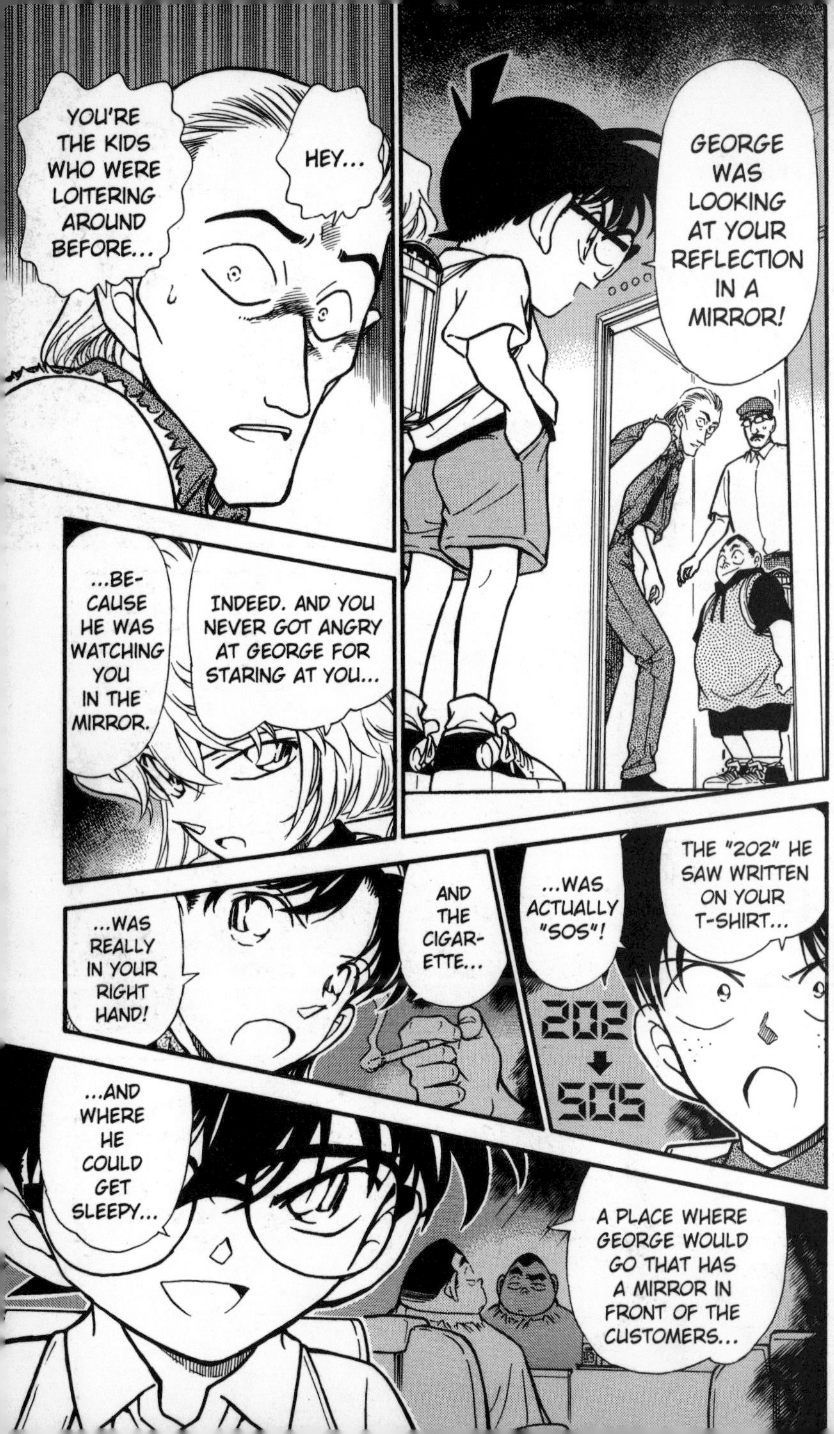
GEORGE WAS LOOKING AT YOUR REFLECTION IN A MIRROR!
HEY...
YOU'RE THE KIDS WHO WERE LOITERING AROUND BEFORE...
INDEED. AND YOU NEVER GOT ANGRY AT GEORGE FOR STARING AT YOU...
...BE-CAUSE HE WAS WATCHING YOU IN THE MIRROR.
THE "202" HE SAW WRITTEN ON YOUR T-SHIRT...
...WAS ACTUALLY "SOS"!
202
SOS
AND THE CIGAR-ETTE...
...WAS REALLY IN YOUR RIGHT HAND!
A PLACE WHERE GEORGE WOULD GO THAT HAS A MIRROR IN FRONT OF THE CUSTOMERS...
...AND WHERE HE COULD GET SLEEPY...

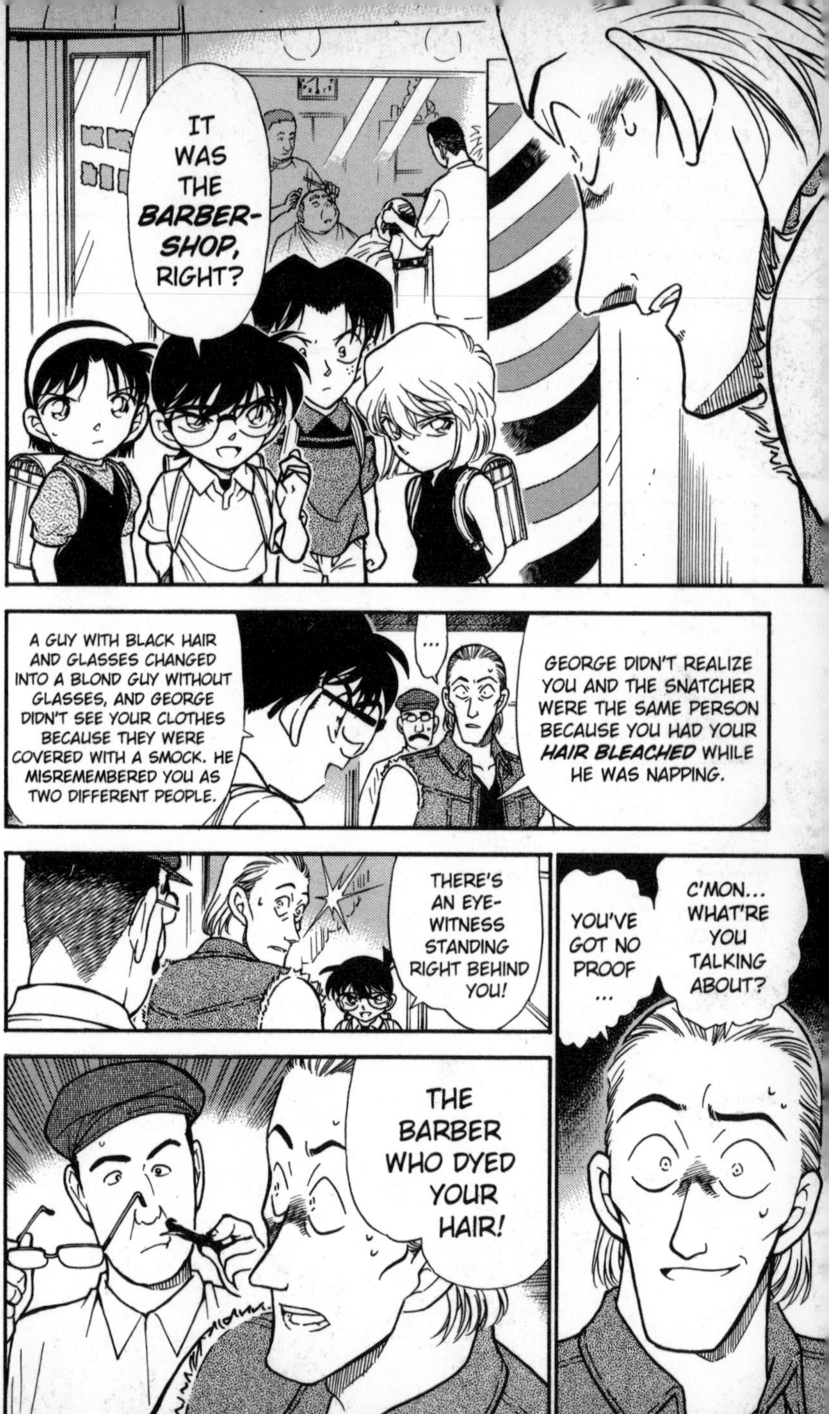
IT WAS THE BARBER-SHOP, RIGHT?
GEORGE DIDN'T REALIZE YOU AND THE SNATCHER WERE THE SAME PERSON BECAUSE YOU HAD YOUR HAIR BLEACHED WHILE HE WAS NAPPING.
...
A GUY WITH BLACK HAIR AND GLASSES CHANGED INTO A BLOND GUY WITHOUT GLASSES, AND GEORGE DIDN'T SEE YOUR CLOTHES BECAUSE THEY WERE COVERED WITH A SMOCK. HE MISREMEMBERED YOU AS TWO DIFFERENT PEOPLE.
C'MON... WHAT'RE YOU TALKING ABOUT?
YOU'VE GOT NO PROOF ...
THERE'S AN EYE-WITNESS STANDING RIGHT BEHIND YOU!
THE BARBER WHO DYED YOUR HAIR!

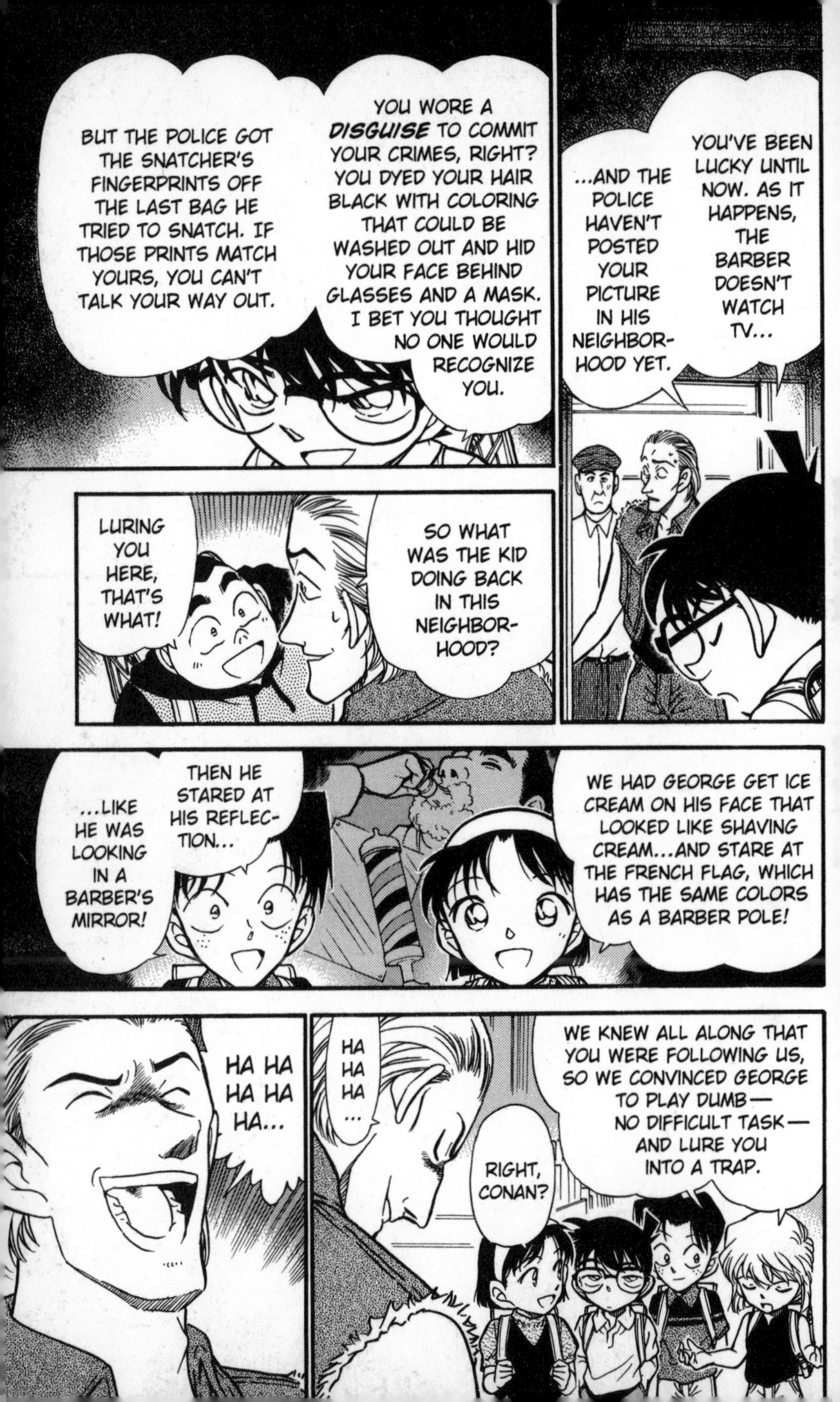
YOU'VE BEEN LUCKY UNTIL NOW. AS IT HAPPENS, THE BARBER DOESN'T WATCH TV...
...AND THE POLICE HAVEN'T POSTED YOUR PICTURE IN HIS NEIGHBORHOOD YET.
YOU WORE A DISGUISE TO COMMIT YOUR CRIMES, RIGHT? YOU DYED YOUR HAIR BLACK WITH COLORING THAT COULD BE WASHED OUT AND HID YOUR FACE BEHIND GLASSES AND A MASK. I BET YOU THOUGHT NO ONE WOULD RECOGNIZE YOU.
BUT THE POLICE GOT THE SNATCHER'S FINGERPRINTS OFF THE LAST BAG HE TRIED TO SNATCH. IF THOSE PRINTS MATCH YOURS, YOU CAN'T TALK YOUR WAY OUT.
SO WHAT WAS THE KID DOING BACK IN THIS NEIGHBORHOOD?
LURING YOU HERE, THAT'S WHAT!
WE HAD GEORGE GET ICE CREAM ON HIS FACE THAT LOOKED LIKE SHAVING CREAM...AND STARE AT THE FRENCH FLAG, WHICH HAS THE SAME COLORS AS A BARBER POLE!
THEN HE STARED AT HIS REFLECTION...
...LIKE HE WAS LOOKING IN A BARBER'S MIRROR!
WE KNEW ALL ALONG THAT YOU WERE FOLLOWING US, SO WE CONVINCED GEORGE TO PLAY DUMB— NO DIFFICULT TASK— AND LURE YOU INTO A TRAP.
RIGHT, CONAN?
HA HA HA ...
HA HA HA HA HA...

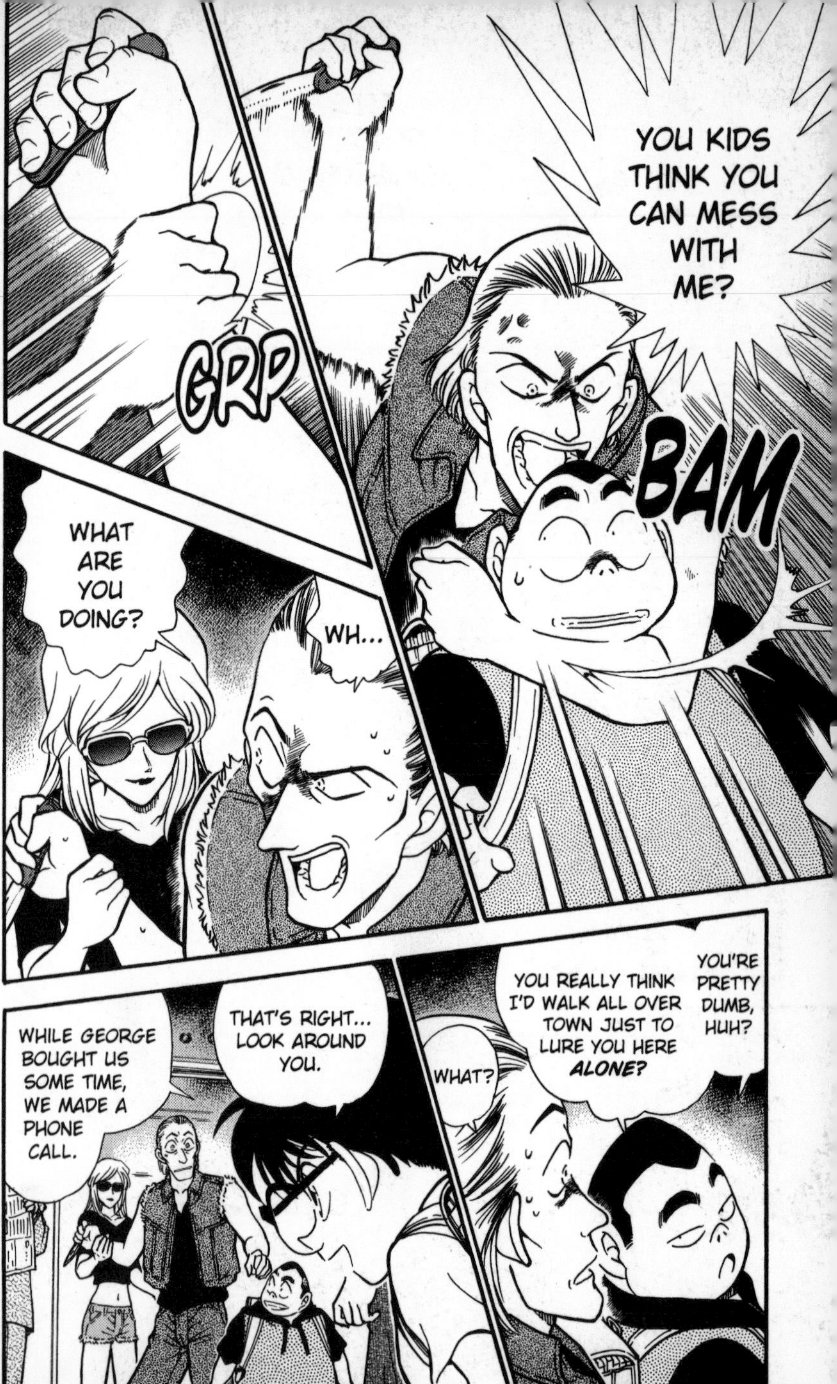
YOU KIDS THINK YOU CAN MESS WITH ME?
BAM
GRP
WHAT ARE YOU DOING?
WH...
YOU'RE PRETTY DUMB, HUH?
YOU REALLY THINK I'D WALK ALL OVER TOWN JUST TO LURE YOU HERE ***ALONE?***
WHAT?
THAT'S RIGHT... LOOK AROUND YOU.
WHILE GEORGE BOUGHT US SOME TIME, WE MADE A PHONE CALL.

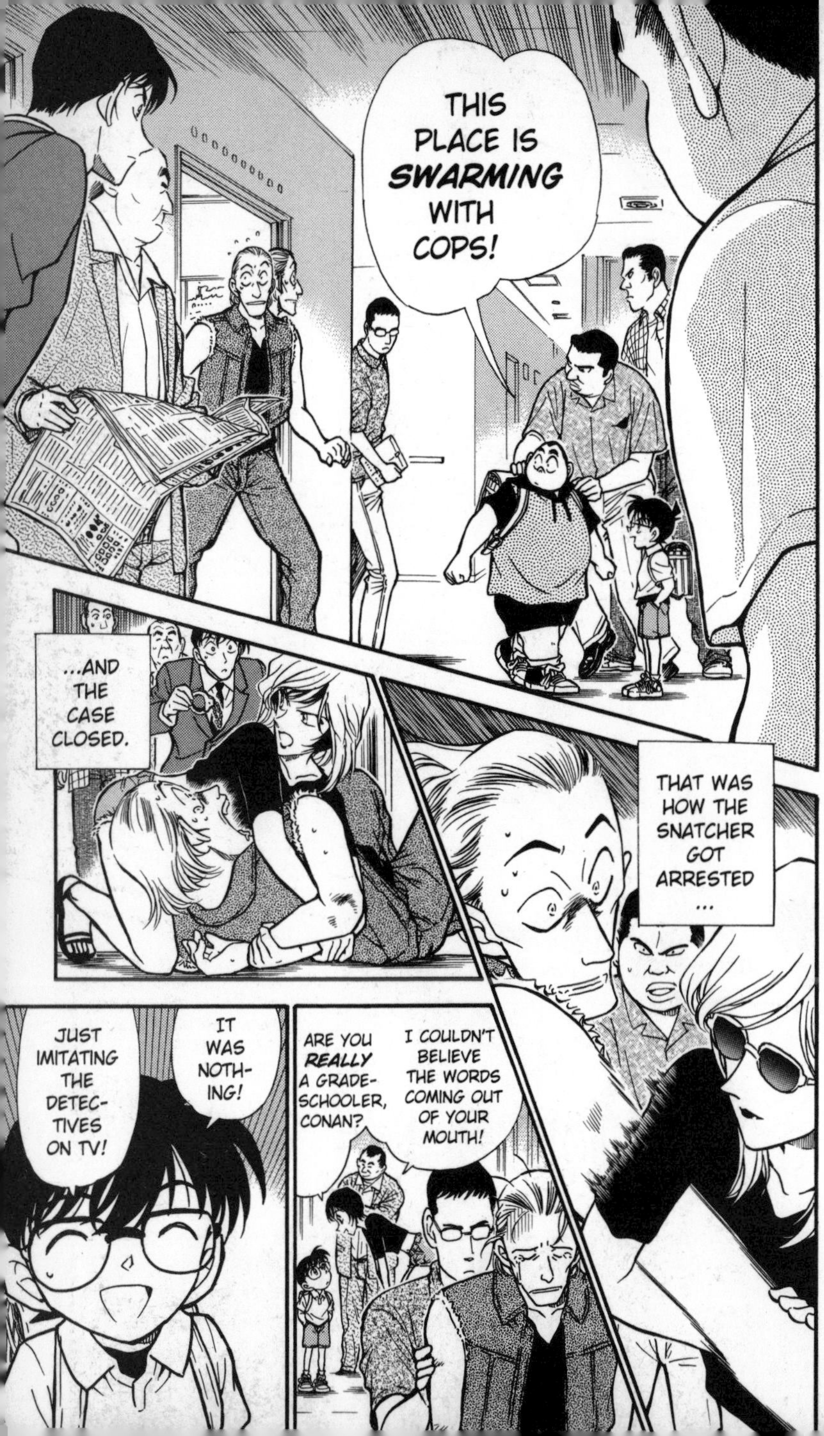
THIS PLACE IS SWARMING WITH COPS!
THAT WAS HOW THE SNATCHER GOT ARRESTED ...
...AND THE CASE CLOSED.
I COULDN'T BELIEVE THE WORDS COMING OUT OF YOUR MOUTH!
ARE YOU REALLY A GRADE-SCHOOLER, CONAN?
IT WAS NOTHING!
JUST IMITATING THE DETECTIVES ON TV!

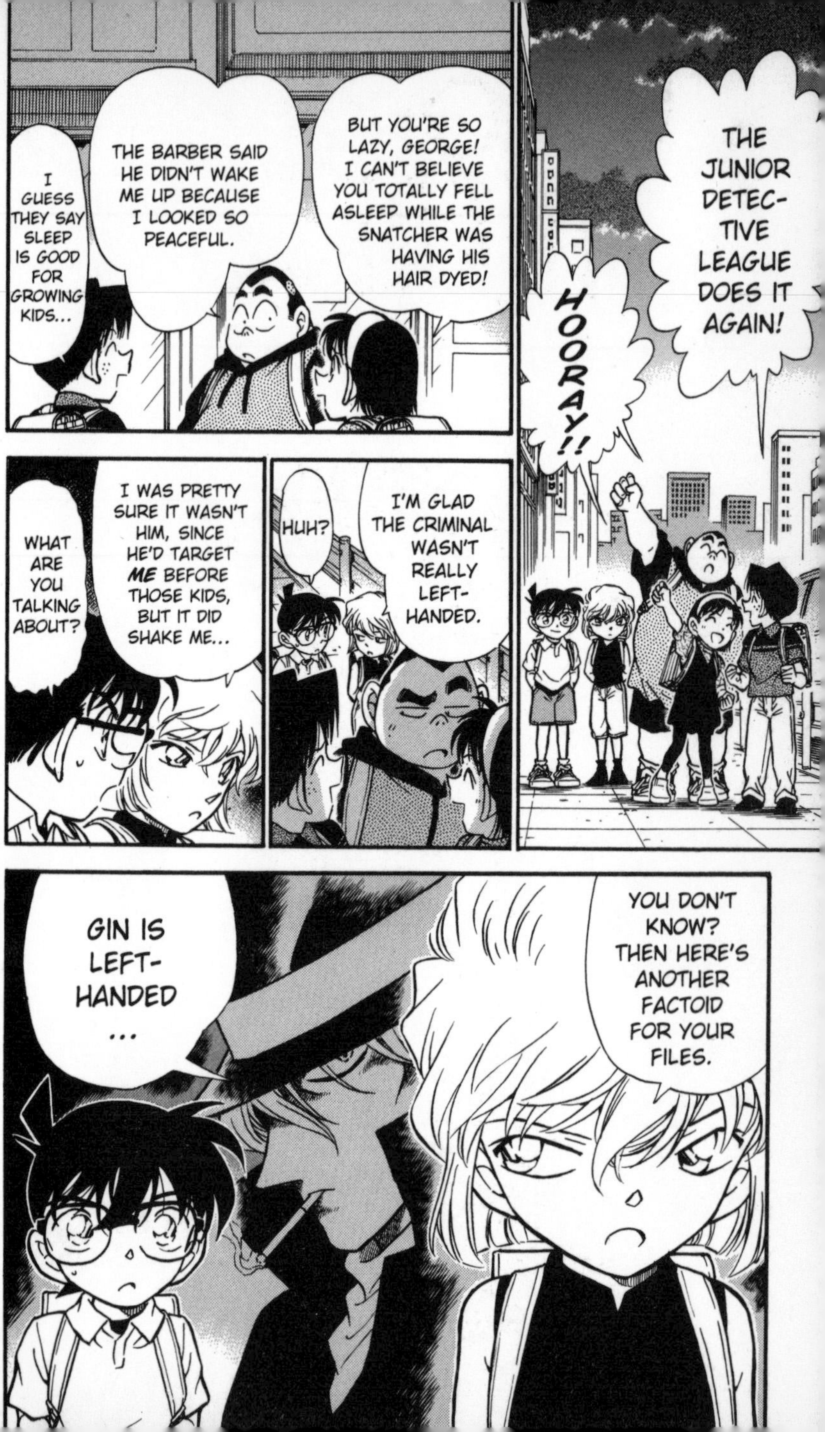
THE JUNIOR DETECTIVE LEAGUE DOES IT AGAIN!
HOORAY!!
BUT YOU'RE SO LAZY, GEORGE! I CAN'T BELIEVE YOU TOTALLY FELL ASLEEP WHILE THE SNATCHER WAS HAVING HIS HAIR DYED!
THE BARBER SAID HE DIDN'T WAKE ME UP BECAUSE I LOOKED SO PEACEFUL.
I GUESS THEY SAY SLEEP IS GOOD FOR GROWING KIDS...
I'M GLAD THE CRIMINAL WASN'T REALLY LEFT-HANDED.
HUH?
I WAS PRETTY SURE IT WASN'T HIM, SINCE HE'D TARGET *ME* BEFORE THOSE KIDS, BUT IT DID SHAKE ME...
WHAT ARE YOU TALKING ABOUT?
YOU DON'T KNOW? THEN HERE'S ANOTHER FACTOID FOR YOUR FILES.
GIN IS LEFT-HANDED ...

FILE 10: THERE...

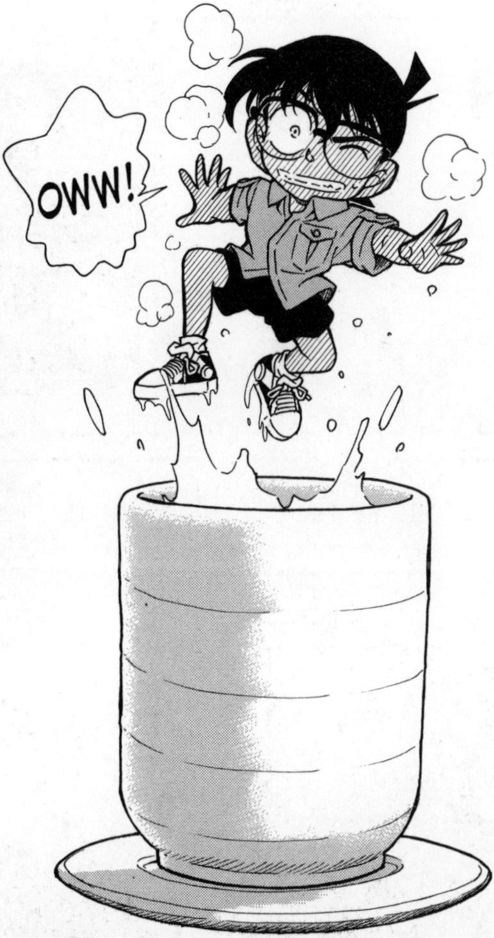
OWW!

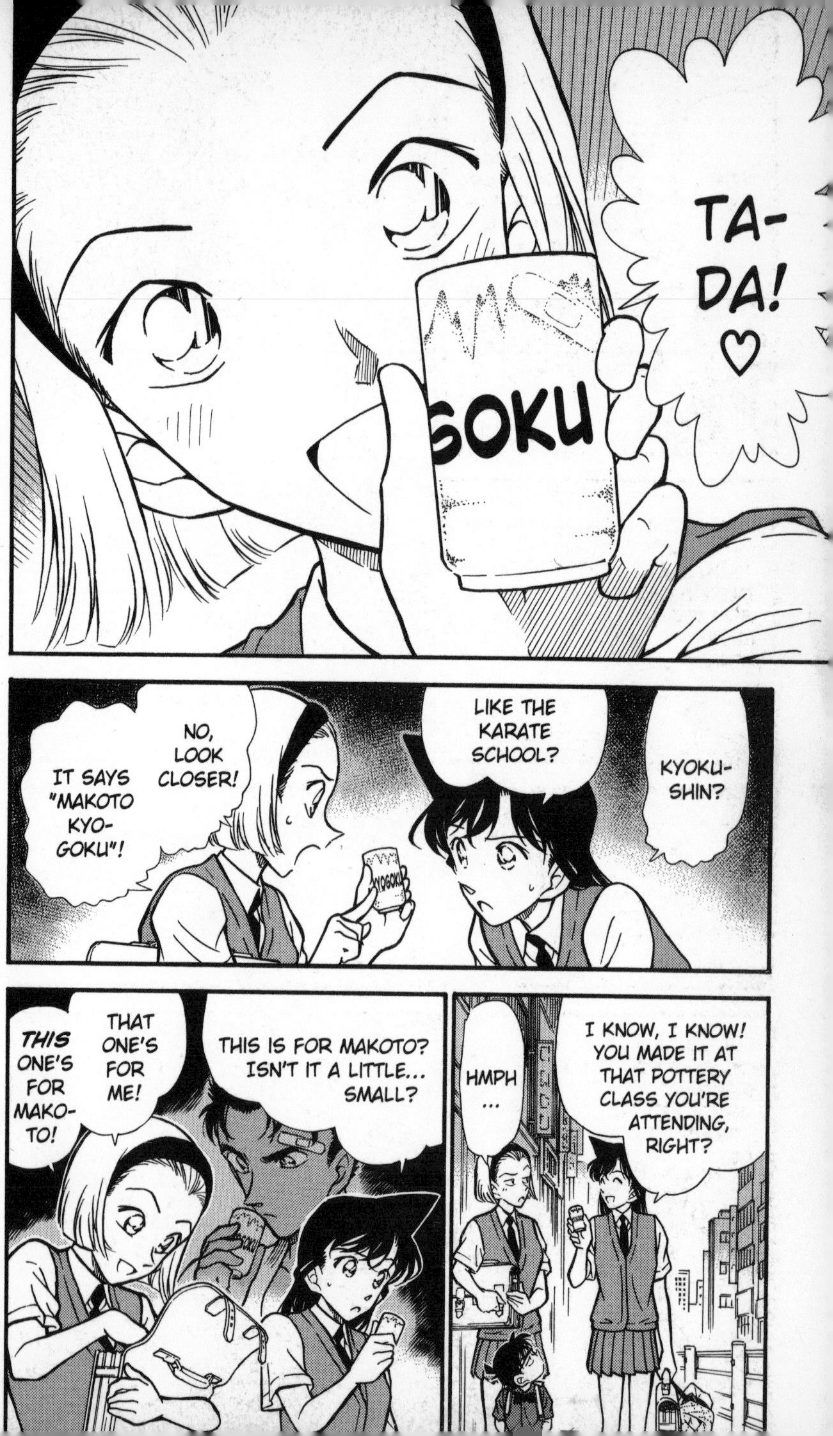
TA-DA! ♡
GOKU
KYOKU-SHIN?
LIKE THE KARATE SCHOOL?
NO, LOOK CLOSER!
IT SAYS "MAKOTO KYO-GOKU"!
I KNOW, I KNOW! YOU MADE IT AT THAT POTTERY CLASS YOU'RE ATTENDING, RIGHT?
HMPH...
THIS IS FOR MAKOTO? ISN'T IT A LITTLE... SMALL?
THAT ONE'S FOR ME!
THIS ONE'S FOR MAKO-TO!

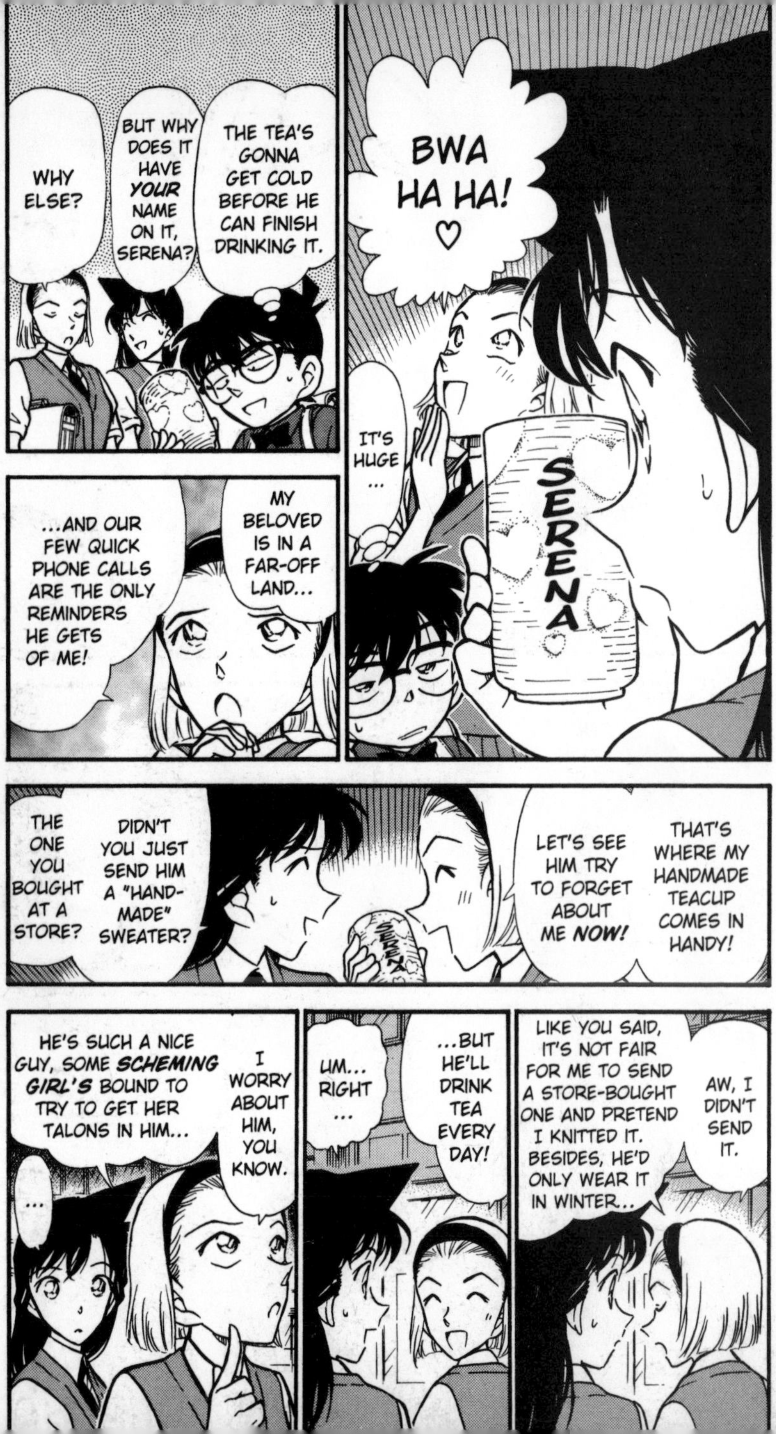
BWA HA HA! ♡
IT'S HUGE ...
SERENA
THE TEA'S GONNA GET COLD BEFORE HE CAN FINISH DRINKING IT.
BUT WHY DOES IT HAVE YOUR NAME ON IT, SERENA?
WHY ELSE?
MY BELOVED IS IN A FAR-OFF LAND...
...AND OUR FEW QUICK PHONE CALLS ARE THE ONLY REMINDERS HE GETS OF ME!
THAT'S WHERE MY HANDMADE TEACUP COMES IN HANDY!
LET'S SEE HIM TRY TO FORGET ABOUT ME NOW!
DIDN'T YOU JUST SEND HIM A "HAND-MADE" SWEATER?
THE ONE YOU BOUGHT AT A STORE?
AW, I DIDN'T SEND IT.
LIKE YOU SAID, IT'S NOT FAIR FOR ME TO SEND A STORE-BOUGHT ONE AND PRETEND I KNITTED IT. BESIDES, HE'D ONLY WEAR IT IN WINTER...
...BUT HE'LL DRINK TEA EVERY DAY!
UM... RIGHT ...
I WORRY ABOUT HIM, YOU KNOW.
HE'S SUCH A NICE GUY, SOME SCHEMING GIRL'S BOUND TO TRY TO GET HER TALONS IN HIM...
...

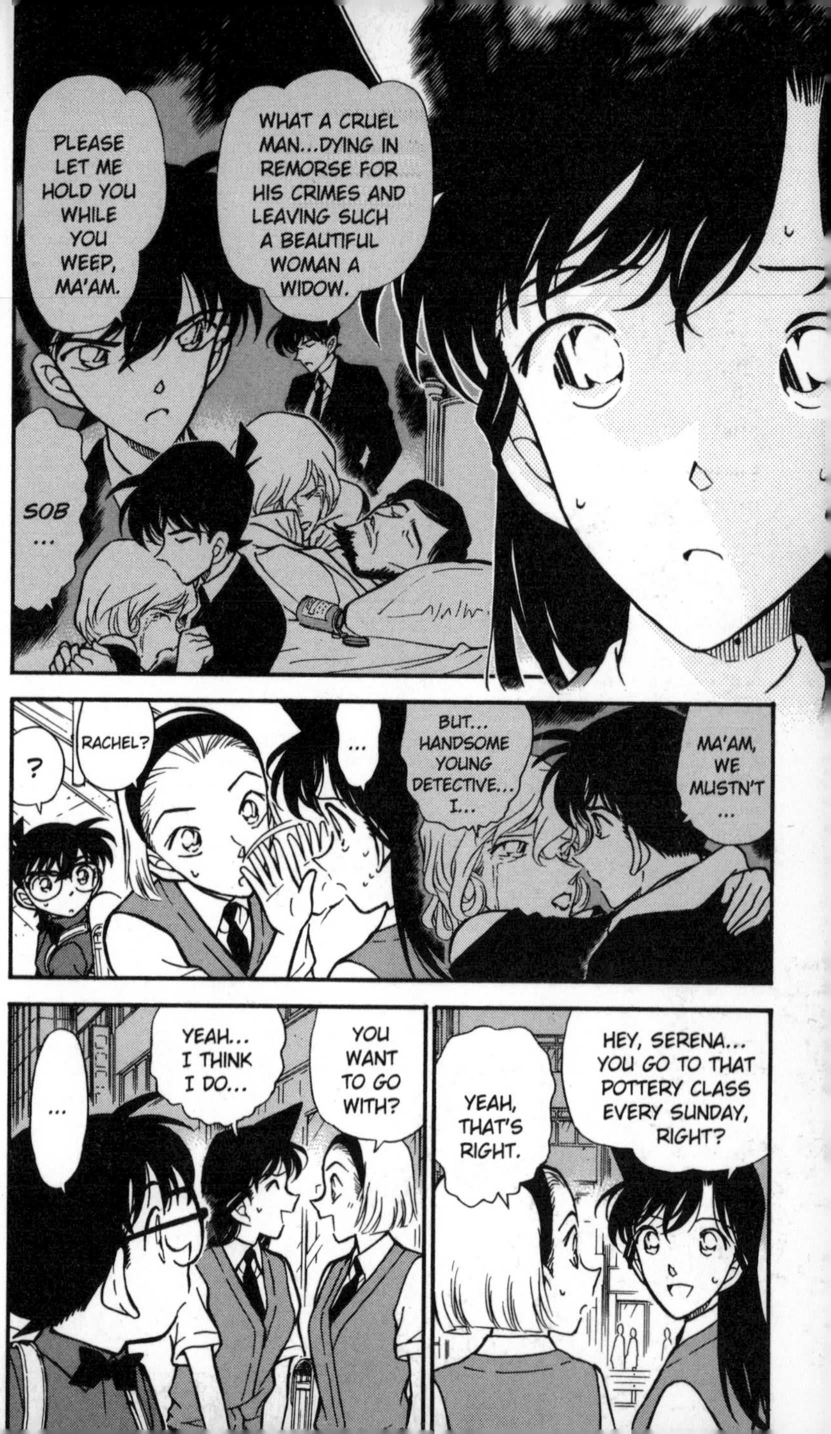
WHAT A CRUEL MAN...DYING IN REMORSE FOR HIS CRIMES AND LEAVING SUCH A BEAUTIFUL WOMAN A WIDOW.
PLEASE LET ME HOLD YOU WHILE YOU WEEP, MA'AM.
SOB...
MA'AM, WE MUSTN'T...
BUT... HANDSOME YOUNG DETECTIVE... I...
...
RACHEL?
?
HEY, SERENA... YOU GO TO THAT POTTERY CLASS EVERY SUNDAY, RIGHT?
YEAH, THAT'S RIGHT.
YOU WANT TO GO WITH?
YEAH... I THINK I DO...
...

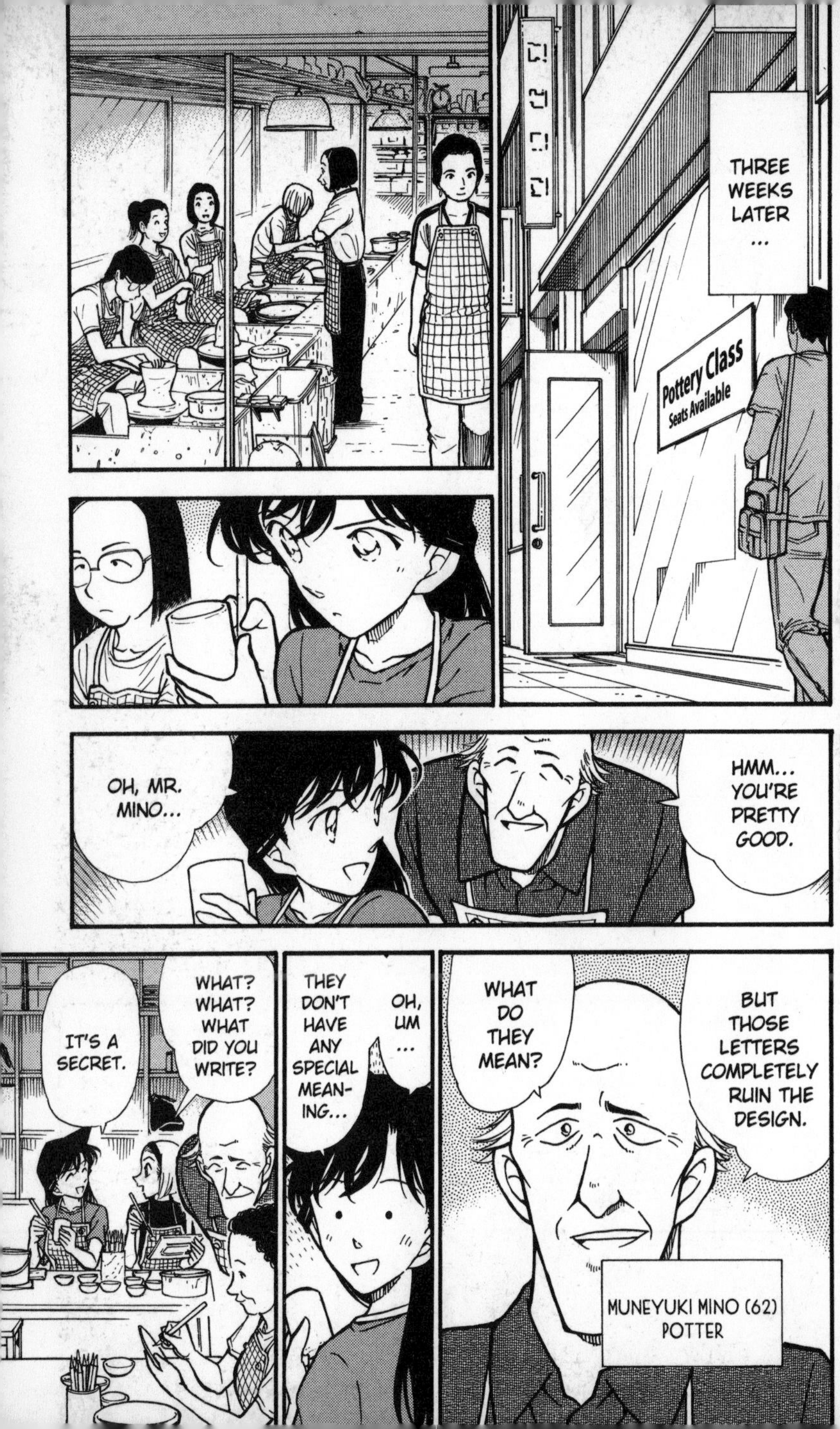
THREE WEEKS LATER ...
Pottery Class
Seats Available
HMM... YOU'RE PRETTY GOOD.
OH, MR. MINO...
BUT THOSE LETTERS COMPLETELY RUIN THE DESIGN.
WHAT DO THEY MEAN?
MUNEYUKI MINO (62) POTTER
OH, UM ...
THEY DON'T HAVE ANY SPECIAL MEAN-ING...
WHAT? WHAT? WHAT DID YOU WRITE?
IT'S A SECRET.

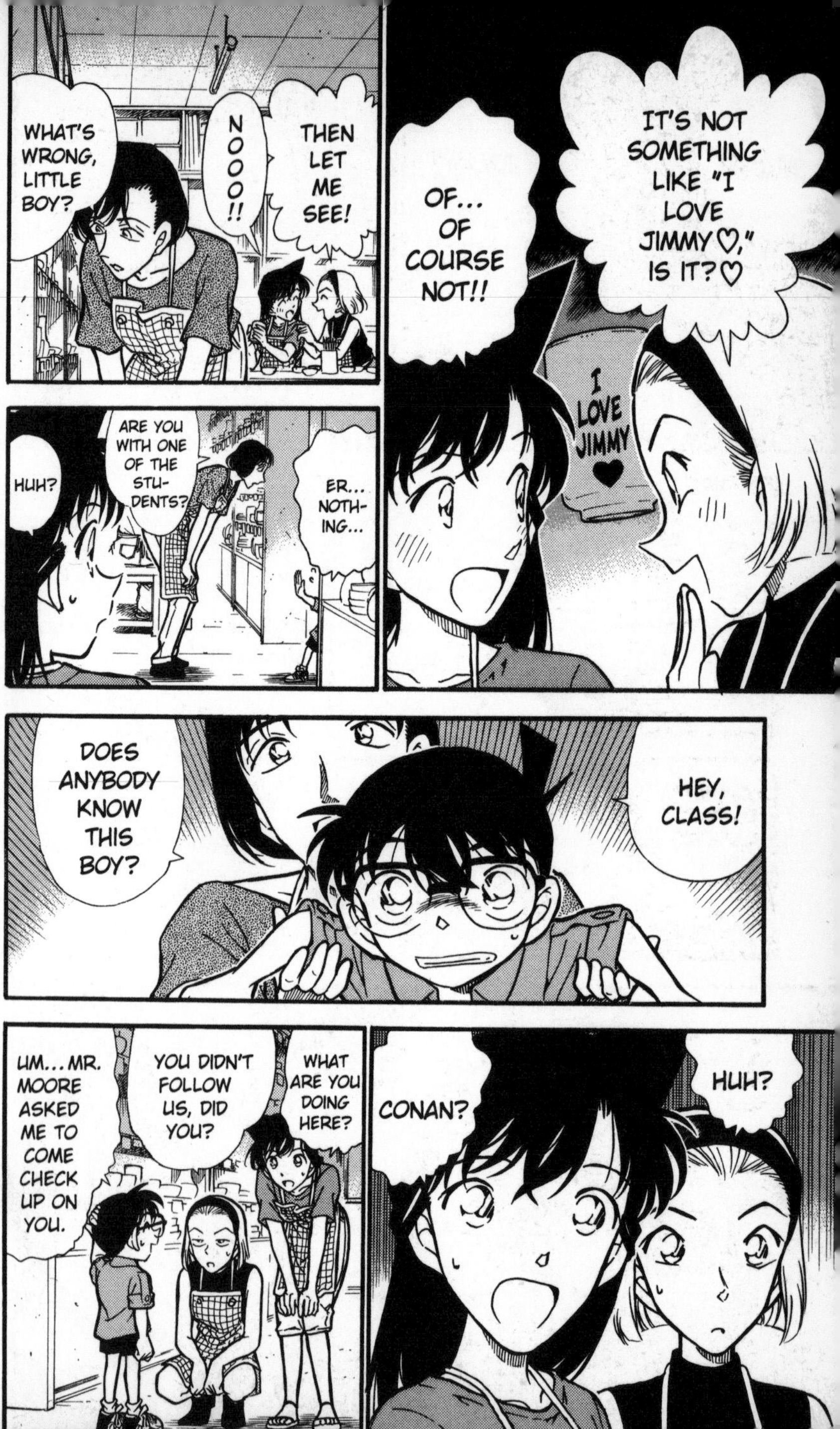
IT'S NOT SOMETHING LIKE "I LOVE JIMMY♡," IS IT?♡
OF... OF COURSE NOT!!
I LOVE JIMMY ♥
THEN LET ME SEE!
NOOOO!!
WHAT'S WRONG, LITTLE BOY?
ER... NOTHING...
ARE YOU WITH ONE OF THE STUDENTS?
HUH?
HEY, CLASS!
DOES ANYBODY KNOW THIS BOY?
HUH?
CONAN?
WHAT ARE YOU DOING HERE?
YOU DIDN'T FOLLOW US, DID YOU?
UM... MR. MOORE ASKED ME TO COME CHECK UP ON YOU.

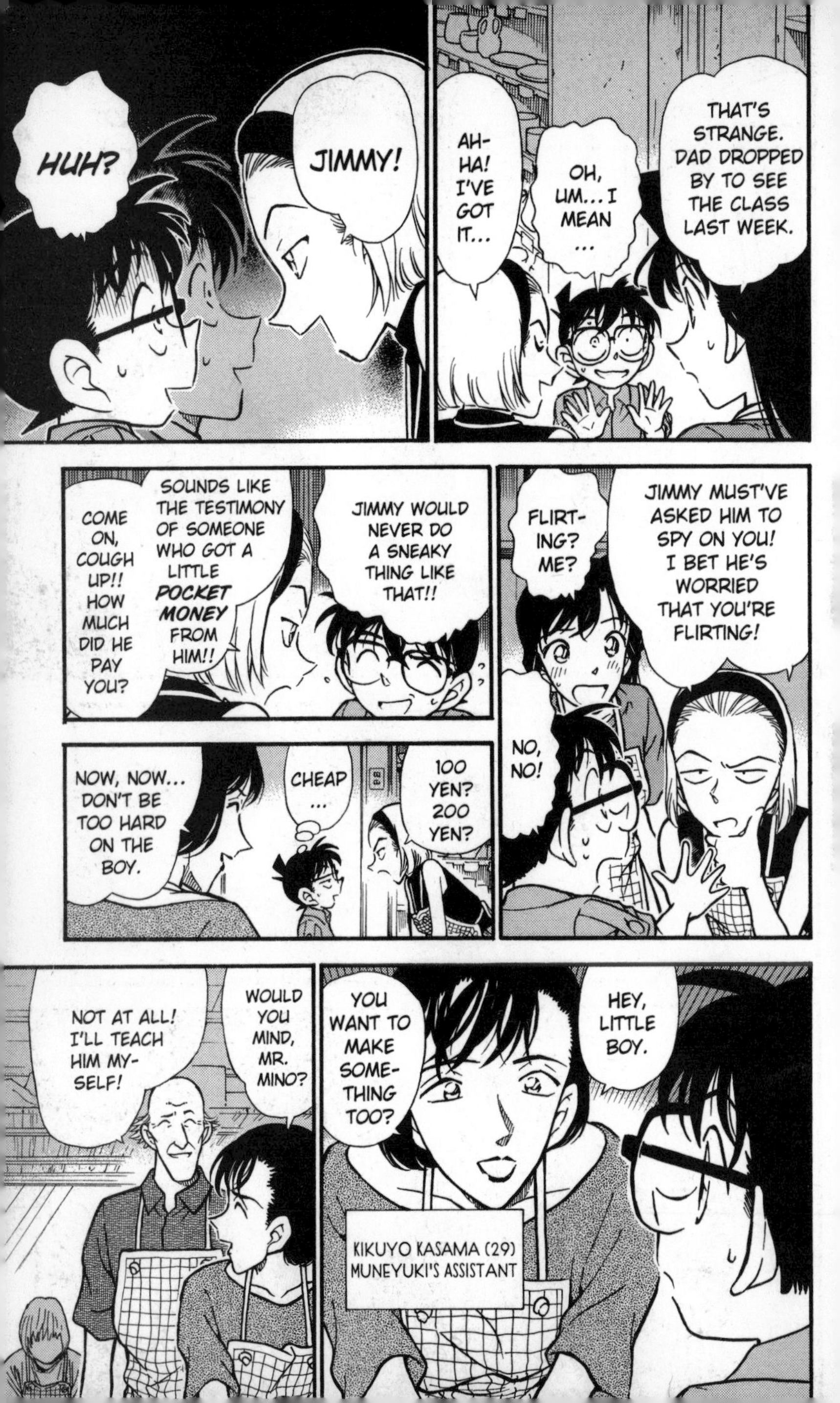

THAT'S STRANGE. DAD DROPPED BY TO SEE THE CLASS LAST WEEK.
OH, UM... I MEAN ...
AH-HA! I'VE GOT IT...
JIMMY!
HUH?
JIMMY MUST'VE ASKED HIM TO SPY ON YOU! I BET HE'S WORRIED THAT YOU'RE FLIRTING!
FLIRT-ING? ME?
NO, NO!
JIMMY WOULD NEVER DO A SNEAKY THING LIKE THAT!!
SOUNDS LIKE THE TESTIMONY OF SOMEONE WHO GOT A LITTLE POCKET MONEY FROM HIM!!
COME ON, COUGH UP!! HOW MUCH DID HE PAY YOU?
100 YEN? 200 YEN?
CHEAP ...
NOW, NOW... DON'T BE TOO HARD ON THE BOY.
HEY, LITTLE BOY.
YOU WANT TO MAKE SOME-THING TOO?
KIKUYO KASAMA (29) MUNEYUKI'S ASSISTANT
WOULD YOU MIND, MR. MINO?
NOT AT ALL! I'LL TEACH HIM MY-SELF!

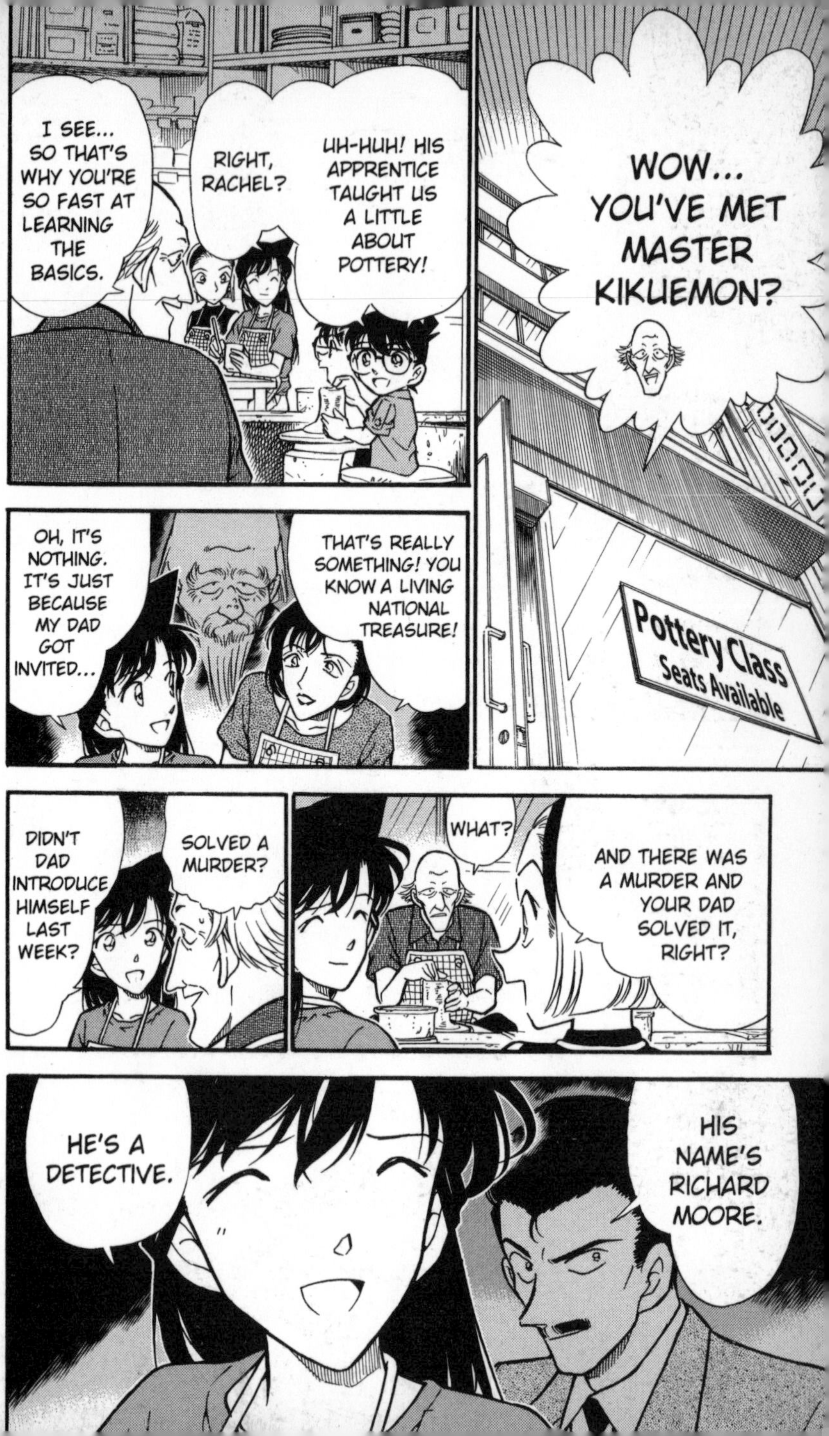
WOW... YOU'VE MET MASTER KIKUEMON?
Pottery Class
Seats Available
UH-HUH! HIS APPRENTICE TAUGHT US A LITTLE ABOUT POTTERY!
RIGHT, RACHEL?
I SEE... SO THAT'S WHY YOU'RE SO FAST AT LEARNING THE BASICS.
THAT'S REALLY SOMETHING! YOU KNOW A LIVING NATIONAL TREASURE!
OH, IT'S NOTHING. IT'S JUST BECAUSE MY DAD GOT INVITED...
AND THERE WAS A MURDER AND YOUR DAD SOLVED IT, RIGHT?
WHAT?
SOLVED A MURDER?
DIDN'T DAD INTRODUCE HIMSELF LAST WEEK?
HIS NAME'S RICHARD MOORE.
HE'S A DETECTIVE.

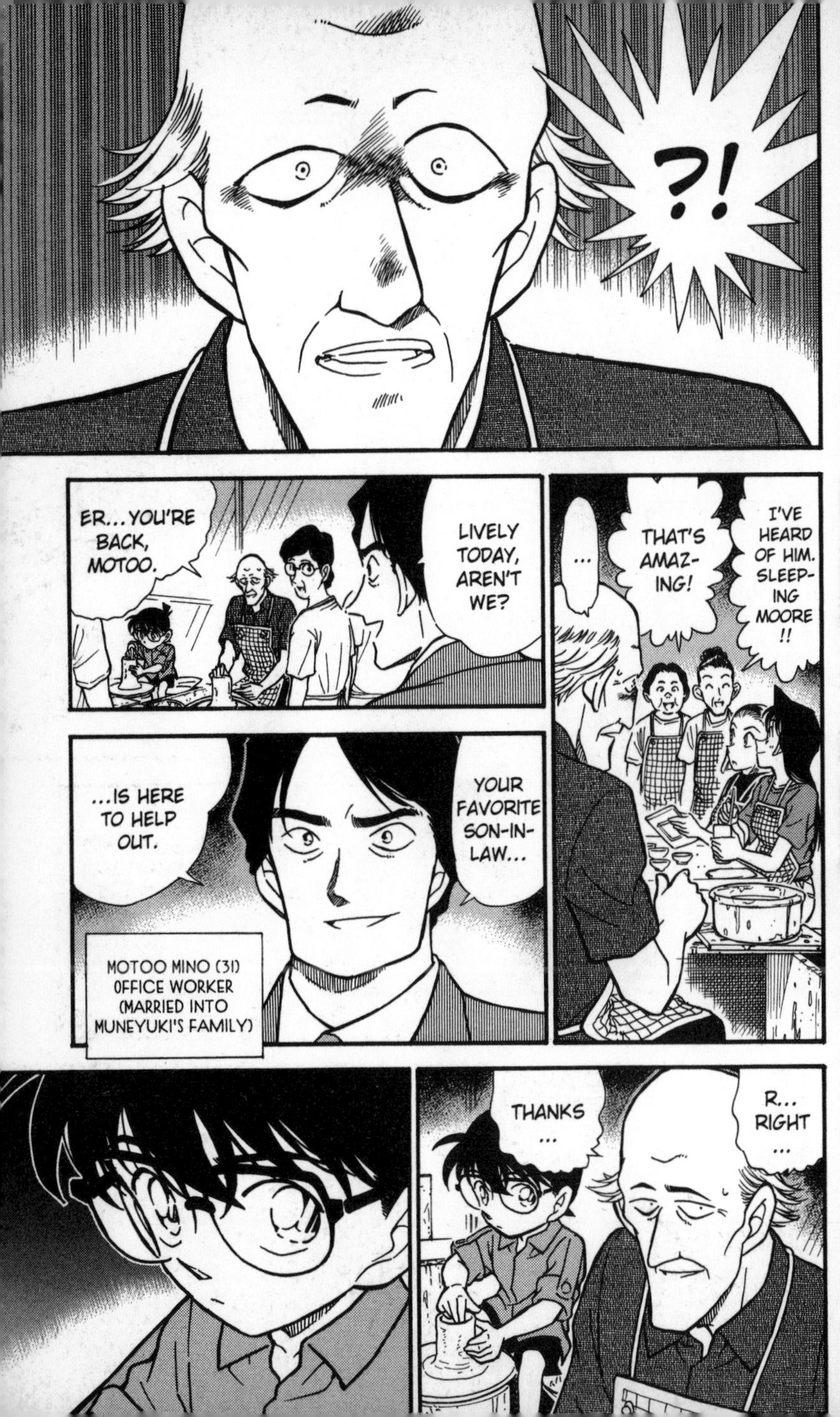
?!
I'VE HEARD OF HIM. SLEEPING MOORE!!
THAT'S AMAZING!
...
LIVELY TODAY, AREN'T WE?
ER... YOU'RE BACK, MOTOO.
YOUR FAVORITE SON-IN-LAW...
...IS HERE TO HELP OUT.
MOTOO MINO (31) OFFICE WORKER (MARRIED INTO MUNEYUKI'S FAMILY)
R... RIGHT...
THANKS...

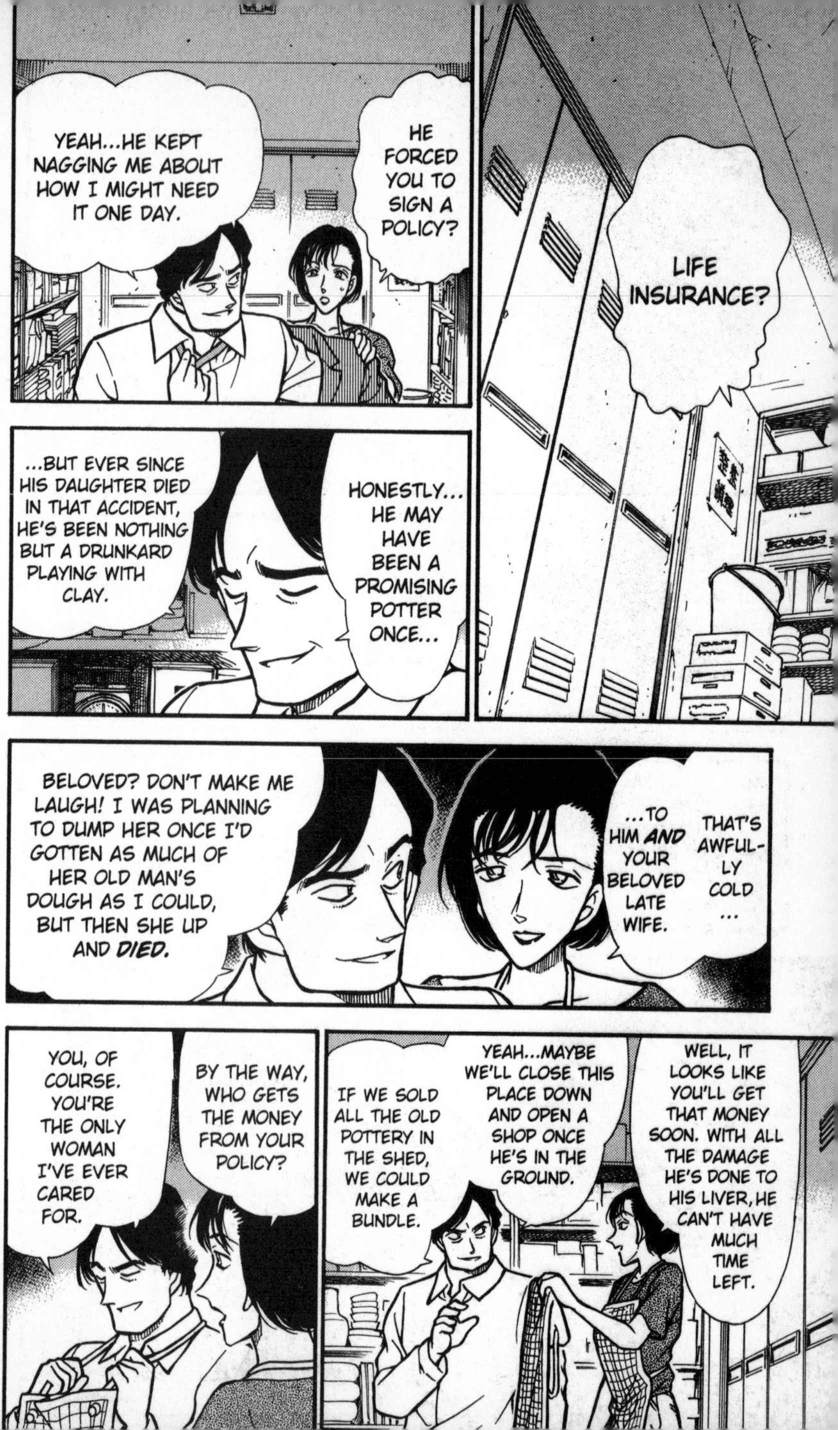
LIFE INSURANCE?
HE FORCED YOU TO SIGN A POLICY?
YEAH...HE KEPT NAGGING ME ABOUT HOW I MIGHT NEED IT ONE DAY.
HONESTLY... HE MAY HAVE BEEN A PROMISING POTTER ONCE...
...BUT EVER SINCE HIS DAUGHTER DIED IN THAT ACCIDENT, HE'S BEEN NOTHING BUT A DRUNKARD PLAYING WITH CLAY.
THAT'S AWFULLY COLD ...
...TO HIM *AND* YOUR BELOVED LATE WIFE.
BELOVED? DON'T MAKE ME LAUGH! I WAS PLANNING TO DUMP HER ONCE I'D GOTTEN AS MUCH OF HER OLD MAN'S DOUGH AS I COULD, BUT THEN SHE UP AND *DIED.*
WELL, IT LOOKS LIKE YOU'LL GET THAT MONEY SOON. WITH ALL THE DAMAGE HE'S DONE TO HIS LIVER, HE CAN'T HAVE MUCH TIME LEFT.
YEAH...MAYBE WE'LL CLOSE THIS PLACE DOWN AND OPEN A SHOP ONCE HE'S IN THE GROUND.
IF WE SOLD ALL THE OLD POTTERY IN THE SHED, WE COULD MAKE A BUNDLE.
BY THE WAY, WHO GETS THE MONEY FROM YOUR POLICY?
YOU, OF COURSE. YOU'RE THE ONLY WOMAN I'VE EVER CARED FOR.

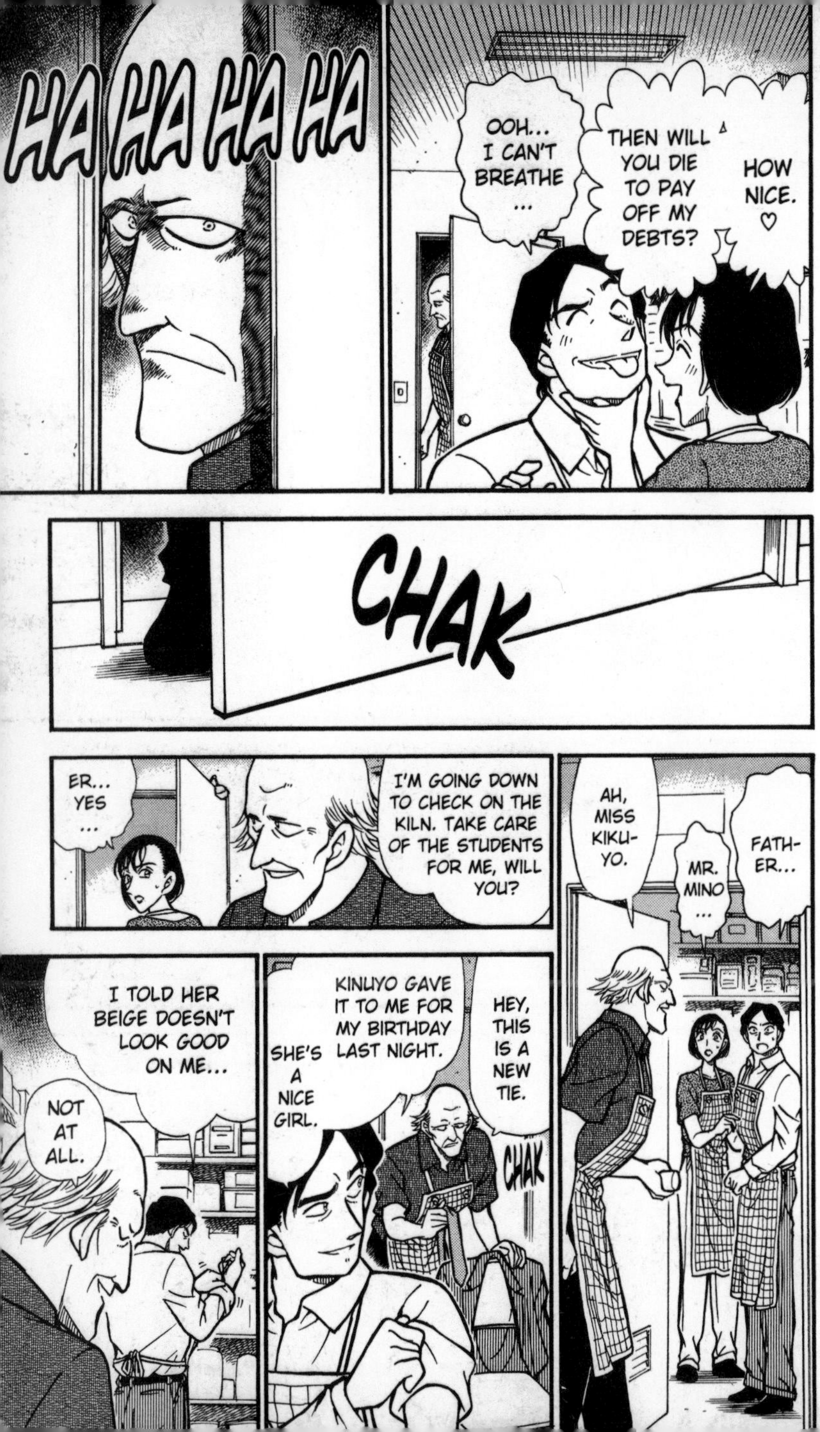

HOW NICE. ♡
THEN WILL YOU DIE TO PAY OFF MY DEBTS?
OOH... I CAN'T BREATHE ...
HA HA HA HA
CHAK
FATHER...
MR. MINO ...
AH, MISS KIKUYO.
I'M GOING DOWN TO CHECK ON THE KILN. TAKE CARE OF THE STUDENTS FOR ME, WILL YOU?
ER... YES ...
HEY, THIS IS A NEW TIE.
CHAK
KINUYO GAVE IT TO ME FOR MY BIRTHDAY LAST NIGHT.
SHE'S A NICE GIRL.
I TOLD HER BEIGE DOESN'T LOOK GOOD ON ME...
NOT AT ALL.

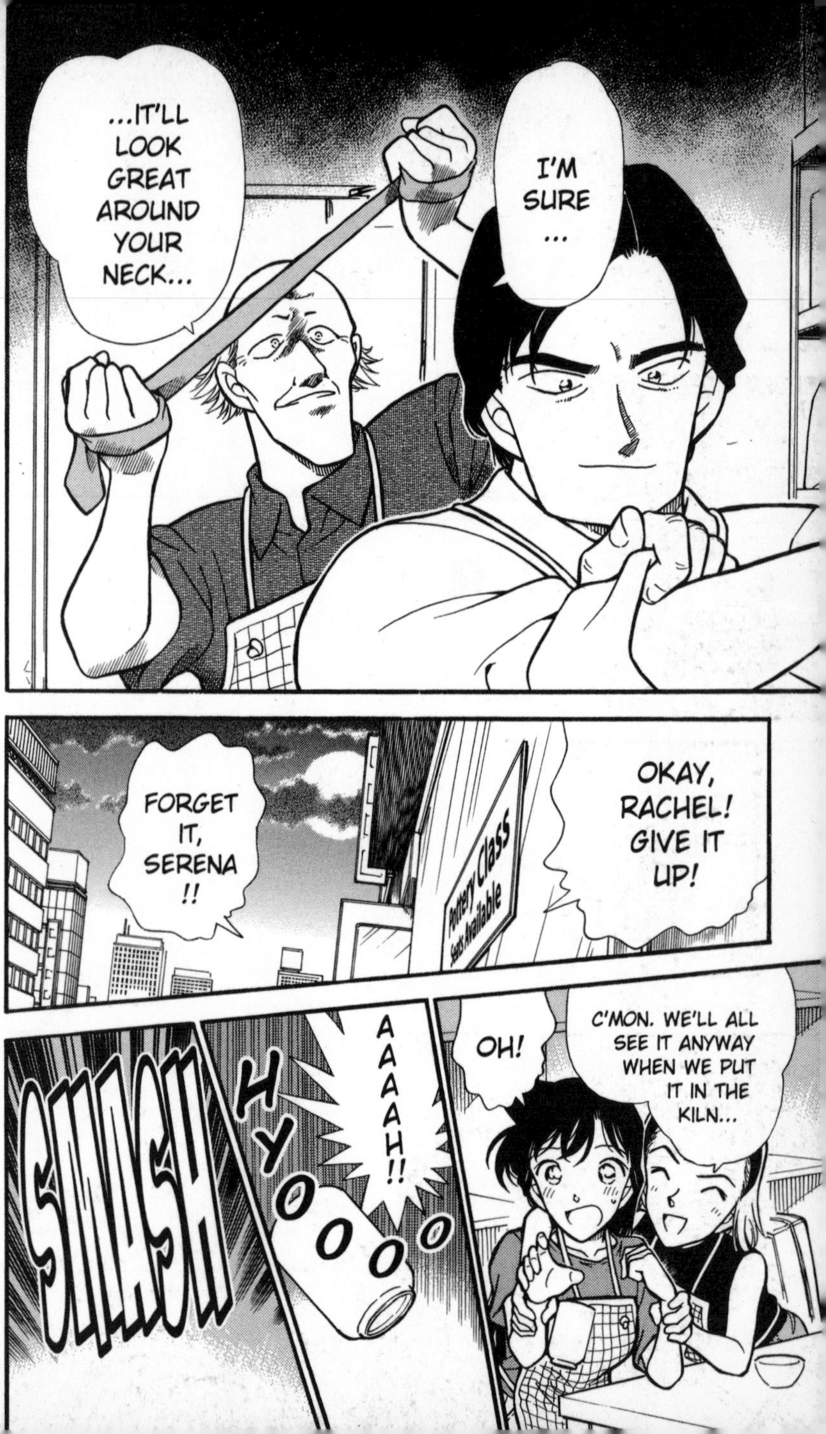
I'M SURE ...
...IT'LL LOOK GREAT AROUND YOUR NECK...
OKAY, RACHEL! GIVE IT UP!
Pottery Class Seats Available
FORGET IT, SERENA !!
C'MON. WE'LL ALL SEE IT ANYWAY WHEN WE PUT IT IN THE KILN...
OH!
AAAAAH!!
HYOOOOO
SMASH

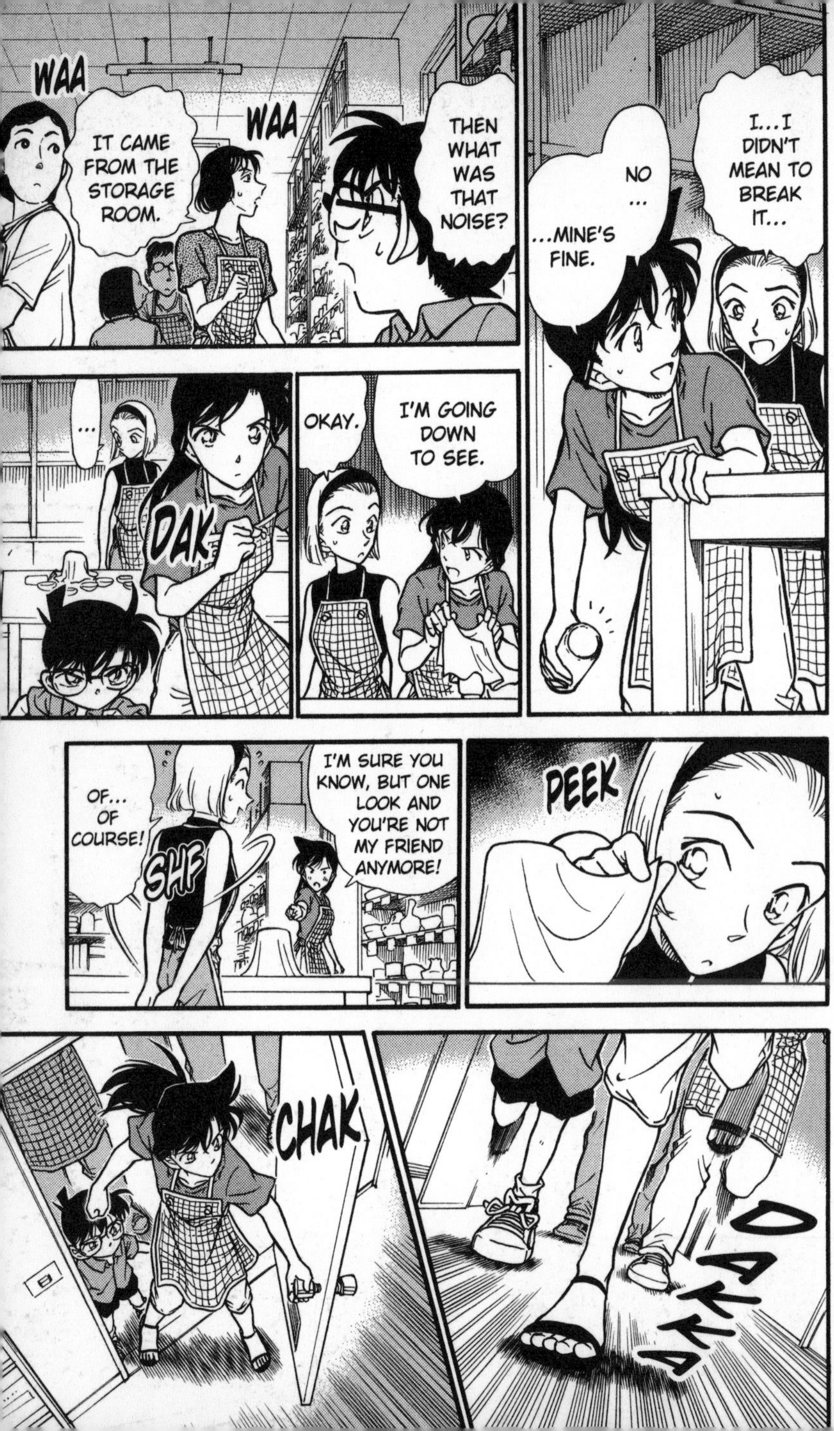
I…I DIDN'T MEAN TO BREAK IT…
NO …
…MINE'S FINE.
THEN WHAT WAS THAT NOISE?
WAA
IT CAME FROM THE STORAGE ROOM.
WAA
I'M GOING DOWN TO SEE.
OKAY.
…
DAK
PEEK
I'M SURE YOU KNOW, BUT ONE LOOK AND YOU'RE NOT MY FRIEND ANYMORE!
OF… OF COURSE!
SHF
DAKKA
CHAK

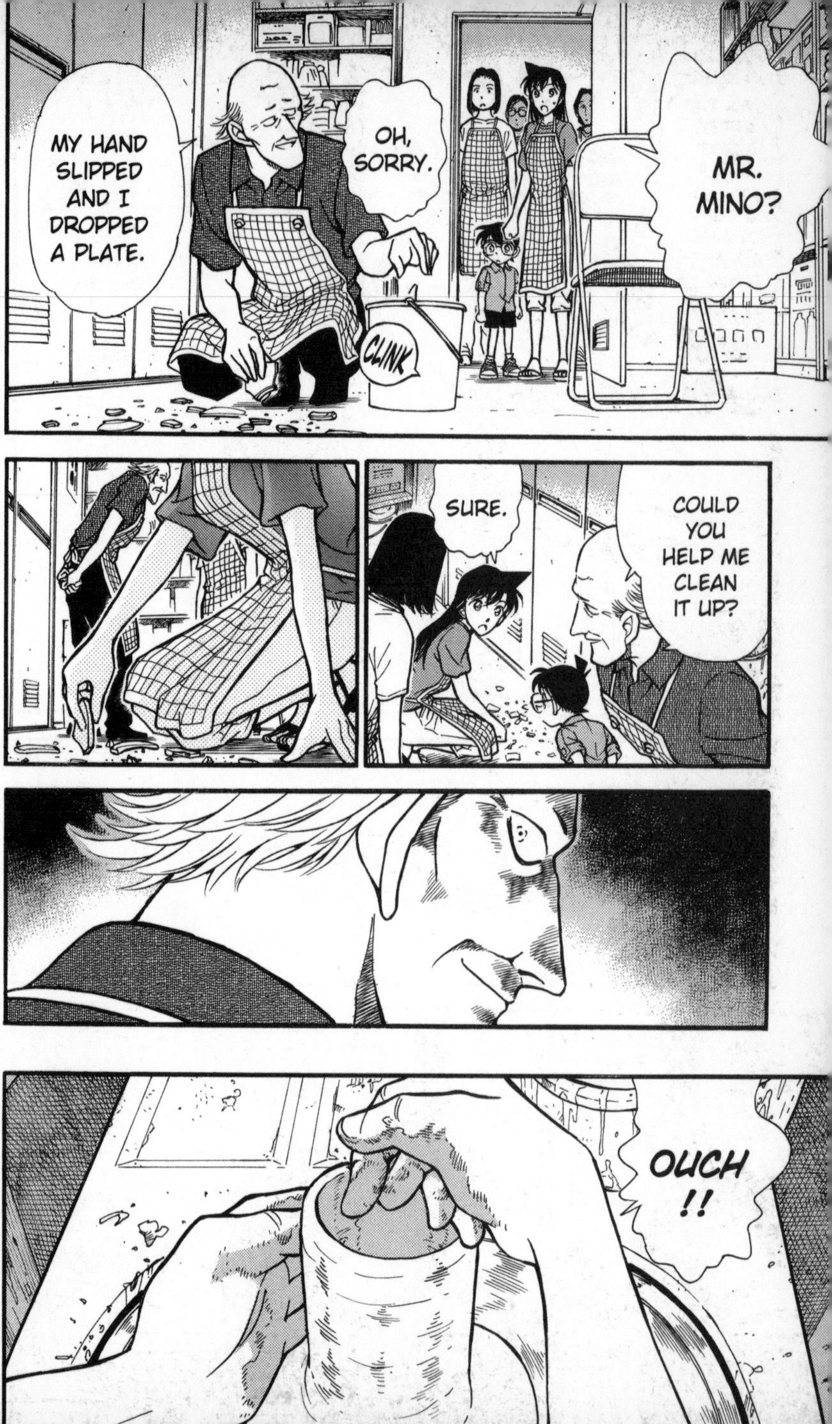
MR. MINO?
OH, SORRY.
MY HAND SLIPPED AND I DROPPED A PLATE.
CLINK
COULD YOU HELP ME CLEAN IT UP?
SURE.
OUCH !!

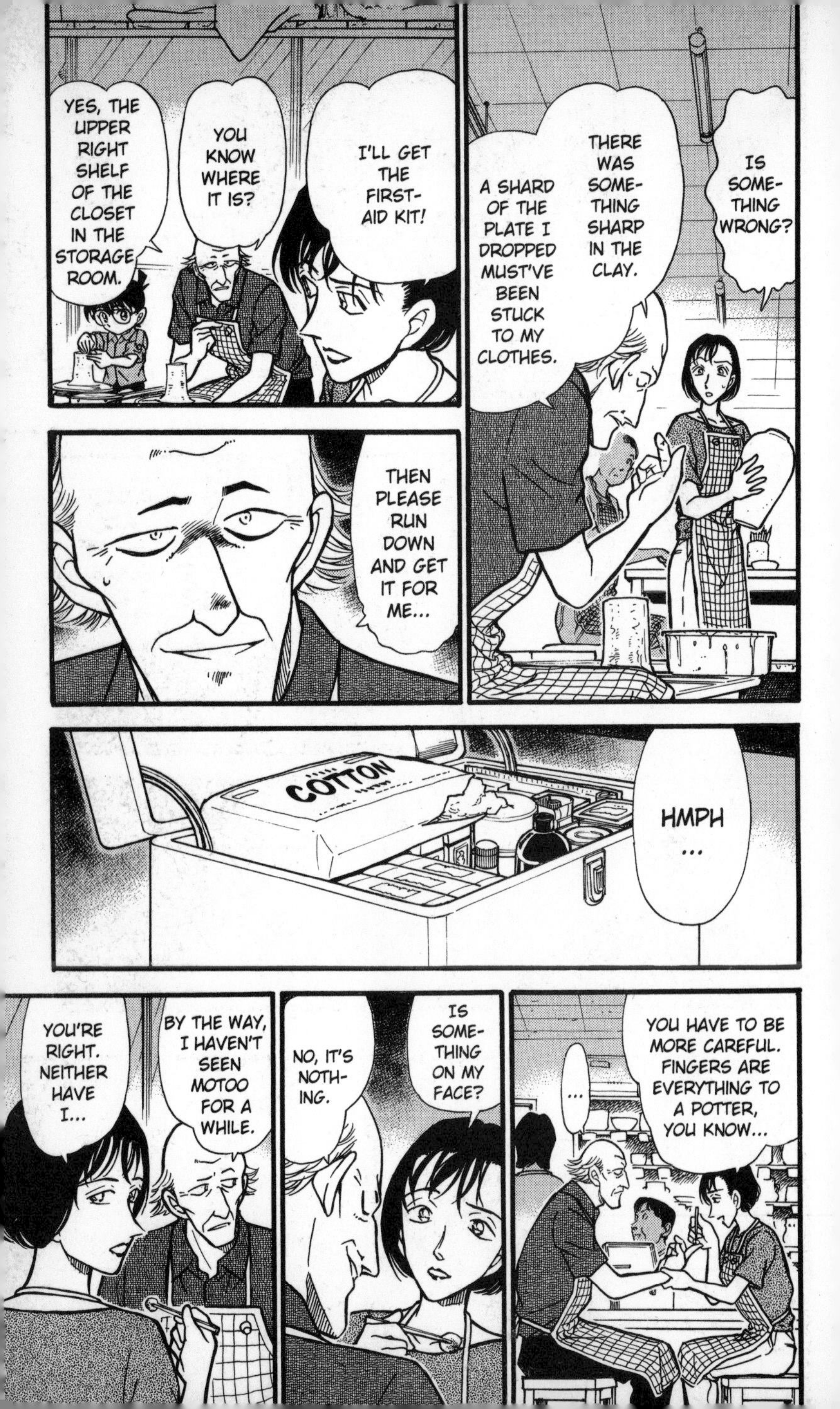
IS SOMETHING WRONG?
THERE WAS SOMETHING SHARP IN THE CLAY.
A SHARD OF THE PLATE I DROPPED MUST'VE BEEN STUCK TO MY CLOTHES.
I'LL GET THE FIRST-AID KIT!
YOU KNOW WHERE IT IS?
YES, THE UPPER RIGHT SHELF OF THE CLOSET IN THE STORAGE ROOM.
THEN PLEASE RUN DOWN AND GET IT FOR ME...
HMPH ...
COTTON
YOU HAVE TO BE MORE CAREFUL. FINGERS ARE EVERYTHING TO A POTTER, YOU KNOW...
...
IS SOMETHING ON MY FACE?
NO, IT'S NOTHING.
BY THE WAY, I HAVEN'T SEEN MOTOO FOR A WHILE.
YOU'RE RIGHT. NEITHER HAVE I...

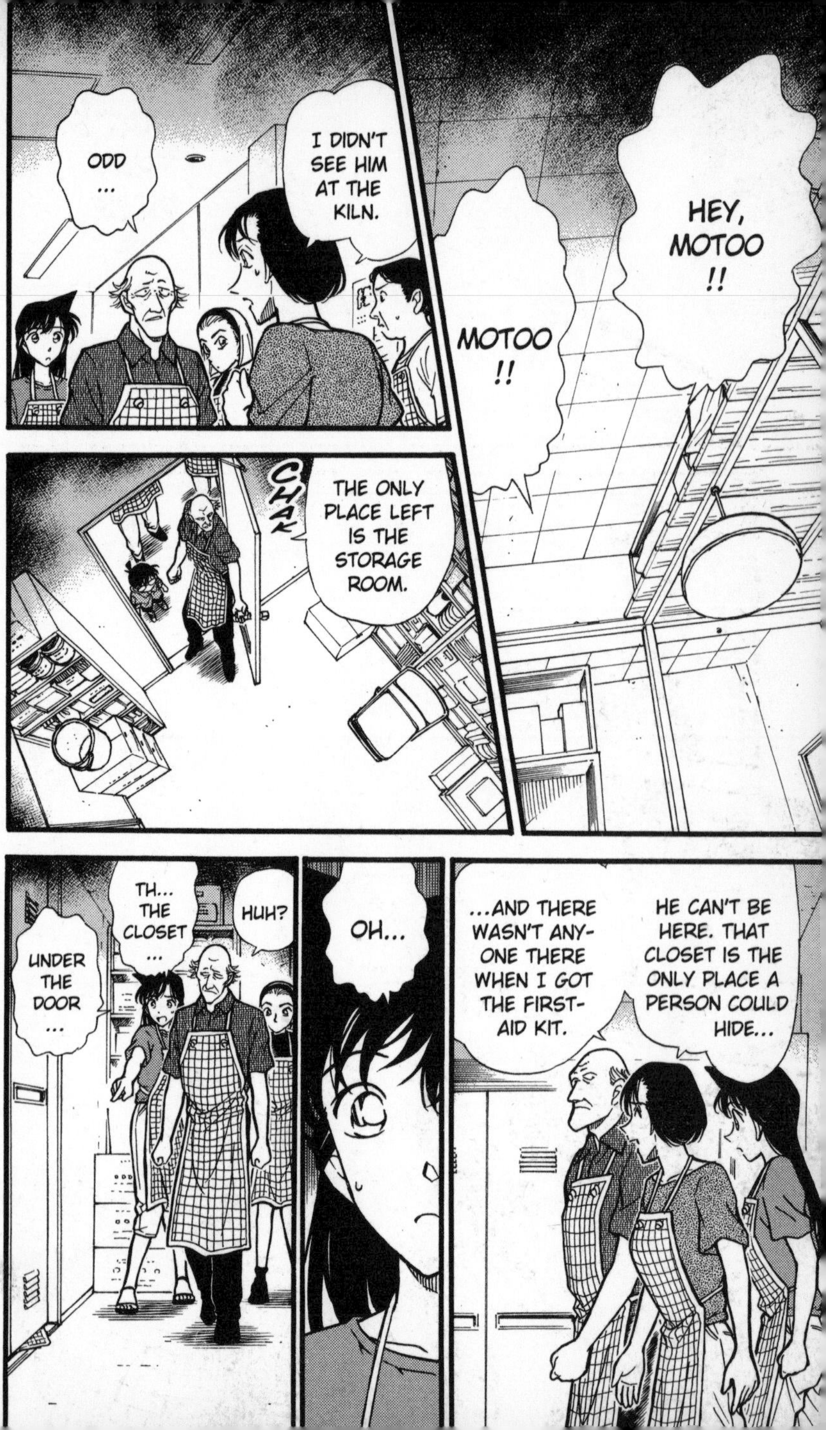
HEY, MOTOO !!
MOTOO !!
I DIDN'T SEE HIM AT THE KILN.
ODD ...
CHAK
THE ONLY PLACE LEFT IS THE STORAGE ROOM.
HE CAN'T BE HERE. THAT CLOSET IS THE ONLY PLACE A PERSON COULD HIDE...
...AND THERE WASN'T ANY-ONE THERE WHEN I GOT THE FIRST-AID KIT.
OH...
HUH?
TH... THE CLOSET ...
UNDER THE DOOR ...

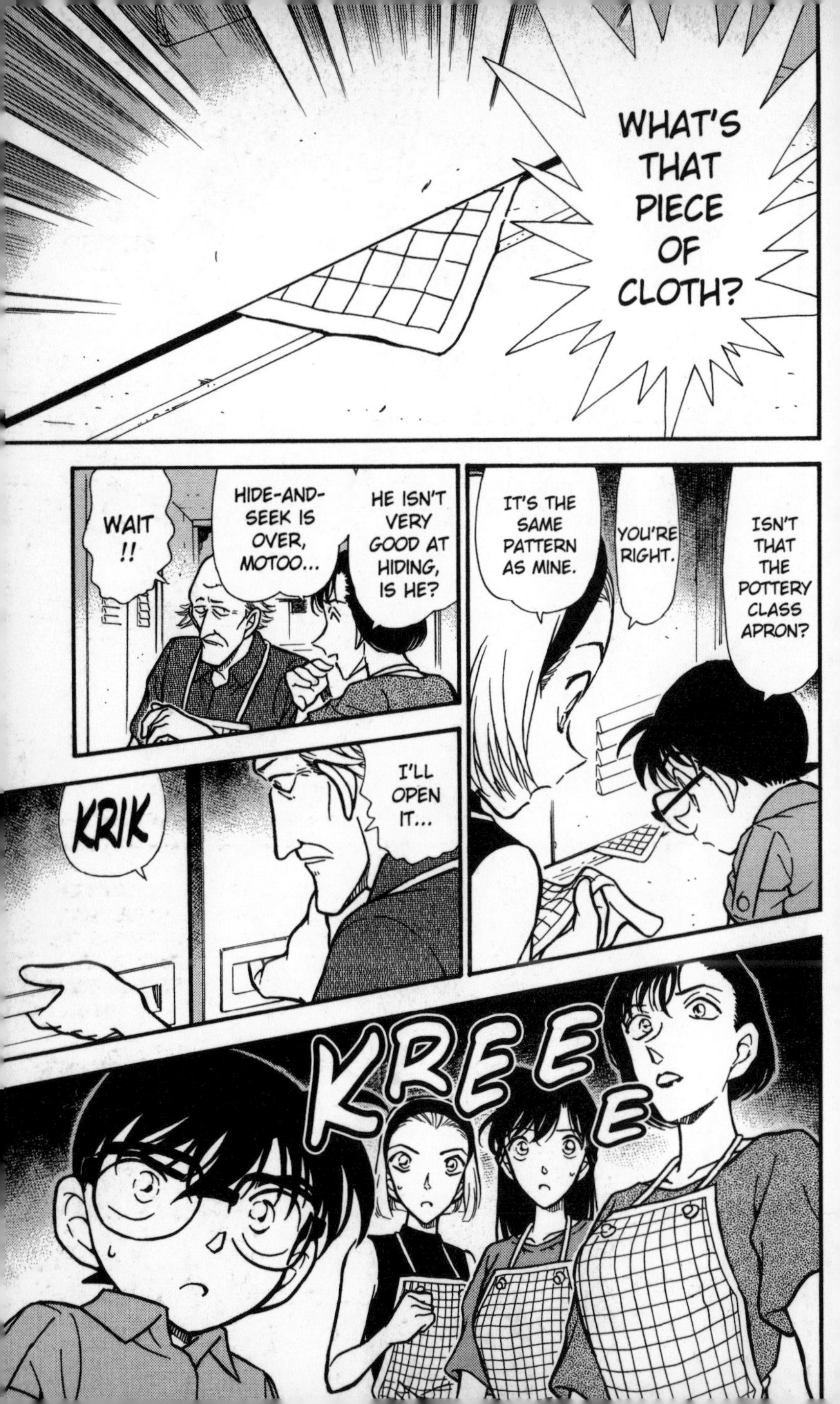
WHAT'S THAT PIECE OF CLOTH?
ISN'T THAT THE POTTERY CLASS APRON?
YOU'RE RIGHT.
IT'S THE SAME PATTERN AS MINE.
HE ISN'T VERY GOOD AT HIDING, IS HE?
HIDE-AND-SEEK IS OVER, MOTOO...
WAIT !!
I'LL OPEN IT...
KRIK
KREEE

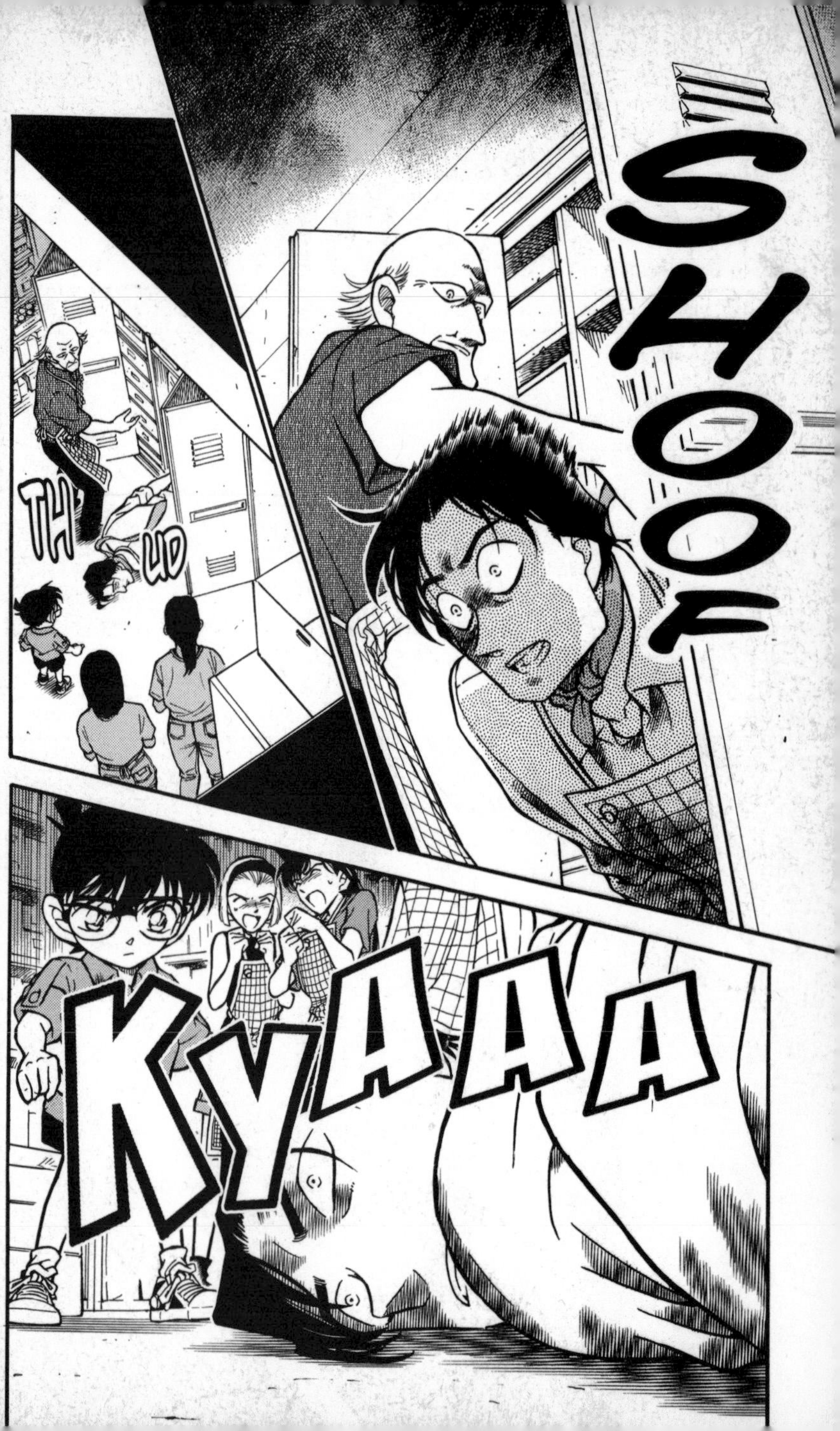

SHOOF
THUD
KYAAA

ENCIRCLED BY PROOF

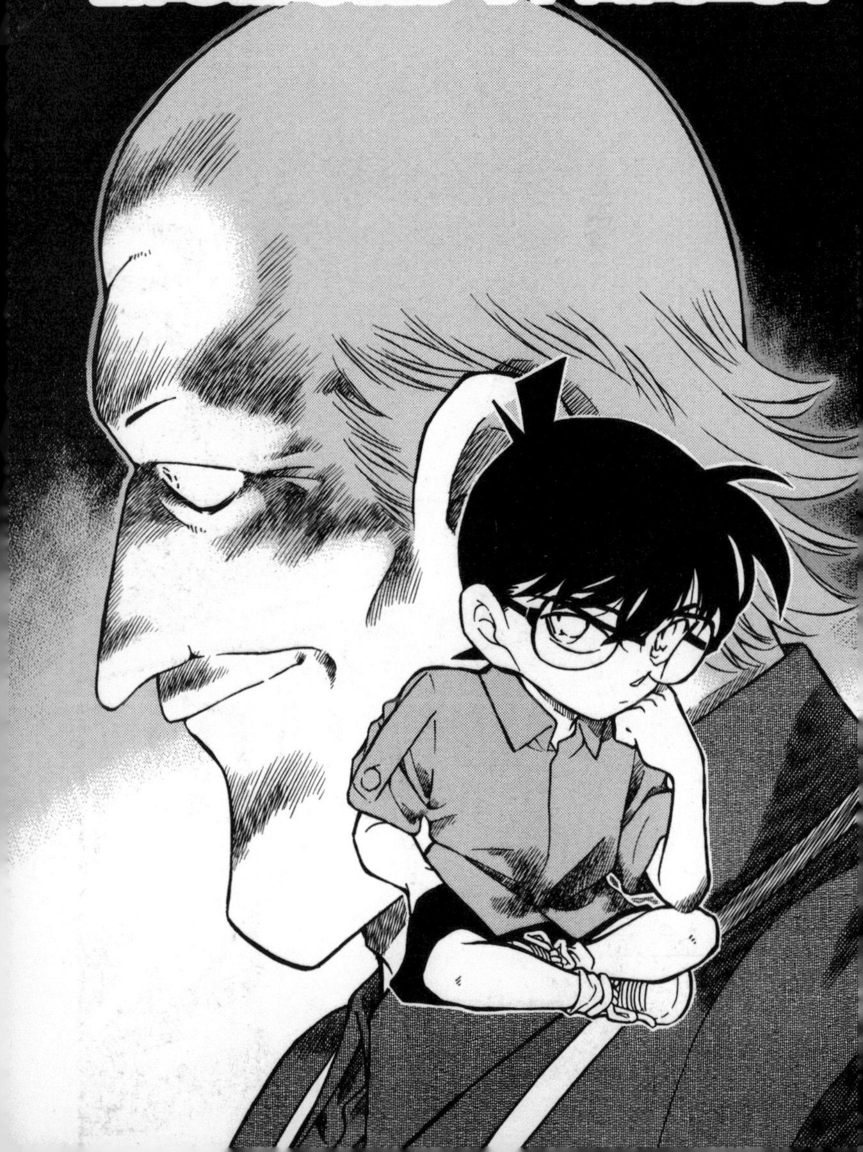

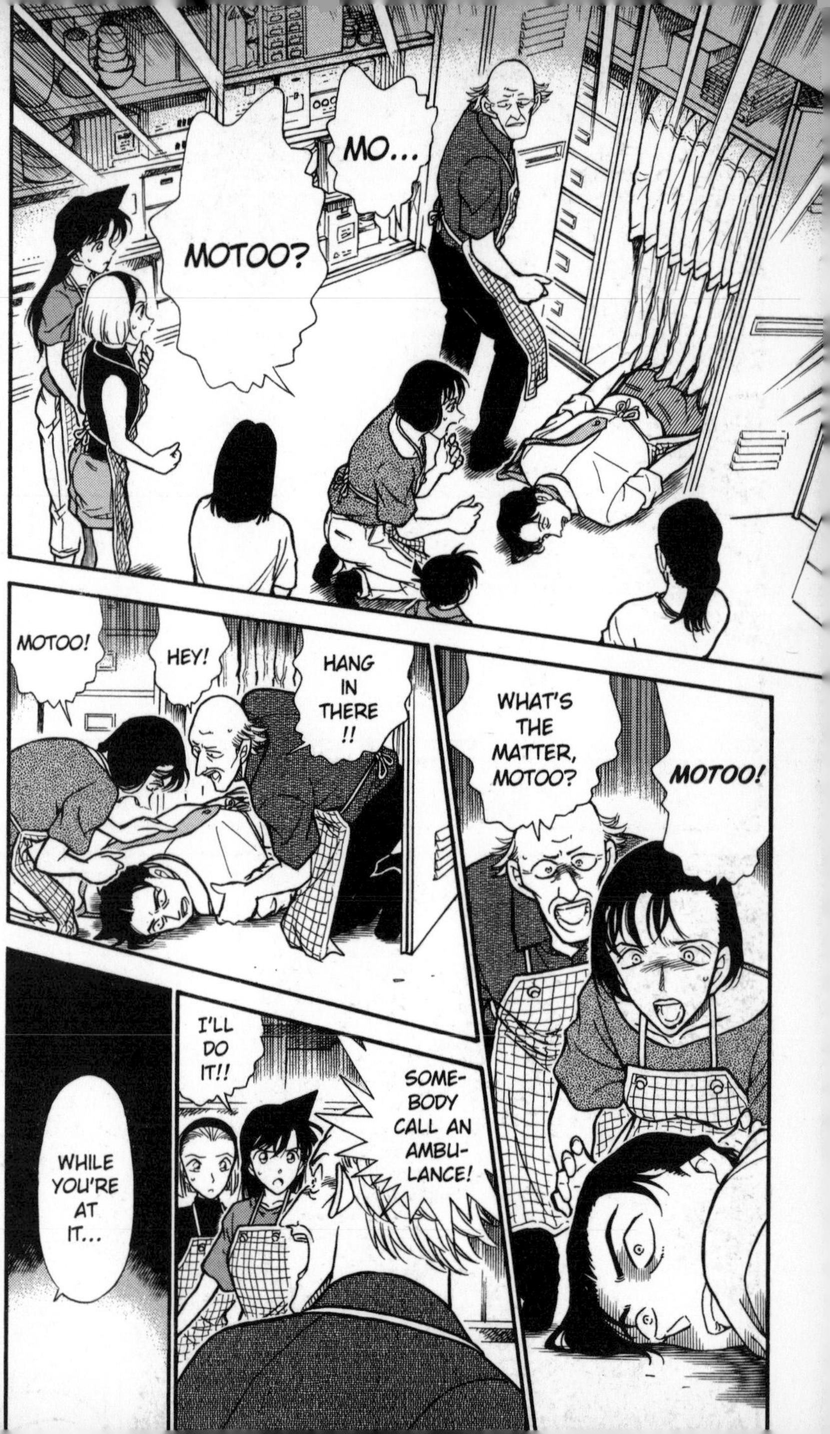
MO...
MOTOO?
MOTOO!
WHAT'S THE MATTER, MOTOO?
HANG IN THERE!!
HEY!
MOTOO!
SOMEBODY CALL AN AMBULANCE!
I'LL DO IT!!
WHILE YOU'RE AT IT...

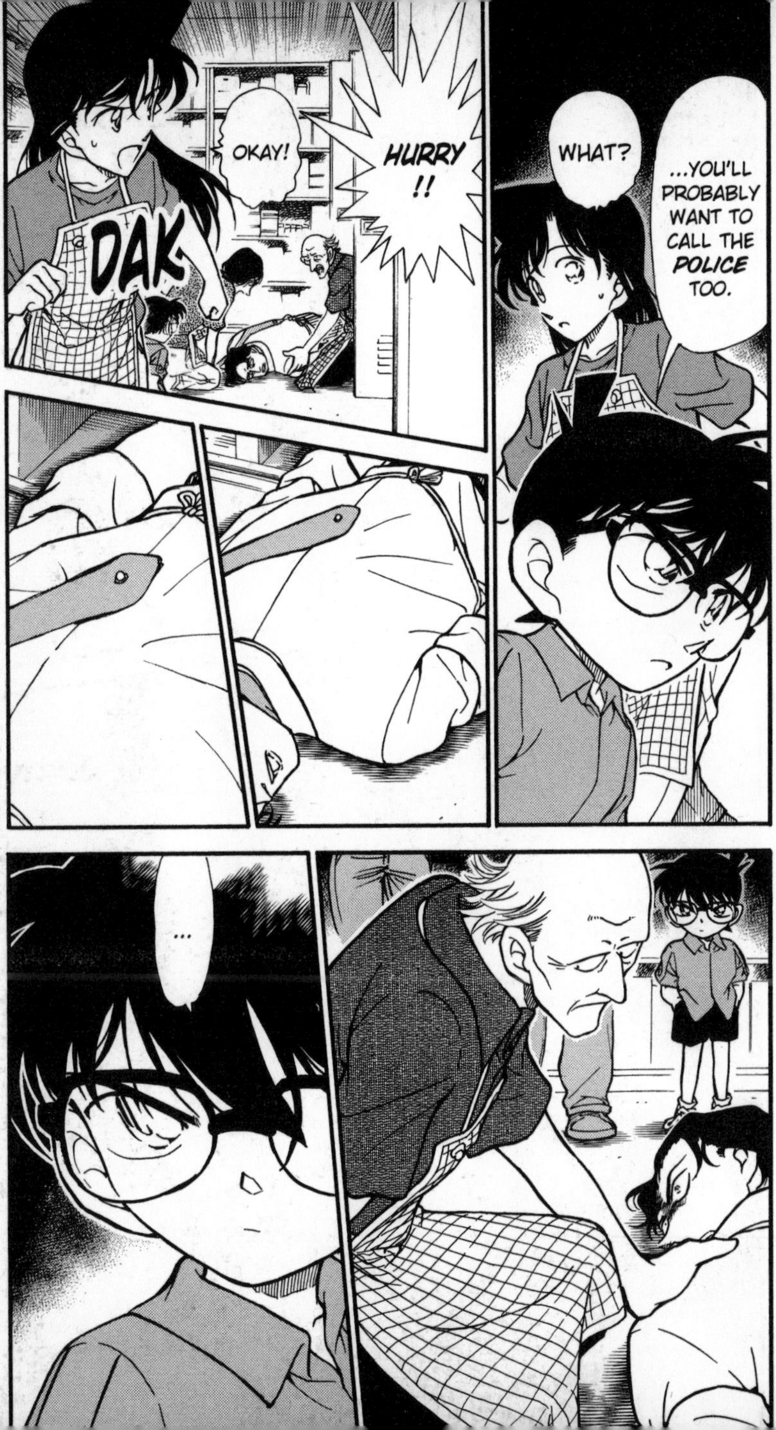
WHAT?
...YOU'LL PROBABLY WANT TO CALL THE POLICE TOO.
HURRY!!
OKAY!
DAK
...

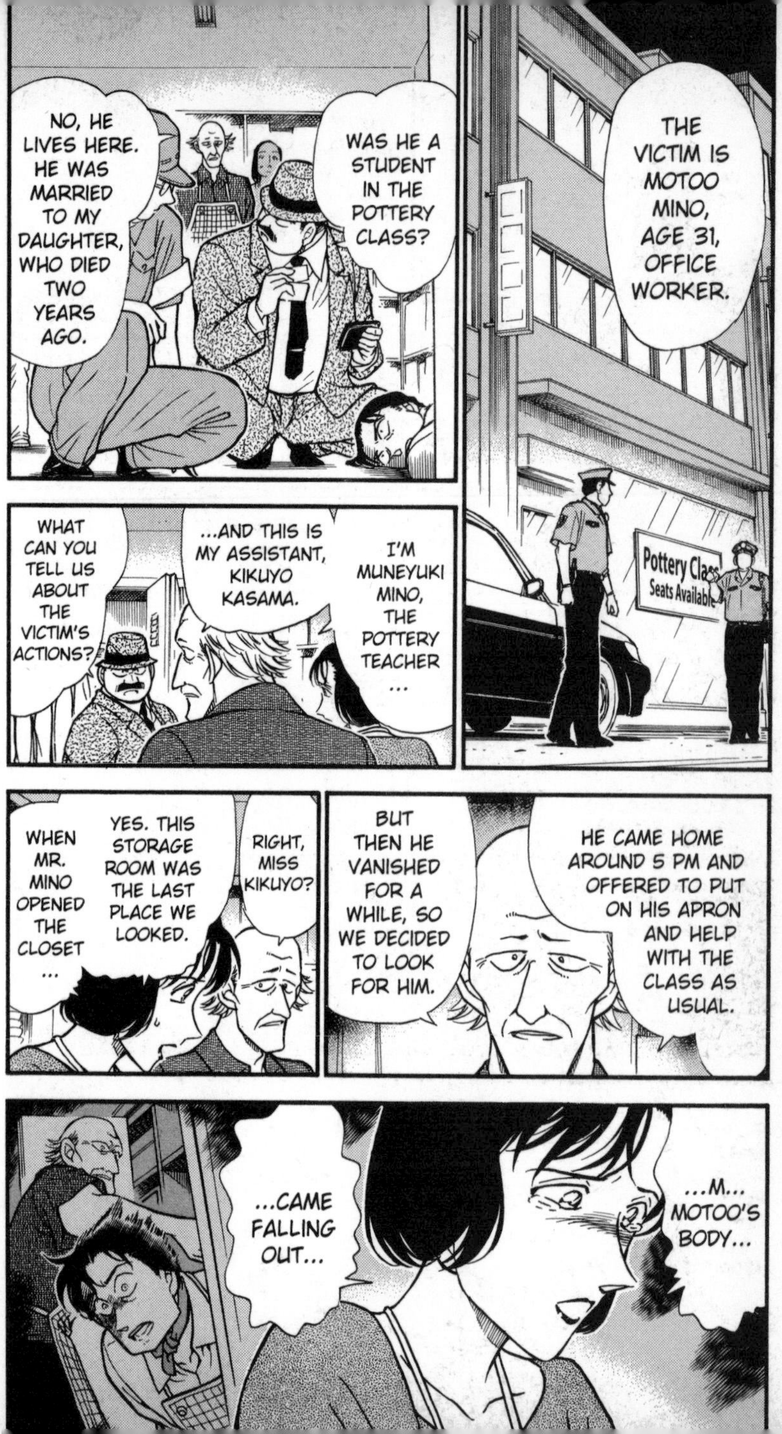
THE VICTIM IS MOTOO MINO, AGE 31, OFFICE WORKER.
Pottery Clas
Seats Availabl
WAS HE A STUDENT IN THE POTTERY CLASS?
NO, HE LIVES HERE. HE WAS MARRIED TO MY DAUGHTER, WHO DIED TWO YEARS AGO.
I'M MUNEYUKI MINO, THE POTTERY TEACHER ...
...AND THIS IS MY ASSISTANT, KIKUYO KASAMA.
WHAT CAN YOU TELL US ABOUT THE VICTIM'S ACTIONS?
HE CAME HOME AROUND 5 PM AND OFFERED TO PUT ON HIS APRON AND HELP WITH THE CLASS AS USUAL.
BUT THEN HE VANISHED FOR A WHILE, SO WE DECIDED TO LOOK FOR HIM.
RIGHT, MISS KIKUYO?
YES. THIS STORAGE ROOM WAS THE LAST PLACE WE LOOKED.
WHEN MR. MINO OPENED THE CLOSET ...
...M... MOTOO'S BODY...
...CAME FALLING OUT...

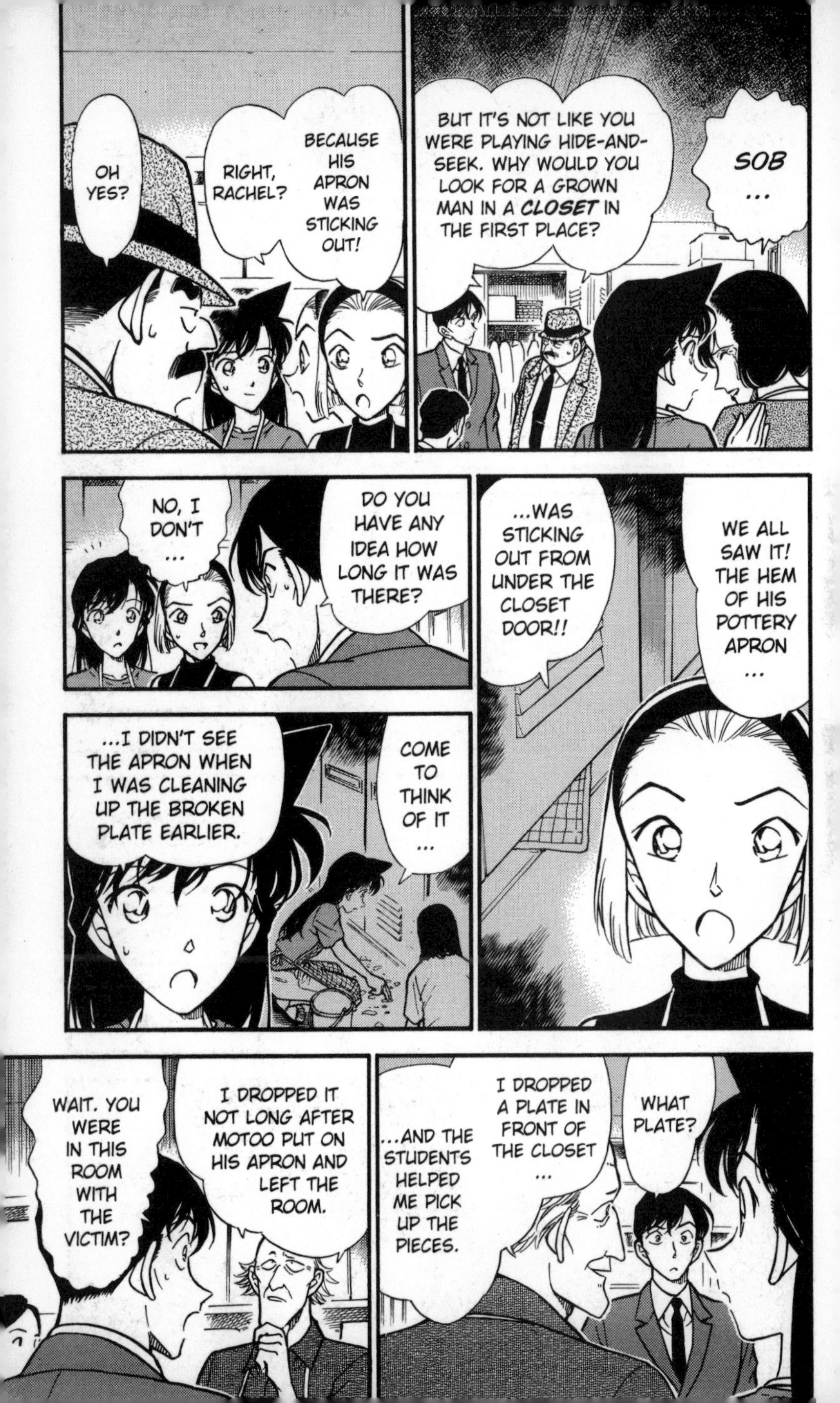
SOB ...
BUT IT'S NOT LIKE YOU WERE PLAYING HIDE-AND-SEEK. WHY WOULD YOU LOOK FOR A GROWN MAN IN A CLOSET IN THE FIRST PLACE?
BECAUSE HIS APRON WAS STICKING OUT!
RIGHT, RACHEL?
OH YES?
WE ALL SAW IT! THE HEM OF HIS POTTERY APRON ...
...WAS STICKING OUT FROM UNDER THE CLOSET DOOR!!
DO YOU HAVE ANY IDEA HOW LONG IT WAS THERE?
NO, I DON'T ...
COME TO THINK OF IT ...
...I DIDN'T SEE THE APRON WHEN I WAS CLEANING UP THE BROKEN PLATE EARLIER.
WHAT PLATE?
I DROPPED A PLATE IN FRONT OF THE CLOSET ...
...AND THE STUDENTS HELPED ME PICK UP THE PIECES.
I DROPPED IT NOT LONG AFTER MOTOO PUT ON HIS APRON AND LEFT THE ROOM.
WAIT. YOU WERE IN THIS ROOM WITH THE VICTIM?

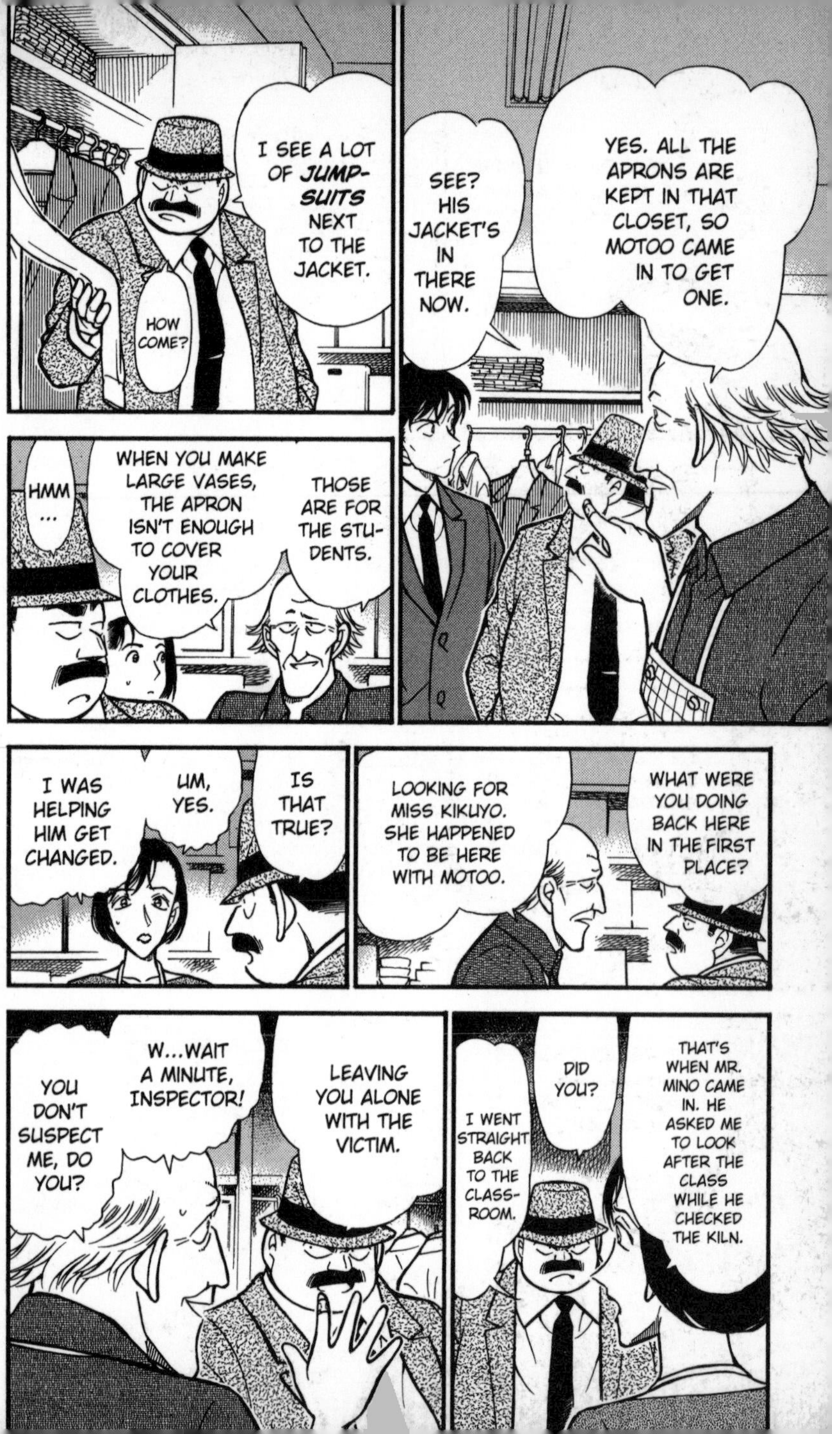
YES. ALL THE APRONS ARE KEPT IN THAT CLOSET, SO MOTOO CAME IN TO GET ONE.
SEE? HIS JACKET'S IN THERE NOW.
I SEE A LOT OF **JUMP-SUITS** NEXT TO THE JACKET.
HOW COME?
THOSE ARE FOR THE STU-DENTS.
WHEN YOU MAKE LARGE VASES, THE APRON ISN'T ENOUGH TO COVER YOUR CLOTHES.
HMM ...
WHAT WERE YOU DOING BACK HERE IN THE FIRST PLACE?
LOOKING FOR MISS KIKUYO. SHE HAPPENED TO BE HERE WITH MOTOO.
IS THAT TRUE?
UM, YES.
I WAS HELPING HIM GET CHANGED.
THAT'S WHEN MR. MINO CAME IN. HE ASKED ME TO LOOK AFTER THE CLASS WHILE HE CHECKED THE KILN.
DID YOU?
I WENT STRAIGHT BACK TO THE CLASS-ROOM.
LEAVING YOU ALONE WITH THE VICTIM.
W...WAIT A MINUTE, INSPECTOR!
YOU DON'T SUSPECT ME, DO YOU?

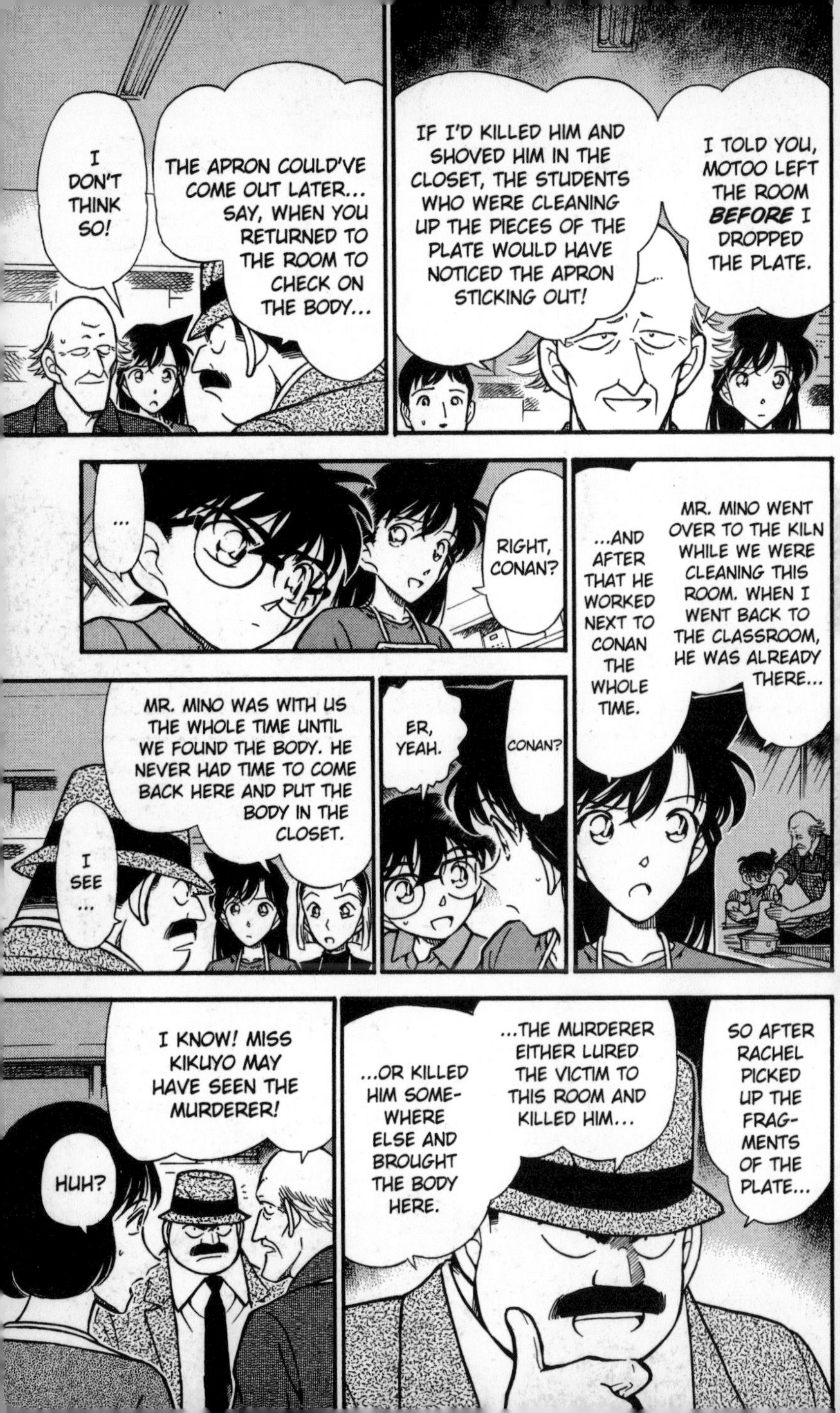
I TOLD YOU, MOTOO LEFT THE ROOM *BEFORE* I DROPPED THE PLATE.
IF I'D KILLED HIM AND SHOVED HIM IN THE CLOSET, THE STUDENTS WHO WERE CLEANING UP THE PIECES OF THE PLATE WOULD HAVE NOTICED THE APRON STICKING OUT!
THE APRON COULD'VE COME OUT LATER... SAY, WHEN YOU RETURNED TO THE ROOM TO CHECK ON THE BODY...
I DON'T THINK SO!
MR. MINO WENT OVER TO THE KILN WHILE WE WERE CLEANING THIS ROOM. WHEN I WENT BACK TO THE CLASSROOM, HE WAS ALREADY THERE...
...AND AFTER THAT HE WORKED NEXT TO CONAN THE WHOLE TIME.
RIGHT, CONAN?
...
CONAN?
ER, YEAH.
MR. MINO WAS WITH US THE WHOLE TIME UNTIL WE FOUND THE BODY. HE NEVER HAD TIME TO COME BACK HERE AND PUT THE BODY IN THE CLOSET.
I SEE...
SO AFTER RACHEL PICKED UP THE FRAG-MENTS OF THE PLATE...
...THE MURDERER EITHER LURED THE VICTIM TO THIS ROOM AND KILLED HIM...
...OR KILLED HIM SOME-WHERE ELSE AND BROUGHT THE BODY HERE.
I KNOW! MISS KIKUYO MAY HAVE SEEN THE MURDERER!
HUH?

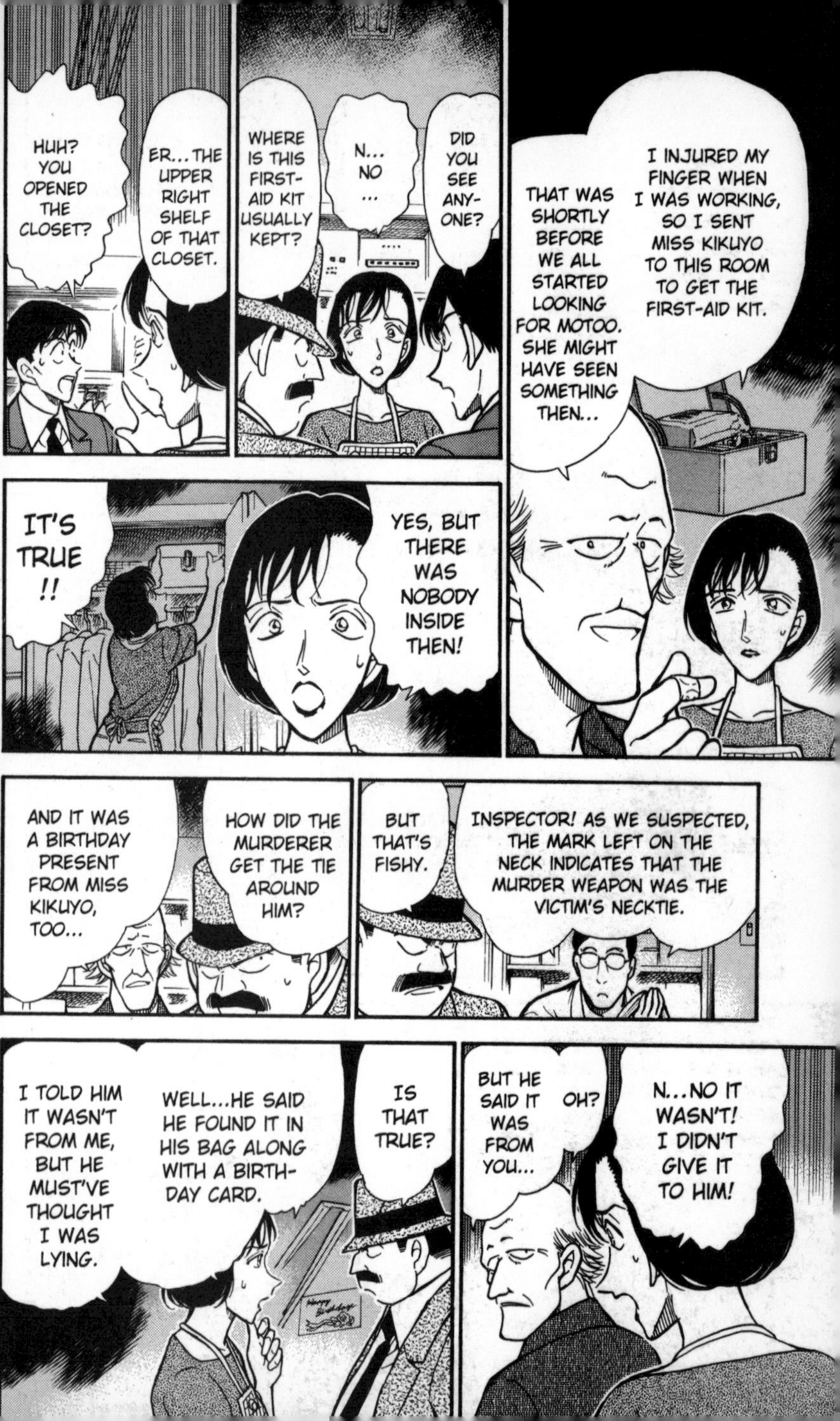
I INJURED MY FINGER WHEN I WAS WORKING, SO I SENT MISS KIKUYO TO THIS ROOM TO GET THE FIRST-AID KIT.
THAT WAS SHORTLY BEFORE WE ALL STARTED LOOKING FOR MOTOO. SHE MIGHT HAVE SEEN SOMETHING THEN...
DID YOU SEE ANYONE?
N... NO ...
WHERE IS THIS FIRST-AID KIT USUALLY KEPT?
ER... THE UPPER RIGHT SHELF OF THAT CLOSET.
HUH? YOU OPENED THE CLOSET?
YES, BUT THERE WAS NOBODY INSIDE THEN!
IT'S TRUE !!
INSPECTOR! AS WE SUSPECTED, THE MARK LEFT ON THE NECK INDICATES THAT THE MURDER WEAPON WAS THE VICTIM'S NECKTIE.
BUT THAT'S FISHY.
HOW DID THE MURDERER GET THE TIE AROUND HIM?
AND IT WAS A BIRTHDAY PRESENT FROM MISS KIKUYO, TOO...
N...NO IT WASN'T! I DIDN'T GIVE IT TO HIM!
OH?
BUT HE SAID IT WAS FROM YOU...
IS THAT TRUE?
WELL...HE SAID HE FOUND IT IN HIS BAG ALONG WITH A BIRTH-DAY CARD.
I TOLD HIM IT WASN'T FROM ME, BUT HE MUST'VE THOUGHT I WAS LYING.

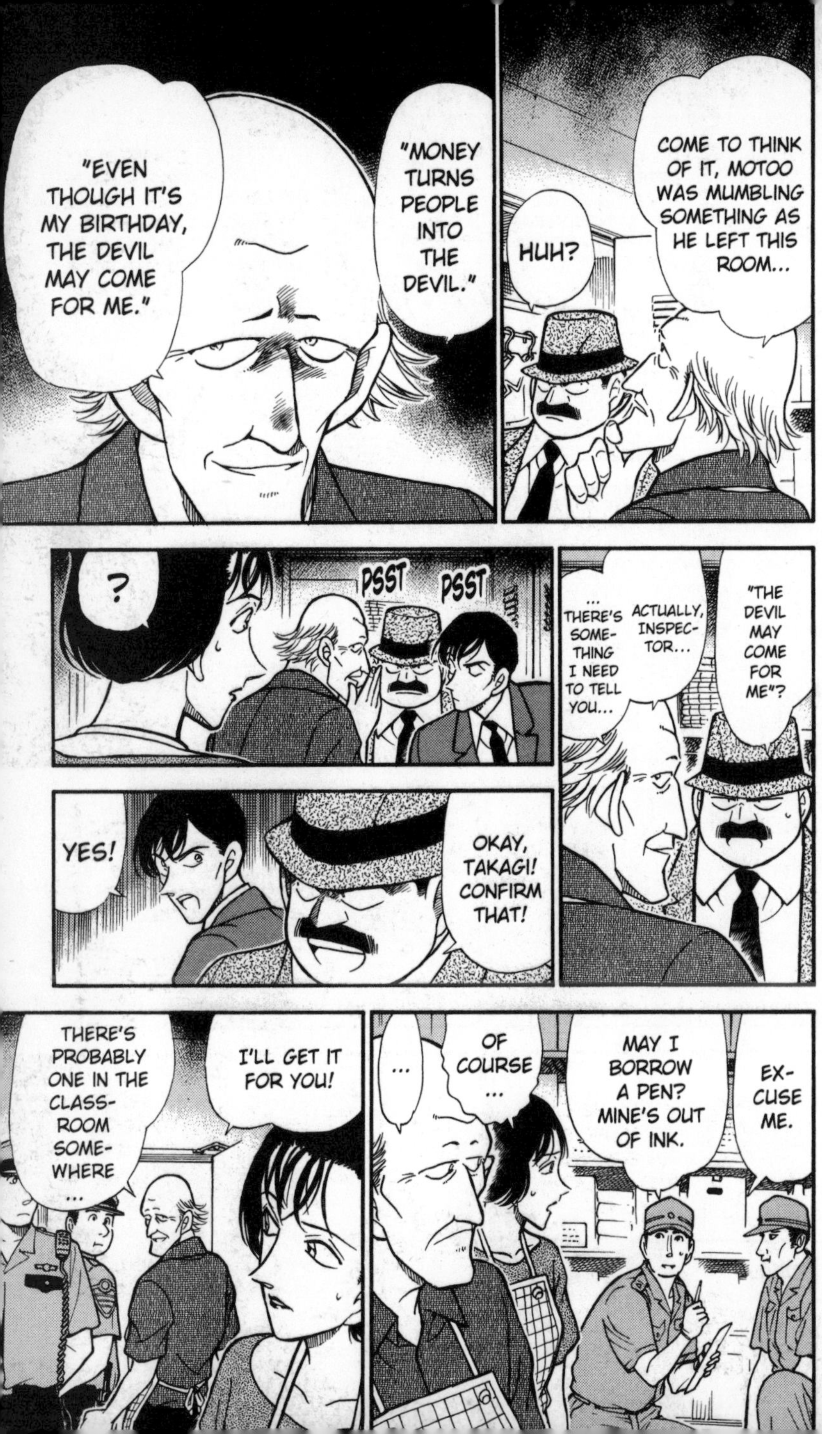
COME TO THINK OF IT, MOTOO WAS MUMBLING SOMETHING AS HE LEFT THIS ROOM...
HUH?
"MONEY TURNS PEOPLE INTO THE DEVIL."
"EVEN THOUGH IT'S MY BIRTHDAY, THE DEVIL MAY COME FOR ME."
"THE DEVIL MAY COME FOR ME"?
ACTUALLY, INSPECTOR...
... THERE'S SOMETHING I NEED TO TELL YOU...
PSST
PSST
?
OKAY, TAKAGI! CONFIRM THAT!
YES!
EXCUSE ME.
MAY I BORROW A PEN? MINE'S OUT OF INK.
OF COURSE...
...
I'LL GET IT FOR YOU!
THERE'S PROBABLY ONE IN THE CLASSROOM SOMEWHERE...

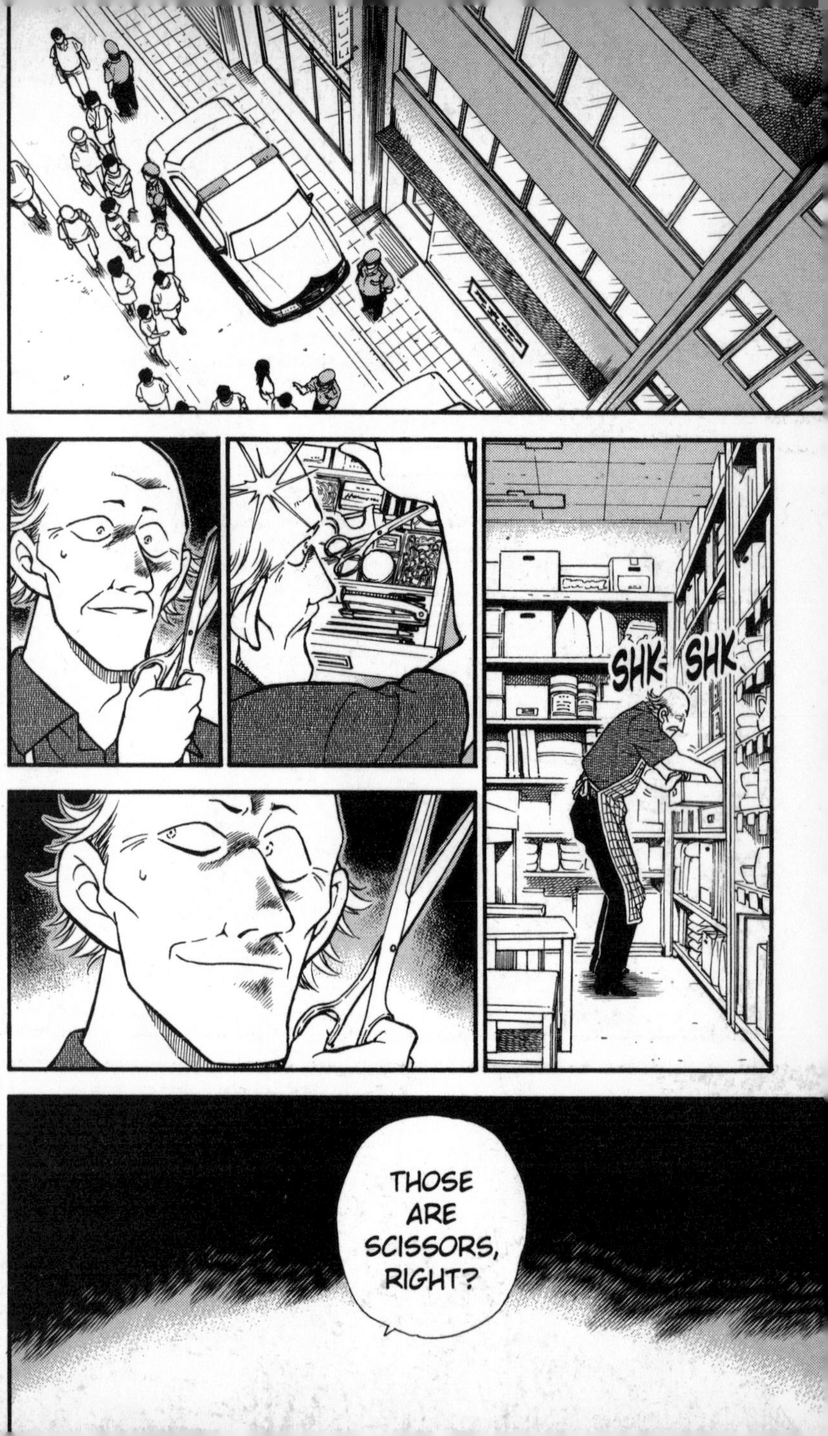
SHK SHK
THOSE ARE SCISSORS, RIGHT?

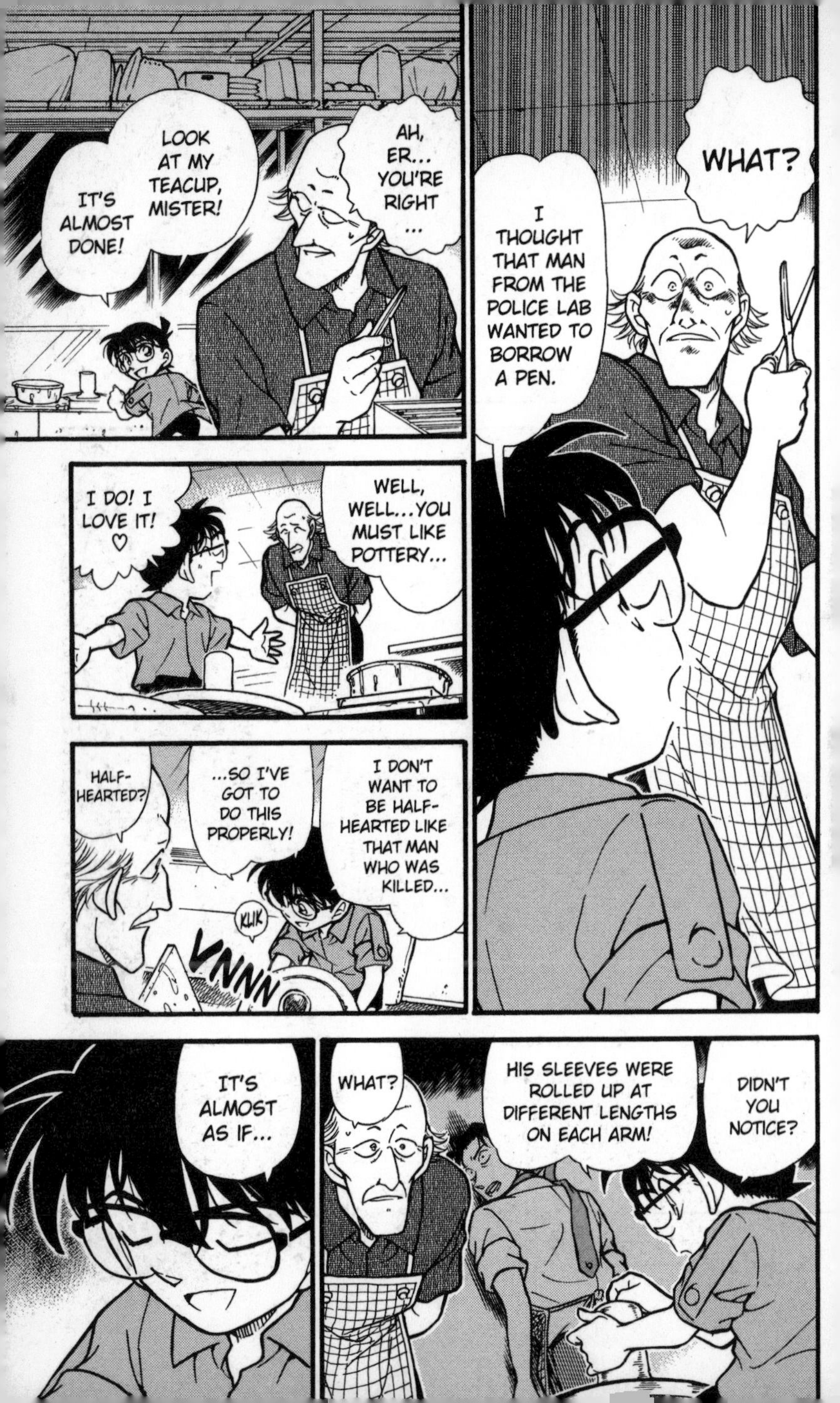
WHAT?
I THOUGHT THAT MAN FROM THE POLICE LAB WANTED TO BORROW A PEN.
AH, ER... YOU'RE RIGHT...
LOOK AT MY TEACUP, MISTER!
IT'S ALMOST DONE!
WELL, WELL...YOU MUST LIKE POTTERY...
I DO! I LOVE IT! ♡
I DON'T WANT TO BE HALF-HEARTED LIKE THAT MAN WHO WAS KILLED...
...SO I'VE GOT TO DO THIS PROPERLY!
HALF-HEARTED?
KLIK
VNNNN
DIDN'T YOU NOTICE?
HIS SLEEVES WERE ROLLED UP AT DIFFERENT LENGTHS ON EACH ARM!
WHAT?
IT'S ALMOST AS IF...

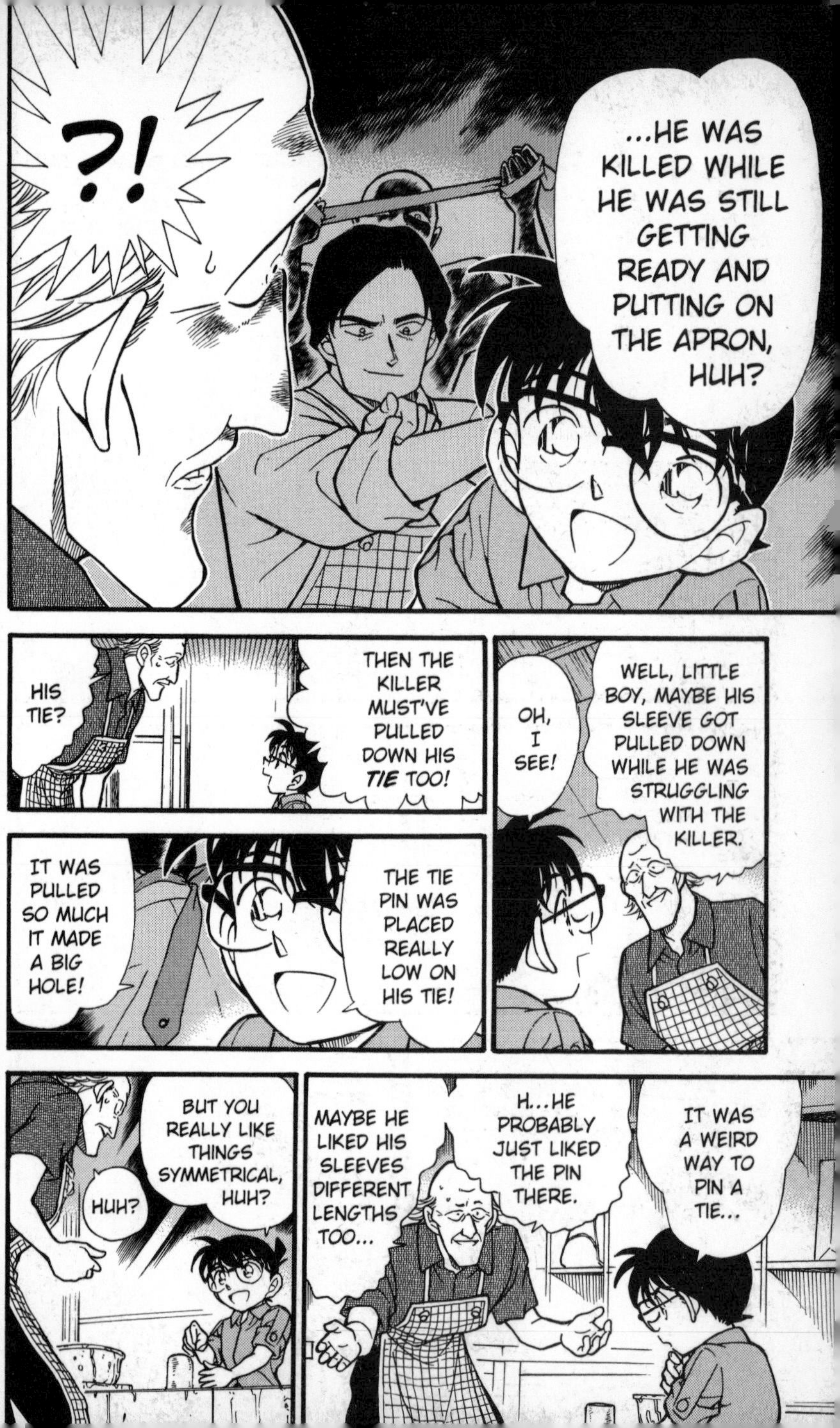
...HE WAS KILLED WHILE HE WAS STILL GETTING READY AND PUTTING ON THE APRON, HUH?
?!
WELL, LITTLE BOY, MAYBE HIS SLEEVE GOT PULLED DOWN WHILE HE WAS STRUGGLING WITH THE KILLER.
OH, I SEE!
THEN THE KILLER MUST'VE PULLED DOWN HIS *TIE* TOO!
HIS TIE?
THE TIE PIN WAS PLACED REALLY LOW ON HIS TIE!
IT WAS PULLED SO MUCH IT MADE A BIG HOLE!
IT WAS A WEIRD WAY TO PIN A TIE...
H...HE PROBABLY JUST LIKED THE PIN THERE.
MAYBE HE LIKED HIS SLEEVES DIFFERENT LENGTHS TOO...
BUT YOU REALLY LIKE THINGS SYMMETRICAL, HUH?
HUH?

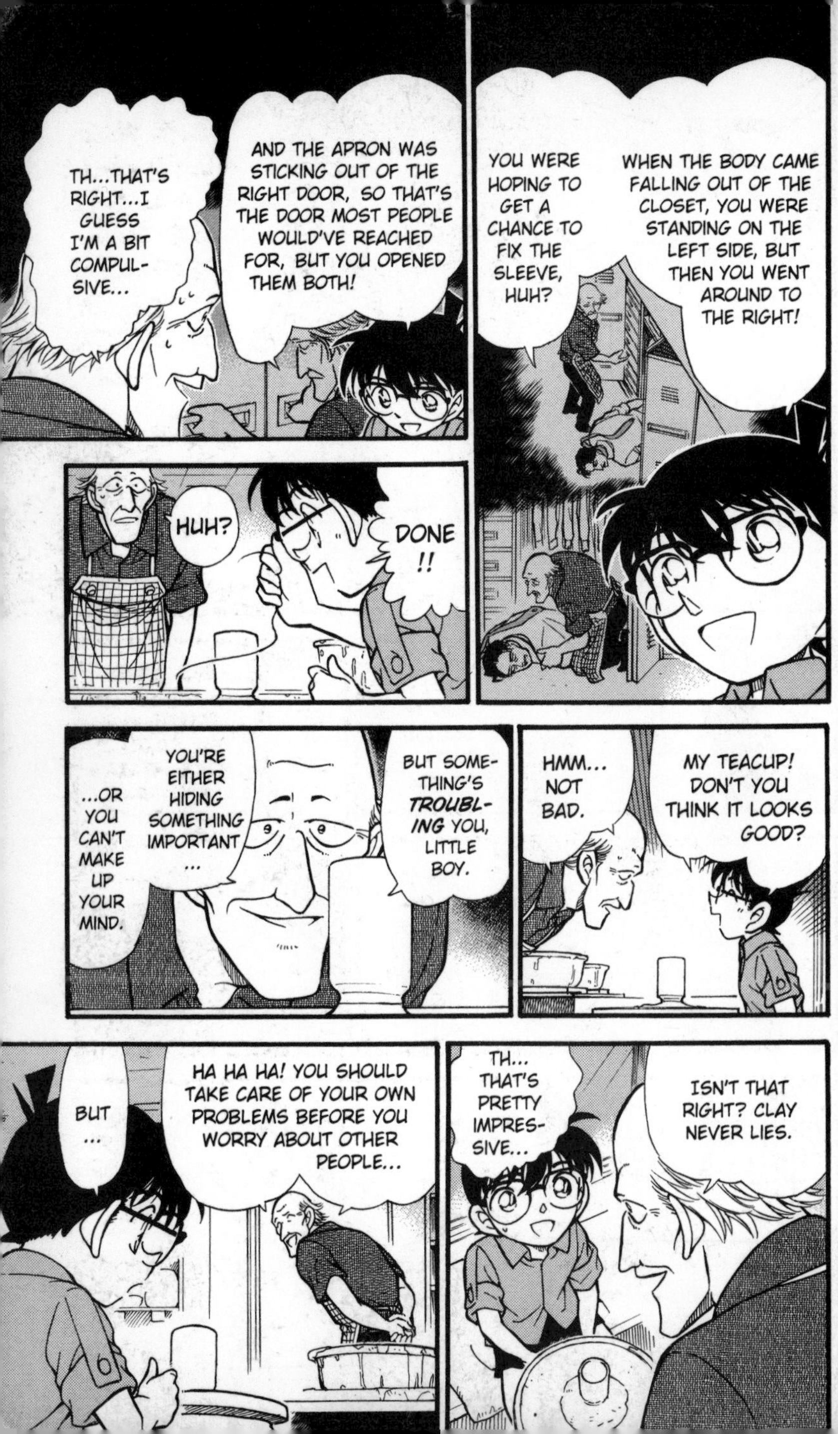
WHEN THE BODY CAME FALLING OUT OF THE CLOSET, YOU WERE STANDING ON THE LEFT SIDE, BUT THEN YOU WENT AROUND TO THE RIGHT!
YOU WERE HOPING TO GET A CHANCE TO FIX THE SLEEVE, HUH?
AND THE APRON WAS STICKING OUT OF THE RIGHT DOOR, SO THAT'S THE DOOR MOST PEOPLE WOULD'VE REACHED FOR, BUT YOU OPENED THEM BOTH!
TH...THAT'S RIGHT...I GUESS I'M A BIT COMPUL-SIVE...
DONE !!
HUH?
MY TEACUP! DON'T YOU THINK IT LOOKS GOOD?
HMM... NOT BAD.
BUT SOME-THING'S *TROUBL-ING* YOU, LITTLE BOY.
YOU'RE EITHER HIDING SOMETHING IMPORTANT ...
...OR YOU CAN'T MAKE UP YOUR MIND.
ISN'T THAT RIGHT? CLAY NEVER LIES.
TH... THAT'S PRETTY IMPRES-SIVE...
HA HA HA! YOU SHOULD TAKE CARE OF YOUR OWN PROBLEMS BEFORE YOU WORRY ABOUT OTHER PEOPLE...
BUT ...

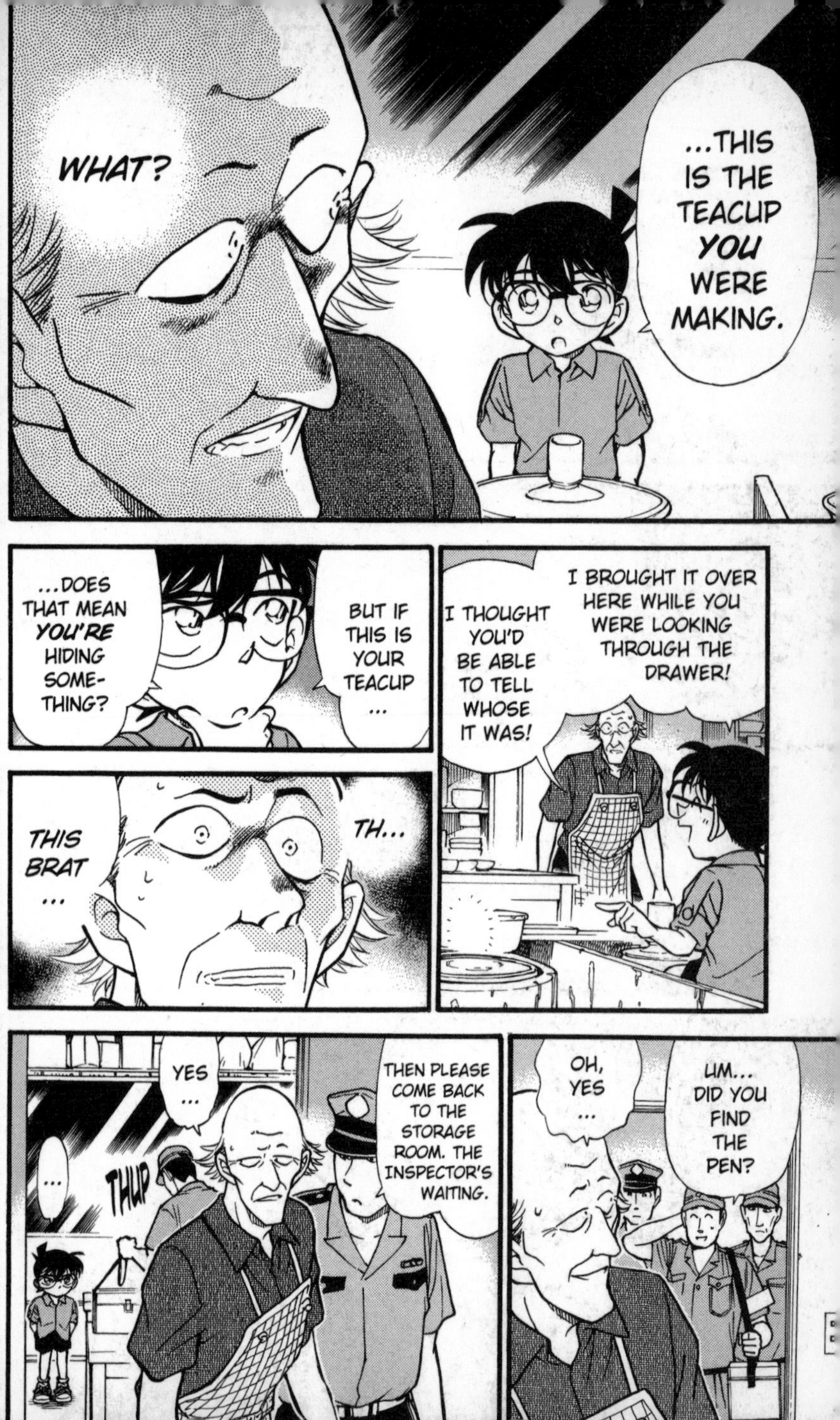
...THIS IS THE TEACUP YOU WERE MAKING.
WHAT?
I BROUGHT IT OVER HERE WHILE YOU WERE LOOKING THROUGH THE DRAWER!
I THOUGHT YOU'D BE ABLE TO TELL WHOSE IT WAS!
BUT IF THIS IS YOUR TEACUP...
...DOES THAT MEAN YOU'RE HIDING SOMETHING?
TH...
THIS BRAT...
UM... DID YOU FIND THE PEN?
OH, YES...
THEN PLEASE COME BACK TO THE STORAGE ROOM. THE INSPECTOR'S WAITING.
YES...
THUP
...

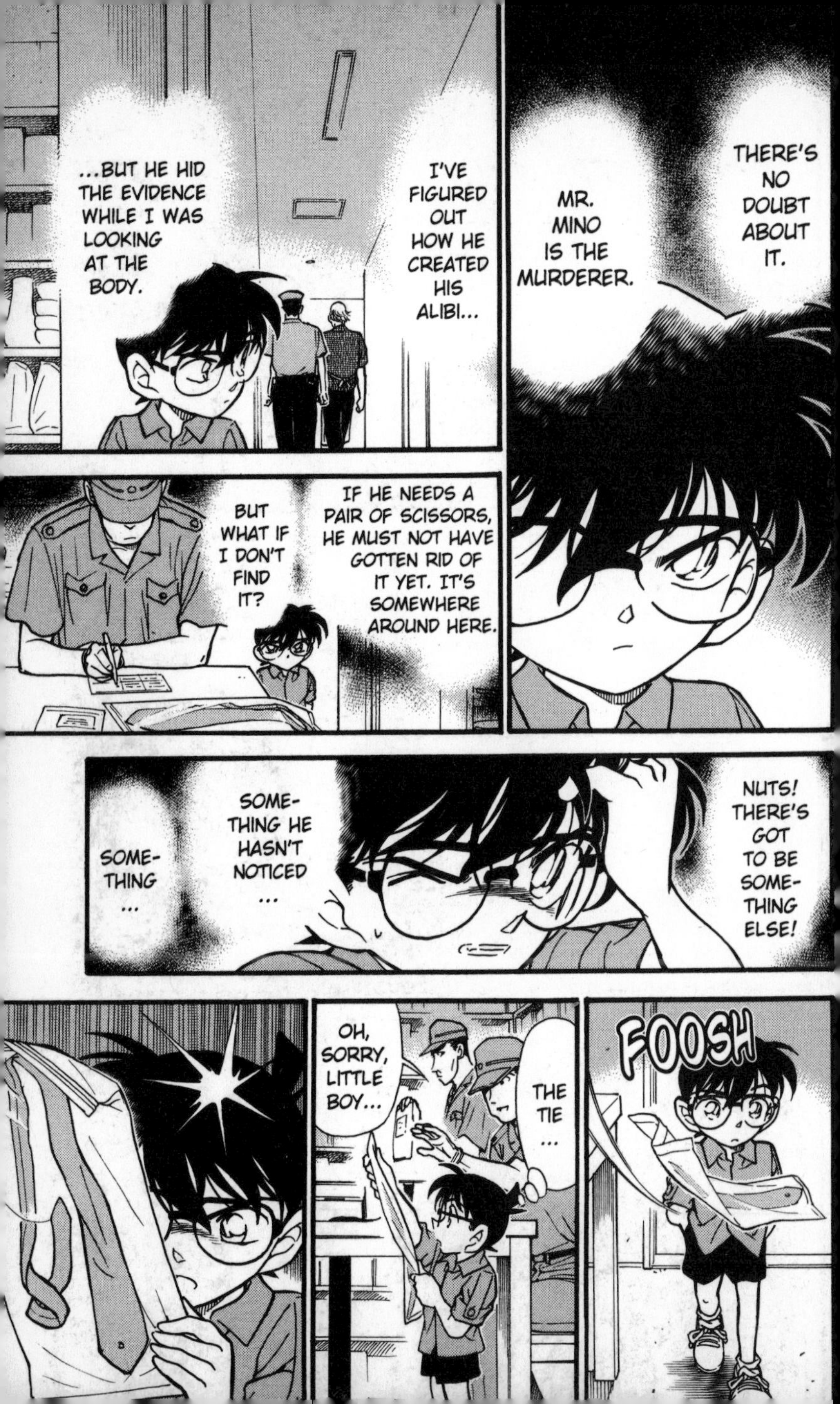

THERE'S NO DOUBT ABOUT IT.
MR. MINO IS THE MURDERER.
I'VE FIGURED OUT HOW HE CREATED HIS ALIBI...
...BUT HE HID THE EVIDENCE WHILE I WAS LOOKING AT THE BODY.
IF HE NEEDS A PAIR OF SCISSORS, HE MUST NOT HAVE GOTTEN RID OF IT YET. IT'S SOMEWHERE AROUND HERE.
BUT WHAT IF I DON'T FIND IT?
NUTS! THERE'S GOT TO BE SOME-THING ELSE!
SOME-THING HE HASN'T NOTICED...
SOME-THING...
FOOSH
THE TIE...
OH, SORRY, LITTLE BOY...

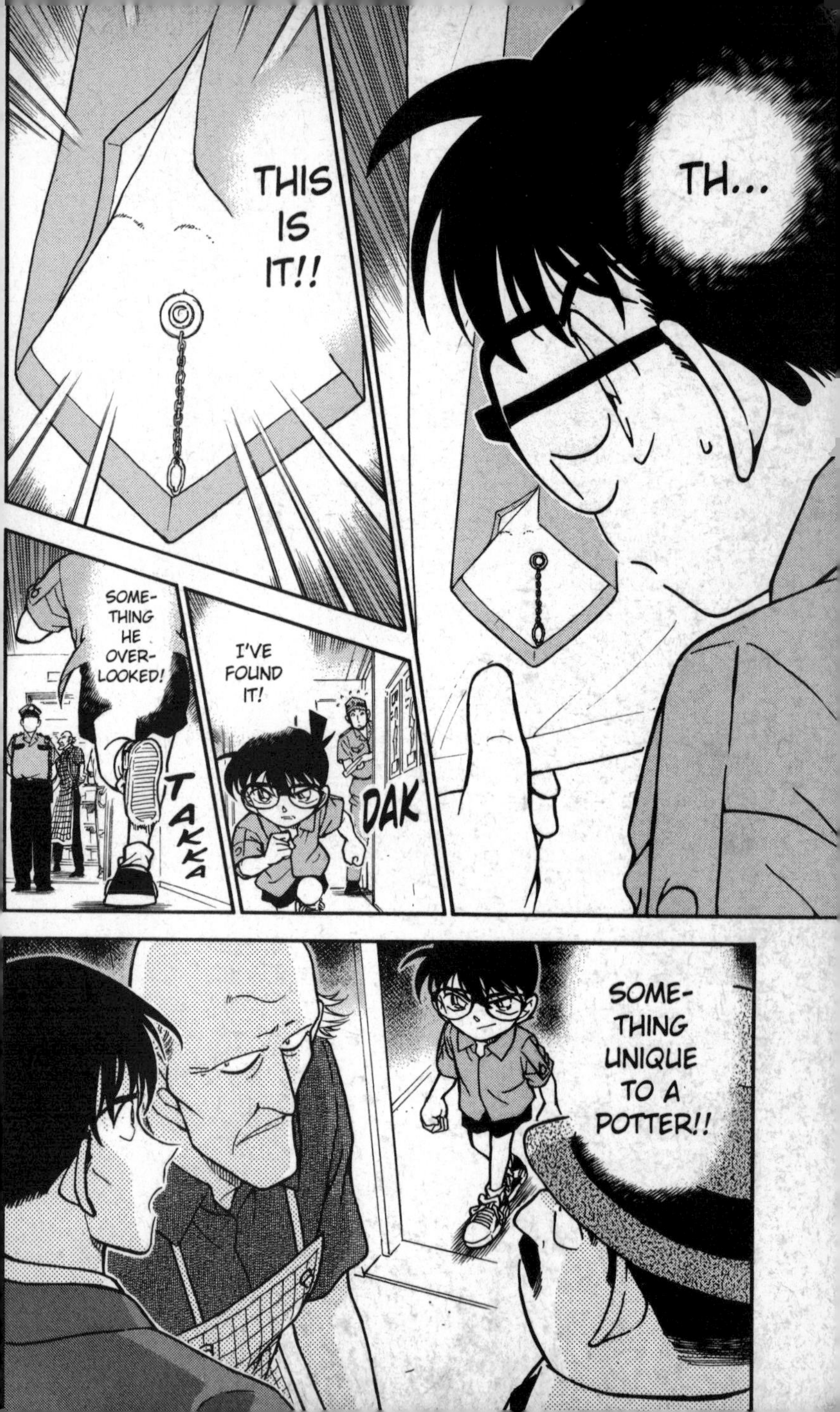
TH...
THIS IS IT!!
I'VE FOUND IT!
DAK
SOME-THING HE OVER-LOOKED!
TAKKA
SOME-THING UNIQUE TO A POTTER!!

Hello, Aoyama here.

Case Closed has finally reached volume 30! Wow!! To commemorate this event, a whole bunch of sleuths who are parodies of famous detectives appear in this volume!

One of them is Harufumi Mogi, whose name is a pun on Humphrey Bogart, a.k.a. "Bogie." He was famous for playing Philip Marlowe. There are more, so try to figure out which character is a parody of which famous sleuth!

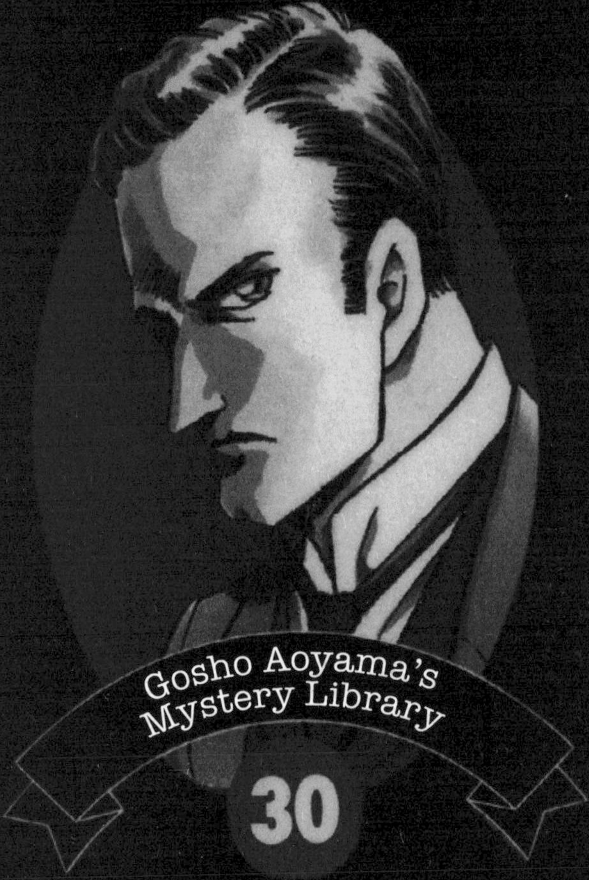
Gosho Aoyama's
Mystery Library
30

JOHN THORNDYKE

Forensic science is an important investigation method, and Dr. John Thorndyke was one of the first forensic scientists in fiction! A former professor and authority on forensic medicine, he is also a qualified lawyer. He carries out investigations with his able assistant Polton and his friend Dr. Jervis. As a "medical jurispractitioner," he uses his keen insight to gather data and his medical and scientific knowledge to solve the most baffling cases. He always carries a green case filled with fingerprint dusters, microscopes, and other equipment and chemicals, making him a "walking laboratory." Author R. Austin Freeman is famous as the creator of the inverted detective story, which starts by describing the crime and then shows the detective solving it, so Dr. Thorndyke is the ancestor of Columbo and Furuhata.

I recommend *The Singing Bone.*

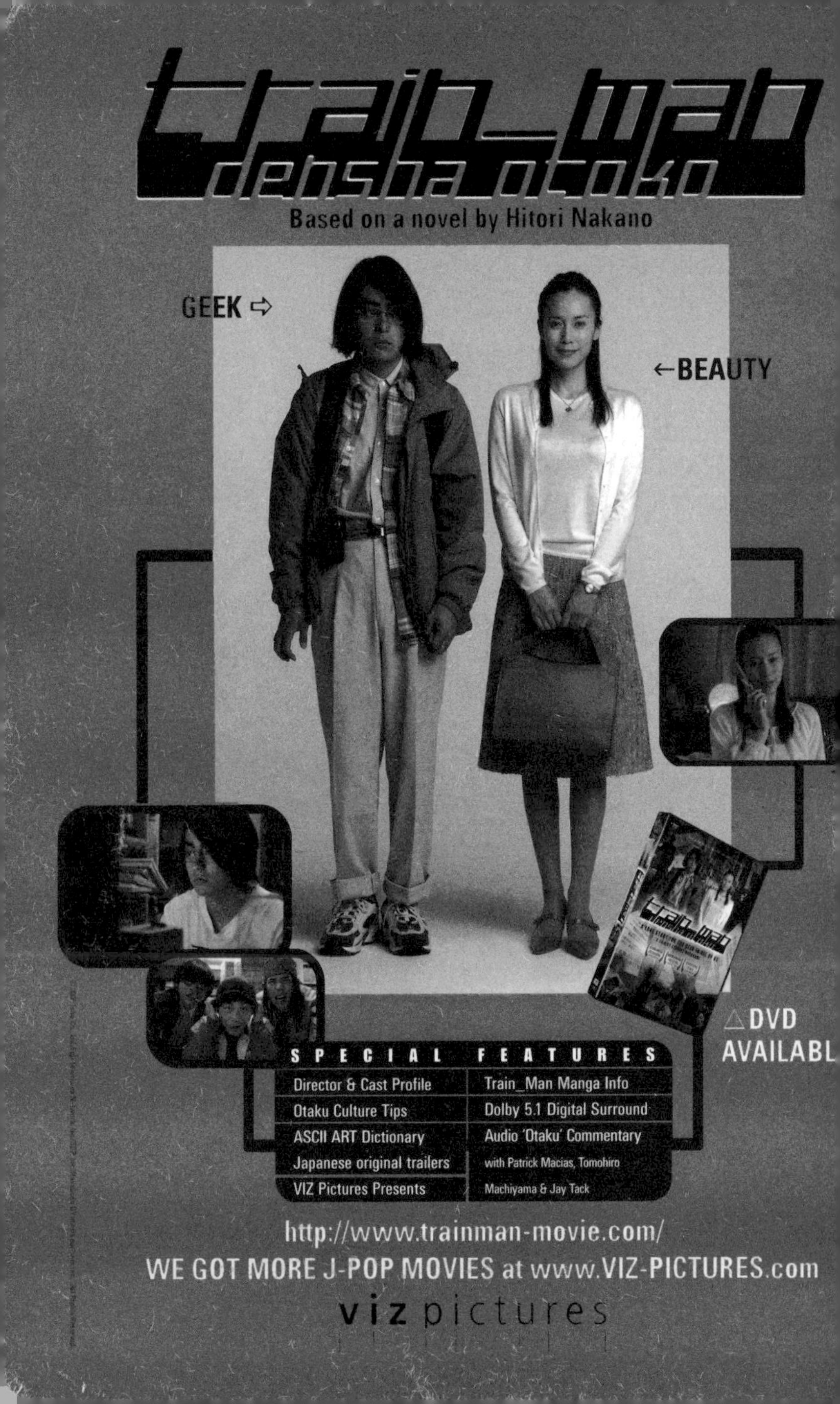
train_man
densha otoko
Based on a novel by Hitori Nakano
GEEK ⇨
←BEAUTY
△DVD
AVAILABL
SPECIAL FEATURES
Director & Cast Profile
Otaku Culture Tips
ASCII ART Dictionary
Japanese original trailers
VIZ Pictures Presents
Train_Man Manga Info
Dolby 5.1 Digital Surround
Audio 'Otaku' Commentary
with Patrick Macias, Tomohiro Machiyama & Jay Tack
http://www.trainman-movie.com/
WE GOT MORE J-POP MOVIES at www.VIZ-PICTURES.com
viz pictures

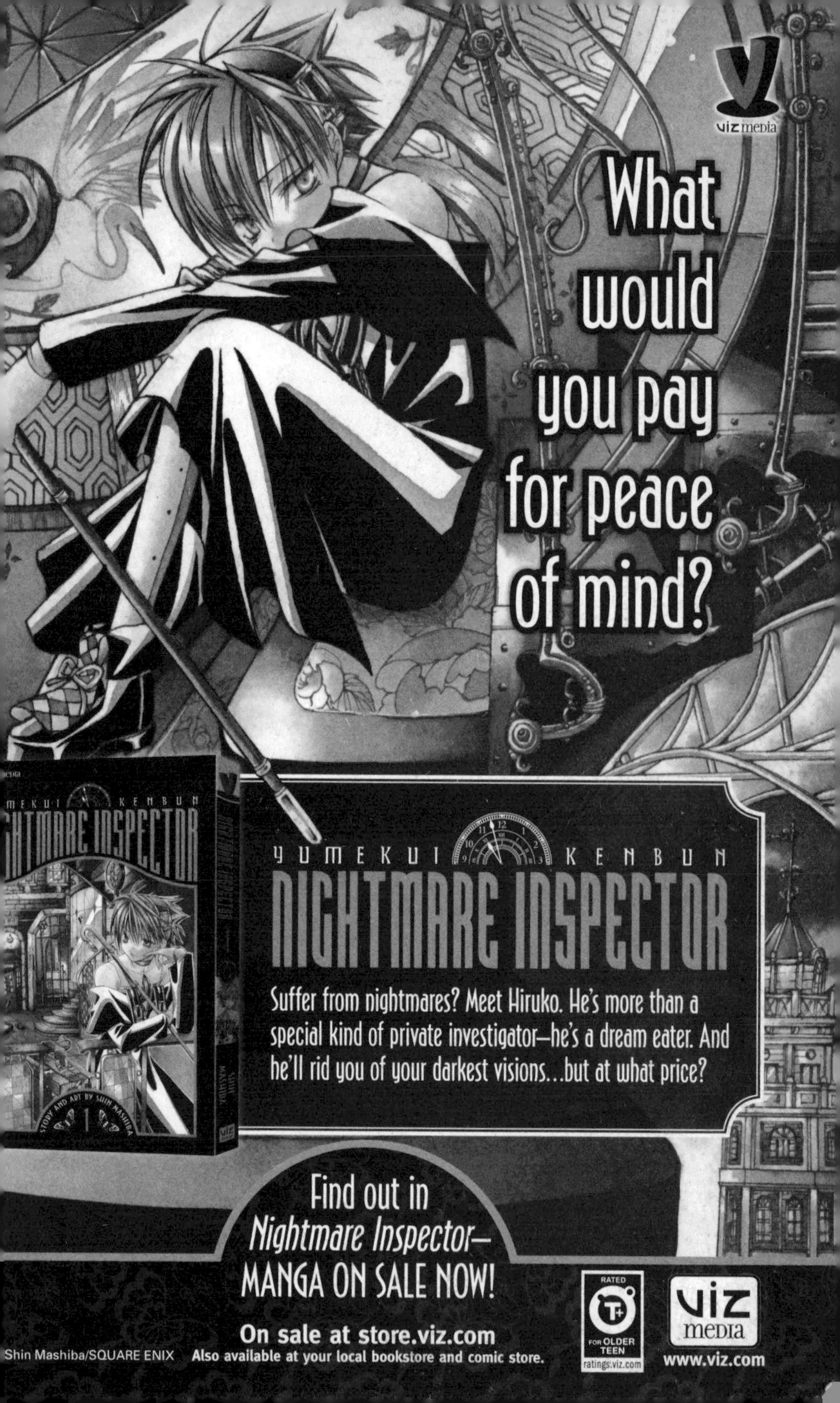

viz media
What would you pay for peace of mind?
STORY AND ART BY SHIN MASHIBA
YUMEKUI KENBUN
NIGHTMARE INSPECTOR
Suffer from nightmares? Meet Hiruko. He's more than a special kind of private investigator—he's a dream eater. And he'll rid you of your darkest visions...but at what price?
Find out in *Nightmare Inspector*—
MANGA ON SALE NOW!
On sale at store.viz.com
Also available at your local bookstore and comic store.
Shin Mashiba/SQUARE ENIX
RATED T+ FOR OLDER TEEN
ratings.viz.com
viz media
www.viz.com